To Weave a
Web of Magic

To Weave a Web of Magic

CLAIRE DELACROIX
LYNN KURLAND
PATRICIA A. MCKILLIP
SHARON SHINN

BERKLEY BOOKS, NEW YORK

A Berkley Book
Published by The Berkley Publishing Group
A division of Penguin Group (USA) Inc.
375 Hudson Street
New York, New York 10014

First edition: July 2004

Library of Congress Cataloging-in-Publication Data

To weave a web of magic / Claire Delacroix . . . [et al.].—1st ed.
    p. cm
    ISBN 0-425-19615-1
    1. Fantasy fiction, American. 2. Love stories, American.
I. Delacroix,   Claire.
PS648.F3T6 2004
813'.08766083543—dc22   2004041003

Printed in the United States of America

10   9   8   7   6   5   4   3   2   1

Contents

The Gorgon in the Cupboard

PATRICIA A. McKILLIP

HARRY could not get the goat to stay still. His model, who was an aspiring actress, offered numerous impractical suggestions as she crouched beside the animal. In fact, she rarely stopped talking. Harry didn't like the look in the goat's eye. It wasn't very big, but it seemed to him arrogant beyond its age, and contemplating mischief.

"Give it something to eat," Moira suggested. "Goats eat anything, don't they? That old leather sack, there."

"That's my lunch," Harry said patiently. "And the less we put into the goat, the less will come out of it. If you get my meaning."

She giggled. She was quite charming, with her triangular elfin face, her large green eyes with lashes so long they seemed to catch air like butterfly wings as they rose and fell. She dealt handily with the goat, who was eyeing Harry's lunch now. It strained against the rope around its neck, occasionally tightening it so that its yellow eyes verged on the protuberant. A bit like hers, Harry thought.

"Try to remain serious," he pleaded. "You're a scapegoat; you've been falsely accused and spurned by the world. Your only friend in the world is that goat."

"I thought you said you were just sketching the outlines today. Putting us in our places. So why do I have to be serious?" The goat, in whose rope her wrists were supposedly entangled, gave an obstinate tug; she loosed one hand and smacked it. "You should have gotten a female. They're sweet-natured. Not like this ruffian." She wrinkled her nose. "Stinks, too, he does. Like—"

"This one was all I could borrow. Please."

They were still for a miraculous moment, both gazing at him. He picked up charcoal, held his breath and drew a line of the goat's flank onto the canvas, then continued the line with her flank and bent knee. She swatted at a fly; the goat bucked; they both seemed to *baa* at once. Harry sighed, wiped sweat out of his eyes. They had been there half the morning, and little enough to show for it. The sun was high and dagger-bright; the tavern yard where he had set his poignant scene was full of sniggering critics. Idlers, he reminded himself, resuming doggedly when the pair settled again. They wouldn't know a brush from a broom straw. Still. He paused to study his efforts. He sighed again. There was something definitely wrong with her foot.

"It's hot," she said plaintively, shaking her heavy hair away from her neck, disturbing the perfect, nunlike veil across her face.

"Ah, don't—"

"And I'm starving. Why can't you paint like Alex McAlister? He lets me sit inside; he dresses me in silks; he lets me talk as much as I want unless he's doing my face. And I get hung every time, too, a good place on the wall where people can see me, not down in a corner where nobody looks."

The goat was hunkered on the ground now, trying to break its neck pulling at the rope peg. Harry glanced despairingly at the merciless source of light, looked again at his mutinous scapegoats, then flung his charcoal down.

"All right. All right."

"You owe me for Thursday, too."

"All right."

"When do you want me to come again?"

He closed his eyes briefly, then fished coins out of his pocket. "I'll send word."

One of the critics leaning against the wall called, "Best pay the goat, too; it might not come back otherwise."

"I might have work," Moira reminded him loftily. Mostly she worked early mornings selling bread in a bakery and took elocution lessons in afternoons when she wasn't prowling the theaters, or, Harry suspected, the streets for work.

"That goat won't get any younger neither," another idler commented. Harry gritted his teeth, then snapped his fingers for the boy pitching a knife in a corner of the yard. The boy loosened the goat from the peg, got a good grip on its neck-loop to return it to its owner. He held out his other hand for pay.

"Tomorrow then, sir?" he asked indifferently.

"I'll send word," Harry repeated.

"Don't forget your dinner there, sir."

"You have it. I'm not hungry."

He dropped the charcoal into his pocket, tucked the canvas under one arm and the folded easel under the other, and walked home dejectedly, scarcely seeing the city around him. He was a fair-haired, sweet-faced young man, nicely built despite his awkward ways, with a habitually patient expression and a heart full of ravaging longings and ambitions. He was not talented enough for them, this morning's work told him. He would never be good enough. The girl was right.

His paintings, if chosen at all to be hung for important exhibits, always ended up too high, or too close to the floor, or in obscure, badly lit corners. He thought of McAlister's magnificent *Diana,* with the dogs and the deer in it looking so well-behaved they might have been stuffed. And Haversham's *Watchful Shepherd:* the sheep as fat as dandelions and as docile as—as, well, sheep. Why not scapesheep? he wondered despondently, rather than scapegoats? No goat would stand still long enough for mankind to heap their crimes on its head.

Then he saw that which drove every other thought out of his head.

Her.

She was walking with her husband on the other side of the street. He was speaking fervidly, gesturing, as was his wont, probably about something that had seized his imagination. It might have been anything, Harry knew: a poem, the style of an arch, a pattern of embroidery on a woman's sleeve. She listened, her quiet face angled slightly toward him, her eyes downturned, intent, it seemed, on the man's brilliance. He swept fingers through his dark, shaggy hair, his thick mustaches dancing, spit flying now and then in his exuberance. Neither of them saw Harry. Who had stopped midstream in the busy street, willing her to look, terrified that she might raise her dark, brooding eyes and see what was in his face. She only raised her long white fingers, gently clasped her husband's flying arm and tucked it down between them.

Thus they passed, the great Alex McAlister and his wife Aurora, oblivious to the man turned to stone by the sight of her.

He moved at last, jostled by a pair of boys pursued through the crowd, and then by the irate man at their heels. Harry barely noticed them. Her face hung in his mind, gazing out of canvas at him: McAlister's *Diana,* McAlister's

Cleopatra, McAlister's *Venus.* That hair, rippling like black fire from skin as white as alabaster, those deep, heavy-lidded eyes that seemed to perceive invisible worlds. That strong, slender column of neck. Those long fingers, impossibly mobile and expressive. That mouth like a bite of sweet fruit. Those full, sultry lips . . .

I would give my soul to paint you, he told her silently. But even if in some marvelous synchronicity of events that were possible, it would still be impossible. With her gazing at him, he could not have painted a stroke. Again and again, she turned him into stone.

Not Aurora, he thought with hopeless longing, but Medusa.

He had tried to speak to her any number of times when he had visited Alex's studio or their enchanting cottage in the country. All he managed, under that still, inhuman gaze, were insipid commonplaces. The weather. The wildflowers blooming in the garden. The stunning success of McAlister's latest painting. He coughed on crumbs, spilled tea on his cuff. Her voice was very low; he bent to hear it and stepped on her hem with his muddy boot sole, so that whatever she had begun to say was overwhelmed by his apologies. Invariably, routed by his own gracelessness, he would turn abruptly away to study a vase that McAlister had glazed himself, or a frame he was making. McAlister never seemed to notice his hopeless passion, the longing of the most insignificant moth for fire. He would clap Harry's shoulder vigorously, spilling his tea again, and then fix him in an enthusiastic torrent of words, trying to elicit Harry's opinion of some project or profundity, while the only thought in Harry's head was of the woman sitting so silently beyond them she might have been in another world entirely.

He walked down a quiet side street shaded by stately elms, opened the gate in front of the comfortable house he had inherited from his parents. Looking despondently upon his nicely blooming hollyhocks, he wondered what to do next.

If only I could create a masterwork, he thought. An idea no one has thought of yet, that would attract the attention of the city, bring me acclaim. Make me one of the circle of the great . . . Now I'm only a novice, a squire, something more than apprentice yet less than master. Harry Waterman, dabbler at the mystery of art. If only I could pass through the closed doors to the inner sanctum. Surely She would notice me then . . .

He went across the garden, up the steps to his door, and stopped again, hand on the latch, as he mused over an appropriate subject for a masterpiece. The goat, while original and artistically challenging, held no dignity; it would not rivet crowds with its power and mystery. At most, viewers might pity it and its ambiguous female counterpart, and then pass on. More likely they would pity the artist, who had stood in a sweltering tavern yard painting a goat.

Aurora's face passed again through his thoughts; his hand opened and closed convulsively on the door latch. Something worthy of those eyes he must paint. Something that would bring expression into them: wonder, admiration, curiosity . . .

What?

Whatever it was, he would dedicate his masterpiece to Her.

The door pulled abruptly out of his hold. Mrs. Grommet, his placid housekeeper, held a hand to her ample bosom as she stared at him. "Oh, it's you, Mr. Waterman. I couldn't imagine who was making that racket with the door latch." She shifted aside, opened the door wide for him to enter.

"Sorry, Mrs. Grommet," he murmured. "Throes of creation."

"Of course, Mr. Waterman. I didn't expect you back so soon. Have you had your lunch, sir?"

"No. Just bring me tea in my studio, please. I expect to be in the throes for the rest of the afternoon."

"Yes, sir."

In the highest floor of the house, he had knocked down walls, enlarged windows to give him space and light, views from a city park on one side, the broad, busy river on the other. Mrs. Grommet came panting up with a great silver tray. He slumped in an easy chair, sipped tea as he flipped through his sketchbooks for inspiration. Faces, dogs, flowers, birds, hills, rocks, pieces of armor, horses, folds of heavy tapestry, drifting silk, hands, feet, eyes . . . Nothing coherent, nothing whole, nothing containing the lightning bolt of inspiration he craved.

He read some poetry; words did not compel an image. He paced for a while, his mind a blank canvas. He beseeched his Muse. Anybody's Muse. Inspiration failed to turn her lovely face, her kindly attention, toward him. He wandered to his cupboards, pulled out old, unfinished canvases, studied the stilted figures, the fuzzy landscapes for something that he might redeem to greatness.

One caught at memory: a head without a mouth. He placed it on the easel, stood studying it. The head, when completed, would have belonged to Persephone at the moment she realized that, having eaten of the fruits of the Underworld, she was doomed to spend half her life in that gloomy place. The young model he had chosen for it had vanished before he could finish it. Harry gazed at her, struck by her beauty, which had inspired his normally clumsy brushwork. The almond-shaped eyes of such pale gray they seemed the color of sun-kissed ice, the white-gold hair, the apricot skin. A true mingling of spring and winter, his model, who had disappeared so completely she might have been carried away into the netherworld herself.

He tried to remember her name. May? Jenny? She had gotten herself into trouble, he suspected. Harry had noticed a certain heaviness in her walk, the frigidity of terror in her expression. Moved, he had offered, in his nebulous, hesitant way, to help. But she had fled. Or died, perhaps, he was forced to consider. In childbirth, or trying to get rid of the child, who could know? He had tried to find her so that he could finish the painting. But no one seemed to know anything at all about her.

He wondered if it might be worth finishing. Her eyes, gazing straight out at the viewer, compelled attention. Idly, he traced a mouth with his forefinger, rifling through all the likely mouths he might borrow to finish it. There was Beresford's cousin Jane . . . But no, even at her young age, her lips were too thin to suggest the hunger that had caused Persephone to eat forbidden fruit. . . . Or was that a different tale?

He recognized the invisible mouth his finger had outlined, and swallowed.

Some passing Muse, a mischievous sprite, tempted him to reach for crimson paint. The lips that haunted him burned like fire in memory . . . but darker than fire, darker than rose, darker than blood. He toyed guiltily with all those colors on his palette. Only paint, he told himself. Only memory. The color of wine, they were, deep, shadowy burgundy, with all the silken moistness of the rose petal.

Vaguely he heard Mrs. Grommet knock, inquire about his supper. Vaguely he made some noise. She went away. The room darkened; he lit lamps, candles. Mrs. Grommet did not return; the streets grew even quieter; the river faded into night.

He blinked, coming out of his obsessive trance. That full, provocative splendor of a mouth was startling beneath the gentle, frightened eyes of his Persephone. But the likeness transfixed him. Aurora's mouth it was; he had succeeded beyond all dreams in shifting it from memory into paint. He could not use it. Of course he could not. Everyone would recognize it, even on some other woman's face. Which he would need to go out and find, if he wanted to finish this Persephone. Maybe not his masterwork, but far easier to manage than the goat; she would do until inspiration struck.

He lingered, contemplating that silent, untouchable mouth. He could not bring himself to wipe it away yet. He would go down and eat his cold supper, deal more ruthlessly with the mouth after he had found a replacement for it. It did not, after all, belong to him; it belonged to the wife of his dear friend and mentor. . . . He tore his eyes from it, lifted the canvas from the easel and positioned it carefully back in the cupboard, where it could dry and be forgotten at the same time.

He closed the door and the lips spoke.

"Harry!" Its voice was sweet and raucous and completely unfamiliar. "You're not going to leave me here in the dark, are you? After calling me all afternoon? Harry?"

He flung himself against the door, hearing his heart pound like something frantic trying to get out of him, or trying to get in. He tried to speak; his voice wouldn't come, only silent bleats of air, like an astonished sheep.

"Harry?"

"Who—" he finally managed to gasp. "Who—"

"Open the door."

"N."

"You know I'm in here. You can't just keep me shut up in here."

"N."

"Oh Harry, don't be so unfriendly. I won't bite. And even if I did—" The voice trilled an uncouth snigger, "you'd like it, from this mouth."

Harry, galvanized with sudden fury, clutched at the cupboard latch, barely refraining from wrenching it open. "How dare you!" he demanded, feeling as though the contents of his inmost heart had been rifled by vulgar, soiled hands. "Who are you?"

"That's it," the voice cooed. "Now lift the latch, open the door. You can do it."

"If you force me to come in, I'll—I'll wipe away your mouth with turpentine."

"Tut, Harry. How crude. Just when I'm ready to give you what you want most."

"What I want—"

"Inspiration, Harry. You've been wishing for me ever since you gave up on the goat and gave me a chance to get a word in edgewise."

"You're a mouth—" He was breathing strangely again, taking in too much air. "How can you possibly know about the goat?"

"You called me."

"I did not."

"You invoked me," the voice insisted. "I am the voice of your despair. Your desire. Why do you think I'm coming out of these lips?"

Harry was silent, suddenly breathless. A flash went through him, not unlike the uncomfortable premonition of inspiration. He was going to open the door. Pushed against it with all his strength, his hands locked around the latch, he was going to open . . . "Who are you?" he pleaded hoarsely. "Are you some sort of insane Muse?"

"Guess again," the voice said cooly. "You looked upon your Beloved and thought of me. I want you to paint me. I am your masterwork."

"My masterwork."

"Paint me, Harry. And all you wish for will be yours."

"All I wish . . ."

"Open the door," the voice repeated patiently. "Don't be afraid. You have already seen my face."

His mouth opened; nothing came out. The vision stunned

him, turned him into stone: the painting that would rivet
the entire art world, reveal at last the depths and heights of
his genius. The snake-haired daughter of the gods whose
beauty threatened, commanded, whose eyes reflected inex-
pressible, inhuman visions.

He whispered, "Medusa."

"Me," she said. "Open the door."

He opened it.

DOWN by the river, Jo huddled with the rest of the refuse,
all squeezed under a butcher's awning trying to get out of
the sudden squall. In the country, where she had walked
from, the roads turned liquid in the rain; carriages, wagons,
horses, herds of sheep and cows churned them into thick,
oozing welts and hillocks of mud deep enough to swallow
your boots if you weren't careful. Here the cobbles, though
hard enough, offered some protection. At least she was off
her aching feet. At least until the butcher saw what took up
space from customers looking in his windows and drove
them off. Jo had been walking that day since dawn to finish
her journey to the city. It was noon now, she guessed,
though hard to tell. The gray sky hadn't changed its morose
expression by so much as a shift of light since sunrise.

Someone new pushed into the little group cowering under the awning. Another drenched body, nearly faceless under the rags wrapped around its head, sat leaning against
Jo's shoulder, worn shoes out in the rain. It wore skirts;
other than that it seemed scarcely human, just one more
sodden, miserable, breathing thing trying to find some protection from life.

They all sat silently for a bit, listening to the rain pound-
ing on the awning, watching the little figures along the
tide's edge, gray and shapeless as mud in their rags, darting
like birds from one poor crumb of treasure the river left

behind to the next. Bits of coal they stuffed into their rags to sell, splinters of wood, the odd nail or frayed piece of rope.

The bundle beside Jo murmured, "At least they're used to being wet, aren't they? River or rain, it's all one to them."

Her voice was unexpectedly young. Jo turned, maneuvering one shoulder out from beneath a sodden back. She saw a freckled girl's face between wet cloth wrapped down to her eyebrows, up to her lower lip. One eye, as blue as violets, looked resigned, calm. The other eye was swollen shut and ringed by all the colors of the rainbow.

Jo, her own face frozen for so long it hardly remembered how to move, felt something odd stirring in her. Vaguely she remembered it. Pity or some such, for all the good it did.

She said, "Whoever gave you that must love you something fierce."

"Oh, yes," the girl said. "He'll love me to death one of these days. If he finds me again."

There was a snort from the figure on the other side of Jo. This one sounded older, hoarse and wheezy with illness. Still she cackled, "I'd one like that. I used to collect my teeth in a bag after he knocked them out. I was so sorry to lose them, I couldn't bear to give them up. I was that young, then. Never smart enough to run away, even when I was young enough to think there might be a place to run to."

"There's not," Jo said shortly. "I ran back home to the country. And now I'm here again."

"What will you do?" the girl asked.

Jo shrugged. "Whatever I can."

"What have you done?"

"Mill work in the country. I had to stop doing that when my mother died and there was no one else to—to—"

"Care for the baby?" the old woman guessed shrewdly.

Jo felt her face grow cold again, less expression on it than on a brick. "Yes. Well, it's dead now, so it doesn't matter."

The girl sucked in her breath. "Cruel," she whispered.

"After that I got work at one of the big houses. Laundry and fires and such. But that didn't last."

"Did you get your references, though?"

"No. Turned out without."

"For what? Stealing?"

"No." Jo leaned her head back against the wall, watched rain running like a fountain over the edge of the swollen awning. "I wasn't that smart."

The old woman gave her crow-cackle again. "Out of the frying pan—"

Jo nodded. "Into the fire. It would have been, if I hadn't run away. If I'd stayed, I'd have had another mouth to feed when they turned me out. So I came back here."

Another voice came to life, a man's this time. "To what?" he asked heavily. "Nothing ever changes. City, country, it's all the same. You're in the mill or on the streets from dark to dark, just to get your pittance to survive one more day. And some days you can't even get that." He paused; Jo felt his racking cough shudder through them all, piled on top of one another as they were. The old woman patted his arm, whispered something. Then she turned to Jo, when he had quieted.

"He lost his wife, not long ago. Twenty-two years together and not a voice raised. Some have that."

"Twenty-two years," the man echoed. "She had her corner at the foot of the Barrow Bridge. She sang like she didn't know any better. She made you believe it, too—that you didn't know anything better than her singing, you'd never know anything better. She stopped boats with her voice; fish jumped out of the water to hear. But then she left me alone with my old fiddle and my old bones, both of us creaking and groaning without her." He patted the lump under his threadbare cloak as though it were a child. "Especially in this rain."

"Well, I know what I'm going to do when it quits," the girl said briskly. "I'm going to get myself arrested. He'll never get his hands on me in there. And it's dry and they feed you, at least for a few days before they let you out again."

"I got in for three months once," a young voice interposed from the far edge of the awning.

"Three months!" the girl exclaimed, her bruised eye trying to flutter open. "What do you have to do for that?"

"I couldn't get myself arrested for walking the streets, no matter how I tried, and I was losing my teeth and my looks to a great lout who drank all my money away by day and flung me around at night. I was so sick and tired of my life that one morning when I saw the Lord Mayor of the city in a parade of fine horses and soldiers and dressed-up lords and ladies, I took off my shoe and threw it at his head." The old woman crowed richly at the thought. "I let them catch me, and for three months I had a bed every night, clean clothes, and food every day. By the time I got out, my lout had moved on to some other girl and I was free."

"They don't make jails nowadays the way they used to," the fiddler said. "They never used to spoil you with food or a bed."

Jo felt the girl sigh noiselessly. "I'd do three months," she murmured, "if I knew where to find a Lord Mayor."

Jo's eyes slid to her vivid, wistful face. "What will you do," she asked slowly, "for your few days?"

"I've heard they take you off the streets if you break something. A window, or a street lamp. I thought I'd try that."

Jo was silent, pulling a tattered shawl around her. Jo had made it for her mother, years earlier, when her father had been alive to tend to his sheep and his cows, make cheese, shear wool for them to spin into thread. When she'd gone back, her mother had given the shawl to her to wrap the baby in. The sheep and cows were long gone to pay debts after her father died. Her mother's hands had grown huge and red from taking in laundry. Alf, they called the baby, after her father. Alfred Fletcher Byrd. Poor poppit, she thought dispassionately. Not strong enough for any one of those names, let alone three.

The man who was its father showed his face in her thoughts. She shoved him out again, ruthlessly, barred that entry. She'd lost a good place in the city because of him, in a rich, quiet, well-run house. A guest, a friend of the family, who had a family of his own somewhere. He'd found her early one morning making up a fire in the empty library. . . . The only time she'd ever seen him, and it was enough to change her life. So she'd run out of the city, all the way back home to her mother. And all she had left of any of that time was an old purple shawl.

That was then, she thought coldly. This is now.

Now, the rain was letting up a little. The young girl shifted, leaning out to test it with her hand. Jo moved, too, felt the coin or two she had left sliding around in her shoe. Enough for a loaf and a bed in some crowded, noisy, dangerous lodging house run by thieves. Might as well spend it there, before they found a way to steal it.

Or she could break a window, if she got desperate enough.

A door banged. There was the butcher, a great florid man with blood on his hands and a voice like a bulldog, growling at them to take their carcasses elsewhere or he'd grind them into sausages.

The girl wrapped her face close again, hiding her telltale eye. The fiddler coughed himself back into the rain, his instrument carefully cradled beneath his cloak. The old woman, wheezing dreadfully, pulled herself up with Jo's help. Jo picked up her covered basket for her. Flowers, she thought at first, then caught a pungent whiff of it. Whatever it was she sold, it wasn't violets. The woman winked at her and slid the basket over her arm. She trailed off after the rest of the bedraggled flock scattering into the rain.

Jo saw a lump of masonry, or maybe a broken cobblestone, half the size of her fist near the wall where the old woman had been sitting. She picked it up, slipped it into her pocket in case she needed it later.

You never knew.

HARRY stood in the enchanted garden of the McAlister's cottage in the country. Only a few miles from the city, it might have existed in a different time and world: the realm of poetry, where the fall of light and a rosebud heavy with rain from a passing storm symbolized something else entirely. The rain had stopped in the early afternoon. Bright sun had warmed the garden quickly, filled its humid, sparkling air with the smells of grass and wild thyme, the crushed-strawberry scent of the rambling roses climbing up either side of the cottage door. The cottage, an oddly shaped affair with no symmetry whatsoever, had all its scattered, mismatched windows open to the air. There was no garden fence, only a distant, rambling stone wall marking the property. The cottage stood on a grassy knoll; in nearby fields the long grass was lush with wildflowers. Farther away, brindled cows and fluffy clouds of sheep pastured within rambling field walls. Farther yet, in a fold of green, the ancient village, a bucolic garden of stone, grew along the river. On the next knoll over, John Grainger was battling the winds trying to paint the scene. Occasionally, as a puff of exuberant air tried to make off with Grainger's canvas, Harry could hear his energetic swearing.

Harry had come up for the day to look for a face for his Medusa among the McAlisters' visitors. Painters, their wives and families, models, friends who encouraged and bought, and brought friends who bought, wandered around the

gardens, chatting, drinking wine and tea, sketching, painting, or watching McAlister paint.

McAlister was painting his wife. Or rather, he was painting her windblown sleeve. She stood patiently against the
backdrop of climbing red roses, all of which, Harry noticed,
were the exact shade of her mouth. He tried not to think of
that. Thinking of her mouth made him think of the monstrous creation in his cupboard. In the sweet light of day,
there in the country, he was willing to attribute his Gorgon
to the morbid churning of his frustrated romantic urges.
But she had inspired him, no doubt about that. Here he was
in McAlister's garden, looking at every passing female, even
the young girl from the kitchen who kept the teapot filled,
for his Medusa.

McAlister was unusually reticent about his own subject
matter. Whatever figure from myth or romance he was por-
traying, he needed her windblown. He had captured the
graceful curves of his wife's wrist bone, her long, pliant fingers. The flow of her silky sleeve in the contrary wind
proved challenging, but he persevered, carrying on three
discussions at once with his onlookers as he painted. Aurora,
her brooding eyes fixed on some distant horizon, scarcely
seemed to breathe; she might have been a piece of garden
statuary.

Harry drifted, trying not to watch.

He sat down finally next to John Grainger's mistress, Nan
Stewart. She had modeled many times for John's drawings
and paintings, as well as for other artists who needed her
frail, ethereal beauty for their visions. Grainger had discovered her sitting in the cheaper seats of a theater one evening.
A well-brought-up young girl despite her class, she refused
to speak to an artist. Undaunted, he found out who she was
and implored her mother's permission to let her model for
him. Her mother, a fussy lump of a bed mattress, as Grainger
described her, accompanied Nan a few times, until she

realized that the girl could make as much in an hour model-
ing for artists as she could sewing for a week in a dress-
maker's shop. Eventually Nan came to live with the brilliant,
volatile Grainger, which explained, Harry thought, her pallor and her melancholy eyes.

She had fine red-gold hair and arresting green eyes. With
marriage in view at one point in their relationship, Grainger
had hired someone to teach her to move and speak properly.
She smiled at Harry dutifully as he filled the empty chair
beside her.

"More tea?" he asked.

A vigorous, incoherent shouting from the knoll beyond
made them both glance up. Grainger, hands on his easel,
seemed to be wrestling with the wind.

Nan shook her head. She had a bound sketchbook on her
lap, as well as a pencil or two. Grainger encouraged her to
draw. She had talent, he declared to the world, and he was
right, from what Harry had seen. But that day her sketchbook was shut.

"Not inspired?" he ventured.

"Not today." She turned her attention from the painter
on the knoll finally. "How are you, Harry?"

"Flourishing."

"Are you painting?"

"I have a subject in mind. I'm prowling about for a face."

"What subject?"

"It's a secret," he said lightly. "I'm not sure I can pull it
off. I don't want to embarrass myself among you artists."

Her smile touched her eyes finally. "You're a sweet man,
Harry. I'm still such a novice myself."

"John praises your work to the skies. He thinks very
highly—"

"I know." Her face was suddenly angled away. "I know.
I only wish he still thought so highly of me."

"He does!" Harry said, shocked. "He's loved you for years.

You live together, you work together, you are twin souls—"

"Yes." She looked at him again, her expression a polite mask. "Yes."

He was silent, wondering what was troubling her. His eyes strayed to the group beside the rose vines. Children ran out of the cottage door; he recognized Andrew Peel's gray-eyed little beauty, and her baby brother trundling unsteadily after. Nan sighed absently, her eyes on the children. Harry's own eyes strayed. Across the garden, the statue came to life; the dark, unfathomable eyes seemed to gaze straight at him.

He started, his cup clattering, feeling that regard like a bolt from the blue, striking silently, deeply. He became aware of Nan's eyes on him, too, in wide, unblinking scrutiny. Then she set her cup down on a table; it, too, rattled sharply in its saucer.

"She's pregnant, you know," Nan said. Harry felt as though he had missed a step, plunged into sudden space. He started again, this time not so noisily. Nan added, "So am I."

He stared at her. "That's wonderful," he exclaimed finally, leaning to put his cup on the grass. He caught her hands. That's all it was then: her inner turmoil, her natural uncertainties. "Wonderful," he repeated.

"Is it?"

"Of course! You'll marry now, won't you?"

She gave him an incredulous stare. Then she loosed her hands, answered tonelessly, "Yes, quite soon. Next week, perhaps, and then we'll go away for a bit to the southern coasts to paint."

"I couldn't be happier," Harry told her earnestly. "We've all been expecting this for—"

"For years," she finished. "Yes." She hesitated; he waited, puzzled without knowing why. Something about the event, he supposed, made women anxious, prone to fear disasters, or imagine things that were not true.

Grainger's voice, sonorous and vibrant, spilled over the group. He appeared tramping up the knoll, his hat gone, his canvas in one hand, easel in the other, paints in the pockets of his voluminous, stained jacket. He blew a kiss to Nan, leaving a daub of blue on his bushy, autumn-gold mustaches. Then he turned to see how McAlister's sleeve was coming. Above his broad back, Harry saw the statue's eyes come alive again; her cheeks had flushed, in the wayward wind, a delicate shade of rose. Ever the consummate professional, she did not move, while Grainger, lingering in the group, expounded with witty astonishment how like a wing that sleeve seemed, straining for its freedom on the wind.

Harry turned back to Nan, breath indrawn for some pleasantry.

Her chair was empty. He looked around bewilderedly. She had flown herself, it seemed, but why and on what wayward wind, he could not imagine.

JO walked the darkening streets, fingering the broken cobble in her pocket. The day had been dryer than the previous one; that was as much as she could say for it. Sun seemed to linger forever as she trudged through the noisy, stinking streets. She asked everyone for work, even the butcher who had driven her out from under his awning, a shapeless, faceless, unrecognizable bundle he didn't remember in the light. But he only laughed and offered the usual, smacking with the flat of his hand the quivering haunch of meat he was slicing into steaks.

"Come back when you get desperate," he called after her, to the amusement of his customers. "Show me how fine you can grind it."

She got much the same at inns and alehouses. When she stopped at crossings to rest her feet and beg for a coin or two, she got threats from sweepers' brooms, screeches from ancient heaps of rags whose territory she had invaded, shoves from lean, hollow-cheeked, cat-eyed girls with missing teeth who told her they'd cut off her hair with a rusty knife if they saw her twice on their street.

Toward late afternoon she was too exhausted to feel hungry. She had money for one more night's lodging, or money for food. Not both. After that—she didn't think about it. That would be tomorrow, this was not. Now she had her two coppers, her two choices. And she had the stone in her pocket. She drifted, waiting for night.

When the street lamps were lit, she made up her mind. Just in that moment. She was sitting in the dark, finally safe because nobody could see her nursing her blistered, aching soles. Nobody threatened, yelled, or made lewd suggestions; for a few precious moments she might have been invisible.

And then the gas lamps went on, showing the world where she was again. Caught in the light, she didn't even think. She was on her feet in a breath, hand in her pocket; in the next she had hurled the broken stone furiously at the light. She was startled to hear the satisfying shatter of glass. Someone shouted; the flare, still burning, illumined a couple of uniformed figures to which, she decided with relief, she would yield herself for her transgression.

There was a sudden confusion around her: ragged people rushing into the light, all calling out as they surrounded the uniforms. Jo, pushing against them, couldn't get past to reveal herself to the law.

"I did it," a woman shrieked.

"No, it was me broke the lamp," somebody else shouted. The crowd lurched; voices rose higher. "Give over, you great cow—it was me!"

"I did it!" Jo shouted indignantly. "It wasn't them at all!"

The crowd heaved against her, picked her off her feet. Then it dropped her a moment later, as it broke apart. She lost her balance, sat on the curb staring as the uniforms escorted the wrong woman entirely out of the light. She went along eagerly enough, Jo noted sourly. She pulled herself up finally, still smarting over the injustice of it all.

Then she realized that her purple shawl was gone.

She felt her throat swell and burn, for the first time in forever. Even when her mother had died she hadn't cried. Not even when the baby had died. She had taken the shawl off her mother, and then off the baby. It was all she had left to remember them by. Now that was gone. And she was blinded, tears swelling behind her eyes, because the tattered shawl had borne the burden, within its braided threads, of her memories.

Now she was left holding them all herself.

She limped to find some private shred of shadow, refusing to let tears fall. All the shadows seemed occupied; snores and mutterings warned her before she could sit. She wandered on and on through the quieting streets, unable to stop the memories swirling in her head. Her innocent young self, cleaning the ashes out of the fireplace in the fine, peaceful library. The handsome stranger with the light, easy voice, asking her name. Asking about her. Listening to her, while he touched her cuff button with his finger. Shifted a loose strand of her hair off her face. Touched her as no one had, ever before. Then gone, nowhere, not to be seen, he might have been a dream. And she, beginning to wake at nights, feeling the panic gnawing at her until she could bear it no longer, and upped and ran.

But there was something else. A street name dredged it up as she walked. Or the night smell of a great tree in a line of them along the street. She had run from someone else. Oh, she remembered. Him. The young painter. He had a gentle voice, too, but he only touched her to turn her head, or put her loose hair where he wanted it. He paid well, too, for the random hour or two she could spare him. It was his money she saved to run with, when she knew she could no longer stay. When her skirts grew tight. When the other girls began to whisper, and the housekeeper's eyes drew up tight in her head like a snail's eyes at the sight of Jo.

What was his name?

She walked under the great, dark boughs that shielded her from the streetlights. She could sleep under them, she thought. Curl up in their roots like an animal; no one would see her until dawn. The street was very quiet; a sedate carriage or a cab went by now and then, but she heard no voices. He lived on a street like this; she remembered the trees. She'd walk there from the great house, his housekeeper would let her in, and she would climb the stairs to his—his what was it? His studio. He painted her with that strange fruit in her hand, with all the rows of little seeds in it like baby teeth.

He told her stories.

You are in the Underworld, he said. You have been stolen from your loving mother's house by the King of Hades. You must not eat or drink anything he offers you; if you refuse, he will have no power over you, and he must set you free. But you grow hungry, so hungry, as you wait . . .

"So hungry," she whispered.

You eat only a few tiny seeds from this fruit, thinking such small things would do no harm. But harm you have done for now he can claim you as his wife and keep you, during the darkest months of the year, in his desolate and lonely realm. . . .

What was her name?

Her eyes were closing. Her bones ached; her feet seemed no longer recognizable. Not feet any longer, just pain. Pain she walked on, and dark her only friend. . . . She didn't choose; she simply fell, driven to her knees in the damp ground beneath a tree. She crawled close to it, settled herself among its roots, her head reeling, it felt like, about to bounce off her shoulders and roll away without her.

What was its name?

She closed her eyes and saw it: that bright, glowing fruit, those sweet, innocent seeds . . .

Pomegranate.

Would he want to finish his painting? she wondered.

But there was someone guarding her passage out of the Underworld. Someone stood at the gates she must pass through, protecting the serene upper realms from the likes of her. Someone whose word was law on the border between two worlds. . . .

What was her name?

Her eyes. Jo could not remember her eyes, only felt them watching as she fled into the ancient, timeless dark. Only her bun, the light, glossy brown of a well-baked dinner roll, and her chins and the watch pinned to her bosom, at one corner of her apron.

What would her eyes say when she saw Jo?

She remembered as she felt the strong arms seize her, pull her off the earth into the nether realms of sleep.

Mrs. Grommet.

HARRY, having returned from the country without his Medusa, avoided his studio. He did not want to open the cupboard door again. He couldn't decide which might be worse: his painting talking to him or his painting not talking to him. Was expecting a painting to speak to him worse than having it speak to him? Suppose he opened the cupboard door with expectations, and nothing happened? He would be forced to conclusions which, in the cheery light of day, he did not want to think about.

So he left the house at midmorning and dropped in at a gallery where a new painting by Thomas Buck was hung. The gallery, recently opened, had acquired pieces indiscriminately in its desire to become fashionable. It aimed, it

declared affably, to encourage the novice as well as to celebrate the artist. Tommy Buck's work showed promise. It
had been showing promise for years. Harry, studying the
new painting called *Knight Errant,* was gratified to see that
Buck still could not draw to save his life. The horse was
absurdly proportioned; its wide, oblong back could have
been set for a dinner party of six. And the knight's hands,
conveniently hidden within bulky gauntlets, gripped the
reins awkwardly, as though he were playing tug-of-war. The
young woman tied to a tree, toward whom the knight rode,
seemed to be chatting amiably with the dragon who men-
aced her.

I could do better than that, Harry thought.

He felt the urge, remembered the anomaly in the cupboard, and was relieved when some friends hailed him. They
carried him away eventually to dine, and from there to another friend's studio where they drank wine and watched
the painter struggle with his Venus, a comely enough young
woman with something oddly bland about her beauty. She
bantered well, though, and stayed to entertain them over a
cold supper of beef and salad. Harry got home late, pleasantly tipsy, and, inspired, went immediately up to his studio to view his work within the context of his friends'.

The Gorgon spoke when he opened the cupboard, causing him to reel back with a startled cry: he had actually forgotten her.

"Hello, Harry."

"Hlmph," he choked.

"Have you found me yet?"

He tugged at his collar, tempted to slam the cupboard
shut and go to bed. But he answered, venturing closer, "No.
Not yet."

"Did you even look for me?"

"Of course I did! I looked for you in every female face
I passed. I didn't see you anywhere." Except, he thought, in

McAlister's garden, where Her eyes had immobilized him once again. "You aren't easy to find," he added, speaking now into the shadows. "You're a very complex matter."

"Yes, I am, aren't I?" she murmured complacently. "Harry, why don't you let me out?"

"I can't. What if someone sees?"

"Well, I don't intend to pass the time of day with Mrs. Grommet, if that's what worries you."

"No, but—"

"Hang a cloth over my face or something. Pretend I'm a parrot."

"I don't think so," he sighed, sitting down on the floor because he had been standing much of the day. A lamp on the wall above his head spilled some light into the open cupboard; he could see the edge of the canvas, but not the moving mouth. Less afraid now, lulled by wine and company, he asked her curiously, "Where do you think I should look for you?"

"Oh, anywhere. You'll know me when you see me."

"But to see you is to be—"

"Yes," she said, laughing a little. "You'll recognize your model when she turns you, for just a tiny human moment, into stone."

"Only One can do that," he said softly.

"Maybe. You just keep looking."

"But for what? Are you—were you, I mean, really that terrible? Or that beautiful? Which should I be searching for?"

"Oh, we were hideous," she answered cheerfully, "me and my two Gorgon sisters. Stheno and Euryale, they were called. Even in the Underworld, our looks could kill."

"Stheno?"

"Nobody remembers them, because nothing much ever happened to them. They didn't even die, being immortal. Do you think anyone would remember me if that obnoxious boy hadn't figured out a way to chop my head off without looking at me?"

Harry dredged a name out of the mists of youthful education. "Perseus, was it?"

"He had help, you know. He couldn't have been that clever without divine intervention. Long on brawn, short on brains, you know that type of hero."

"That's not what I was taught."

"He forced our guardian sisters, the gray-haired Graie, to help him, you must have heard. He stole their only eye and their tooth."

"They had one eye?" Harry said fuzzily.

"They passed it back and forth. And the tooth. Among the three of them." She gave an unlovely cackle. "What a sight that was, watching them eat. Or squabble over that eyeball. That's what they were doing when they didn't see that brat of a boy coming. He grabbed their goods and forced them to give him magic armor and a mirror to see me in, so he wouldn't have to meet my eyes. Then he lopped my head off and used me to to kill his enemies. Even dead, I had an effect on people."

"He doesn't sound so very stupid."

"He had help," she repeated with a touch of asperity. "Anyway, it was loathsome, gray-haired old biddies who armed him to fight me. Not lissome, rosy-fingered maidens. You remember that when you paint me."

"I will." He added, brooding over the matter, "If I can find you."

"Oh, you will," she said more cheerfully. "Never fret. I do wish you would take me out of here and let me watch, though."

"No."

"I could advise you."

"You'd scare my model."

"I wouldn't talk, I promise you! And if I forget, just

cover me up. Please, Harry? After all, I have inspired you. You could do me a favor. It's awfully dark in here."

"Well."

"Please? Harry?"

"Well." He got to his feet again, dusted off his trousers, yawning now and forgetting why he had come up. "I'll think about it. Good night."

"Good night, Harry."

He closed the cupboard door and went to bed.

The next morning, his ambition inflamed by what the gallery seemed to think worth hanging, he ate his breakfast hastily and early. He would not come home without his Medusa, he was determined, even if he had to search the ravaged streets and slums for her. No, he told Mrs. Grommet, she should not expect him home before evening. If then. He would go as far as he must to find his inspiration, even as far, he admitted in his inmost heart, as the country, to see if he might find that unexpected face in Aurora's shadow.

He got as far as the street. He paused to latch the garden gate behind him and was turned to stone.

A woman appeared out of nowhere, it seemed. She murmured something to him; he hardly knew what. He looked at her and time stopped. The normal street noises of passing carriages, birds, doors opening, voices calling, simply vanished. He heard the faint hum of his own blood in his ears and recognized it as a constant, unchanging sound out of antiquity. The sound heard when all else is silent; nothing moves.

Her face was all bone and shadow, full of stark paradoxes: young yet ancient with experience, beautiful yet terrifying with knowledge, living yet somehow alive no longer. Whatever those great, wide-set eyes had seen had left a haunting starkness in them that riveted him where he stood. She spoke again. She might have been speaking Etruscan, for all the words made sense to Harry. Her mouth held the same contradictions: it was lovely, its grim line warned of horror, it hungered, it would never eat again.

Sound washed over him again: a delivery wagon, a yowling cat, a young housemaid chasing after it down the street. He heard his stammering voice. "Where—where did you come from?"

She gestured. Out of a tree, out of the sky, her hand said. She was very poorly dressed, he realized: her thin, tight jacket torn at both elbows, the hem of her skirt awash with dried mud, her shoes worn down and beginning to split. She spoke again, very slowly, as if to a young child, or a man whose wits had badly strayed.

"I wondered if you had some work for me, sir. If maybe you could use me for your paintings. Anything will do. Any amount of time—"

One of his hands closed convulsively above her elbow; his other hand pulled the gate open.

"Oh, yes," he said unsteadily. "Oh, yes. Miss. Whoever you—"

"Jo, sir."

"Jo. Come in." He swept her down the walk, threw the door wide, and shouted, "Mrs. Grommet! Mrs. Grommet! We need you!"

"YOU have lice," Mrs. Grommet said.

Jo, hearing her within a cascade of lukewarm water, thought her voice sounded simply matter-of-fact. The kitchen maid stopped pouring water, began to pass a hard, lumpy bar of soap over Jo's wet hair. It took time to work up a lather.

"I'm not surprised," Jo murmured. She knelt in her tattered chemise beside a huge tub, allowing Mrs. Grommet the sight of her cracked, filthy feet. She could only hope that whatever vision had possessed Mr. Waterman to let her in the house would not be washed down the drain. But, she told herself coldly, if that happens then I will be no worse than I was before, and at least I will be clean.

"Go on, girl," the housekeeper said. "Give it a good scrub. Pretend you're doing the front steps."

"There's such a lot of it," the maid ventured. Jo closed her eyes, felt the blunt, vigorous fingers work away at her until she imagined herself underwater, floating in some river god's grip, being flailed back and forth like water weed.

"Rinse now," Mrs. Grommet ordered, and the water flowed again, copious and mercilessly cold. "There," the housekeeper said at last with satisfaction. "That should do it."

Freed, Jo straightened. The maid tossed a towel over her head and began to pummel her again.

"Go and boil some water," Mrs. Grommet told her. She added to Jo when the girl had gone, "Sometimes they work and sometimes they don't, these new hot water pipes. He didn't recognize you, did he?"

Jo swallowed. Mrs. Grommet's eyes, green as unripe tomatoes, said very little beyond her words. She knows, Jo thought. She knows why I ran away. But what Mrs. Grommet felt about that, Jo could only guess. Anyone else in the housekeeper's position would have made her sentiments about this immoral, unwashed bit of dredge crossing her employer's threshold very plain, very soon.

"No," Jo said simply. "He doesn't. He saw my face and wants to paint it. That's all. I don't know if he'll feel the same when he sees it again. If not, I'll go."

Mrs. Grommet did not comment on that. "I'll see what I can find for you to wear while you wash."

"Mrs. Grommet—" Her voice faltered; the housekeeper, hand on the doorknob, waited expressionlessly. "I know my clothes are a disgrace, but they're all I've got, if I go. Please—"

"Don't worry, girl," Mrs. Grommet said briskly, "I won't turn you out naked into the street, whatever becomes of you."

An hour later, Jo sat at the kitchen fireplace, letting her hair dry while she ate some cold beef and bread. She was dressed in a dark, shapeless gown which had made its way, some time in the distant past, to Harry's costume closet. Made to fit tight at wrists and neck and beneath the bosom, it hung on Jo like a sack. The kitchen maid, chopping onions for a pie, could not stop staring at her. Jo, too weary to eat much, didn't wonder at her staring, until the cook, a great mound of a woman with cheeks the color of raw beef, who was rolling out pastry, made as though to swat the maid with a floury hand.

"Leave her be, then," she grunted.

"I'm sorry, miss," the girl murmured to Jo. "I can't help it. It's your hair."

Jo glanced sideways at it, as it fell around her face. It did look unfamiliar clean, but other than that it was just her hair.

"What's the matter with it? Have I got the mange, too?"

"No," the maid whispered, flicking her eyes to it again. "It's so beautiful, all long and gold and curly."

Jo blinked, at a loss. Her eyes rose helplessly, sought Mrs. Grommet's.

The housekeeper, sipping tea at the table and still inscrutable, gave a brief nod. "Oh, yes. He'll like that."

Jo, suddenly terrified, stood abruptly, her meal scattering out of her fingers into the fire. "I have to go, then," she heard herself babble. "I have to go. Where are my shoes? I had a couple of coppers in my shoes—"

Mrs. Grommet gazed at her wordlessly. Her eyes came alive suddenly, as she pushed herself to her feet. "There now, Jo," she said faintly, rounding the table to Jo's side. "Mr. Waterman's not like that. You know that. There's no need to run away from him again." She put her hand on Jo's arm and pointed to a grubby little pile near the hearth. "There's your shoes and clothes. The coins are in there, just as I found them. If you need them, you'll have them."

"Why," Jo asked her wildly, "are you treating me this way?"

"What way?" Mrs. Grommet asked, astonished.

It took Jo a moment to remember the word. "Kind." Spoken, it seemed to surprise them both. "Why are you being kind to me? You know—you—"

Mrs. Grommet's eyes went distant again. But she kept her hand on Jo's arm, patted it a little. "Stay a bit," she said finally, eluding the question. "Mr. Waterman will think we drove you away if you leave now. He'll only go looking for you."

"But I don't understand—"

"Well, you might ask him what he has in mind. You might stay long enough to listen to him. Whatever it is, I'm sure it's nothing more than a painting."

Jo, still trembling, sat down at the hearth again. She heard whispering; after a moment, the little maid brought her a cup of tea. She sipped it wordlessly, the kitchen silent behind her but for the thump of the rolling pin. When she knew she could stand again, she knew it was time. She rose, set the cup on the table. Mrs. Grommet looked at her.

"I'll take you up," she said briefly. Jo nodded gratefully, too lightheaded to speak.

She passed familiar hallways, paintings, patterns of wallpaper, carpets that seemed more real in memory. It was, she thought dazedly, like being in two places at once; she was uncertain, from one step to the next, if she were moving backward or forward in time. They went up the second flight of steeper stairs into the top of the house. There, as Mrs. Grommet opened the door, Jo saw another memory that was real: the long rows of windows overlooking the street, the park across from them, and on the other side of the house, the river. She could see the tree under which she had wakened in the other world at dawn. She smelled oils and pungent turpentine, saw the untidy shelves of books and sketches, the oddments everywhere—peacock feathers, beads, baskets, seashells, tapestries, rich shawls of taffeta, goblets, moth-eaten furs.

She saw Harry. He stood across the room, watching her silently as she entered. She had never seen anyone look at her like that before, as though she were something not quite human, a piece of dream, maybe, that he had to step into to see her properly.

He said absently, "Thank you, Mrs. Grommet."

"Yes, sir." She lingered. "Will you need—"

"Nothing. Thank you."

She closed the door behind her. Harry crossed the room, came close to Jo. Still in his dream, she saw, he reached out, touched her hair with one finger. She felt herself stiffen. He drew back hastily. She saw his eyes again, anxious now, tentative, fascinated. Like some mooncalf boy in love for the first time, she realized, and not even sure with what.

"Will you let me paint you?" he asked huskily.

"Of course," she answered, so amazed she forgot her terrors.

"I see you—I see you as a very ancient power, a goddess, almost, who is herself mortal, but who can kill with a look. To see her is to die. But not to see her is to live without living. I see you, in all her terrible, devastating beauty, as Medusa."

"Yes, Mr. Waterman," she said, completely mystified, and thought with wonder: he doesn't recognize me at all.

MUCH later that day, almost into the next, Harry sat on the floor beside the open cupboard door, babbling to the Gorgon.

"The lines of her face are stunning. They transfixed me

the moment I saw them. They seem shaped—sculpted—by primal forces, like stone, yet very much alive. They are beauty, they are death, they are youth, they are ancient beyond belief. And her eyes. Medusa's eyes. They gaze at you from another world, the Underworld perhaps; they are portals to that grim world. Of the palest gray, nearly colorless, like the mist between life and death—" He heard a vague noise from within the cupboard, almost as if the Gorgon had sneezed. "I beg your pardon. Did you speak?"

"No," she said faintly.

"And her hair. I've never seen anything like it. White gold, rippling down from her face to her knees. Again that suggestion of youth and antiquity, knowledge gained too early from unearthly places—"

"Harry."

"Her mouth—there again—"

"Harry."

"Yes, what is it?"

"I think you should let me see her."

"Her mouth is like—"

"I promise, by Perseus's shield that bore my reflection and killed me, that I won't speak a word in her presence."

"Again, it contradicts itself—it should be mobile, plump, alluring, the delicate pink of freshwater pearls—"

"You can put me in a dark corner where she won't notice me."

"But it has long forgotten how to smile; its line is inflexible and determined—"

"Harry. It's me you're painting. I haven't seen myself in thousands of years. Have a heart. Let me see what humans think of me these days. I'm not used to being associated with beauty."

Harry was silent. He thought he perceived the faintest undertone in the Gorgon's plea, as though she were laughing at him. But her words argued otherwise. And it did seem an appropriate request. She had, after all, inspired him; how could he deny her his vision of herself?

"You'll forget," he said guardedly, "and say something impulsive and frighten her away."

"I won't. I have sworn."

"I'll think about—"

"Harry. Stop thinking about it. Just do it. Or I'll yell my head off here in the cupboard like one of Bluebeard's wives."

Harry blinked. "You could have done that—"

"Today, while she was here. Yes. But I didn't, did I? I am capable of controlling myself. I won't say a word in her presence, no matter how—"

"How?"

"No matter what."

"Do I amuse you?" Harry demanded indignantly.

"No, no," the Gorgon said soothingly. "No. I'm just incredibly old, Harry, and my sense of humor is warped. I'm very ignorant of the modern world, and it would do me good to see even a tiny corner of it."

Harry sighed, mollified. "All right. Tomorrow morning, before she comes."

"Thank you, Harry."

He got up early to hang the Gorgon above some high bookshelves, among other old sketches and watercolors scattered along the wall. The contradictions in the face startled him anew: the frightened eyes, the pale, anxious brows, the lush, voluptuous, wine-red mouth. His eyes lingered on that mouth as he descended the ladder. He would make a trip to the country soon, he decided. She was down there with Alex nearly every weekend. The mouth seemed to crook in a faint smile; his foot froze on the bottom rung.

"No," he said sharply. "You must be absolutely still."

The mouth composed itself. The eyes gazed unseeingly across the room. He had placed the painting where most often his model would have her back to it. She would only glimpse it as she faced the door to leave. And few people looked that high without reason, Harry had learned to his chagrin when his work had been hung near the ceiling in exhibits. She would never notice the peculiar face with its mismatched features unless she looked for it.

He spent a few days sketching Jo, learning every nuance of her face, experimenting with various positions, draperies. He decided, in the end, simply to paint her face at the instant she saw herself reflected in the young hero's shield. The Medusa turning her baleful gaze upon herself and realizing in that instant that she had slain herself. The shield would frame her within the canvas. The pale, rippling beauty of the model's hair would transform itself easily into gorgeous, dangerous snakes. Jo's stark-white skin, drained of life force it seemed, hollowed and shadowed with weariness and strain, hinted of the Medusa's otherworldly origins. He positioned black silk in graceful folds about her neck to emphasize the shadows. That would be her only costume. That and the snakes in her hair, which might suggest, in their golden brilliance, the final light of the sun upon her dying and deadly face.

So lost he was in the excitement of inspiration that he scarcely remembered to speak to his model. She came in the mornings, murmured, "Good morning, Mr. Waterman," and sat in her chair beside his easel. He arranged the silk about her throat, giving her a greeting or a pleasantry. Then she became so still she hardly seemed to breathe. He worked, utterly absorbed, until the light began to fade. Then, her pallor deep by then, her humanity began to intrude upon him. She is tired, he would realize. She must be hungry. I am.

He would put his palette down and open the door. "Mrs. Grommet," he would call down the stairs. Then he would study the day's work until the housekeeper hove into view, bearing a tea tray and Jo's wages for the day. Jo would follow her down. Mrs. Grommet would feed her in the kitchen, for Harry was reluctant to glimpse, at this sensitive stage, his Medusa with her cheeks full of mutton.

The Gorgon above their heads watched all this silently, refraining from comment.

She hardly saw Jo, Harry knew, except when she rose to leave. Then the wan, beautiful face would be visible to the painting above her head. Jo never looked that high; she seemed oddly incurious about the studio. Other models had prowled around peering at his canvases, opening books, trying on bits of finery, fingering this and that. But Jo just came and left, as though, Harry thought, she truly vanished into another world and was not much interested in his.

The Gorgon finally asked one evening, after Jo had followed Mrs. Grommet downstairs, "Where does she go?"

"What?" Harry asked through a bite of sandwich.

"Your model. Where does she sleep at night?"

"How should I know?" He was sitting in a soft stuffed chair, weary from standing all day, and devouring sandwiches and cakes, he suspected, like a well-brought-up vulture. He could see the Gorgon's face from that position if he wanted. Her voice startled him; she hadn't said much for days.

"Aren't you pleased with me, Harry?"

"For being so quiet? Oh, yes, I'm very grateful." He swallowed another mouthful of hot, sweet tea, and looked up at her. "What do you think of her?"

"Oh, a great deal," the painting answered vaguely, and gave a sudden, crude snort of a laugh. "She's far too beautiful for the likes of me, of course. But I see your point in her."

"Do you?"

"Beauty that can kill. But Harry, she's bone-thin and she's not much use to you dead. She might sleep in an alley for all you know. Anything could happen to her, and you'd never know what."

Harry was silent, blinking. He took another scalding sip. "I hadn't thought of that."

"Well, think of it. What would you do if tomorrow she didn't appear?"

The thought brought him out of his chair to pace a little, suddenly edgy. "Surely I pay her enough for decent lodgings. Don't I?"

"How much is enough?"

"I don't—"

"And suppose she has others dependent on her? Who need every coin she brings to them?"

"Well, maybe—" He paused, still tramping across the room; then he dropped into his chair again. "I'll ask Mrs. Grommet."

"You could ask your model."

Harry rolled his head to gaze up at the painting. "How?" he pleaded. "She is my Medusa. She exists only in this little world, only to be painted. I dare not make her real. She might lose all her power, become just another woman in my eyes."

The Medusa snorted again, this time without amusement. "She'd still be there for you to paint her. Your brush knows how to lie. If she vanishes into the streets out there, where will you go to look for her? You might at least ask her that."

Harry tried, at least three times, the next morning, before he got a question out. His model, whose name he kept forgetting, sat silently gazing as he had requested, at the back of his easel. What she saw, he could not begin to guess. Her wide, eerily pale eyes seemed to glimpse enormities in his peaceful studio. Until now, he had absently confused her expression with the Gorgon seeing herself for the first time and the last. Now he wondered, despite his better judgment, what those eyes had truly seen to make them so stricken.

He cleared his throat yet again. Her eyelids trembled, startled, at the sound of his voice. "Tell me, er—Jo?"

"Yes, sir?"

"Do you have a decent place to stay at night? I mean, I do pay you enough for that, don't I?"

She kept her face very still, answered simply, "Yes, Mr. Waterman. I go to a lodging house on Carvery Street."

"Alone?"

Her eyes flicked up, widening; he caught the full force of the Gorgon's stare. "Sir?"

"I mean—I only meant—Do you have other people to care for? Others dependent on you?"

"Oh." The fierce gaze lowered once again to the middle distance. "No, sir. They're dead."

"Oh," he said inanely. He painted in silence a while, aware, though he told himself he imagined it, of eyes boring into his head from above the bookshelves. He glanced up finally, was appalled to see the full red lips moving wildly in a grotesque parody of speech.

He cleared his throat again hastily. "Do you get enough to eat? I mean, you're very thin."

"I'm eating better now," she answered.

The question sent a faint, unwelcome patina of color into her white face that at first alarmed him. Then he thought, Why not? Medusa, seeing her own beauty for the first time, may well flush with pleasure and astonishment before she turns herself into stone.

"Do you know," he asked aimlessly, trying to make conversation, "the story of Medusa?"

"Something of it," she said hesitantly. "Some sort of monster who turned people into stone?"

"Yes."

"Ugly, wasn't she?"

"Hideous," he answered, "by all accounts."

He heard her take a breath or two then, as if to speak. Then she grew still again, so still that he wondered if he had somehow turned her into stone.

HE let his model rest a day or two later and spent a tranquil afternoon in the country, watching others work. Arthur Millidge was there, putting a honeysuckle background to what would be his *Nymph Dying for Love of a Shepherd.* He kept knocking his easel over swatting at bees. John Grainger was there as well, to Harry's surprise, back on his windy knoll painting the distant village. McAlister had finished his wife's windblown sleeve; now he was engrossed in her bare feet and ankles, around which green silk swirled and eddied. Harry, after his first glimpse of those long marble toes and exquisite anklebones, took the first chair he found and tried not to think about them.

Arthur Millidge's wife Holly handed him a cup of tea and sat down beside him. She was a pretty, good-natured, giddy-headed thing, who could pull out an arrow and hit an astute social bull's-eye just when she seemed at her most frivolous. She was watching her suffering husband with a great deal of amusement.

"Oh, poor Arthur," she cried, when he batted at a wasp with his brush and actually hit it; it stuck, struggling, to the yellow-daubed bristles. "At least it's the right color."

Her husband smiled at her wanly.

"I thought," Harry said blankly, "that Grainger and Nan would still be at the south coast."

"Oh, no," Holly answered briskly. "They only spent a few days there."

"But they are—they did get married?"

"So it seems. She's wearing a ring."

"Is she here?"

"No, poor thing, the traveling exhausted her in her condition, so she let John come alone."

Harry's eyes crept back to Aurora. Her condition, as well, he remembered; he could not, for a prolonged moment, stop studying her. The flowing, voluminous silk hid everything. Her face seemed a trifle plumper, but then he had been gazing at his emaciated model for days, he reminded himself. Aurora's face seemed exquisitely serene, he realized, ivory, full and tranquil, like a midsummer moon.

"The condition suits Aurora," Holly said, reading Harry's thoughts in her uncanny way. "I think poor Nan will have a great deal of difficulty with it. She's frail anyway and suffers from imagination."

Harry pulled his eyes away from McAlister's wife, dipped his hand into a bowl full of cherries. "Which of us doesn't?" he asked lightly.

"I'm sure I don't." Holly laughed and helped herself to a cherry or two from Harry's hand. "I heard you're painting something mysterious, Harry. Tommy Buck said that he and some friends came to visit you, and you refused to let them into your studio."

"They frightened my model," Harry said, remembering the shouts, Mrs. Grommet's flurried protest, the stampede up the stairs. "I thought she might faint, she was trembling so badly."

Holly maneuvered a cherry pit daintily from lips to palm and tipped it into the grass. "But who is she? Someone we know?"

"No. I found her in the street."

"How exciting! And what are you making of her?"

"Oh, I'm experimenting with this and that," he answered airily. "Nothing much, yet."

"She must be very pretty."

"In a wild kind of way. She's very shy. Not used to company."

"Everyone," Holly sighed, "is full of secrets. Alex won't tell what he's working on, either. You should bring her here, Harry."

"I should?"

"It might calm her, knowing others like her who model. Besides, if you decide you can't make anything of her, someone else might, and then she wouldn't have to go back into the streets."

"True," he said absently, flinging a cherry pit at a bee buzzing in the honeysuckle. "Oh, sorry, Arthur. I was aiming for the bee."

"Don't try to be helpful, Waterman."

"I won't, then."

"Will you bring her, Harry?"

"I might," he answered vaguely and changed the subject. "What do you think McAlister is making out of his wife?"

"Oh, who knows?" Holly said, waving midges away from her face. "Blind Justice? Aphrodite? Maybe even he doesn't know. The point is to keep her here, don't you think?"

"Here?" Harry repeated, mystified. Holly turned her head, regarded him blithely a moment, chin on her fist. Abruptly she laughed and got to her feet.

"Oh, Harry. You are so unbearably sweet. Arthur, come into the shade with us and have something to drink before you melt in all that light. I'm trying to worm secrets out of Harry."

"Harry has secrets?" John Grainger's deep, vigorous voice intoned incredulously behind them. *"Mirabile dictu!"* He dropped into a chair, dipped into the cherries with cerulean blue fingertips and demanded of the hapless Harry, "Tell all."

JO sat in Harry's kitchen, eating her supper after he had returned from the country and began to paint her again. At his request, she had given Mrs. Grommet explicit instructions about where to find her if Harry needed her. Mrs. Grommet dutifully wrote the address down. Then, to Jo's surprise, she poured herself a cup of tea and pulled out a chair at the end of the table near Jo, where she sat close to the fire.

Mrs. Grommet said, "I know Mrs. Atkins, the woman who owns the lodging house on Carvery Street. She's a good, honest woman. Or at least she was when we worked together, in a great house over on Bellingham Road."

Jo's eyes slid uncertainly to her face. She managed an answer, after a moment. "She seems kind."

"She married unexpectedly. Lucky for her, her husband had saved a little money. And had a very loving heart. Married they were for thirty years before he died, and never a word passed his lips that their child wasn't his."

Jo coughed on a bit of pickled beet. The kitchen maid was on the far side of the kitchen, banging pots noisily in weltering dishwater. The cook was in the pantry counting spoons, which was her way of saying resting her feet and having a nip. Mrs. Grommet's green eyes opened meaningfully upon Jo, then lowered again. She sipped tea, half-turned at a splash from the sink.

"Go easy, girl! You're washing pots, not the flagstones."

Jo put two and two together, cleared her throat. Still, words came out with difficulty. "That's why—" She drew a breath, met the housekeeper's eyes. "That's why you're kind to me."

"Things happen," Mrs. Grommet said, the corners of her mouth puckering a moment. "They're not always our fault."

"No." She lifted her cup. It trembled badly; she put it down again quickly before she spilled. She folded her hands tightly, said to them, "It takes a special heart to see it that way, though."

Mrs. Grommet patted her hands. "I saw how you were with Mr. Waterman the first time you came here. So quiet and nicely behaved. Some of his models—well, the less said. Not that he was that way, at least not under his own roof. But I hear the young men talking about the girls they paint, about which would only pose and go, and which might stay around after for their bit of fun." She became aware of the maid handling the pots as gently as possible, and raised her voice again. "Finish up there, Lizzie, then go and see if Cook needs help in the pantry."

"Yes, Mrs. Grommet."

Jo said very softly, "You were friends, then, you and Mrs. Atkins, when you worked on Bellingham Road."

"Mary. Mary Plum she was, then. We started there very young, you see, and during the same summer. We were there together for five years. What happened to her seemed so unfair to me. It was one of the young friends of the family—"

"Yes," Jo whispered.

"Nothing to him, of course. He told her he loved her and would care for her. He couldn't even remember her name or her face, next time he came. He looked straight at her, she said, when she was serving dinner, and didn't even see her. She was at the point then when she had to leave. She had no choice. But then Martin—Mr. Atkins—found her weeping under the privet hedge when he went to trim it. He was a gardener there, then, and very well thought of. He'd saved all his money for years for an investment, he said. He asked Mary to be his investment." She paused, watching Jo's struggling face. "I've never seen you smile before."

"I've nearly forgotten how. Did he really put it like that?"

"She was a pretty thing," Mrs. Grommet said reminiscently. "He said he'd had his eye on her, but never thought he'd have a chance. Well, chance came, wearing an unexpected face, and he was brave enough to take it. She had a daughter who looked just like her. After some years, he'd worked so hard that—" She stopped abruptly. "Oh, dear."

The tears came out of nowhere Jo could name, hot, fierce and seemingly unstoppable. She put her hands over her mouth, turned her back quickly to face the fire again. She heard Mrs. Grommet say something sharply to Lizzie; all sounds faded in the kitchen. Jo felt a tea towel pushed into her hand.

She buried her face in it, seeing, feeling, smelling all at once, as though memory, locked so carefully away, had crashed and blundered out of its door. His warm, slight weight in her arms, the smell of milk in his hair, his wide, round eyes catching at hers.

"Poor Alf," she whispered into the towel. "Oh, poor Alf. Poor little poppit. Oh, Mrs. Grommet, I did love him despite everything—"

"Now, then."

"He was just too frail to go on."

"There now." Mrs. Grommet patted her shoulder.

"I'm sorry."

"It's all right; Lizzie's gone. You have a good cry."

"I haven't—I forgot to cry, when—when—" Her voice wailed away from her, incoherent. She shook hair over her face and eyes like a shroud, trying to hide in it while tears came noisily, messily, barely restrained under the wad of tea towel. "Poor mite, he was all my heart. I think we must have gotten buried together, and I have been just a ghost ever since. No wonder Mr. Waterman sees me as that stone-eyed monster—"

"What?"

She drew a raw, ragged breath that was half sob. "Some—Medusa—who turns people into stone with her eyes. That's what he sees when he looks at me." Then she felt an odd bubble in her chest; loosed, it sounded strangely like a laugh. "I'd terrify anyone with these eyes now—"

"Let me see," Mrs. Grommet said faintly. Jo lifted her face from the towel, pulled wet strands of hair from her cheeks.

Her throat ached again at the housekeeper's expression. But it was not grief so much as relief that she could still cry, she could still laugh. Which she found herself doing again amid her tears, in a damp, inelegant snort. "Look what I've done to you. You're stunned. . . . "

"You do look a bit fiery around the eyes," Mrs. Grommet admitted. "But no wonder Mr. Waterman doesn't remember you, with all that happened to you since."

"I was a maid when he began his first painting. Now, I'm Medusa." She sat again, drew a shuddering breath as she mopped her eyes.

"Maybe. But you look all the younger now for those tears." She refilled their cups. "Not that you're much more than a girl. But you just seemed . . . like you'd seen a Medusa, yourself. And lived to tell about it."

Jo wrapped her fingers around the cup, managed to raise it without spilling. "Mrs. Grommet, you've been so good to me," she said huskily. "I don't know how to thank you."

"Well. You reminded me so of Mary, when you disappeared like that. I couldn't see that you could have found any way to help yourself, except maybe into the river. Mr. Waterman looked for you when you left. He fretted about you. And not only for his painting. He wanted to help."

"I know." She got a sip past the sudden burn in her throat. "I was too frightened to think then. And now, I don't care if he never recognizes that terrified waif. I don't want him feeling sorry for me. I'm glad he doesn't know me."

"I did," Mrs. Grommet said, "the moment I saw you. I don't see how he can't. Being a painter as he is. Faces are his business."

"He doesn't see me. He sees the woman he wants to see. And I hope—" She touched her swollen eyes lightly. "I hope she's still there, in spite of my tears."

"Now he's got you thinking that way," Mrs. Grommet said roundly. "As if you're not yourself."

"But I never am, when he paints me. I am always the woman he has in mind. I think that's why he doesn't like to talk to me. He only wants to know the woman in his head. The dream he has of me. If I told him too much about"— she swallowed, continued steadily—"about Alf, about the streets, the mill, about my mother's hands all cracked from taking in laundry, about the purple shawl, the dream would be gone. All he'd have left is me."

HARRY was gazing at his Medusa, a ham sandwich forgotten in one hand. With the other hand he was pointing out to the Medusa overhead various examples of his brilliance or his clumsiness, which seemed, judging by the Gorgon's expression, to be running about neck and neck that day.

"Look there. Putting that fleck of pure white just so, I've captured perfectly the suggestion of ice in her gray eyes. Do you see it? Of course the delicate line of the inner eye is a bit blurry, there; I'll have to rework it." Raptly, he took a bite of sandwich. "And there . . ." he said with his mouth full, overcome. "You see what I did?"

"Harry. You still don't know anything about this woman."

"I told her to give Mrs. Grommet her address. You made a good point about that. Now, her hair. I shall have to go to the zoological gardens, observe some snakes." He paused, chewing, added regretfully, "I should have brought a few back with me from the country. I didn't think of it. Perhaps because I don't see the point of them. They just begin and go on and keep going on the same way they began, and then they end without any reason whatsoever." He paused again.

"Don't say it," the Gorgon pleaded.

Harry glanced at her, took another bite. "All right, I won't. But it is a bit like life, isn't it?"

"Harry!"

He smiled. "I'd give a lot to see your snakes, though. What color were they?"

"Ugly."

"No color is ugly."

"Maybe," the Medusa sighed, "but you must remember that I was hideous. I never looked at myself, of course, and my snakes were usually twined around my head. But now and then a loop or a head would lose its direction and slide near my eyes. They were fairly drab: brown, black, gray, without any interesting patterns. Big, they were, though. Thick as your wrists."

"Really? What did they eat?"

"Air, I suppose. Thoughts. They were my hair, Harry; they weren't meant to exist like ordinary creatures. Your hair feeds on you."

"I'll make hers like treasure," Harry said, studying the magnificent, haunting eyes again, the dangerous, irresistible mouth. "Gold, white gold, silver, buttercup, lemon. A shining, glittering swarm of colors. Tomorrow morning, I'll go—"

"She's coming tomorrow."

"I'll paint her in the morning then and visit the snakes in the afternoon."

"You could," the Gorgon suggested, "take her with you. You might get a better perspective on the snakes as hair if you see them both together."

Harry grunted, struck. "Possible . . ." Then he blinked. "No. What am I saying? I can't possibly watch this devastatingly powerful creature wandering around looking at snakes in the zoological garden. Something would happen."

"Like what?"

"She'd step in a puddle, get a paper stuck to her shoe, some such. She'd mispronounce the names of things, she'd want tea and a bun, or peanuts for the bears—"

"I can't see that frozen-eyed woman tossing peanuts to the bears. But what you're saying, Harry, is that she would be in danger of turning human."

"Exactly," Harry said adamantly. "I don't want her human, I want her Gorgon—"

"I bet she'd be a charming human."

Harry opened his mouth. As though one of the Medusa's snakes had streaked down quick as thought and bit him, he glimpsed the potential charms in those eyes, warming in a smile, that hair, piled carelessly on her head, tendrils about her face playing in a breeze. He clenched his fists, pushed them in front of his eyes. "No," he said fiercely. "No, no, and no. This is my masterwork, and nothing—" He lowered his hands as suddenly. "What on earth is that hubbub downstairs?"

There seemed to be a good deal of shouting and thumping coming up the stairwell. Mrs. Grommet's voice joined it and it resolved itself easily then, into any number of friends in every stage of revelry pushing their way upstairs to join Harry.

He threw open the door, heard their chanting as they ascended. "Where is she, Harry? We must see her. We want to see your painting, foul as it may be. We have come to kneel at the feet of your Muse, Harry!"

Harry had just enough time to remove the painting from the easel and slide it carefully into the cupboard. Where, he hoped fervently, it would not also acquire a voice. He opened his study door, stepped into the landing. Half a dozen friends, a couple of them painters, one planning a gallery, others budding poets or philosophers, or whatever was fashionable this week, reeled into one another at the sight of him. Then, they rushed the second flight of stairs.

Harry glimpsed Mrs. Grommet below, flinging her hands in the air, turning hastily back to the kitchen.

"Don't you dare lock your door this time," the honey-haired, sloe-eyed Tommy Buck called. "We'll sit on your stairs and hold them hostage until you reveal her. We'll—"

"She's not here," Harry said, with great relief. "She left an hour ago."

"Then let's see your painting."

"No. It's too dreadful." He turned adroitly as they reached the landing, and locked the door behind him. "You'll laugh, and I'll be forced to become a bricklayer."

"She's in there." Tommy Buck paused to hiccup loudly, then banged upon the door. "You've hidden her."

"I have not. She's a shy, sensitive woman and you lot would cause her to turn into a deer and flee."

"Prove it."

"Prove what?"

"Prove she's not there."

"All right, I will. But I don't want you all rummaging about my studio and tossing my bad paintings out the window. You can look in and see, Tommy. The rest of you go downstairs and wait."

"No," said one of the poets, a burly young man who looked like he might have flung bricks around in an earlier life. "Open up, Harry boy. Show us all."

"No. I shall defend all with my life."

"What's that in your hand?" Tommy asked, swaying as he squinted at it.

Harry looked. "My ham sandwich."

"Ham. He has ham in there," someone said wistfully. "I'm hungry."

"Here," Harry said, tossing him the remains.

"I saw it first," Tommy said indignantly. "I'm hungrier." He paused, still swaying lithely, like a reed in a breeze. "I've got an idea."

"He has an idea."

"I'd rather have a sandwich."

"Silence! I will speak! My idea is this. We all leave—" He waved his arms, fending off protests. "Listen. If we all go out to dinner, and Harry goes out to dinner with us, and then goes wherever we happen to go after that, it will prove that he hasn't got a model locked up in his studio. Won't it?"

"He could get the Grommet to unlock her," someone muttered.

"I won't speak to her," Harry promised. "And—" he dangled it. "I have the only key."

Tommy made a snatch at it. Harry tucked it out of reach. "She really has gone home," he told them. "And I think Tommy has an excellent idea. Maybe, if we hurry out, we'll catch a glimpse of her on the street."

They were quiet, staring at him, faces motionless in the stair lights.

Then, as one, they turned, clattered furiously back down the stairs. Harry followed more slowly, brushing crumbs off his shirt and rolling down his sleeves. He heard the street door fly open, voices flow down the hall and out. Someone called his name, then the sounds faded. He didn't hear the door close. He wondered if Mrs. Grommet had taken refuge in a closet until the barbarian horde had gone.

He reached the hall and nearly bumped into his Medusa, coming quickly out of the kitchen with Mrs. Grommet at her heels.

"Jo—" he exclaimed, startled.

She pulled up sharply, staring at him, just as surprised.

"Mr. Waterman," she breathed. "I thought you had left with them."

He was silent, studying her. Something was awry with her face. It seemed streaked, flushed in odd places; her cold, magnificent eyes looked puffy and reddened, oddly vulnerable. He caught his breath, appalled.

"What have you done?"

"Sorry, Mr. Waterman," she said tremulously, brushing at her eyes. "It'll be gone by morning."

"But—" Something else was happening to her face as he stared. Lines shifted. Memory imposed itself, rearranging a curve here, a hollow there. He swallowed, feeling as though the world he knew had vanished for an eye blink, and then returned, subtly, irrevocably altered.

"Jo," he said, feeling his heart beat. "Jo Byrd."

She said simply, "Yes."

SHE returned the next morning as she promised, though not without misgivings. She looked for the same apprehension in the artist's eyes, searching for his Medusa in her face while he arranged the black silk around her neck, to draw out her pallor as he said. She wasn't certain about the pallor. The face in the tiny mirror above her washstand had been more colorful than usual. Nor was she at all certain what Mr. Waterman was thinking. He was very quiet, murmuring instructions now and then. She would have described his expression as peculiar, if he had asked. He looked like someone who had swallowed a butterfly, she thought: a mixed blessing, no matter how you turned it.

She said finally, hesitantly, "Mr. Waterman. If you can't see your Medusa now for seeing me, I'll understand."

He gave his head a quick little shake, met her eyes. "As the Gor—as someone pointed out, I tell lies with my brush. Let's see how well I can do it."

"But—"

"We'll give it a try," he insisted calmly. "Shall we?"

"If you say so, sir." She subsided, prepared herself to sit as silently as usual.

But, strangely, now he seemed in a mood to talk. "I am," he said, touching white into the black around the Medusa's throat, "incredibly embarrassed that I didn't recognize you."

"I've gotten older."

"By how much? A year? I'm a painter! I've been staring at you daily. Not to mention—" His lips tightened; whatever it was, he didn't mention it.

"Yes, sir."

He looked at her again, instead of the silk. "I can't imagine what you've gone through. Or, rather, I can only try to imagine it. The child . . . it must have died?"

Her voice caught, but she had no tears left for that, it seemed. "Yes. He was never strong."

"Where did you go, when you vanished in the middle of my painting?"

"I went home to my mother's, in the country."

"I looked for you."

"I know. Mrs. Grommet told me."

His mouth crooked ruefully. "So she recognized you."

"The way I see it," Jo explained, "Mrs. Grommet was protecting your household. She has to know what she opens your door to. You remember what I looked like, then."

"Yes."

"She had to make decisions in her own mind about me. You were only seeing your painting. She was seeing a hungry, filthy wreck of a girl and trying to judge all in a moment whether I would steal the silver, eat with a fork or my fingers, go mad and break all the crockery. She was looking for reasons not to be afraid to let me through the door. You just saw your dream and let me walk right in."

He ran his hand through his hair, nearly tangling the brush in it. "Makes me sound like a fool."

She thought about that, shrugged. "I don't know. How do you like your painting?"

He looked at it, his eyes going depthless, still, like water reflecting an empty sky. They were, she realized suddenly, the exact blue of the dragonflies in the stream behind her parents' cottage. She'd lie and watch them dart and light, little dancing arrows as blue as larkspur.

Mr. Waterman blinked; so did she. They both drew back a little from what they'd been examining. She recognized that expression on his face; it was how he had been looking at her until now.

"I think—" he said, still gazing at his painting, and stammering a little, "I think—I wasn't a fool, after all. I think it's at least better than anything I've done so far. Jo . . ." He turned to her abruptly. "I have such amazing visions of your hair. Are you afraid of snakes?"

"No more or less than anything else that might bite me. But, sir," she amended warily, "surely you're not going to put them in my hair? I don't think I want to wear them."

"No, no." His thoughts veered abruptly. "I have to fix that eye before I go on. Look at me. Don't blink." He added, after a moment or two, "You can talk."

"About what?"

"Anything that won't make you cry." She felt her eyes flush at the thought; he looked stricken. "I'm sorry, Jo."

"It's just—somehow I never got around to crying before."

"Tell me something, anything you remember, that once made you happy. If there was anything," he added carefully.

"Well." The tide retreated; she gazed, dry-eyed, at her past. "When my father was alive, he kept a small flock of sheep for wool. I liked to look at them, all plump and white in their green field, watch the lambs leap for no reason except that they were alive. He'd shear them and we'd spin the wool into yarn to sell. Sometimes we'd look for madder root to dye it purple."

"We?" he asked, busy at the corner of her eye, from what she could see. "Sister?"

"My mother. I didn't have sisters. I had a little brother for a couple of years once, but he died."

"Oh. But you chose not to stay with your mother? To come back here instead?"

"She died, too."

"Oh. I'm sorry."

"Yes," she said softly, but without tears. "So was I. So I came back here. And you rescued me."

He looked at her, oddly surprised. "I did?"

"You did," she said huskily. "I couldn't find work, I was exhausted, I had two coppers to my name. I found my way to your street just muddling around in the dark, and then I remembered you. I slept under a tree, that night before I came to your door. I didn't have any hope, but I didn't have anything left to do. I even—I even tried to get myself arrested for breaking a street lamp, to have a place to sleep."

He was watching her, brush suspended. "When you do that—"

"What, sir?"

"Even when you only think about smiling, you change the shape of your eye. Medusa does not smile." He stopped abruptly, cast an odd glance above her head, and amended, "At least we have no recorded evidence that she smiled."

"You asked me to think about something happy."

"You didn't smile, then. It was irony, not happiness, that made you smile."

She mulled that over. "You mean trying to get into jail for a bed?"

"Yes. What happened? Did you miss the street lamp?"

"No. I hit it dead-on. But a dozen others stepped up on the spot and swore it was them that threw the stone. Someone else got my bed. So I wandered on—"

"And," he said softly, his brush moving again, "you found me."

"You found me," she whispered.

"No tears. Medusa does not cry."

She composed her face again, summoned the icy, gorgeous monster to look out of her eyes. "She does not cry."

"But," he said after a while, "she might perhaps like to come with me this afternoon to look at snakes. No blinking."

"No blinking."

"But snakes?"

"Looking at snakes," she said, suddenly aware of his own fair, tidy hair, on a nicely rounded head, his young face with its sweet, determined expression, "would make Medusa happy."

HARRY stood on the ladder in his studio, detaching the Gorgon from her nail. He had gotten in late. After spending a few hours among the reptiles and other assorted creatures, he had walked Jo to her lodging house on Carvery Street. Then he had wandered aimlessly, oddly light-headed, dropping in at studios here and there to let his friends tease him about his imaginary model, his hopeless daub of a painting so dreadful he was forced to keep it hidden behind locked doors. He laughed with them; his thoughts kept straying back to his studio, sometimes to the reptiles, none of which had done justice to his Medusa's hair.

But my brush can lie, he told himself. He had insisted on buying Jo peanuts in the zoological garden. But instead of throwing them to the animals, she had simply given them to a wiry, dirty-faced boy who had somehow wriggled his way in and was begging near the lions' den.

His elbow hit a book on top of the shelves as he maneuvered the painting down and under his arm. The book dropped with a thud that probably woke the house. He breathed a curse, trying to be as quiet as possible. The ladder rungs creaked ominously.

The Gorgon, who had been blessedly silent until then,

said sharply, her mouth somewhere under his armpit, "Harry, you're not putting me back into the cupboard."

"Sh—"

"Don't shush me. Just because you don't need me anymore."

"What do you mean I don't need you?"

"I saw the way you looked at her."

"I was not aware that I looked at her in any particular way."

"Ha!"

"Shhh," Harry pleaded. "Mrs. Grommet will think I'm up here entertaining lewd company."

"Thank you," the Gorgon said frostily. But once started, she could never be silent for long, Harry knew. He felt the floor beneath his foot at last, and her curiosity got the better. "Then what are you going to do with me?"

"I just want to look at you."

He positioned a wooden chair beside the easel, propped the painting on it. Then he drew the black silk off the new Medusa. Side by side, Jo past and Jo present, he studied them: the young, terrified girl; the haunted, desperate woman. A year in the life . . . "What a life," he breathed, moved at the thought of it.

The Gorgon spoke, startling him again. "What are you looking for?"

"I wanted to see why it was I didn't recognize her. I understand a little better now. That hair—I should have known it anywhere. But the expressions are completely different. And the skin tone . . . She was at least being fed when she came to me the first time." His voice trailed away as he studied them: Persephone who had innocently eaten a few seeds and transformed herself into the doomed Medusa. He asked, suddenly curious himself, "Where do you live? I mean, where were you before you took up residence in my painting?"

"Oh, here and there," she answered vaguely.

"No, really."

"Why? Are you thinking of ways to get rid of your noisy, uncouth Gorgon?"

He thought about that, touched the Medusa on the easel. "Who inspired this out of me? No. Stay as long as you like. Stay forever. I'll introduce you to my friends. None of them have paintings that speak. They'll all be jealous of me."

"You invited me," she reminded him.

"I did."

"I go where I'm invited. Where I am invoked. When I hear my name in someone's heart, or in a painting or a poem, I exist there. The young thug Perseus cut my head off. But he didn't rid the world of me. I've stayed alive these thousands of years because I haven't been forgotten. Every time my name is invoked and my power is remembered anew, then I live again, I am empowered."

"Yes," Harry said softly, watching those full, alluring lips move, take their varying shapes on canvas in ways that he could never seem to move them in life. "I understand."

"You understand what, Harry?" the Gorgon asked so gently that he knew, beneath her raucous ways, she understood a great deal more than he had realized.

"I understand that I must go to the country again soon."

"Good idea. Take Jo with you."

"Should I? Really? She might be uncomfortable. And Grainger will try to seduce her away from me. He tries to steal everyone's models."

"That will happen sooner or later in any case, unless you are planning to cast her back into the streets once you've finished with her."

"No. I don't want to do that. I hadn't really thought ahead. About sharing her. Or painting her as someone else. Until now she was just my inspiration." He paced a step or two, stopped again in front of the paintings. Jo then. Jo now. "She's changed again," he realized. "There's yet another face. I wonder if that one will inspire another painting."

"Something," the Medusa murmured.

"Something," Harry agreed absently. "But you're right. I certainly can't put her back on the streets just so that she stays my secret. If she can get other work, she should. If I decide I don't—"

"Harry," the Gorgon interrupted. "One thing at a time. Why don't you just ask her if she'd like to come to the country with you and be introduced to other painters? She'll either say yes or she'll say no. In either case, you can take it from there."

Harry smiled. "That seems too simple."

"And find her something nice to wear. She looks like a bedpost in that old dress. Went out of style forty years ago, at least. I may not have a clue about what to do with my hair, but I always did have an eye for fashion. Though of course, things were incredibly boring in my day, comparatively speaking. Especially the shoes! You wouldn't believe—"

"Good night," Harry said, yawning, and draped the black silk over her. "See you in the morning."

JO sat in the McAlisters' garden, sipping tea. She felt very strange, as though she had wandered into a painting of a bright, sunny world strewn with windblown petals, where everyone laughed easily, plump children ran in and out of the ancient cottage, and a woman, still as a statue at the other side of the garden, was being painted into yet another painting. Some guests had gathered, Harry among them, to watch Alex McAlister work. Jo heard the harsh, eager voice of the painter, talking about mosaics in some foreign country, while he spun a dark, rippling thundercloud of his wife's hair with his brush. Aurora McAlister, a windblown Venus, it looked like, her head bowed slightly under long, heavy hair, seemed to be absorbed in her own thoughts; her husband and guests might have been speaking the language of another world.

Someone rustled into the wicker chair next to Jo. She looked up. People had wandered up to her and spoken and wandered off again all afternoon; she was struggling hopelessly with all the names.

"Holly," this one said helpfully, "Holly Millidge." She was a pretty, frothy young woman with very shrewd eyes. She waved a plate of little sandwiches under Jo's nose; Jo took one hesitantly. "They're all right. Just cucumber, nothing nasty." She set the plate back on the table. "So you're Harry's secret model. We've all been wondering."

"I didn't know I was a secret," Jo said, surprised.

"I can see why."

"Why what?"

"Why he tried to keep you secret. Tommy Buck said he'd been twice to Harry's studio trying to see you, and Harry locked the door on him."

Jo remembered the clamoring voices, the thunder up the stairs. "Why," she asked warily, "did he want to see me that badly?"

"To see if he should paint you, of course." Holly was silent a little, still smiling, studying Jo. "They're noisy, that lot. But they're good-hearted. You don't have to be afraid of them."

"I'm used to being afraid," Jo said helplessly. "I'm not used to this."

"It's not entirely what you think," Holly said obscurely, and laughed at herself. "What am I trying to say? You're not seeing what you think you see."

"Painters don't, do they?"

"Not always, no." She bit into a strawberry, watching the scene on the other side of the garden. "They'd see how pretty you are and how wonderful and mysterious the expression is in your eyes. But they wouldn't have any idea how that expression got there. Or the expression, for instance, in Aurora's eyes."

Jo looked at the still, dreaming face. "She's very beautiful."

"She is." Holly bit into another strawberry. "Her father worked in the stables at an inn on Crowdy Street. Aurora was cleaning rooms for the establishment when Alex met her. Barefoot, with her hair full of lice—"

A sudden bubble of laughter escaped Jo; she put her hands over her mouth. "Her, too?"

"And whatever her name was then, it was most certainly not Aurora. Most of us have a skewed past. As well as a skewed present." She gave a sigh, leaned back in her chair. "Except for me; I have no secrets. No interesting ones, at any rate. When they put me in their paintings, I'm the one carrying the heartless bride's train, or one of the shocked guests who finds the thwarted lover's body in the fish pond."

Jo, feeling less estranged from her surroundings, took another glance around the garden. Seen that way, if the goddess had been a chambermaid, then everyone might be anyone, and no telling what anybody knew or didn't know about life. Except for Harry, she thought. And then she glimpsed the expression on his face and had to amend even that notion.

Nothing, apparently, was plain as day, not even Harry. While the other guests were laughing and chatting, Alex's voice running cheerfully over them all, Harry was standing very quietly among them, his eyes on the tall, dark goddess. Jo drew a breath, feeling an odd little hollow where her certainty had been.

"Harry," she said, hardly realizing she'd spoken aloud.

Holly nodded. "Oh, yes, Harry. And John Grainger, and half the painters in the McAlister constellation, including one or two of the women. Dreamers, all of them, in love with what they think they see instead of what they see."

"John Grainger. The one with the wild hair and rumbly voice and the black, black eyes?"

"Yes, that's him."

"He talked to me earlier."

"Everyone talked to you earlier," Holly said lightly. "I was watching. They're making their plans for you, don't you fret."

"I didn't like him," Jo said. "He has a way of putting his hand on you as though it's supposed to mean something to you. It made me uncomfortable."

Holly laughed. "Then he'll have to watch his manners with you. He's a fine painter, though, and very generous; if you let him paint you, you'll be noticed. Others will find you, if you want." She lifted her bright face to greet a lovely, red-haired woman with somber green eyes. "Nan! Have you met Harry's painting yet? Jo Byrd. Nan Grainger."

"Jo Byrd. Why do I know that name?" Nan eased herself into a chair, gazing at Jo. "Harry must have talked about you. But that was some time ago. Oh." She gave a little start, her pale skin flushing slightly. "I remember now."

"I ran away."

"Yes. In the middle of his Persephone. He was bereft."

"Yes, well," Jo said, her mouth quirked, for everyone seemed to know everything anyway. "So was I."

Nan was silent, gazing at her without smiling. What have I said? Jo wondered, and then saw what lay beneath Nan's hands clasped gently over her belly.

Holly interrupted Nan's silence adroitly, with some droll story about her husband. Jo sighed noiselessly, her eyes

going back to the group around the goddess. John Grainger
stood closest to Aurora, she saw. They did not look at one
another. But now and then the trailing green silk around
her bare feet, raised by a teasing wind, flowed toward him to
touch his shoe. He would glance down at that flickering
green touching him, and his laugh would ring across the
garden.

Secrets, she thought. If you look at this one way, there's a
group of cheerful people standing together on a sunny afternoon in a garden. That's one painting. If you look at them
with a different eye, there's the story within the painting. . . .
She looked at Harry again, wanting the uncomplicated friend
she thought she knew, who got excited over the golden
snakes in the reptile house, and who made her go shopping
with Mrs. Grommet for a dress, he said, that didn't look as
if his grandmother had slept in it.

Unexpectedly, as though he'd felt her thoughts flow in
his direction, against the wind, he was looking back at her.

"What beautiful hair you have," Nan said, watching the
white-gold ripple over Jo's shoulders. "I'd love to paint it."
Her green eyes were gathering warmth, despite the silk fluttering over her husband's shoe, despite her fears and private
sorrows; for a moment she was just a woman smiling in the
light. "Jo, have you ever tried to draw? You might try it
sometime. I forget myself when I do; it makes me very tranquil."

I might try it, Jo thought, after I lose this feeling that
I've just fallen off the moon.

But she didn't say that, she said something else, and then
there was another cup of tea in her hand, and a willowy
young man with wayward locks the color of honeycomb
kneeling in the grass at her feet, who introduced himself as
Tommy Buck . . .

*   *   *

HARRY watched Tommy kneel beside Jo's chair. Their two faces seemed to reflect one another's wild beauty, and he thought dispassionately: I would like to paint them both together. Then, he felt a sharp flash of annoyance at Tommy, who could barely paint his feet, dreaming of capturing that barely human face of Jo's with his brush.

His attention drifted. He watched the green silk touch Grainger's shoe, withdraw, flutter toward him again. Seemingly oblivious, Aurora watched the distant horizon; seemingly oblivious, her husband orated in his hoarse, exuberant crow's voice about the architectural history of the arch. Harry thought about Aurora's long, graceful hands, about her mouth. So silent, it looked now; he had gotten used to it speaking. He wondered if he could ever make this mouth speak.

And then she moved. The little group was breaking up around McAlister. "Too sober," he proclaimed them all. "Much too sober." Lightly he touched his wife, to draw her with him toward the cottage. As lightly, she slipped from his fingers, stayed behind to find her shoes under the rose vines. Grainger glanced at his wife across the garden, then at Aurora, then at his wife again. In that moment of his indecision, Aurora put her hand out to steady herself on Harry's arm as she put on her shoes.

"She's lovely, Harry," he heard her say through the blood drumming in his ears. "I like her. Where did you find her?"

"In the street," he stammered. "Both times. She—she has been through hard times."

"I know." She straightened, shod, but didn't drop her hand. Behind her, Grainger drifted away. Her voice, deep and slow and sweet, riveted Harry. "I know those times. I hear them in her speech, I see them in her eyes. I know those streets."

"Surely not—"

She smiled very faintly. "Harry, I grew up helping my father shovel out the stables until I was old enough to clean up after humans. Didn't you know that? I thought everybody did."

"But the way you speak," Harry said bewilderedly. "Your poise and manners—"

"A retired governess. Alex hired her to teach me. Beyond that I have my own good sense and some skills that Alex finds interesting. He likes my company."

"He adores you."

"He thinks he does. He adores the woman he paints. Not the Livvie that I am."

"Livvie?"

Her mouth crooked wryly; he saw her rare, brief smile. "Olive. That's my real name. Livvie, they called me until I was seventeen and Alex looked at me and saw painting after painting. . . . He said I was the dawn of his inspiration. So Olive became Aurora."

"Why," he asked her, his voice finally steady, "are you telling me this?"

"Because I've often thought I'd like to talk to you. That I might like having you as a friend, to tell things to. But for the longest time you could only see me the way Alex sees me. But then I saw how you looked at Jo today, knowing all you know about her. So I thought maybe, if I explained a thing or two to you, you might look at me as a friend."

She waited, the dark-eyed goddess who had pitched horse shit out of stables and whose name was Livvie. Mute with wonder, he could only stare at her. Then his face spoke, breaking into a rueful smile.

"I hope you can forgive my foolishness," he said softly. "It can't have been very helpful."

"I do get lonely," she confessed, "on my pedestal. Come,

let's have some tea with Jo, and rescue her from Tommy Buck. He's not good enough for her."

"Will you come some day and see if I'm good enough to paint her? I would value your opinion very much."

"Yes, I will," she promised and tucked her long sylph's hand into the crook of his arm, making him reel dizzily for a step. He found his balance somewhere in Jo's eyes as she watched them come to her.

MUCH later, he reeled back into his studio, stupefied with impressions. Jo had promised, sometime before he left her at her door, to sit for the unfinished Persephone as well. So he would see her daily until—until he dreamed up something else. Or maybe, he thought, he would do what Odysseus's Penelope had done to get what she wanted: weave by day, unweave by night. He pulled the black silk off Persephone's head, saw the lovely, wine-red mouth and smiled, remembering the real one speaking, smiling its faint sphinx's smile, saying things he never dreamed would come out of it. But he no longer needed to dream, and he did not want Jo to see that mouth on her own face and wonder.

He was wiping it away carefully with cloth and turpentine when he remembered the Gorgon.

Horrified, he dropped the cloth. He had erased her entirely, without even thinking. What she must be trying to say, he could not imagine. And then he realized that the voluble Gorgon, who had talked her way out of his cupboard and into his life, had said not a word, nothing at all, to rescue herself.

Perhaps, he thought, she had nothing left to say. Perhaps she had already gone. . . .

He picked up the cloth, gazing at the clean, empty bit of canvas where Persephone's mouth would finally appear. He heard the Gorgon's voice in his head, having the last word as usual.

If you need me, Harry, you know how to find me.

He left them side by side, his unfinished faces, and went to bed, where he would have finished them, except that he could not keep Persephone from smiling in his dreams.

The Tale of the Two Swords

LYNN KURLAND

Prologue

HAROLD needed an adventure.

He rolled over onto his belly and contemplated the potential for such a thing. All the elements necessary for the planning of an important quest were about him: foul weather outside; a hot fire inside; his own enthusiasm for the idea at a fever pitch; and the luxury of planning his scheme in a cozy chamber in what was otherwise a very drafty castle.

Now, if he had been a man of five-and-twenty, well-armored, well-horsed, and well-trained in the arts of war, he might have commanded the adventure himself. Unfortunately, he was just an eight-year-old boy who found himself quite generally being swept out from underfoot by those more suited to the doing of mighty deeds than he. But he was a clever lad, so his age would not be a detriment to his ambitions.

He looked at his brother, Reynauld, a supremely focused but otherwise unimaginative lad of ten-and-five who currently studied a complicated battlefield peopled with wooden warriors not of his own making.

Nay, Harold decided, there would be no aid from that quarter.

He looked at his sister, Imogen, a beautiful, dreamy girl of twelve summers who loved lavish fabrics and abhorred dirt of all kinds. Imogen's idea of a good adventure was limited to pressing him and his grubby self into service as a mannequin so she might see how an endless array of itchy materials might grace her slight shoulders. Harold knew that asking her to cast her lot in with him would entail a repayment of hours spent doing just that kind of wearisome labor, and there were some things that even he would not do for the sake of a noble quest. He would have to look elsewhere.

He turned his piercing gaze upon his mother. She sat in a chair near him, fashioning some sort of needlework. He stared at her hands and felt warmth rush into his heart. He suspected it wasn't a manly thing to admit—that he loved his mother's hands—so he kept the sentiment locked inside his heart where he could examine it privately. Serving, creating, soothing; his mother's hands were never still. He liked the soothing best, but that was another unmanly sentiment he would never admit to unless death loomed.

Not that his mother's hands were limited to those gentler arts. He had, on one glorious occasion earlier that winter, seen his mother snatch up a fire iron and impale an enormous spider with it. If he hadn't known better, he would have sworn his mother looked as skilled with a poker as any member of the king's guard was with a sword (not that he'd ever seen a member of the king's guard, mind you, but he could imagine their skill quite well). It had been a deed worthy of song, that one.

He stroked his chin thoughtfully. (He did that often. He was certain it made him look wise beyond his years.) *Had* his mother more skills than she let on? Those thin white scars she bore on her hands; could those have come from learning to use a sword?

He paused.

He considered.

Then he shook his head. Impossible. This was his mother, after all, and as jolly a fellow as he considered her to be, the thought of her hefting a sword and tramping about in the mud to master its use was simply too far beyond even the vast reaches of his formidable imagination for serious contemplation. Her scars had likely come from the innumerable things she did to keep their household with its small battalion of servants, not to mention the secret messengers his father received at all hours that Harold wasn't supposed to know about, in top form.

But in spite of the origin of her scars, and because of her love for him, he knew he could count on her to aid him in whatever business he might be about. She had done it often enough in the past.

She had also been up half the night tending him whilst he puked his guts out into various pots, so perhaps he should give her a rest for the day.

He turned to his sire. Here were riper pickings.

"Father," he said, sitting up and using his most polite tone, "would you have a mind for an adventure?"

His father slowly lowered the missive he'd been reading, blinked a time or two at Harold as if he wasn't quite seeing him, then frowned. "Hmmm?"

"An adventure, Father."

"An adventure? In the snow?"

Harold suspected that if his sire looked that unwilling to tramp about outside in a blizzard, then he likely wouldn't be interested in tramping about inside, either. Obviously, a compromise would have to be made.

"A story, then," Harold said, thinking quickly. If he couldn't live out his own epic compilation of events, then he would hear about someone else's and be content. "Bloodshed . . . great daring . . . aye, I have it. *The Tale of the Two Swords.*"

Reynauld groaned loudly. "Nay, not that. Too much romance."

"I like romance," Imogen said quickly. "Aye, Father, that one."

"The Two Swords," their father said thoughtfully. "Very well, if you like." He rose and fetched a very well-used leather-bound volume from a shelf. *"The Two Swords,"* he muttered as he sat and gingerly turned the yellowing sheaves of parchment. "Aye, here it is. Now, Harold," he said, looking over the top of the book at him, "where shall I start? With bloodshed? Mayhem? Long marches in the dead of night through marshy wastes infested with bugs of uncommonly potent stings?"

"Bloodshed," Reynauld said absently, moving his cavalry to a more advantageous locale.

"Romance," Imogen said with a dreamy sigh. "I like those parts—"

"Nay, begin where she flees the castle on one of Angesand's finest steeds," Reynauld interrupted. "There's a goodly bit of excitement there." He looked up at his sire. "And Angesand *does* produce the finest of horses, Father."

"Aye, son, he does," their sire agreed. "Harold, have you an opinion on where we should begin?"

"Any time during those first few days of her harrowing escape would suit me, Father," Harold said obligingly.

"As you will, then." He cleared his throat, then began. "This chapter is entitled 'How Mehar of Angesand Escaped

Her Father's Keep and Earned His Bounty on Her Head in One Night.'"

Harold settled himself more comfortably on the rug, placed his toes a bit closer to the fire, and smiled. Could his evening improve?

He doubted it.

Chapter One

*In which Mehar of Angesand Escapes Her
Father's Keep and Earns His Bounty on Her
Head in One Night . . .*

THUNDER rolled in the distance, driving before it an unwholesome air.

In answer, the great horse gathered itself onto its
haunches and leapt up and over the upturned faces of half a
dozen astonished peasants who lingered at the mouth of the
only visible track into a densely populated bit of forest.

Mehar flattened herself against Fleet's back as he flew, lest
she find herself becoming too acquainted with any of the stray
branches that brushed past her. The last time Fleet had taken
such a mighty leap, it had been over a dozen of Angesand's gate
guards, but then it had been the rapidly lowering portcullis to
catch at her, not the branch of a tree. If she hadn't managed to
free the catch of her cloak, she would have surely been pulled
backwards off her horse and sent sprawling onto the cobble-
stones. But luck had been with her that night; she had left her
coat and her prison behind and galloped madly down the road.

There was no chance for such speed now. All she could do was plunge her mount farther into the underbrush, then turn and whisper the one feeble spell she had at her command and hope it would do.

The air began to pulse against her ears, as if some strong wind behind it pushed it relentlessly on. The feeling of tension increased and with it the thunder until both turned into a company of horsemen who galloped up the road towards her hiding place. Leaves and peasants alike scattered before them.

She thought she had ridden hard.

Apparently, her father had ridden harder.

She held her breath as the company halted, then regrouped directly before her. She didn't dare try to escape. She might have outridden her sire and his men, but then again, she might not have, and that didn't bear thinking on. All she could do was hope that her spell would hold. She was no mage; she was a weaver, and she suspected the spell of un-noticing she'd woven about herself and Fleet might be nothing more than words hopefully spoken but yielding nothing of substance.

Damn her sire. Could he not have found a convenient tavern to loiter in and thereby save himself from the rain? Another pair of days would have served her well. Though she supposed the fact that she'd even come this far wasn't far short of a miracle.

That miracle she owed to the steed beneath her who had flown as if on wings. Her father had never produced his like before, and likely never would again. Much the same could have been said about her, but no doubt in far less inspired tones of awe and admiration.

She scowled at Fleet's equine cousins who bore the company of men before her. A pity they hadn't done a bit of loitering as well. They had followed Fleet at first, given that she'd liberated them from her father's stables along with

Fleet, but they'd been no match for his speed. She'd known her father would catch his horses soon enough, but she'd intended that even once he did, he would find no gear to put on them. The bridles, saddles, and other pertinent items in the stables had worn a spell of un-noticing that had been guaranteed to last at least two full days.

Then again, the mage who had taught her the spell hadn't been all that sure of the wording, and the times she'd tried to weave the spell over her sisters' things she hadn't been all that successful, but considering how attached her sisters were to their combs, beautifying herbs, and steel implements made to mold noses into pleasing shapes during sleep, it was difficult to determine if the spell had worked or not.

It was also hard to imagine her father being more intent on finding his gear than his daughters had been, but there you had it.

All of which left her standing where she was, under a dripping tree, watching the men before her and trying not to sneeze.

"My lord," one of the horsemen said carefully, "surely we have searched long enough—"

"Silence, Peter, you fool," Robert of Angesand barked. "It will be enough when we find that . . . that . . ." His fury obviously burned brightly even now. "I vow I'll kill her for this! Damn her for the trouble she's caused me!"

Mehar wondered what irritated him more: the inconvenience of having had to catch his horses or the embarrassment of not having had the goods to deliver to a wooing Prince of Hagoth.

"But, my lord," Peter said, aghast, "surely you don't mean—"

"I mean to hunt until I find her," Robert snarled. "And if I don't find her, I'll put a price on her head that a hundred hunters couldn't resist—if it beggars me to do it!"

Damn that Hagoth. Couldn't he have turned his clouded

eye elsewhere? She had three quite serviceable sisters of marriageable age and tractable mien. Surely the dotard could
have found one of them more suitable to his purposes than
she.

He finds you . . . pretty. Her father had choked on that last
word when he'd spewed it at her. He'd washed the taste of it
out of his mouth with a hefty tankard of ale taken in one
long, slow draught.

She wasn't pretty; she knew it. Her fingers were stained
from dye, her skin rough from carding and spinning, and
her hair (piled haphazardly on her head usually) and her
clothes (piled haphazardly on her person always) left her
looking more like a scullery maid than a lord's daughter.
But she had sisters aplenty for wedding off to make alliances; that should have left her free to dress like a beggar
and weave miracles.

It had, for quite some time. Until the Prince of Hagoth
had taken one look at her and decided she was a filly begging to be broken to his brutal hand.

"In truth, I don't know why Hagoth would want her,"
Robert grumbled. "She's too much like her dam. Fey
wench."

"Elfine had many gifts," Peter said quietly. "She wove
beautiful things for your hall and your guests."

Mehar half expected her sire to run his captain through.
Instead, he merely snorted. "You were half in love with her
yourself, you fool," he said contemptuously. "I should have
let you have her, her with her endless weaving and muttering and scribbling in that bloody book of hers." He paused.
"I wonder what became of that . . . ?"

Mehar put her hand to her breast, where that small book
safely resided. It was the one thing of her mother's she'd
managed to save, when her sire had destroyed all her posses-
sions in an effort to convince her that Hagoth truly was the
man for her.

"Never should have let the wench take up her dam's work," her sire continued darkly. "I should have burned El—" He cursed, which was his usual alternative to saying his dead wife's name. ". . . the woman's gear the moment she drew her last."

At least he hadn't and for that, at least, Mehar was grateful. She'd had a dozen years to enjoy creating her own magic with her mother's tools. And she'd had like number of years to puzzle over the small book her mother had kept ever near her.

A traveling mage, the one who had taught her the spell of un-noticing in return for a cloak, had said the book contained spells, but they weren't ones he could read. The wizard who had written them down for her mother would be the one who could, he had said. The king's finest court mage might be another, he had offered. Then he'd said that given the ease with which she'd learned his spell, perhaps one day even she might be able to read the book. But a simple man such as himself? Nay, it was far beyond his art.

Mehar had considered his words long after he'd gone. She was quite certain no wizard had written her mother's book. The characters were in her mother's fine hand. She hadn't dared ask her sire about it. She'd been content to allow him to focus his attentions on her three younger, more beautiful, more empty-headed sisters and leave her to losing herself in the feel, the smell, and the work of her hands.

Of course, that had been before Hagoth had decided she was to be his, before her father had destroyed all her mother's weaving tools, before she had decided that flight was her only choice. Pulling away the cloak of mystery covering her mother's book had seemed like a fine idea as she'd freed herself from her bedchamber by clouting the guardsman outside over the head with a leg from her mother's ruined spinning wheel. Fleeing to the king's palace had seemed an even more brilliant plan as she'd silently slipped down the stairs and out through the kitchens whilst her father and the Prince of Hagoth were drinking themselves into insensitivity at her father's table. Remaking herself into a powerful mage had seemed the best plan of all as she'd raced down the road on her father's finest steed as if she really was in great haste to be about starting her future.

This all assumed, of course, that a court mage would help her; that she would find the king's palace in spite of the magic that was rumored to protect it; and, most pressingly, that she might keep her throat free of her father's clutching fingers long enough to search.

Back on the road in front of her, her father was vowing several more black oaths. He topped even himself as he contemplated aloud a proper reward for her head (attached or not), before he called his company to turn around and head back down the road to that inn they'd recently passed where he had damn well better find something strengthening before he decided upon a final price. Mehar had little trouble imagining how the rest of her father's se'nnight would go.

He would retreat to Angesand, call for every bounty hunter in the land, offer them a ridiculous sum for the doing of the deed, then try to bargain with them before they exited the hall. After that, he would sit about and curse them as weak-stomached fools who couldn't track a feeble wench for the sport of it and if he were younger, he would do it himself, but what with his stables to attend to and three other daughters to see properly married, and also the Prince of Hagoth to see appeased . . .

And all that would lead him back to wanting to kill her and then he might up the price a bit until there actually might be a fool who would think it worth his time.

It would behoove her to make haste whilst her father fingered the coins in his purse, bemoaning their scarcity.

Mehar swung up onto Fleet's back and turned him

deeper into the forest. They would take the road again in another day or so, when she felt it was safe. But for now, with apologies to her mount, she drove him farther into the darkness of the thick undergrowth.

IT was hunger that almost undid her, hunger and a desperate need for warmth. After ten days, she had long since exhausted what little food she had brought with her. She had tried to forage for food, but she wasn't a hunter, and she hadn't dared make a fire to cook anything she might have caught.

At least she'd had no sightings of her sire, nor heard anyone making the stomping noises a tracker makes whilst hunting game he knows is far too simple-minded to realize it is being stalked.

She smelled a rabbit, nicely toasted, before she saw the fire. She pulled Fleet up quickly and hoped she hadn't been heard. The fire was built in a little clearing not far from where she could see the road ahead. A man sat there, examining the meal on the end of his stick, but he didn't look overly dangerous and she supposed she wouldn't have cared if he had. She dug about in her purse, then spurred Fleet on. She burst through the trees and flung one of her precious coins at the man, who gaped at her as he fumbled for it. His spit went up into the air and she snatched it on her way by.

She left the forest behind her and thundered down the road.

It was only then she realized that her breakfast was hot as hellfire.

She almost lost her seat *and* her meal, but she managed to get her skirts up and around the hare without finding herself sprawled in the dirt. Her hand burned, but it burned far less than her belly gnawed, so she ate and was very glad for the food and the warmth.

She rode for the rest of the morning without incident. The sun had just passed noon when she came to a fork in the way. Fleet chose the right hand. She had no sure plan in mind, and one way was the same as the other to her mind. At the worst, she might find a comfortable inn, have a good sleep, then be forced to retrace her steps and take the other fork on the morrow.

At least she hoped that might be the worst.

The road widened as she traveled until it became a large, well-tended thoroughfare. It was paved with smooth stone and lined by large, shapely trees that now bore the last of fall's vivid colors. Rain dripped off the leaves, misted down to soak her hair, rolled down Fleet's forelock onto his forehead, and finally dripped off his nose.

Large, wrought-iron gates appeared suddenly out of a mist before her. She passed under them, unchecked. Smooth bluish-gray stone stretched out before her, wet and slick, unmarred by either muddy footstep or hoofprint. No merchant's wagon rolled along, no knight cantered by on his proud steed, no freeman walked off to the side with his gear on his back and his liberty leaving him with his head held high. It was as if the entire world slept.

Was this the magic people spoke of when they talked about the vale of sorcery that protected the palace of Neroche? She had thought there might have been paths that dead-ended, terrible monsters that faded in and out of the mist, ghostly shapes that led travelers into deep bogs and trapped them there. This mere bit of emptiness was, in her opinion, not very substantial and certainly nothing to inspire legends and nervous whispers.

She hadn't gone but a mile farther when the road turned into a formal approach. She lifted her eyes and saw what she could only assume was the king's palace, standing in the distance. A heavy mist hung over the parapets, obscuring the towers. Darkness crept down the walls and pooled at the footings of the bulwarks.

Mehar shivered.

She rode slowly up to the entrance. Magic lay draped over the massive palace like a loosely woven piece of very soft cloth that fell onto and covered every stone, sank into every crenellation, cascaded down onto every flat surface. Mehar slid down off Fleet's back and walked up the dozen very wide steps that led to the front door. She reached out and smoothed her hand over the illusion, finding it as soft as cottonwood fluff but strong, as if it had been forged by a steelsmith at the height of his powers.

Mehar looked back at Fleet and decided she would leave him where he was. There was grass where he stood and he would be safe enough there for a time.

She turned back to the palace and studied the illusion that covered it. Suddenly, she saw where it might be parted, as if it were two curtains that had been drawn together. She lifted one side of the spell, then came to an abrupt halt, staring in horror at the ruin the spell had concealed.

The king's crest that had no doubt once hung proudly over the massive front doors now lay shattered on the steps. She picked her way over the shards of fine plaster and eased past doors that hung drunkenly from twisted hinges.

Where was the king?

Where was his mage?

She found, to her shame, that it troubled her far more that the mage might be lost than the king. She supposed there were a handful of princes or perhaps a cousin or two in line for the throne, but what would they do without a mage to guide them?

She picked her way through the ruined corridors, stumbling a time or two quite heavily over large bits of tumbled marble she hadn't seen in the gloom. Her hands bore the brunt of those falls, but her knees wound up bloody in time as well. But she found that she couldn't turn back, so she pressed on until she reached what had obviously been the palace's great hall.

She stepped inside the doorway, then froze.

Stones from the hall floor had been tossed up and about without care for where they landed. Furniture had been reduced to firewood. Tapestries were shredded, plates and bowls scattered like seeds on the wind, walls were pockmarked. She walked into the hall in a daze, tripped over a stone, and sat down heavily on a bit of something that crunched beneath her. She remained where she was for some time and simply marveled at the extent of the destruction.

And then she realized with a start that she was not alone. A man had come into the hall from an entrance across from her. Who was he? A palace servant? A common peasant? A trespasser? She watched his shadowy figure as he kindled a fire in a hollow of the floor that had once been a no-doubt quite lovely bit of polished stone. He seemed perfectly comfortable in his surroundings, which gave her pause. Did he know that everyone in the palace was dead?

Had he been the one to do the deed?

"Cousin, damn you, where are you—"

The voice came closer, accompanied by sounds of various bits of flesh encountering various other bits of unyielding palace—and that accompanied by a litany of very inventive curses—until the voice and its creator stumbled into the great hall with a final *damnation.*

Mehar recognized the man instantly. He could possibly add an empty belly to the list of things that had bothered him during the past few hours.

"What the devil have you been doing?" the man demanded. "I've been out scouting, I was *assaulted* by a band of ruffians who stole my breakfast, and here you sit as if you have nothing better to do than sulk!"

"I am not sulking," the other man said, sitting down with a sigh. "I am thinking."

"Well, you should think less and *do* more," the other man said in a disgruntled voice as he stomped into and across the chamber. He righted a bench only to realize that it was missing a leg. He tossed it aside with another curse, then sat on a wobbly stone that looked as if it had erupted from the floor. "What a bloody mess!" he exclaimed, holding his hands against the fire. "Why don't you *do* something—"

Mehar looked over her shoulder and contemplated the distance to the doorway. It would only take one good leap to gain it, then she could flee and count the cost in bruises and blood later. What had she been thinking to come in here alone? For all she knew, these two had murdered her king and would next turn their blades on her. She crawled to her feet slowly and eased her way toward the yawning opening—

"Where's the light?" a voice said sharply. "How's a body to bring in a meal without a proper light?"

Mehar jumped out of the way as a brisk, gray-haired woman of indeterminate age marched through the doorway and over to the fire carrying a tray laden with things that made Mehar's mouth water. Despite her meal that morning, she still had days to make up for and what was over there looked fit for the king's finest table.

Maybe she'd said as much aloud without realizing it because quite suddenly the woman, as well as the men, turned and looked at Mehar with varying degrees of surprise.

The man with a thousand curses dredged up a few more. "Thief," he said, pointing an accusing finger at her. "She stole my breakfast!"

"It looks as if she could have used it, Alcuin," the older woman said curtly. She handed him the tray, then marched across the chamber purposefully and pulled Mehar back along behind her toward the fire. "Come, gel, and eat."

"Nay, cast her from the hall," said the man named Alcuin. "Better yet, toss her in the dungeon. Nay, even better yet, put her to work. There's aught to be shoveled out of the stalls."

Mehar had certainly done enough of that over the course of her life—a daughter of Robert of Angesand took her turn like everyone else in caring for the family business—so she wasn't completely opposed to the idea, but she was opposed to losing her life and she couldn't say with any degree of confidence that she trusted any of the chamber's occupants.

"Mucking out the stalls?" the old woman echoed doubtfully. "Nay, what the gel needs is a rest. Alcuin, up and give her your seat."

"Won't," said Alcuin stubbornly.

The other man rose silently. "Take mine, lady."

Mehar opened her mouth to thank him, then caught a full view of him by the weak light of the fire. And whatever else she might have said, along with her few remaining wits, slipped through her grasp like fine silk.

It wasn't that he wasn't beautiful, for he was. It wasn't that he wasn't well-made and tall, for he was that as well. It was his eyes, crystal blue eyes full of shards of deeper blue and veins of white, eyes that laid her soul bare.

Fey. Fey and otherworldly. She didn't doubt that if this man had possessed any magery at all, he could have been the one to wreak the havoc she stood in. Any thoughts of gratitude she had fled, to be replaced by ones of dread. She tried to speak. She croaked instead, something quite unintelligible.

He frowned at her. "Are you unwell?"

She gestured weakly around her. "Did you do this?"

"I should be flattered you think so, but nay, I did not."

"And why in the world would he—" Alcuin interrupted, but he was cut off by a sharp movement of the other's hand.

"What do you seek here, lady?" asked the man with the fathomless eyes.

Her answer came tumbling out before she could stop it. "I came to see the king. Well," she amended, "not the king really. One of his mages. The best mage, if possible, for I've questions for him. I suppose I could do with one less skilled, if I had to." She paused for a moment or two. "I don't suppose any of his mages still live," she said slowly.

"Unfortunately, they don't," the man said.

"And the king?"

"Dead as well."

Hope extinguished itself in her breast. Now the illusion hanging over the castle made sense. It was obviously just the remnants of a former magic.

"What of his son, the prince?" she asked.

"He was with the king," came the answer.

"Of course," she said. "And what of others—"

"Enough of this," said the old woman. She took Mehar by the arm and pulled her away from the fire. "What you need, gel, is a seat by a proper cooking fire with as much to eat as you like and I, Cook, will see as you gets it. Did you come on a horse? Does it need tending?"

"She did," Alcuin said. "It's trimming the flowerbeds near the hall door."

"Then one of you lads can go see to him," Cook said. "For now, my gel, you should eat. Everything will seem better with something in your belly."

Mehar couldn't answer. Not only did Cook not offer her the opportunity, she doubted she could have found words if she'd needed them.

The king was dead.

Worse still, his mage was dead.

And if that wasn't enough, her father had a price on her head.

She doubted those were things Cook's stew could change.

She paused at the archway that led to the kitchens and looked back over her shoulder. The two peasants were still there, the taller one still standing where she'd left him, staring at her with those odd eyes of his. She shivered, her former doubts about him returning. He looked infinitely capable of a great number of sinister things. She supposed if she'd had any sense at all, she would have fled as fast as her feet would carry her.

But apparently her common sense had been left behind with her cloak. She was cold, hungry, and exhausted. Perhaps if she remained in the kitchen, she would avoid any of that man's untoward magic—for she was almost positive he had some.

The thought that she might possibly ask him for aid flitted across her mind, but she let it disappear on its way just as quickly. She turned away from that perilous stranger and followed Cook to the promise of peace and safety—or at least a decent meal, which would give her the strength to find peace and safety.

It would have to do.

Chapter Two

*In Which Gilraehen the Prince Finds Himself
Pretending to be Someone He's Not . . .*

THE lights twinkled in the deep blue vault of the palace ballroom. The dancers, garbed in luxurious silks of rainbowed
hues, swirled about the marbled floor; the sweet strains of
song played on rare instruments by the realm's finest players
wove themselves through the air, in and out of the dancers'
patterns. Lights floated on the air, occasionally fluttering
down to land on the delighted faces of the occupants of the
chamber. The lady of the hall looked over the guests; it was
she who made the lights dance with the slightest movement
of her fingers. The lord looked on as well, watching his
guests with a benevolent smile, pleased at their pleasure.

"Dam*nation*!"

And so the spell was broken. Gil blinked and looked at
his cousin, who had tripped over something and gone
sprawling. He sighed. The only things dancing now were
tumbled bits of marble; the only things floating presently

through the air were dust motes up by the passage of his cursing cousin. His mother, the queen, was dead. His father, the king, was dead as well. His brothers had vanished on the field of battle and his father's palace was in ruins. If he'd had a sense of humor, he would have said he'd had better days. But he didn't have a sense of humor. In fact, he wondered if he would ever again smile at anything, much less laugh. Any merriment he'd possessed had been lost somewhere on that horrendous journey back from Pevenry, whence he'd fled like a kicked whelp—

Someone must be left alive, Gilraehen, his father had gasped as his life ebbed from him. *Flee, hide, gather your strength to fight another day.*

Gil hadn't wanted to flee, nor hide, nor take the time to gather his strength. He'd wanted to turn, ride onto the field, and find his enemy to run him through. Never mind that his enemy was his great-great-uncle. Never mind that the power Lothar wielded was immense, or that he had twisted the same to his own ends until it had become something unrecognizable and evil. Never mind that Gil had exhausted almost all the reserves of his power trying to protect his father's army. Lothar deserved death and Gil had been more than willing to aid him in finding it and finish the war his sire, Alexandir, had begun with that vast, well-trained army.

The army that had almost completely perished.

And why was it that he, Gilraehen the Fey, prince of the house of Neroche, had survived whilst all around him were lost? It was because he'd taken the bloodied hilt of the sword his father had managed to lift up toward him and bolted, leaving those about him to die in agony of soul and body both. Last night, he'd led that woman to believe that the prince had died on the field with his father. In a certain sense, he wasn't sure that wasn't true—

A sharp slap brought him to himself without delay. Alcuin, his cousin and part of the reason he himself was still alive, damn him, stood with his hand pulled back, apparently prepared to deliver another bracing blow.

Gil glared at him. "You dare much."

Alcuin grunted, unimpressed. "Brooding on the past serves nothing. Put it behind you."

Aye, put it behind him like the smoking field he'd put behind him. With one last, vast sweep of his matchless power, he'd set the whole bloody place afire. For anyone to have survived that—be he man, beast, or monster—would have been a miracle. Unfortunately, he knew there would be at least one to survive, the one man alive with power greater than his, who would no doubt come seeking him in his own good time.

"In truth, I don't much care to remember that escape," Alcuin muttered. "Don't know why you do."

Because it was constantly before him, the sight of that endlessly thick wall of Lothar's misshapen men, the smell of their sweat, the feel of his boots sloshing through their blood that soaked the ground, the heat of the fire behind him, driving him forward without choice. He and Alcuin had started with twenty men of their household, but by the end of his flight, it had been naught but him and Alcuin on their own legs, with only Alcuin's stubbornness to keep them alive.

Alcuin clapped a hand on his shoulder and shook him. "Gil, stop," he said. "Stop thinking so damned much."

"What else do you suggest I do?" Gil demanded, irritated. "Go on holiday to the seaside and leave my realm in shreds?"

"You have no realm," Alcuin said pleasantly. "You haven't even found your father's crown—not that anyone with any authority is about to put it on your head should you find it, though I suppose I would do in a pinch—and you have no army. You don't even have anywhere to sleep, unless you've been scooping up feathers and stuffing them back into your mattress whilst I was out taking my life in my hands and scouring the countryside for ne'er-do-wells."

"And finding yourself and your breakfast bested by a girl half your size," Gil noted. "Some scout, you."

"She caught me unawares. Now," Alcuin continued, "since you insist on squandering all that magic you have at your disposal in a misguided effort to appear as a common man— a useless exercise, if you ask me, for even I can sense what you are—then you must rely on the paltry skills of those sworn to serve you to keep the kingdom safe. At least my scouting, such as it was, yielded nothing but an empty belly. None of Lothar's minions—unless you want to count the wench. What do you think of her, by the by?" he added with a look of unwilling interest. "She could do with a tidy-up, I daresay, though I suppose Lothar's spies have looked worse—"

"She isn't one of his spies," Gil said. He had no idea who she was, nor why she was riding a beast such as the one he'd put away in the stable the evening before, but she had no taint of evil on her. He took a deep breath that was suddenly full of her, full of the smell of herbs and flowers, and the sweet scent of sunshine.

He pulled his mind abruptly away from that image. He rubbed his gritty eyes and cast about for something else to think on.

Her horse, aye, that was it. Now, there was a beast to dream about; never had he seen its equal. Last night he'd wondered if he would get it to cover without it tearing him to shreds. He'd managed it only because he'd finally con-vinced the beast—in less than dulcet tones—that his bloody mistress was filling her belly at a fine fire and would be along afterwards to see to him.

Whether she had done the like he didn't know because he'd put the horse up, then spent half the night walking through his ruined gardens. He'd finally cast himself upon his previously quite plump goose-feather mattress and partaken of two full hours of sleep before nightmares had driven him out of dreaming, and he'd come back to the great, formerly grand hall to brood.

"Isn't this the first place he'll look for us?" Alcuin asked suddenly. "You know," he said, his voice lowering, "*him*."

"Aye, I knew of whom you spoke," Gil said wearily. "And what I'm hoping is that he'll think I died on the field. He'll realize soon enough I didn't, but by then I will have a plan."

"If you say so," Alcuin said, sounding quite doubtful that Gil might manage something that complicated. "And I suppose I'll follow you, just as I have since we were five and both had our arses blistered because of *your* damned idiotic idea to try a few spells from one of your mother's locked books. How did you open the lock on that large, black, obviously-unsuitable-for-wee-lads book of sorcery anyway?"

The memory of that was almost enough to lighten Gil's heart. "I touched it and it fell open."

Alcuin stared at him in silence. Well, not complete silence. There was the incessant *drip, drip, drip* of something leaking onto the unyielding marble of the floor. Gil wondered what the floor would look like when the rains of fall truly began.

"Then perhaps," Alcuin said finally, "someday you will touch Lothar's defenses and they will fall open in like manner. It could happen." He smiled grimly. "I could also march into the kitchen and find myself something delicious to eat that hadn't come from things that we've been storing for just such a disaster as this. Cook is a wonder, but even she can't make sprouted grain any less unappetizing than it is." He turned and started toward the far door, the one that led to the kitchens. "Perhaps unappetizing is the wrong word. It would just be a damned sight more interesting if I just had a bit of fancy marmalade to go with it. Currant jam, perhaps. A smidgen of honey . . ."

Gil left the hall by a different door. He had no stomach for either currant jam or honey, even if any could be found. He picked his way around the heaps of rubble strewn all about the formerly quite impressive passageway that led from the front doors to many of the king's other receiving chambers, and wished for a large broom.

He left the palace, ignoring the ruin of his father's crest on the front steps, and continued on to the stables. There, at least, something had been left standing. It was puzzling, the extent of the destruction. No one could have wreaked this kind of havoc without either a vast army or a goodly amount of magery at his disposal. Lothar's army had been on the field. Perhaps one of Lothar's sons had come calling whilst he was away.

It was almost more than he could bear to think on.

He entered the stables, stopped, and breathed deeply. Ah, to have nothing more pressing demanding his attention than a few horses needing to be groomed. He'd certainly passed much of his youth doing just that. At the moment, he would have given much to work in the stables and ignore the burdens of his birthright.

Though the claiming of that duty was still before him, as Alcuin had so pointedly reminded him. He did have his father's crown (hidden cunningly under what was left of his bed) but he had no one to install that fine bit of jewel-encrusted metal atop his head, unless he was to send for his mother's father, a feisty old man of impeccable lineage and questionable wisdom in matters of his personal safety; or his uncle, his mother's brother, who had sequestered himself on an island half a kingdom away where he might think deep thoughts in peace. Neither man would come willingly, but perhaps they could be persuaded. Later, when Gil had found a kingdom to rule. For now, he had more pressing matters to attend to.

Mainly that of watching the woman sitting beneath the

poor light coming in from a stable window, poring over a book.

He stood in the shadows and stared at her, wondering who she was and how it was she had come to the palace by herself. He knew few women who traveled alone in such perilous times; it must have been something overwhelmingly compelling to have driven her from her home without aid.

Especially given the look of her.

He scrutinized her whilst he had the chance. To be sure, she had not the painful type of beauty of those who regularly came to court—generally at their fathers' insistence—to present themselves to him and curry his favor. He had, in his long, weary existence as the heir to the throne, seen more beautiful women than he cared to number. But never had he met a woman who troubled his dreams after a mere glance into her eyes.

He jumped slightly when he realized she was looking at him. He bowed. "My pardon, lady. I came to make sure you were well."

She shut her book and stood, looking as if she might just flee. "My thanks, good sir," she said quickly. "I've had a fine meal or two, so I'll soon be on my way."

Nay was almost out of his mouth before he grasped at the few remaining shreds of good sense he normally possessed and stopped himself. Nay, he was loath to let her leave, but there was no good reason to force her to stay.

At least none that he could come up with at present.

All the same, there was no sense in her rushing off hastily. Better that she continue on her quest fully fed and much better rested. It was only common courtesy that demanded that he offer her the chance for both. His mother would have been greatly impressed by his comportment.

And appalled by his subterfuge.

The woman shifted, as if she intended to bolt for the door. "Sit," he commanded, and she flinched. He took a deep breath. "Please sit," he amended, "and take your ease. No need to rush off."

She sat slowly, but didn't look away, as if she expected him to leap upon her at any moment and throttle her.

He smiled, trying to project an air of harmlessness. It wasn't something he did well, but he tried. He cast about for something to distract her. "Your book," he said, nodding at it. "It looks well worn."

She ran her hand carefully over the leather cover. "It was my mother's."

"Is it a tale about her life?"

She studied him for a moment before she answered slowly. "Nay, 'tis a book of spells."

He blinked. Books of spells were rare and guarded jealously. "Are they interesting spells?"

"I don't know. I can't read them."

"Then 'tis for that reason you sought the king's mage?"

"Aye, but now I find that my journey was in vain."

He hesitated. To reveal his skill with magery was to reveal his own identity and he found himself with a sudden desire to be, for a day or two, simply Gil and not the fey Prince of Neroche. It wouldn't hurt to let this woman believe him to be less than he was and allow his skill with spells to lie fallow, would it? He found the plan to his liking and proceeded with its implementation without hesitation. Ordinary, unremarkable conversation was to be the order of the day.

"Well," he said, "at least your journey was made on a fine horse."

"Aye," she agreed.

He waited, but she offered nothing else. "Is he yours?" he asked.

"He is now."

His eyebrows went up of their own accord. "Did you steal him?"

She smiled briefly and the sight of her faint smile did

something to his heart, something he feared he might not recover from anytime soon.

"Steal him?" she asked, then shook her head. "I wouldn't call it that. I needed to flee an unsavory betrothal and Fleet was the fastest way to do it."

An unsavory betrothal? That was nothing unusual, but fleeing it on such a steed certainly was. "And how will your sire feel about that?" Gil asked.

"I've no doubt it inspired him to put a price on my head for the deed."

He was surprised she seemed so at ease with that. "Who is this sire who is so ruthless?"

She shifted on her seat. "No one of importance."

"I'm curious."

"I fear you'll need to remain so."

He smiled to himself; her lack of deference was quite refreshing. "Then I don't suppose you'll give me your bridegroom's name, either, will you?"

"I don't suppose I will."

"Was he young or old?"

She smiled briefly, without humor. "Old enough to be my sire, and quite cruel."

He pursed his lips. Somehow the thought was one that seemed particularly loathsome in regards to the woman before him. She deserved sunshine, youth, long days spent searching for flowers for her table, not a cold existence in some dotard's mean hall devoid of even the smallest comforts.

The mystery of her was becoming unsettlingly compelling. "What is your name, lady?" he asked. "Might I have that at least?"

"And what would you do with that name, if you had it?"

"Use it," he said simply.

She looked into the distance for so long, he began to wonder if she had forgotten his question. Then she sighed suddenly and looked at him. "I am trusting you with more than just my name, if I give it to you."

He nodded seriously. "Aye."

She put her shoulders back and took a deep breath. "Mehar. My name is Mehar."

"Mehar," he repeated. "A beautiful name. An unusual name." One he desperately wished he recognized, but there were, as he could personally attest, a staggering number of unwed maidens in his kingdom, so not being able to fix a place to a name wasn't unthinkable. Perhaps it would come to him in time.

"And what of your name?" she prompted. "Cook called you Gil—"

". . . bert," he supplied promptly. "Gilbert. Or Gilford, if you like better. My father never could decide. Gilford was his favorite hound and Gilbert was a mighty rooster that pleased him and so he had a goodly amount of trouble selecting what he thought would suit . . ." He trailed off with a shrug, wondering if he was lying well.

She only stared at him suspiciously.

Apparently he wasn't a good liar. "Call me Gil," he finished.

"Gil," she repeated. "Is that your name?"

"It will do until you trust me enough to tell me who your sire is."

She smiled and seemed to thaw just a bit. "Very well. For now, Gil, who may or may not be named after a mighty fowl, favor me with an answer or two. Why do you find yourself in this ruined place?"

"I was born here," he admitted.

"Did you serve the king?"

"Aye, that as well."

"What happened to his kingdom?"

"He gathered his army and went to battle Lothar of Wychweald."

"In truth?" she asked, surprised. "I thought the black mage of Wychweald was long dead by now."

"Oh, nay, he is very much alive," Gil said, pushing aside the vision of Lothar's fathomless black eyes and the mocking smile he'd worn as he'd watched Gil pay the price for daring to battle him. "I daresay the king grew tired of losing his people to Lothar's service. Lothar does that, you know. Presses innocent souls into serving him. By the time he's finished with them, you wouldn't recognize them as human."

She shivered. "I daresay. Then did you go to battle as well?"

"Aye, with my father. But my father did not return."

"I'm sorry."

"Aye, I am as well."

She stared at him for a moment or two in silence, then she sighed and stood. "Thank you for your name, and the pleasant conversation, but I should now be about seeing to my charges, so I can earn my supper."

He watched her look for a place to put her book. "I could hold that," he offered. "I could also help you with the horses."

"Are you a stable's lad, then?" she asked.

"I have spent my share of time here," he said.

She hesitated, looked at him carefully a moment or two more, then handed him her book. "I'll see to the horses. You look a bit soft."

He spluttered before he realized she was teasing him.

"If you flee with my book, Fleet will hunt you down," she added. "You would regret it."

Gil didn't doubt it. He accepted the book with what he hoped was a look of trustworthiness and sat down with a manly grunt on the hay. He turned to the first page, fully prepared to find some obscure village witch's spells, scribbled in an illegible hand.

Instead, he found a hand that was learned; the characters

were neat and precise, with a flowing script that pleased the eye. He read through several pages, his wonder growing with each until he finally stopped halfway through the book, closed the halves together slowly, and stared off into the stable's gloom thoughtfully.

The spells were of Camanaë. He was so surprised to find something of theirs in his hand, he hardly knew what to think. There were few of that particular school of magic left in the world.

They being one of Lothar's preferred targets.

He knew none of them personally. By reputation, he knew them to be mostly wizardesses. There was the occasional mage who'd been gifted his mother's power, of course, when occasion required, but for the most part they were women, keepers of a surprisingly strong magic. If the magic he had inherited from his sire was full of ruling, Camanaë's was full of healing, of protection, of restoring after the ruling hand had done its brutal work.

He looked at Mehar thoughtfully as she groomed her horse and wondered if the genealogy kept by the court mage would aid him in discovering the identity of her mother. Unfortunately, he feared that Tagaire of Neroche was dead, which meant that he himself would be the one doing the searching. He had a brief vision of Tagaire's terrifyingly unorganized chamber, with stacks of paper, pots, and sundry falling off tables and spilling out of shelves, and decided that he would let the search alone.

For the moment.

He watched Mehar for a bit longer, before he rose and took over her tasks. He groomed the rest of the horses, feeling her eyes on him, and finding his hands fumbling much more than they should have.

A very unsettling feeling, on the whole.

But an hour later, the tasks were done and he was walking with her back to the palace.

"I think I can aid you with a spell or two," he offered casually.

"You?"

He smiled at her disbelief. "Aye, me. I'm not completely ignorant of things magical." Though Camanaë was not his own magic, his schooling had demanded that he learn the languages of all the schools of wizardry. He could not only decipher Mehar's book, he could likely weave a spell or two from it.

A dreadful hope bloomed in her face. "Could you?"

"I could." That hope touched a place in his heart he'd been sure Lothar had incinerated along with his hand. He had to take a deep, steadying breath before he could speak again. "I could also see to your hand, the one you favor. A bad burn?"

"From Alcuin's rabbit."

"A high price to pay for something that probably took him all morning to catch."

"I paid him well for that hare."

Gil grunted. "Trust him not to say as much. Come, then, and let us find you somewhere more comfortable to stay than a mean scrap of floor in Cook's domain."

She walked with him along the ruined path, holding tightly to her book. "Where? In the roosting place of some fine noble perhaps?"

"Nothing less. When the king is out, peasants shout."

She smiled. "Did you make that up yourself?"

"This very moment."

"Then you'd best hope none of the king's relations return, or they'll have your head for the shouting you've done in the hall."

"I've tried to tidy up the place as best I could."

"Hmmm," she said, sounding quite unconvinced. "Well, perhaps some of the king's people will come back and see to things."

"Aye," he said, but he found himself less distracted by the thought of his people returning to see to work he could manage with a slight bit of effort himself than he was by the sight of Mehar-of-someplace-she-wouldn't-name—with her riotous hair and her serious gray eyes.

Which was so completely inappropriate considering who he was and what his future held that he could only shake his head at himself.

But that didn't stop him from inviting her and her book to come with him to supper where they might all become better acquainted.

Poor fool that he was.

Chapter Three

In Which Mehar Finds More Than Dust Under the Prince's Bed . . .

MEHAR sat at the high table in the palace's grand hall and watched as a long-fingered hand followed the words written on a page, then traced a pattern on the wood of the table, showing her how the spell should be woven. It was a spell of protection.

Mehar didn't wonder that it was the first spell in her mother's book.

She did wonder, however, how it was that a mere peasant, his youth spent in the king's palace aside, should know how to weave such a spell with such unfaltering confidence. She looked up at him, met his searing blue eyes and felt herself being woven into a weft that seemed like threads of a destiny she'd never anticipated.

"Here," he said, nodding toward his hand, "watch again, then copy me."

He traced the pattern again, a simple pattern that seemed suddenly to make perfect sense to her. Mehar copied his motions, then stared in astonishment as silver lines appeared where she had traced, as if she'd written with ink that shimmered and glittered and was slow to fade.

She looked at Gil. He was staring at her in astonishment.

"Well," he said at length. "Apparently you have a gift. I daresay you have it from your mother."

"Why do you say that?"

"Because Camanaë is a matriarchal magic. If your dam had it, then so would you. Do you have sisters?"

She looked up at him. "Aye."

"Then they have it as well, unless they're completely dim-witted."

"I'll have to think on that," she said. "I tried a spell of un-noticing on them and it failed miserably. I thought it was because I'd woven it poorly, but perhaps they merely possessed the wherewithal to see through it." She smiled, chagrined. "I never credited them with any skill at all beyond the ability to attend to their potions and beautifiers for great stretches of time. Perhaps I misjudged them."

"Perhaps, or they might be totally lacking in any imagination at all," he conceded. "In which case it would take a great need to awaken whatever magic is in their blood. Have they any great needs?"

"None beyond accurate looking glasses," she said dryly. It was quite an extraordinary thought, though, to imagine that her sisters might have inherited something from their mother besides her perfect beauty.

It was also a marvel to find herself tracing lines on a table, beautiful lines that looked as if a wizard had done the like, yet they had come from her humble, work-roughened hand with its chipped fingernails and cracked skin.

"Well," she said, finding herself at quite a loss. Then she looked at Gil and found herself traveling even farther down that uncharted path to complete bewilderment.

How could she have known two weeks ago that a fortnight passed in fear would find her sitting in the palace at Neroche, at the high table no less, sketching bits of magic on that royal table and having it come to her hand as if it found her pleasing to its purposes?

"I think I like this," she said finally.

He smiled. "I imagine you do."

She gestured at the table. "My lines are better than yours."

He laughed. "Aye, and so they would be, for my magic is not of Camanaë, lady. And that is a good thing, else we would have no . . . else we would be—"

She watched him squirm as he found himself pinioned quite thoroughly by a lie he was obviously not equipped to spew forth.

"Magic? You have magic?" she asked politely. "What kind? Educate me, good sir."

He pursed his lips. "I inherited a few bits from my sire."

"A little prevarication, that," she noted.

"And a bit more from my dam."

She waited patiently.

"All right," he grumbled, "a great bit from both parents, but I'll not tell you more until you tell me why a woman of your beauty travels alone to the king's palace on a horse Angesand himself would salivate over, with a book of magic that dark mages far and wide would kill her for, and she hides her name as if revealing it to a soul as trustworthy as myself might endanger her to just those sorts of villains." He looked at her crossly. "You tell me that first."

Beauty. Had he said beauty? Mehar found herself with an alarming redness creeping with unnerving speed up her throat and onto her cheeks.

Gil nodded in satisfaction. "I agree. 'Tis quite embarrassing when one realizes that one is being unnecessarily stubborn."

"I told you there was a price on my head," Mehar said evenly, her blush receding at the thought, "and how do I know you wouldn't find it a sum worthy of your attention? It isn't as if you're dressing yourself in embroidered silks and reclining upon cushions of uncommon softness with covers woven of cashmere."

He looked at the table and traced her pattern with his own. The lines faded after his passing, but they didn't disappear. Instead, they glowed a deep blue, shot with silver.

That was an uncommon magic, his.

But then he brushed his hand over the wood and the lines disappeared. He looked at her.

"There is no sum that I would consider to be worth your head."

"Are you so rich?" she asked.

"Nay, I am so honorable."

She pressed her hand flat on the table, over the place where they'd both woven her mother's spell, but found no adequate reply to his words.

"And if you would learn them from me," he continued, "I can teach you a spell or two of ward, another of strengthening whatever weapon you have to hand, and perhaps one or two that might aid you when someone is set to come upon you."

"Where did you learn all this?" she asked. "You, a simple peasant."

He smiled at her and a dimple appeared in his cheek, a mark of such easy charm that she found herself quite enchanted. It was with an effort that she looked away from it.

"Haimert of Wexham, the court mage, wasn't always about the king's business," he said. "When he had a free moment, I bribed him for knowledge with Cook's most easy-to-carry pasties. It seemed to us both a fair trade."

"Do you have great power?"

He opened his mouth to speak, then shut it, and smiled at her. "Enough for my purposes, and telling more would tell you all—" He stopped and looked up as Alcuin came into the hall and walked quickly over to the table. "Aye?" he asked.

Mehar watched Alcuin's gaze flick to her and back to Gil. Gil turned to smile at her.

"Perhaps you would care for a bit of peace," he offered, "in that luxurious chamber I promised you."

She was tempted to tell them she would rather stay and listen, but she forbore. "I'll leave you lads to your plotting," she said as she rose, "though what two peasants would have to plot about I can't imagine, unless you're bent on making off with the king's finest silver in which case I should likely put a stop to it. Are you planning thievery?"

Alcuin snorted. "Nay, we are not."

"Nay, nothing untoward," Gil assured her.

Well, it was obvious they had business together, and as she just couldn't believe anything foul of Gil truly, her first impressions aside, she left the grand hall with an untroubled heart. Soon deep whispers were sliding along the walls to either side of her and rising up to flutter against the ceiling, whispers that carried the hint of subterfuge.

There was more to those peasants than met the eye.

She threaded her way through the rubble in the corridor, wandering down passageway after passageway, becoming hopelessly lost, but she suspected that had less to do with Gil's directions than it did with her own distracted state.

She had woven a spell from her mother's book and had it fall easily from her hand.

She felt as if she had just put her foot to a path that had been laid out before her all along; she just hadn't been able to see it. It was, on the whole, a vastly unsettling feeling, but even that had an air of familiarity that sent chills down her spine.

She paused before the door she thought might be the correct one, then eased it open and peeked inside. The chamber was empty. She entered it, then slowly shut the heavy door behind her. The ruin here was not so terrible as it was in other places. The tapestries, for the most part, were still intact. The furniture was merely overturned, not destroyed. She pushed away from the door and wandered about the chamber, putting things to rights. She sat on the bed and wondered just whose chamber she was in. The king's, perhaps?

But nay, there were no kingly trappings, no gilding, no banners with his crest, no furs and luxurious silks hanging on the walls. But the colors on the rugs, the hangings, and the bedclothes had been dyed with difficulty and at no doubt great expense.

There was a bench sitting under the window, and next to that a chair sporting quite worn cushions, as if it had seen much use by one who sat and stared out the window to contemplate deep thoughts. She stared at the chair for a moment, then realized what struck her as odd. There was a blanket draped over its arm, as if it had been just recently used and not quite put away properly. It was a cloth she recognized.

She likely should, given that she'd been the one to weave it.

She floated over to the chair, feeling as if her legs were no longer beneath her. She lifted the cloth and held it to her cheek, remembering vividly the weaving of it.

It had been for the eldest of Alexandir the Bold's sons, a gift sent to comfort him after his mother had been slain. Fey, that eldest prince had been rumored to be, fey and wild. People tended to make all manner of signs to ward off any stray spells or whatnot when they spoke of him. Mehar had imagined that he was less strange than sorrowful, and it was for that reason that she'd woven her gift for him.

She sank down into the chair, set her book onto the nearby bench, and pulled the prince's blanket over herself. She had one of her own, something her mother had woven for her the month before she'd died, but hers had been destroyed along with everything else. She fingered the cloth. It was frayed in places, faded by the sun in others, missing bits of the fringe she had painstakingly tied. She leaned her head back against the chair, closed her eyes, and spared a brief thought for the prince who had obviously used this often.

Had he died alongside his father, or had he been alone? Was he in a better place? She'd often wondered where a man went when his task here was finished. Her mother had told her, with her eyes full of its vision, that she saw a land far beyond the eastern deserts, where the air was cool and the waters clear, and there was no more suffering.

She hoped, as she rubbed the prince's soft blanket against her cheek, that he had found such a place. Perhaps he now sat at table with his mother who had gone before him. She closed her eyes and wept, not daring to hope that such a place existed, or that she might one day feel her own mother's arms around her yet again, smell the sweet scent of her, feel the gentle caress of her hand on her own hair.

She wept until the wool was damp and began to disturb her. She sat up, folded the blanket over the arm of the chair, then winced at the brightness of the setting sun streaming through the window. She turned away from the window and watched the motes of dust dance. They glinted and sparkled as they swirled and slid toward the floor.

Then other things began to glint.

She blinked at the sight of something sparkling beneath the bed.

She rose from the chair, then dropped to her hands and knees and peered more closely under the wooden railing. She reached in and drew out something quite unexpected.

A crown.

She put her hand under again and drew out, with quite a bit more difficulty, a sword.

She stared down at the treasures before her and wondered why they found themselves under this bed instead of upon the king's head and by his side where they should have been. Had the king left them behind? The crown, she could understand. It had to get in one's way, when one was trying to avoid having his head cut off in battle. Though with the gems that encrusted that substantial circle of metal, she was surprised the king hadn't worn it in hopes that the glint of gemmery would have blinded his enemies and won him the day by its virtue alone.

The sword was a deeper puzzle. That the king should have left that behind was unthinkable. Gil had said he was a servant of the king, so perhaps he had brought his liege's sword back from the field of battle for him, that he might give it to one who might in future times come to claim the kingship.

Odd, though, that they should find themselves here.

She returned both the sword and the crown to their places, then turned her mind from the king's gear to things that concerned her more closely.

She had found someone who could help her to understand her mother's book. She had a warm place to sleep and decent food in return for work she could readily do. It was enough, at least, for the moment.

She rose, fetched the prince of Neroche's blanket, then cast herself upon the bed and fell asleep, its softness surrounding her with a quiet peace.

Chapter Four

*In Which Gilraehen Finds Himself Fixed
Quite Firmly on the Horns of a Dilemma . . .*

GIL had never considered himself a poor horseman, but he
found himself quite out of his depth at present. He watched
Mehar fly, and he meant that quite literally, over a hedge
that any sensible gardener would have trimmed whilst
standing upon a ladder. He himself chose quite wisely to direct his own mount around the greenery instead of over it.
Mehar's horse, that fleet beast, was truly a miracle, and his
rider was his equal in every respect. Robert of Angesand
would have been proud to call her his.

Gil hauled back on his reins, then blinked in the manner
he normally reserved for the break of day when it came too
early.

Was Fleet one of Angesand's beasts?

It was possible.

Was Mehar one of Angesand's daughters?

That was possible as well.

He cast back to the times he'd been to Angesand's hall, but could only bring to mind three daughters; three beauties who were perfectly coiffed, perfectly mannered, and perfectly clean at all times. Not at all like the woman before him who had turned Fleet around and come cantering back his way.

She pulled up and laughed at him. "I thought you were for a goodly bit of speed this morn," she chided, "especially after the past three days you've spent just ambling through the gardens, yet here I find you merely sitting and admiring the divots in the grass."

Nay, I was admiring you was almost off his tongue before he thought better of it. Aye, admiring her with her hair tumbling down over her shoulders, her clothes splattered with mud, the cloak he'd loaned her also splattered with mud. Aye, and there went her cheek, just as muddy, thanks to the back of her hand brushing away a stray bit of hair.

What he really needed was Tagaire alive and well and pouring over pages of the realm's genealogy so he might answer Gil's question for him. Gil ran through a list of evil dotards as potential suitors for Mehar—the same list he'd been contemplating during those three days spent ambling through the garden with her—but no one came immediately to mind save Uirsig of Hagoth. Hagoth was hardly out of mourning for his fourth wife, so there was little chance he was looking for another. Perhaps Mehar's undesirable betrothed was an elderly farmer with grown children who had looked to her for a bit of pleasure after his own wife's death.

The thought, unsurprisingly, left Gil with a rather strong desire to grind his teeth.

"Come on," she said, turning Fleet back toward the garden. "Keep up, if you can. And given your showing this morning, I very much doubt you'll manage it."

He couldn't remember the last time a woman had spoken

to him with such an appalling lack of respect. He laughed just the same and tried to keep up.

And, as she had predicted he would, he failed.

But as he struggled to follow her over shrubbery, around fallen benches, and over large pits in his father's garden, he came more surely to the conclusion that Fleet was no simple horse breeder's finest and Mehar was no simple horse breeder's daughter. He watched in awe as she sent Fleet over another jump that no sensible woman would have attempted and no horse with any fear at all would have dared.

He finally managed to draw alongside her. "You are magnificent," he said simply.

" 'Tis the horse," she said, with a breathless laugh. "He is unmatched."

"As are you. No wonder Angesand was loath to let either of you go."

The blood drained from her face. With a cry of dismay, she wheeled Fleet around and galloped off before he could gather his wits to call an apology after her. He congratulated himself on being right, but that glowing feeling was somewhat lost in the effort it took to chase her. He wouldn't have caught her at all if she hadn't ridden straight for the front door and been stopped by the large contingent of souls loitering there.

Damnation. He wasn't even going to have a chance to apologize before all hell broke loose. Gil sighed heavily. His future had arrived—and far too soon for his taste.

He reined his horse in and squared his shoulders against the frowns of disapproval he was receiving from an older man and a younger woman who sat at the head of the company that blocked the door. He moved next to Mehar. "Allow me to introduce you," he said, inclining his head toward his guests. "His Majesty, King Douglass of Penrhyn and his daughter, the Princess Tiare of Penrhyn."

Mehar looked at him in surprise. "How would you know?" she asked.

"He would know, you grubby little upstart, because I am his betrothed," Tiare said coldly. "Though at the moment I am having grave doubts about the advisability of wedding with . . ."—at this point words seemed to quite fail her as she raked Gil with a gaze that missed no splatter of mud, no matter how slight—"with . . . with a prince who masquerades as a common laborer. It all seems quite inadvisable."

"Prince?" Mehar echoed faintly. "Prince?"

"No longer the prince," Douglass said, chewing on his pipe, then removing it and sending Gil a rather steely glance. "He is the king. The mind reels at such a thought, but is it possible, Gilraehen, that the tales are true and your father is dead? Leaving you in charge?"

Gil had wondered, on previous occasions, if he might have misjudged Douglass, having thought his meanness to be due to a man of his small stature being allotted such a small portion in life. But now, he concluded that Douglass was unfortunately entirely unpalatable on his own merits alone.

How was it, Gil asked himself, that he found himself connected to the pair before him? Penrhyn was an insignificant little country, and it exported nothing save the sour wine that some found a delicacy. Its kings were forever looking for ways to improve their situations, which usually entailed wedding their daughters to those who might pour money into monarchial coffers so the kings might import the things they desired instead of grousing about the fact that they couldn't produce the like themselves.

That had been one reason for Douglass's enthusiasm over Gil's betrothal to the quite tart Tiare.

Penrhyn also held, in a handful of quite inconsequential mountains, several mines of brencara, the sapphire gem that was quite necessary to the weaving of the spell of secrecy that covered the vale of Neroche. Gil's father had counseled him that it would be advisable to cement a supply of that rare gem far into the future. Gil was quite certain that the necessary spells could be cast with naught but his own two hands to aid him (indeed, he had proved that to himself the first time his father had suggested a match with the violently acerbic woman before him), but he supposed his father had, in his heart of hearts, been less taken by the fact that Tiare had also been one of the few who hadn't begged to wed Gil because of his fierce beauty (their words and not his), and the delicious peril of putting themselves in his questionable hands, than he had been taken by the thought of a steady stream of sour wine running into his kingly cup.

Either that, or his father had suffered a complete and utter loss of good sense and betrothed his eldest son to Dour Douglass's nastiest daughter after one too many glasses of that sour wine.

Gil couldn't have said.

All he knew was that he was committed to a course he was quite sure he no longer wanted to pursue, without an out in sight.

Damn it anyway.

He swung down off his horse with a sigh and nodded to his guests. "If I might offer you the hospitality of my hall?" he asked politely.

Tiare rolled her eyes, her father made a sour face and a noise to match, then they both clambered down off horses that had seen far too much wear. And whilst they were about their journeys to the ground, Gil murmured a spell under his breath. The strength of it took a good deal of his own, and it certainly hadn't been a proper job (there was a good deal of screeching coming from inside the corridor in which his name figured prominently in uncomplimentary ways), but at least most of the castle was again put to rights.

He hoped that hadn't been a mistake. If evil eyes had been watching, there had certainly been magic there to be seen.

"Here, wench, come take our horses," Douglass said, gesturing behind Gil.

Gil opened his mouth to speak, but given that his breath had been taken away by what he'd just done, he didn't manage it. He leaned against his horse for a moment or two, then found himself eased aside as Mehar took the reins from him. She looked at him briefly with all the expression wiped off her face.

"With your leave, my liege?" she asked.

He would have scowled at her, or at least reminded her that she hadn't been all that forthcoming with her details (though he supposed he should have been quick enough to know that the only horse breeder who could generate the kind of stallion Fleet was would indeed be Robert of Angesand), but he didn't, mostly because he didn't have the breath for it.

"Gilraehen, go bathe," Tiare said crisply. "You look no better than that filthy peasant there."

He looked at Tiare quietly, quite steadily, and with no lack of warning—or so he intended it. Tiare returned his look, quite unimpressed.

"Can you not try to look the part that is now yours?" she demanded. "Where is the cloak trimmed in ermine? The ruby encrusted scepter? The crown with diamonds and emeralds wrested from the mountains of Fhir Mhoil where dwarfs vie for the mere right to gaze at the map in the hall of Assyent and guess where the truest gems might be mined? I do not see it upon your head."

" 'Tis under his bed."

Gil looked at Mehar in astonishment as she walked past him without so much as a smile. She called to Fleet, clicked to his horse, then led off Tiare and Douglass's horses toward the stables as well. He stood there now without excuse. And as tempting as it was to leave those guests standing before his doors, he knew he couldn't.

"A better welcome we certainly could have expected," Douglass groused pointedly.

"I've been a bit busy," Gil said, then gestured toward his front door. "If you'll follow me, I'll see you settled."

"In heaven only knows what sort of unacceptable accommodations," Tiare said with a heavy sigh.

Gil said nothing more as he led them into the palace. It was almost overwhelmingly tempting to tell them to go find lodging elsewhere—say, in the next kingdom. He tried to lay his finger on a good reason why he couldn't, but the only one he dredged up was that his mother would have been unimpressed by his hospitality and sorely disappointed in his aforementioned comportment and attention to duty. He didn't think that was a good reason, but perhaps it was the best he could do for the moment.

Besides, it was his betrothed he led down the passageway to the great hall.

Damn her anyway.

He tried to concentrate on what was being spewed at him but all he could think about was the fact that he really wished he was out in the stables, inviting Mehar of Angesand to sit whilst he tended their beasts—not showing Tiare of Penrhyn her chamber and listening to her tell him how it (and he) was lacking.

After waiting for his guests to be settled, he led them to the hall so they might soothe their complaining stomachs.

"Is there no supper waiting for us?" Tiare asked, aghast.

Hay, straw, a few choice oats. If those were good enough for their horses, wouldn't they be good enough for Tiare and her sire? Gil closed his eyes, took a deep breath to shore up his dwindling supply of patience, then ushered them toward the table. "If you'll take your ease, I'll see what Cook has on the fire."

"Do you have no servants?" Tiare asked, still quite

unhappily surprised. "And your hall—has no one polished the floors? Scrubbed the walls? Cleaned the tapestries? It looks as if all your people have been on holiday for weeks instead of seeing to their tasks."

He would obviously have to work on that hasty spell he'd thrown together and add a bit of cleaning to it. He was actually quite impressed that the place looked as good as it did and that no one had suffered any cuts or bruises as the stones had replaced themselves in (mostly) their proper places.

"I'll go put the whip to the sweepers," he said dryly.

"I should hope so," Tiare said. She dusted her chair off, accompanied by several noises of disgust, then sat down, and looked around expectantly.

Alcuin appeared at Gil's side. He glared at Tiare and Tiare returned the glare. Gil thought it wise to excuse himself before he found himself in the crossfire.

"I'll see how supper is progressing," he said, making Tiare and her father a low bow, then escaping to the kitchens, wondering why he'd let his father talk him into having anything to do with the woman he quickly left behind him. He had supposed at the time that since he had to wed, he might as well please his father in his choice. Penrhyn was as good as any for the making of alliances.

Then again, so was Angesand.

He wondered if Mehar knew how very rich her father was, or how very powerful. It was no secret that Robert considered himself ruler of his own small kingdom on the edge of the southern forests. Mehar obviously knew little about her sire's reputation, else she never would have dared flee her home. The number of men Angesand could command with a mere frown was impressive. Why they hadn't come thundering down the road right after her, Gil didn't know. All the more reason to keep a close eye on her.

Though to what end, he couldn't have said, given that he wasn't free.

Would that he were.

He walked through the kitchens. "Penrhyn's here," he said, hurrying on his way. He heard something hit the wall behind him and surmised Cook had thrown a pot lid at him. "That could have killed me!" he bellowed back down the outer passageway.

"Save me cooking a wedding feast!" came the response.

True enough, he supposed.

He walked along his preferred path that led to his preferred location and found that his steps were not as light as he might have otherwise wished. He slowed to a stop. What was he doing, going to find a woman he couldn't have? Thinking to pass any more time with a woman who couldn't be his?

He put his hand on the door to the stable, stood there for a very long moment whilst he wrestled with his duty, then sighed and turned away.

That was when he heard Fleet scream in anger.

He flung open the door and sprinted forward, coming suddenly to a skidding halt, sending straw and dirt scattering everywhere.

A man stood over Mehar, the dagger in his upraised arm gleaming wickedly in the lamplight. Fleet was crashing against the stall door.

Mehar was frozen, a look of complete terror on her face.

Gilraehen cleared his throat. "Excuse me," he said politely. "I think you're trespassing."

The man turned, then snarled out a vicious curse.

Gil felt something akin to pity for the fool. If he'd had a better fortnight, he might have been kinder.

As it was, he suspected the man might pay for quite a few things that hadn't been his doing.

Chapter Five

In Which Mehar Loses Her Heart in a
Most Thorough Manner . . .

MEHAR sat on the floor and shivered. It wasn't just from
the terror she felt, though that was certainly flowing through
her abundantly. Nay, it was that she was watching Gilraehen the Fey prove all the rumors about himself to be true.

She'd come to the stables, removed the gear from Gil's
horse, and put him in his stall. She'd done the same to Fleet,
without lingering over his grooming as she usually did.
A pity she hadn't. If she'd still been at her work, she would
have had something in her hand, something she could have
used as a weapon. As it was, she had turned from Fleet's stall
only to face a man of grim and evil mien who announced
himself with nothing more than a drawn dagger pointed at
her. She'd tried to flee past him only to find herself thrown
to the ground.

She'd tried desperately to draw a spell of protection
around herself, but she'd forgotten the words, forgotten

how Gil had taught her to weave the words, forgotten everything but her fear and the knowledge that she was going to die. Either at this man's hand or Hagoth's; it was inevitable.

And then Gil had appeared.

He had brought no sword, but apparently he hadn't needed one. He'd fought the bounty hunter with his hands alone.

Or with one hand, rather.

Mehar was torn between watching his good hand as it now made a casual motion that sent the man's knife flying, and staring in horrified pity at his withered hand as he held it to his side.

It wasn't the first time she'd seen that other hand. She had seen it after he'd worked the magic that had so suddenly and completely put the palace to rights. She'd seen it as he'd leaned wearily against his horse, his ruined hand tangled in its mane. He'd stood there, stripped of all the illusion she now knew he was capable of. A powerful magic, his, if he could maintain it about his person so easily.

The company from Penrhyn had obviously marked nothing amiss. Perhaps they'd been too busy complaining about whatever seemed to fall beneath their critical eyes. Mehar had counted herself lucky to have escaped before they turned upon her like ravaging dogs.

"Think ye can best me?" the bounty hunter demanded angrily, trying to lay his hands on Gil and finding it somehow quite impossible. Wherever he lunged, Gil seemed not to be; wherever he struck, Gil was no longer there. "Use both hands, damn ye, and give me a fair fight."

Mehar found that her breath had returned, and with it a bit of her courage. "He's Prince Gilraehen, you know. He doesn't need two hands."

The man faltered and came to be standing quite still for a moment before he made the usual signs of ward she'd always seen accompany any talk about the eldest prince. Mehar couldn't help but laugh, though she supposed she might have been doing the same thing if she hadn't passed the last few days in Gil's company and found him to be an ordinary sort of fellow.

When he wasn't about his magic, that was.

She looked again at the bounty hunter to judge his reaction to it all. He looked appropriately horrified and was still frantically making signs of ward against Gil.

And then, quite suddenly, the man wasn't there. In his place was a large, quite ugly, quite immobile spider. Gil, his breathing just the slightest bit labored, looked at her.

There was a wildness in his eyes that she might have feared, had it been directed at her.

"He's yours," he said.

"That's a very big spider," she said.

He lifted a single finger in the slightest of gestures and the spider shrank to something that could have easily been squashed under her shoe. Mehar looked down, then took a deep breath.

"I suppose something larger than he might eat him." She looked at him. "Do you think?"

He waited. When she said no more, he stepped forward and ground the spider under his boot.

And so ended the life of one of her father's ruffians.

Gil held out his hand and pulled her up onto her feet. From there, it was all too easy to go into his arms. She closed her eyes, breathed in his wildness, and felt it sink into her soul.

Far, far too easy, indeed.

"Are you hurt?" he asked quietly.

She shook her head and shivered. "I'm not, but that is thanks to you. I wanted to use the spell, but I couldn't remember how to make it work."

"It takes time."

"I don't have time."

He ran his hand gently over her hair. "You have me to look after you until you master what you must. You have time."

She lingered for another exquisite moment, then pulled away, and took a step backward. She didn't have him; there was a woman inside the castle who would make certain of that. And she certainly couldn't ask him for his time when it was promised elsewhere. She looked up at him, into his fell eyes, and wished things were different. If she'd had her sisters' beauty, her mother's grace, her father's blessing and riches . . .

But how could she have ever expected the future king of Neroche to look at her and see past her stained fingers and flyaway hair?

"Thank you for the aid," she said, suddenly finding it easier to look down at his boots than up at his face. "I think I am unprepared for this."

"We all are, in the beginning," he said.

She looked up at that. "Trading the mage lessons for pasties," she said in mock disgust, trying desperately to find a lighter tone. "You are a terrible liar."

He smiled and the dimple in his cheek almost felled her where she stood. "I didn't lie. I did take him all number of treats, for then he would let me from my lessons early."

"Well, you seemed to have managed in spite of that."

He sobered slightly. "The magic in the blood cannot be denied. As you have found."

"You're hedging. You led me astray with that story, diverted me from finding out who you really were. And that business about your name," she said with a snort. "Gilford, indeed."

"It seemed worth the lie, to have you see me differently. I wanted the novel experience of being just Gil the Ordinary," he said, reaching out to tuck a strand of hair behind her ear. "With you."

"And how was it?"

He smiled at her. "Much like you are. Breathtaking."

She stared at him, not wanting to breathe, not wanting to break whatever unbreakable spell he was weaving about them both. He took her hand, casually, as if he feared she would bolt if she realized what he was doing.

She could only look at him, mute, and labor under the thoughts that clamored for her attention: that she might have fallen in love years ago with the prince who had used her mourning gift so thoroughly; that she might have even more fond feelings for the golden peasant she'd passed the past several days with; that she might be becoming unsettlingly enamored of the man who so casually taught her wizard's speak and rode like a demon through palace gardens and over the fallen statues, and ragged hedges.

And to think all those men were merely facets of none other than Gilraehen the Fey, Prince of Neroche.

King of Neroche, now.

She wished that she'd known it from the first; she never would have allowed herself any feelings for him at all if she had.

"I *will* keep you safe," he said quietly.

She shook her head. She would make her way alone soon enough. It was what she had planned on from the start, after all. There was no reason to change that just because she'd found her heart involved in something she hadn't planned on. Magic was her goal and she would just have to continue her search for someone who could teach it to her.

She realized, with a start, that tears were coursing down her cheeks.

Gil put his arms around her and pulled her close again. "Mehar, I'm sorry," he whispered. "I'm sorry."

She shook her head, but found nothing to say. She merely stood there in his arms and contemplated the apology she would have to offer for soaking his shirt.

A throat cleared itself from a safe distance behind them.

"Gil? They grow restless inside and you know I cannot satisfy them."

"In a moment," Gil said. "I'll be there in a moment."

"Well," Alcuin said, "I wouldn't let myself be caught in the stables thusly were I you. No offense, Mehar."

Mehar pulled away from Gil, then pulled her sleeve across her eyes. "Just trying to wash up a bit," she said. "Didn't have any decent water to hand."

Alcuin grunted but said nothing.

Gil dragged his good hand through his hair. "I have to go."

"Aye, you do." She put her shoulders back. "Sorry for the tears. I'm not used to the price on my head, you see."

He was looking at her, she could sense, but she couldn't meet his eyes. Whatever he felt, whatever she might have imagined he felt, he was still set to wed with the Princess of Penrhyn. Even if he hadn't been, that was no guarantee he would turn his clear eye her way.

"Alcuin, watch over her," he said with a sigh. "Who knows what other kind of filth is lurking about. Apparently, my defenses aren't what they should be, but I don't dare do more."

Alcuin steered him back toward the stable doors. "Go. I'll keep watch over her. And I'll entertain her with all sorts of unsavoury things about you after you've gone."

"Sounds treasonous," Mehar said, trying to smile.

Gil muttered something under his breath, shot her a final searing look that made her shiver, then turned on his heel, and walked swiftly from the stables. Mehar looked at Alcuin, who, for once, didn't curse at her. Instead, he handed her a coin.

"Take it back," he said. "If I'd known what you were about, I would have given you the hare freely, and caught you another."

"You're too kind."

"I pity you," he said simply. "Gil, of all people. Don't you know he has more bad habits than I have curses? Now, if you were to cast your eye *my* way, you would find a man of truly impressive lineage, impeccable manners, and diverting antics."

"But I haven't cast my eye his way," she protested.

He stared at her so long that she finally had to look away.

"Hrumph," he grunted. "Poor wench. Well, we'd best be about some sort of training for you. *Never let magic rule when a dagger will do* is my motto."

"Do you have no magic of your own?"

"None that I'll admit to," he said. "Besides, I'm fonder of my blade than all that whispering and muttering under my breath. Bring that dagger lying fallow over there and we'll make for the chicken coop. It's empty and no one will look for us there. Especially no one from Penrhyn, if our luck holds."

She followed him from the stable silently—silently because he seemed to have as many words to hand as he did foul oaths and he seemed determined to talk her to death.

"Thank you," she said, when he finally paused for a few good breaths.

"For that?" he asked, his eyes quite devoid of guile. "You don't really like him anyway, do you? He snores, you know. And he doesn't bathe on long marches. I think you'd be far better off with someone not so afeared of a harmless bit of soap. Take me, for instance. Come along, woman, and I will list my virtues for you. That will occupy the whole of the afternoon."

"Will there be another list on the morrow?"

He smiled, and Gil's dimple showed from his cheek as well. "Of course. I have a quite exhaustive supply."

"Heaven help me."

"Aye, you'll say that as well, when I find you a sword."

"I know where to find a sword," she said.

Alcuin looked at her sharply. "Is it keeping company with a crown?"

"It might be."

He grunted. "Well, then you'd best keep a good eye on both. And we'll go over that spell of protection again, the one Gil taught you this morning. Even I can manage that one in moments of strain, Mehar. Don't know why you can't."

But he patted her companionably on the back as he said it, and she knew she had a friend, at least for a while. She let out her breath slowly. She could do this; she could remain at the castle and learn what she needed to, then be on her way.

And then she would pray she never would have to see Gilraehen the Fey again.

Her heart wouldn't survive it.

Chapter Six

*In Which Gilraehen Finds That Serving Supper
Can Be a Perilous Undertaking . . .*

SEVERAL endless hours later, Gil stood in the shadows of
the kitchen herb garden and watched Mehar go at a helpless
bush with his father's sword.

It was, he had to admit, a novel sight.

Fortunately for the shrub, she didn't seem to be able to
get it and the sword within the same arc, but she made a
valiant effort. She swung, she heaved, she spun.

She landed quite firmly upon her backside.

She looked around quickly, as if to make certain no one
had seen her, but Gil knew he was too far in the shadows to
be seen even despite a very full moon, so he didn't worry.
Besides, he wasn't laughing. He remembered quite well his
first lessons with the sword—a sword that he later realized
had been purposely too heavy for him. Perhaps Master
Wemmit had been trying to teach him humility. He'd certainly never learned the like as a part of more otherworldly

lessons. Nay, sword mastery had come dear, and he prized it the more for the effort.

Mehar might as well, in time, though he couldn't imagine what she might be thinking to do with such a skill. There were shieldmaidens in his father's kingdom, he supposed, but they were seldom made such without grave necessity. A brother, a father, a lover wounded and in need of protection—those were the things that drove a woman to master a blade and bend it to her purposes.

His hand ached suddenly, and then his heart, followed quite hard by a flush of shame. To think that she might have seen his hand he could stomach; that she might want to aid him was moving; that she might have him enough in her heart that she would tramp about in the mud in the middle of the night to pay for that skill so she might protect him made him, by turns, humbled and astonished that he could be so foolish. She was not here for him; she was here for herself.

He wished with all his heart that she needn't be.

Damn that Tiare of Penrhyn and damn him for having agreed to endure her waspish tongue.

Mehar had, whilst he was about his torturous thoughts, picked herself up, taken a firmer grasp on the king's sword, and proceeded to try to demonstrate to it who was in charge.

A goodly while later, when the moon had moved quite a bit more toward the middle of the night, even Gil had to admit that said soul was not her.

He watched her as she sighed heavily, jammed his father's sword into the ground, then turned her attentions elsewhere. She fetched her mother's book and studied a page for a few minutes. She put the book aside, then wove a spell of protection quite beautifully over her chosen bush. Gil was tempted to add his own charm to the shrubbery, but refrained. Let the victory be hers.

She retrieved his father's sword and hacked at the bush with all her strength.

The sword clove it in twain.

Gil held his breath.

Leaves had scattered, branches had split and cracked, and blossoms were lying on the ground.

Or so it seemed.

Then, slowly, the ruin dissipated, and the bush resumed its proper form.

She laughed.

He smiled so hard, tears stung his eyes.

May the stars in the heavens and the pitiless faeries in their sparkling palaces look upon him with mercy, he was lost.

Mehar examined her handiwork another moment or two, then took her book and his sire's sword and trudged back to the house. He watched her go and wished he'd never been born the prince, never agreed to wed Tiare, never given his heart where it couldn't go. If only he could change the present . . . He leaned back against the stone of the palace's outer wall and wished for a miracle.

Unfortunately, given the lack of miracles in his life so far, he didn't hold out much hope.

Eventually, he pushed away from the wall and headed back to the hall himself. Maybe if hope wouldn't be with him, luck might and he would avoid any unpleasant encounters with any of his future in-laws until he had his treasonous heart under control.

He thought about seeking a bed, but found himself suddenly standing before the door to the chamber of records. It didn't matter to him, really, who Mehar's forbearers were. He would have loved her if she'd been a thief or a princess, poor fool that he was. But since he was where he was, there was no sense in not seeing what a little look into Tagaire's impossibly cluttered chamber might yield. He pushed the door open, took a deep breath, then sneezed heartily.

He picked his way around stacks of papers, teetering piles of books, and perilously positioned inkwells. Apparently his spell of restoration had worked all too well inside Tagaire's chamber—taking it back to its former state of glorious disarray.

He spent the rest of the night turning manuscript pages and wishing for better light than the weak magelight he dared conjure up. A candle didn't bear thinking on; he had visions of the entire chamber catching fire due to a stray spark and that kept him from looking for any suitable wicks.

Dawn had broken and the sun was well into his rise toward midmorning before Gil made his way, bleary-eyed but much enlightened, toward the kitchens. He'd found Elfine of Angesand's name entered neatly into Tagaire's books, and thereby knew her claim to a mighty magic. Her line was pure, going back to Isobail of Camanaë, who was the mightiest of her kind in the days when those with gifts had been assembled together and their places decided upon. What would Mehar do, if she knew? Wilt under the pressure or rise to great heights because of it?

He would tell her, eventually, when he thought it would serve her. For now, his curiosity satisfied, he suspected that what would serve him best was a hearty breakfast.

He walked into the kitchens to find Cook in high dudgeon. She banged and clattered and cursed loudly. And that was just when she saw him.

"Have they been awake long?" he asked politely.

He ducked to miss the flying spoon, then loitered with his hip against the work table whilst she made ready a substantial meal.

"I don't think you've ever fed me this well," he remarked.

"I won't be feeding you at all if you don't send them on their way," Cook threatened.

"And how am I to do that?" he asked.

"A finger gesturing toward the front door might do."

He refrained from comment. For all he knew, one of Tiare's spies was lurking behind the flour barrel, waiting for just such an admission of agreement, whereupon the scout would immediately repair to his mistress and tell the full tale. Gil would then find himself begging pardon from a furious Princess of Penrhyn.

He shuddered at the thought.

So instead, he waited, and while he waited, he examined Mehar's lineage and that of his own and speculated on the children such a union might produce. A fruitless and dangerous speculation, to be sure, but he hadn't slept well in a very long time and his poor wits were at their worst.

Such unhealthy contemplation took him through the rest of Cook's grudging meal preparations and on into the great hall where he struggled to carry several dishes in his arms. He wasn't very good at it, given that his maimed hand was of use for little besides trying to keep the plates balanced on his other arm, but he was the king, after all, and not a page, so perhaps it didn't matter what he dropped. Hopefully he would be better at juggling the affairs of his realm than he was at juggling plates of meat and bowls of sauce.

Dour Douglass was already seated and Tiare was preparing to sit when he reached the high table. He started to set down his burdens when Tiare set up a screech so piercing that he dropped everything in surprise.

"Damnation, woman," he exclaimed. "What are you—"

She only made more shrill noises that left him wanting to cover his ears. He looked about him in alarm, half expecting to see an army of trolls marching in to make a breakfast of him and his guests.

But there was nothing in the hall.

Nothing but him, Tiare, and her father.

And then he realized, quite suddenly, what was amiss.

In his haste to see to Tiare's comfort and make the meal presentable, he'd neglected to make himself presentable as well. Tiare was pointing to his maimed hand with a look of complete horror on her face.

"I will not wed with *that*," she howled.

"The dirt will wash off him," her father said placidly. "Look you, he's already cleaner than he was yesterday."

"Look at his *hand,* Father," she cried.

Douglass had his look, then shrugged. "New scars. Freshly healed. They'll fade in time. Lost the use of it as well, lad?"

Gilraehen put his hand behind his back and inclined his head. "For the moment. It will heal."

"It will heal," Douglass agreed dismissively. "Come, Tiare, sit. Perhaps there is drinkable wine in this place to-day. Used to be. Can't say what we'll find now that young Gilraehen is master here. Any wine left below, boy, or have your men sucked it all up?"

Tiare dug in her heels. "I will *not* wed with him," she announced. "I simply will not."

"Aye, you will," Douglass said.

"You'll have to bind me and bring me to the altar. And even then I will not agree, no matter the times you beat me, or stick me with a blade. I will not. I simply will *not.*" She gave Gilraehen a withering look. "I will not wed with a dirty, bedraggled oaf who is so weak he leaves his hall to be overrun by ruffians and so feeble he can't guard even his own hand. Are you to wed me to this, Father? This man who cannot even see to himself? This man who likely left his sire to die on the field so he could escape?"

At that moment, though he suspected it was just a rewishing of things he had wished so many times he'd lost count, Gil heartily wished that she would find someone else to ply her flaying tongue upon and leave him in peace.

Douglass eyed him with disfavor. "Bloody hell, lad, did you hear that? Wouldn't put up with that kind of talk my-self."

"And what is it you suggest I do, lord?" Gil asked. "Beat her?"

"I would."

"I wouldn't."

"Well," Douglass said in disgust, "there is where you've gone wrong."

"I don't care what either of you thinks," Tiare said archly. "I will *not* wed with a man of his . . . his . . . *ilk*," she spat. "Bad enough that he's mad as a loon and fey as a sprite. That he should be so . . . so . . ." Words seemed to fail her at this point. She glared at Gilraehen as if his injury and all the other unsettling things that surrounded him were entirely his fault. "I will not wed with a sorcerer." She turned her glare on her sire. "You cannot make me, Father."

"You'll do what I tell you—"

"I'll kill myself first. See if I don't."

Dour Douglass looked unimpressed.

"He has nothing to give you anyway," Tiare said scornfully. "Look you at his hall. If he could afford my bride price, I would be greatly surprised."

Gil imagined she would be surprised by a great many things, but he refrained from saying as much.

"I have to agree with her about the bride price," Douglass said. "You cannot have the gel for free, and you can't take her dowry then turn about and give it back to me as payment for her. You'll have to buy her with aught of your own, and it doesn't look as if you have aught of your own to spare. At least nothing of this world," he added.

He looked at Gil and Gil supposed it was only vast amounts of self control that kept the man from making some sign of ward against him.

"And then there are the rumors surrounding your father's demise," Douglass continued. "Those are above and beyond the rumors that surround your own self. And I've heard aught about darkness and danger in the north and east, fell, unwholesome things that are coming your way. Perhaps 'tis well that my daughter not be near you, if that is the case."

Gil blinked in surprise. "Are you casting me aside, my lord king?"

"Aye," Douglass said without hesitation. "But serve me some of those fine-looking victuals first, boy. What you can scrape back onto a plate, of course. I daresay I'll need my strength for the journey home." He cast Tiare a quick look before he relieved Gilraehen of the platter he had just picked up and retrieved his own meal from what lay scattered on the table.

For herself, Tiare seemed more interested in fleeing the hall than in shoring up her strength.

Gil wondered wryly what it was he would do without Tiare's dowry of brencara. He gave that some thought as he sat on the edge of the table and swung his leg back and forth. He continued to ponder the problem as Dour Douglass plowed through all the victuals he could manage, burped heartily in kingly fashion, then slapped something down at Gil's elbow before he nodded to him and left the hall.

Gil looked down at the small pouch. He opened it, then laughed to himself. Crushed bits of brencara lay therein, surely enough to serve him should he need it in the near future. Perhaps Douglass felt sorry for him; perhaps he felt sorry for himself. Perhaps he had his eye on a richer prize than the kingdom of Neroche. Gil didn't care. For himself, he felt nothing but relief.

Immense, soul-searing relief.

In fact, he was so relieved, he walked around the table, sat himself down, and set to his own breakfast with vigor and a light heart. He ate, chortled, ate some more, and contemplated how he might arrange his future to suit himself now that he was free.

Then he looked up.

Mehar had just walked into his hall. She hesitated, looked about her, then walked over to the table.

"What happened?" she asked. "The Princess of Penrhyn

fair ran me over in her haste to reach her chamber. Did the meal not suit her?"

"*I* didn't suit her."

She blinked. "You didn't?"

"I didn't."

She brushed crumbs off the table and sat sideways on its edge so she could look at him. "What are you saying?"

"I'm saying she cast me aside."

"But why would she do that?" Mehar asked. "You're the king, for pity's sake."

He slipped his damaged hand under the table before he thought better of it. Perhaps Mehar shared Tiare's revulsion. "Well," he said finally, "apparently the crown didn't make up for my other flaws."

"I understand from Alcuin that you have many."

"He has more. Come, sit, and I'll tell you of them while you eat." He helped himself to a bit more veg under sauce. "Cook never makes this for me. I should ask her to."

She came around the table to sit next to him. "You eat like a man in a great deal of anguish."

"I imagine I feel much as you felt when you fled your home on that winged steed of yours."

"Happy, happy, happy," Mehar murmured.

"Aye, quite," he agreed. He didn't look at her, for he wasn't sure he wanted to look for more in her eyes than he might see.

But he sat next to her just the same and felt happier than he had in days.

He was free.

And he was king.

And he supposed that since his former bride didn't want him anymore, he might be free to wed where he willed—and if that meant looking toward a woman with a price on her head and a hand with beasts that even Angesand himself would admire, then so be it.

"How much would that bounty your sire wanted for you

be, do you suppose?" he asked, absently toying with his knife and watching her from under his eyebrows.

"That depends," she said, helping herself to his ale, "on how much of this he'd been drinking, how long his ire had burned, and how fiercely. And how light his purse was feeling."

He shook his head. Angesand bred magical steeds in his stables and grew gold in his garden, or so the tales said. The man was also notoriously stingy, and exacted exorbitant, though quite deserved prices for his horseflesh. Gil shuddered to think how high a price Angesand would have put on his irritation with Mehar.

Though it was a price Gil would gladly pay. As well as the bride price and whatever it would take to satisfy the jilted bridegroom. He had wealth enough, assuming the vaults under the palace hadn't been plundered. He promised himself a good look in the treasury the first chance he had.

"Who was your betrothed?" he asked. No sense in not knowing all the damage at once. A pity Tagaire wasn't still alive. Along with the realm's genealogy, he kept a running tally of who was betrothed to whom, the odds of the union being finalized, and the possibilities of decent children to come. When Mehar didn't answer right away, he supposed that perhaps she might not be eager to say, perhaps for shame that such a man might be less than worthy.

"Hagoth," she said finally. "And no doubt he's put a price on my head as well."

"Hagoth?" he echoed, dumbfounded. Hagoth was notorious for choosing young, exquisite brides with vast sums of money to their names and accomplishments to match. "Hagoth," he repeated. "I wouldn't have thought—"

"I know," she interrupted. "Me, of all people." She rose suddenly. "I think I have horses to tend. By your leave, my liege?"

And with that, she turned and walked away.

He stood up. "I didn't mean . . . that is, I never meant to imply . . ."

She turned at the doorway. "Don't you have business of the realm to attend to?" she asked briskly.

He paused, considered trying to explain himself, then caught a full view of her glare. He winced. Perhaps the kitchens were the safest place for him at present. "I suppose there are always dishes to wash," he conceded.

She didn't laugh. Instead, she curtseyed to him with all the grace of any of the young, exquisite ingenues who came to present themselves to him, and left the hall.

"Damn," he said to no one in particular.

He almost went after her, but he suspected that anything he might say would go unlistened-to. Perhaps if he gave her time to cool her temper, he might attempt an apology later. So, as penance, he gathered platters and forks, then made his way to where the washing tub resided.

He contemplated his apology as he prepared to be about his task. He could offer to teach her magery. Not just the reading of her mother's book, but the whole business. Spells, changings, the long and illustrious oral tradition that made one anxious to go back out and work with the sword. That might take a very long time. Perhaps years. And perhaps at some point during those years, she might grow to have fond feelings for him.

And perhaps he would learn to check what he planned to say before he said it and avoid any more of the kind of looks he'd received from her after he'd expressed in not so many words his doubt about Hagoth's choice.

Damn it anyway.

Soon, he was deep into his work, his head full of visions of himself with his newly acquired perspicuous and proper tongue contributing to a very happy and unoffended Mehar of Angesand. He had just finished envisioning how she would receive his proposal of marriage when he looked up from the scrubbing of his pots to see his two younger brothers walk into the kitchen, just as they'd done countless times over countless years, seeking something to filch before supper.

"Well," Lanrien said with a laugh, "here we find our good King of Neroche. Up to his elbows in suds."

Tirran laughed as well, snatching a hot cake off the cooling racks and cursing as he juggled it in the air. "He's no fool when it comes to filling his belly or locating the most drinkable ale."

Gil stared at the two men who were currently pestering Cook for things to eat and thought his heart might burst. They were battered and bruised, with rags wrapped about various parts of their forms, but they were whole. Tirran, his dark hair mussed and his bright blue eyes twinkling, looked as if he'd just come in from a ride. Lanrien, fair-haired like their dam, with deep green eyes that held secrets he didn't often share, looked worse for the wear, as if the journey home had been more difficult than he cared to admit. But they were home. Gil could scarce believe it.

They soon left off tormenting Cook and turned to him. He was quite happy for a bucket of suds beneath his hands. It made the tears that fell into it as his brothers hugged him much less noticeable than they would have been had they been dripping with great splats onto the floor.

"You great idiots," Gil said finally, dragging his sleeve across his eyes, "where have you been?"

Tirran shrugged. "Scouting."

"We supposed you didn't have the lads for it," Lanrien added, "what with only Alcuin at your heels."

Gil looked at them unflinchingly. "I ran."

Lanrien returned the look. "We did as well. We had no choice. At least you destroyed most of his army as you left."

"Aye, we just scurried around the side and wished you the best," Tirran agreed cheerfully.

"So I see by the condition of your clothes and yourselves," Gil said dryly.

"Well, at least your hands are clean for the tending of our hurts," Lanrien said pragmatically. "Though you aren't really much on the healing part of it all, are you?"

Gil scowled. "You would think I was the only one in this keep capable of muttering a spell. Why didn't you work on each other?"

"Didn't want to attract attention," Tirran said easily. "And you know we haven't any decent magic. Not for that kind of thing. And, since we haven't bled to death yet, waiting a few more moments won't hurt. Cook, my love, what is it you're creating in that fine copper pot? It smells like heaven."

"It's lunch for Penrhyn and his get," Cook said tartly, "so keep your grubby paws out of it. Your Highness," she added with a nod.

"I'll just taste—"

Gil laughed. *His brothers were alive.* Somehow, that made it all more bearable. He shook water off his hands, reached for a towel, then realized his hand wasn't working. Still.

Silence fell. He looked at his brothers, realizing what they'd seen. He put his hand behind his back. "'Tis nothing."

"Gil," Lanrien said in a low voice, "what happened to you?"

"I put my hand into a fire and scorched it. Which is what will happen to you if you're not careful with Cook's pot. And Cook, Penrhyn and his get have departed."

She looked at him hopefully. "For good?"

"For good."

Cook looked pleased. His brothers looked shocked. For himself, he could only smile.

"Come, lads, and let us repair to the hall where we can talk peacefully. We've much to discuss. Did you bring anyone with you, or is it just you two who wafted back to the palace like a bad smell?"

"Ingle the smith," Lanrien said, "and Tagaire as well."

"In truth?" Gil asked, surprised.

"He wields a mighty pen," Tirran said, chewing industriously on something else he'd poached from Cook's table. "Poked several lads with it that I saw. And there are a few others coming along shortly who might be necessary to the running of the keep."

"Then let's have a parley," Gil suggested. "But later, after you've eaten. Follow me and bring food with you."

His brothers followed, and, fortunately for them, chose to make no more comments. He wasn't sure he could have borne any more discussion of his wound, or how it might come to bear on his kingship.

Or on his ability to weave the spells necessary to keep that kingship intact.

He sat down at the table, grateful beyond measure for their companionship and not a little surprised at how he'd grieved unknowingly for its lack. He watched his siblings eat as if they'd been starved for weeks and was content.

Or at least he was until the questions began.

"What of Penrhyn?" Tirran demanded.

Gil shrugged. "She decided she didn't want me."

"Tiare pitched you?" Lanrien asked in astonishment. "What'd you do to her, Gil, tell her that her face matched her wine?"

He shook his head with a smile. "She didn't care for the new look of my paw."

"Daft wench," Tirran said, shaking his head. "At least you aren't weeping over it."

"I'll survive."

"Any new prospects?" Lanrien asked, studying his brother

with a grave smile. "Vast armies of lassies of all ages coming to vie for the attentions of the new king?"

"Nay."

Tirran leaned forward. "Then why are you so bloody cheerful? Gil, the future of the realm! The continuation of your line, an heir for the throne!" He waggled his eyebrows. "Think on your duty, brother."

Gil thought about that duty and decided it was perhaps time to see to it. He cuffed Tirran affectionately on the back of the head and rose. "If that's the case, then our parley can wait. I've business in the stables."

"Don't tell us you've fallen for a stable wench," Tirran said in disbelief.

"A horse breeder's daughter, actually."

They were silent long enough for him to gain the passageway leading to the kitchens.

"Who?" Lanrien bellowed.

"Gil, wait!" Tirran shouted.

He continued on his way, smiling. His brothers were alive. Could his life improve?

He suspected it could, so he quickened his pace.

He entered the stables and paused in the shadows where he could watch Mehar stroking Fleet's nose. Whatever else might be happening to his realm, whatever horrors awaited him in the future, whatever deep waters he might need to swim in before he reached peace and stability, he didn't care if he could just stand there and look at her for a moment or two more.

For he was, as he had noted earlier, free, and he was the king.

Which surely meant that he could choose his bride where he willed.

He stood there for so long, thinking on that happy prospect, that he failed to notice when exactly it was that Mehar turned to look at him. She was leaning on the stall door and staring at him solemnly.

"My liege?" she queried. "Did your meal not sit well with you?"

"Best one I've had in years," he admitted with a smile. "I was just now lost in thought."

"The weightier matters of the realm?"

"I was considering choosing a bride, actually."

Had her smile faltered? He looked closely, searching for a sign that it had. Unfortunately, all he could decide was that perhaps a bit of dust had floated up and tickled her nose.

"I wish you good fortune," she said, sounding perfectly content that he might be about his choosing and not in the least bit interested that he turn that choosing in her direction.

He decided to take matters into his own hands. It was one of his father's most useful traits and he'd inherited a goodly quantity of it. He walked across the hay-strewn floor and paused a pair of steps away from her and assumed a like pose of leaning with his elbow atop the railing. He stood there and admired her dark gray eyes, her riotous hair that had yet again escaped her plait, and her hands that were cracked, worn, and wearing a fine layer of dirt and other stable-ish kinds of things.

Ah, but what a woman this one was.

Indeed, he was so intent on admiring her that he completely forgot his hand until he saw her gaze fall upon it. But she only looked at it, then looked up at him, neither pity nor disgust on her face. Gil straightened and put his hand behind his back.

"I came to see if you might be willing to aid me," he said formally, all thoughts of proposing a union suddenly gone from his mind. Angesand's daughter she was, and therefore she might have her standards in a husband. King though he might have been, he certainly had flaws enough.

"Aid you?" she repeated. "How, my liege?"

"You called me Gil this morning."

"I'm feeling formal."

"I'm not wearing a crown."

She smiled briefly. "Then how may I aid you, Gilraehen the Fey?"

He wondered why the sound of his name from a woman's lips without a charm or ward attached should please him so much. He dragged his wandering thoughts back to the present with an effort. "I came to discuss wedding you, but perhaps you would prefer to learn a bit of healing so you might see to my brothers."

She blinked.

He did as well, when he realized what he'd said. He was tempted to curse his tongue—for he'd certainly intended a more flowery proposal, one in which he laid out a thorough inventory of his virtues—but perhaps his tongue had things aright where he didn't.

Then Mehar laughed. He supposed he should have been affronted by it, but he couldn't seem to muster up any kind of serious frown.

"Wed me?" she echoed. "Who, you?"

"Is the thought so ridiculous?"

She finally had to sit down, the thought was apparently so ridiculous. He did find an appropriately displeased expression, but that only made her laugh the harder. He finally sat down next to her on an unassuming bale of hay and waited until her mirth had subsided. She sighed finally, wiping the tears from her eyes.

"Wouldn't that be something?" she asked. "Me, wedding you."

"I cannot decide if I should be insulted or not."

She shook her head. "Nay, lord, I am surely not high enough for the likes of you."

"I am king," he said loftily. "I can decide who is high enough for me and who isn't. And perhaps you don't realize your father's place in the kingdom. I may have the crown and the title, but his power and wealth are easily equal to mine."

She blinked. "In truth?"

"Mehar, what have you been doing all your life?"

"Weaving upstairs and avoiding royal guests below."

He took her hand, then suddenly he saw that hand in another place, weaving a blanket to slip around the shoulders of a young prince who had lost his dam. He saw her with a shuttle in her hand, saw the tears that fell from her eyes as she wove love and pity into the plaid of a cloth that would go around him in the dark of night and bring him ease. He took that hand, that tender hand, and held it against his cheek.

"Your gift," he said. "The mourning cloth."

Tears sprang to her eyes. "You used it."

"Endlessly." He kissed the palm of her hand. "Perhaps 'twas when I first touched it that my heart was given and 'tis only now that the strands of fate have woven us together at last." He smiled at her. "I can be grateful your father was so foresighted as to have hidden you away that you might be mine."

"I'm certain it wasn't for that reason," she said dryly.

He rubbed his thumb over her hand, stained as it was from dye and work, then met her eyes.

"Can you not love me, Mehar with the price on her head?"

She looked down at his hand surrounding hers, then nodded slowly. "I could, Gilraehen of Neroche. But about that price on my head—"

"What will I have to sell?"

"What won't you?"

He laughed. "Tell me of it as we wed."

"My father will be furious when he learns," she warned.

"That I wed you, or that I saved him from having to pay someone to deliver you to him?"

"That he wasn't consulted," she said. "But point out to him the gold it saved him and he'll likely toast you with his finest."

"I'll send Alcuin to him to give him the tidings and let him brave both your sire's wrath and his wine. As for you, will you not come with me and let us be about our business whilst the day is yet young?" He didn't wait for an answer, but pulled her to her feet and along behind him for several paces until she dug in her heels so firmly that he was forced to stop and look at her. "Aye?"

"You've said nothing of your heart, my liege."

"Why do you think I was so relieved to see Tiare go?"

"That's hardly an answer."

He pulled her into his arms, kissed her thoroughly, then looked down at her with a smile. "My heart is full of you, Mehar of Angesand. Is that answer enough? It was full of you the moment I saw you. I've spent a completely inappropriate amount of time over the past several days wishing Tiare of Penrhyn would take herself and her sharp tongue and go home so I could wed where I willed."

"Have you?" she asked wistfully.

"Aye," he said, "I have."

She looked down at her hand in his, then met his gaze. "Then I am content."

He led her back to the hall, content as well. Later that day there would be time to talk to his brothers, to face the heavy reality that was his and now would be Mehar's, but for now, for the next few hours, he would put it aside and be glad of a woman who loved him for himself.

It was indeed enough.

Chapter Seven

*In Which Mehar Solves the Mystery of Her
Mother From a Most Unexpected Source . . .*

MEHAR sat across from her newly made husband near the
fire in his grand and glorious hall and wondered if she could
possibly manage what it was he asked of her. His brothers
sat on either side of him, healed and well, and watching her
expectantly. Her healing of them had gone quite well, but
admittedly their wounds had been minor ones. She wasn't
sure she could take confidence from her experience with
them.

Alcuin sat on her right, making noises of impatience that
were so distracting she finally had to glare him into silence.
Then she took Gil's hand in hers, held it gently between
both her own, and looked into his shattered blue eyes.
"I don't think this will hurt."

"I daresay it will."

"How can it? My magic is supposed to be a gentle one."

"Aye, that is the rumor, but the truth may be quite a different thing. But I will bear the attempt." He smiled at her briefly, then nodded once, and closed his eyes.

Mehar looked down at his hand; it was red, twisted, laced with angry weals as if he'd thrust it into a fire full of teeth. She traced her fingers over his skin, felt him shiver. Well, there was no use in waiting. She took a deep breath and started to weave the simple spell of healing Gil had taught her from her mother's book.

She found it difficult to concentrate. The events of the day, leading up to where she now sat, clamored for her attention. She wasn't completely convinced that she wouldn't wake and find herself back in her own cold tower room, buried under blankets that her mother had wrought, and wishing that her future might be other than it promised to be.

That morning, after she'd come back to the palace with Gil, Alcuin had taken her under his wing until all was made ready. His grumbling had been continual, beginning with his reminding her that he was but Gil's cousin ("never will see the damned throne myself"), though captain of his army ("never will see one of *those* of my own either"), dispenser of marital vows ("are you certain you wish to wed with this oaf here, or did he persuade you unfairly?"), and questionable placer of crowns upon the heads of uncrowned kings ("how does it look on *my* head? Better than Gil's, don't you agree?"). He had concluded with an expectant look she'd laughed at, which had incited yet another round of grumbling that had taken her through a hall which had been filled with twinkling lights she hadn't been able to determine the origin of.

"He is fey, you know," Alcuin had reminded her. "I'd think twice about wedding him, were I you."

She had known, and she didn't have to think twice. She had crossed the floor in a gown of Gil's mother's, placed her hand in the hand of her king, and wed him without so much as a breath of hesitation.

Gil's hand twitched and she came to herself, realizing that she had stopped speaking. She looked at him and smiled apologetically.

"Regrets?" he asked.

"Oh, aye," she said with a small laugh. "I'm sure I'll live well into my old age wishing I'd put my hand down to be crushed under Hagoth's heel instead of into yours to be brought close to your heart."

"Will you listen to that?" Alcuin grumbled to Gil's brothers. "I think the girl likes him, poor wench."

Tirran punched Alcuin in the arm. "You just wish she were yours, but you haven't Gil's charm, so shut up."

"It wasn't his charm," Lanrien offered, "it was his sweet temper and handsome face that so resembles my own handsome face that won him the day."

"Not to mention his murky reputation," Mehar added with a smile at her husband of five hours.

That launched an entirely new discussion of Gil's murky reputation and how that might affect the affairs of the realm in the near future. At least they were talking about something else, and quite loudly, too, so she could concentrate on what she was doing.

When she was finished, she looked critically at Gil's hand and her heart sank. "I don't think there's any change."

"It was a very powerful spell that wrought the damage," he said easily. "It will take a spell equally powerful to fashion the healing. You'll manage it—"

"Let her manage it later," Alcuin interrupted. "Cook is bellowing for hands to carry in the wedding feast." He looked pointedly at Gil and found himself cuffed quite enthusiastically by Lanrien.

"Dolt," Lanrien said, "he's the bridegroom."

"And the king," Tirran added.

"Which neither of *you* are," Alcuin groused. "Come help me."

Mehar waited until they'd left before she looked at Gil. "Will he ever show you any deference?"

"He'll muster up a bit of bobbing and scraping when others are about," he assured her. "But other than that, we can count on him treating me as just Gil the Ordinary."

Mehar looked at him, with his terrible beauty, his eyes that contained the shards of sky and water, his face that held secrets she wasn't sure she was ready to know, and thought him anything but ordinary. But she didn't say as much. Instead, she leaned forward and kissed him, easily, as if she'd been doing it all her life—in spite of the fact that the very act of it made her heart feel as if it would never again regain its proper place in her form.

"I suppose," she said pulling back, "that you'll need someone about you to remind you you're merely a man when you begin to take yourself too seriously."

"And you won't?" he asked, cocking his head to one side.

She shook her head. "I am your warp threads, my liege, ever fixed in my affections. Let someone else correct your pattern. My task is to wrap you in peace and comfort, not strip you of it."

He smiled, reached out, and put his hand to her cheek. "I thank you for the safe harbor. Come, and sit by me, that we might enjoy that peace."

While we have it, was what she heard him add, though he didn't say it aloud and she suspected he wasn't talking about insults from his cousin. But she sat next to him just the same, cut his meat as if she'd been his page (and that over his vociferous protests), and listened to Alcuin and his brothers drag out instruments and sing several ballads that she'd never heard, though she was certainly not one for the recognizing of such given her lack of presence in her own father's hall.

After supper, Gil rose. His brothers were conspicuously

silent, his cousin as well, until they had been left a safe distance behind. Then all manner of suggestions were called out. Gil stepped past the threshold, uttered a single, sharp command, and the doors slammed shut behind them with a resounding bang.

"Did you shut them in there for the night?" Mehar asked.

"Aye," he said with a superior smile. "I also filled the hall with a collection of terrifying wildlife that will keep them busy for most of the night."

The curses that immediately began to stream out from under the doorway were proof enough of that. Mehar shook her head, put her hand in her love's, and walked with him to the bedchamber he'd given her in the beginning.

And after their night's work was done, she fell asleep in his arms, wrapped in the bit of weaving that she'd once upon a time sent him to ease his heart.

She'd never imagined it might cover them both.

THE morning came and brought with it an abrupt end to the peace and quiet she'd wished for, though she wasn't surprised and Gil seemed even less so. She washed and dressed without fuss and walked with him quietly to the great hall where an array of grim-faced men awaited their king.

She looked about the circle at the men who had come uncalled to Gil's need. There were men of Gil's father's house who had straggled back from the battle: Ingle, the steelsmith; Laverock, the apprentice keeper of records; Tagaire, his master; Hirsel, the stable master; and Wemmit the Grim, the swordmaster. Others sat there as well, men who had no title and no names that they would offer.

Lords of other kinds had come as well, seemingly in the night. A dwarf with piercing black eyes and a long, slender nose sat across from Gil, caressing the curve of a small knife as he listened. There was another man who sat apart, long-fingered like Gil, but shorter in stature and quite old. He had a jolly face, but she sensed something beneath his worn exterior that bespoke great power.

And then off to one side, quite aloof, but so desperately handsome that she could scarce look at him without shielding her eyes, sat a stranger. If the man hadn't reminded her so much of Gil with his aura of power, she might have felt a little disloyal in the way she couldn't seem to stop herself from staring at him. She finally leaned over to whisper to Alcuin, who sat next to her, silent and watchful.

"Who is that?" she asked.

He grunted. "Bloody elf. Don't see much of them, as they don't usually leave their gilt-edged halls. They must be worried."

She looked at him. "Are you?"

"Never." He smiled a rather fierce smile. "You haven't seen Gil annoyed. Lothar bested him last time; he won't again. I think Gil took pity on him, in some small fashion, because Lothar is his uncle."

She blinked. "His uncle?"

"His great-grandfather's brother."

"Indeed."

"Second thoughts?" Alcuin asked hopefully.

"None."

"Damn," he whispered, but it was lacking in conviction. "That's why Gil's fey, you know. That magic from Wychweald. He has it a hundredfold, by some bit of fate, and that says nothing of what he has from his dam. That magic is something his brothers got little of. You'll notice they aren't exactly overendowed with that look that makes you want to rub your arms and try to get warm."

"Aye, I did notice. Why is that?"

Alcuin shrugged. "Who knows why magic chooses the course it does? Maybe Gil was fated to be king. The lads have

enough magic to reign, should it come to that, I suppose—
and Lanrien more than Tirran—but it would be a far different kingdom."

She nodded, but found herself distracted by the terrible
talk flowing around her, talk of Lothar of Wychweald and
how to go about defeating him.

The dwarf promised a cage of steel and rare mined stone if
Gilraehen would be so good as to strengthen it with a bit of
his magic. Several men agreed with that plan, vowing to
search out lads to build another army, if Gilraehen would lead
it. There was talk of seeking out ancients from the schools of
wizards to strengthen those armies and build a force that
Lothar couldn't best.

The old man with the weathered face suggested patience.

Gil's brothers vowed revenge.

The elf with the terrible beauty and sparkling eyes
cleared his throat and even Gil lifted his gaze to look at
him. Mehar understood completely. She could hardly take
her eyes off him.

"I think," he said, in a melodious voice that made her
wonder if she croaked like a crow when she spoke, "we should
consider his deeper purpose."

"And that would be?" Gil asked. "Tell me, Ainteine,
what deeper purpose he has than to ruin us all?"

"You know it already, Gilraehen," Ainteine said. "Have
you not seen him single out certain races and hunt them until they're gone?" He looked at Mehar and she felt as if her
soul had suddenly become transparent, that he saw all that
she was in one glance. "You've wed a wife of Camanaë out of
love, and you also promised her safety, and that out of love
as well. Perhaps destiny has had a stronger hand in it than
you realize, given her dam's fate."

Alcuin leaned over to her. "Quite fond of destiny, that lot."

Mehar found herself feeling quite cold all of a sudden.

"Why do you speak of my mother?" she asked Ainteine. "Did you know her?"

"We know all of Camanaë," Ainteine said, "for you are more like to us than other men."

"Are they?" Mehar asked, hardly able to believe it. "I mean, are we?"

"You are," Gil said, smiling at her gravely. "Many generations ago, Sgath of Faerië wed with Ealusaid of Camanaë and thus the line of Camanaë was begun."

"That is true, Gilraehen," Ainteine said smoothly. "And you will find yourself, as did Sgath, watching your children bear your lady's magic and searching doubly hard for ways to thwart Lothar that he does not touch them."

Mehar blinked. "What do you mean?"

She felt Gil take her hand. "What he means is that he believes most of your mother's line has fallen to Lothar's hand at one time or another."

"Your mother's was a powerful magic, one that Lothar loathes above all else, but desires likewise," Ainteine said. "Gilraehen was wise to wed you, for he alone has the strength to protect you and the children you will bear him." He looked at her gravely. "Watch yourself, Mehar of Neroche. You will need all the skills you can learn from your lord, as well as many you will only learn from yourself, to survive."

"Well, this is all fine and good," said the crusty old man, "but that hardly solves the larger problem of ridding ourselves of him for good."

Alcuin elbowed her in the ribs until she leaned his way. "Gil's mother's father, Beachan of Bargrenan. He's not much for elves or anyone else who doesn't like to get his boots muddy. We'll move on to practical matters now."

Mehar wasn't sure she wanted to move on to practical matters. She wanted to know if Ainteine had spoken to her mother, if he knew her grandmother, or her mother's grandmother, or all the other women she had never had the chance to know. She wanted everyone to pause until she'd had the answers she desired.

But it was a council of war, not a bit of a chat during supper, so she held her peace and pondered what she'd learned. And she wondered, if there truly was blood from Faerië running through her veins, why Ainteine could be so beautiful and she so not beautiful. Too much of her father in her, she supposed with a sigh.

She leaned her head back against her chair and waited out the discussions, which, true to Beachan's apparent schedule, moved along quite quickly; they adjourned for supper at a most reasonable hour. Mehar picked idly at her food, too overwhelmed by what she'd learned, and what she thought she'd learned, to eat.

She was almost relieved when Gil took her hand, excused them from the table, and left the hall. She was certain Alcuin was going to fill the company in on all of Gil's faults (he apparently didn't like snakes and there had been a full complement of them in Gil's annoying army the night before), but she had little desire to stay and defend her love when she thought he might be heading for the stables and a bit of freedom.

"Is it safe?" she asked, looking at him as he reached for his horse's gear.

He stopped his movements, then looked at her. "Nay, it likely isn't. But I think I can keep us safe enough for a bit of freedom."

She didn't doubt he could. She only wished, as she saddled Fleet and led him out behind Gil's horse, that she had some kind of weapon herself.

Just in case.

But that just in case didn't seem to be waiting for them. Not that it would have mattered if it had been, given the way Gil was riding. Whether he was simply living up to his name, or whether too much talk of things he couldn't yet master had driven him to a strange mood, she couldn't have said. Fleet was the better horse, and she no poor rider, but she was hard-pressed to keep up with her love. It was a cold, crisp day, and there had been no rain in the night. The ground was bare and dry, and the chill seemed only to suit their mounts. Mehar found herself quite glad of Gil's mother's cloak, which now found a home about her own shoulders.

And then she found herself not glad at all.

Everything happened so fast, she hardly knew how to sort the events out and make sense of them.

One moment Gil was on his horse, the next he was on the ground and Fleet was lifting up to leap over him. She wheeled Fleet around and raced back only to have her horse, fearless beast that he was, pull up, and shudder.

Gil crawled to his feet, dazed.

And then, out of the shadows of the trees, came a man.

Mehar knew without being introduced that this was Lothar. He looked, oddly enough, a great deal like the Prince of Hagoth, but Mehar supposed she was beginning to lump all the horrible men she knew into one mass that wore the same sort of face Hagoth and the bounty hunter had.

Hard. Cold. Cruel.

And then, quite suddenly, not a face anymore.

What sort of creature Lothar had become, she honestly couldn't say, but he was no longer a man and just the sight of him made her want to bolt.

But Gil didn't flee. Where he had stood now hovered an enormous bird of prey, its beak outstretched, its terrible, razorlike claws reaching out to shred the beast before it.

And that was just the beginning.

Mehar lost count of the changes, of the nightmares come to life, of the curses that were hurled, the threats that were spewed, the taunts that Lothar gave and Gil ignored.

And then, just as suddenly as before, Lothar was a man again and in his hand was a sword that flashed in the sunlight. It flashed again as it struck out like a snake. Mehar watched in horror as it bit into whatever disjointed mass of creature Gil had chosen in his wrath to become; the creature bellowed and suddenly there was Gil, writhing on the ground with a sword skewering his leg.

Mehar didn't think. She dug her heels into Fleet's side, but that was unnecessary. He was a mount fit for a mighty warrior and he did what her sire had trained him to do long before she'd stolen him and bid him to be her wings. He leaped at Lothar, slashing him across the face with a hoof as he jumped.

Lothar screamed, but pulled her from the saddle by her foot just the same.

As she fell, she wove her spell of protection.

Over herself.

Over Gil.

Over Fleet.

Lothar glared at her as she lay sprawled on the ground before him. He clutched the torn side of his face and spewed forth curses at her. Mehar quailed, but her spell, the simple, blessed thing that it was, held true. Lothar took a step back.

"I will find you," he said coldly, "and when I've taken your magic, I will kill you."

Mehar didn't dare answer him.

He vanished, but his last words hung in the air.

Just as I did your mother.

Mehar crawled over to Gil. He was white and he'd lost a great deal of blood. She hardly dared pull the sword free, though she could only imagine the foul spells it was laced with. Her lord husband looked at her with wonder and sorrow mingled in his eyes.

"I feared that," he said quietly. "About your mother."

"How . . . how did he . . ."

Gil shook his head. "I don't know. She may have kept him from Angesand so thoroughly that he resorted to having some simple soul poison her." He grasped her hand. "All I know is she protected you. As will I."

She clutched his bloody hand with both hers. "I need a sword, Gil. Even if your hand was whole, even when it *is* whole, I'll need some way to guard your back. To guard my own if you're guarding our children. I could weave things into it."

He looked at her quietly for a moment or two, then nodded. "As you will, love. But you'll use none of this metal here. Can you pull this accursed thing free?"

"You'll bleed."

"Better that than have his magic crawling up my leg as it is presently."

"But Gil, how will I—"

Epilogue

HAROLD blinked, then realized his father had stopped reading. He was whispering behind his hand to one of the men in his merchantry business. Then the man departed and his father stood.

"Wait," Harold said, sitting up suddenly, "you can't stop there. What happened? Did she pull the sword out of his leg? Did Gilraehen survive? And what about her sword? The magical sword she made? The Sword of Angesand?" Harold gave his father his most potent look of pleading. "Father, you cannot leave me at this point. Finish before you leave, I beg you."

His sire hesitated, then sat back down. "Very well," he said, "I will humor you. Briefly. Though you've heard this tale a hundred times at least."

"Once more?" Harold asked hopefully.

His father sighed, but it was without irritation. "Once

more," he agreed, taking up the book again. "It says here that
Gilraehen and Mehar managed to get themselves atop Fleet
and let him carry them back to the ruined palace, with Gil's
horse following, where Cook nourished them with all useful
herbs and fine stews. Then our goodly Queen Mehar—"

"The Bold," Harold put in reverently.

"Aye," his father said with a grave smile, "our good
Queen Mehar the Bold descended into the bowels of the castle and there forged her blade, weaving into it the most
powerful of her mother's spells."

"Right away, or did she have to practice sword-making?"
Reynauld asked. "It is, as you might not know Father, a
rather complicated business."

Harold watched their sire look at his eldest son over the
top of the book. "It says that she did take a goodly bit of
time at the task, son. And Ingle, the steelsmith, did take an
especial interest in aiding her, for by then Gilraehen and
Mehar had searched all the pages of Elfine's book and discovered many potent spells of defense and protection—
which Ingle found much to his liking—"

"And what of the bride price?" Imogen interrupted impatiently. "And the price on her head? Did the king pay
both?"

"He would have—" their sire began.

"And likely still would be—" interjected their mother.

"But," their father said with a smile thrown his wife's
way, "the price on Mehar's head was satisfied because the
dastardly Prince of Hagoth was persuaded to take another of
Angesand's daughters to wife."

"How horrible!" Imogen exclaimed.

"Aye, well, Hagoth wed Sophronia of Angesand, beat her
once, then found himself encountering a piece of meat too
large for his throat at table two days later—and there is
some question as to whether or not Sophronia was cutting
his meat that day, though it doesn't say here—and died,

unmourned. Sophronia took over his affairs, corralled his children, and wed herself to a man quite content to let her manage him, so perhaps it wasn't so horrible after all."

"But what of the bride price?" Harold persisted. "The king paid a goodly price for Queen Mehar, didn't he? It seems as if he should have, she being such a capital fellow and all."

"Never fear, son," their father said, "it says here that a premium price was paid. The king gave our good Lord of Angesand a queenly amount of his gold, a pair of the finest brood mares left him, then laid an enchantment of excellence on Angesand's stables—an enchantment, I might add, that took nigh onto two weeks to do properly."

"Still in force, I'd say," Reynauld said pragmatically. "Passing good steeds, those beasts from Angesand. Fleet of foot and fearless in battle. Strong. Courageous. Wouldn't mind having one myself."

At this point, he looked at his father expectantly.

"I'll think on it," his father promised. "Those horses of Angesand's come dear." He looked at Harold. "Any further questions, my lad?"

"What was Queen Mehar's dowry?"

His father smiled. "Why, Fleet, of course."

"And what happened to Lothar?"

His father seemed to choose his words carefully. "He was wounded, but not mortally. He is Yngerame of Wychweald's son, after all, and because of that has untold years to count before his tally is full. He could live on endlessly."

"But you don't think so," Harold said. He'd overheard—very well, he'd eavesdropped, but how else was a lad to find out anything interesting in a hall where the conversations changed course so quickly each time a child appeared within earshot?—he had *overheard* his sire and his dam speculating on this very subject more than once.

His father looked at him sharply—perhaps he hadn't

been careful enough—then sighed. "I think," he said slowly, "that Lothar will continue until he is slain. His evil is strong and he feeds on the fear he inspires in those around him. It is an endless supply of energy to him. How he will meet his end, in the end, I cannot say."

"And his sons?" Reynauld asked, looking, for once, more concerned about affairs of the realm than he was in obtaining the horse of his dreams.

"I don't think they match him in power," their father said quietly.

"But I thought Lothar was a faery tale," Imogen said in a low, quavering voice. "One you made up to frighten us when we asked for that kind of thing. I didn't think he was real."

Their father closed the book and smiled easily at her. " 'Tis perhaps just that, my love. After all, few claim to have seen him. Mayhap he was just a simple man who lived and died long ago—"

There was a knock, then a servant came in, leaned down, and whispered into their sire's ear. Their father excused himself quickly and went out.

"More tradespeople?" Imogen asked hopefully, her face alight with the expression Harold immediately recognized as enthusiasm over the possibility of more fabric. She even shot him a look, assessing no doubt his current state of grubbiness and how that might affect her plans.

"Mother, must I go into the merchant business?" Reynauld asked, kneeling over his battlefield. "I would so much prefer to be a warrior. On one of Angesand's finest war horses," he added casually.

"Merchantry is an honorable profession," his mother said placidly.

"It seems a tiresome business," Reynauld said. "Messengers arriving at all hours, having to closet yourself with them at all hours, endless discussions, endless bolts of cloth. You would think," he added, "that father would have chosen a more likely spot for his house, wouldn't you? Nearer the Crossroads, perhaps in the duchy of Curach, somewhere other than so far north that our most frequent arrivals are snow and ice and the only reason we have green, tender leafy things to eat is because I stoke the fires each day in that accursed glass house to keep them warm!"

And then, apparently fearing he'd said too much, he shot his mother an apologetic look, rose, then trotted off, to no doubt stoke more fires.

Imogen rose as well, with the excuse of needing to go examine her supply of red silk and see if it was sufficient. Harold watched them go, then watched his mother thoughtfully for some time. The Book of Neroche lay on a heavy, richly carved table next to her chair. He glanced at it, then back at his mother's scarred hands. Some of the scars were round, silvery circles of uneven shape, as if she'd been burned by stray sparks.

He blinked, feeling a great mist begin to clear from his mind.

Burns. Stray sparks. Stray sparks from a *smithy* perhaps?

He looked at the rest of his mother. Her hair was dark, piled on top of her head in what at the start of day was a quite restrained bun. By evening, though, it always looked as it did this evening: riotously curly and relentlessly falling off the top of her head to cascade down past her shoulders.

He thought about her killing that spider.

He wondered why indeed it was that they lived so far in the north. Why men came to see his sire at all hours. Why his sire was gone for long periods of time without a better explanation than he'd been off looking at silks.

Something he seemed to have no affinity for when he was home, truth be told.

Harold pondered yet more on questions that suddenly demanded answers. Why had he never met any of his mother's kin? Why did his father command such deference from the men who came to see him? Why did his mother oft sit in her weaving chamber, whispering quietly over what she wove in a tongue he could not understand?

Reynauld never thought past his pretend battles; Imogen was content with her wares, so if they asked and were given vague answers, they never questioned further. Harold suspected the days of his doing that were over.

He sat up, walked across the rug on his knees and knelt before his mother, the questions burning in his mouth. His father called her *my lady,* and his mother always called his father *my lord.* Indeed, as he looked back over his memories, he couldn't remember them calling each other anything else.

At least within his earshot.

Surely there was more to them both than that.

"Who are you?" he asked.

She looked at him in surprise, but it was followed so quickly by a gentle smile that he almost believed he'd imagined her first reaction.

"I am your mother who loves you, son."

He took his mother's hand. "Where did you get these burns?"

"From a fire."

"Is your sire alive? Your dam?"

She tilted her head to one side. "You're full of questions tonight."

"Well?"

"If you'll have the answers to those, then aye and nay."

"Why I have never met them?"

"Travel is perilous."

He frowned at her. "These are not the answers I'm seeking."

"They are the safe answers, Harry."

He frowned at her, then kissed her hand and rose.

"Where do you go, son?"

He paused at the door. "Hunting, Mother."

" 'Tis bedtime, my dear."

"It will be a short hunt."

She laughed softly and he left the warmth of the family's chamber. He wondered where his parents would keep secrets, if they had any, and decided upon their bedchamber. He almost toppled his great-grandsire—his father's mother's sire—over in his haste. He looked at him sharply. Was this Alesone of Neroche's father? He knew the king's genealogy well; it was required learning from his tutor. He'd never dreamed it might apply to him. He returned his attention to the man before him.

"Who are you?" Harold demanded.

"Who do you think I am?" his great-grandsire asked with a look about him that said he'd been long anticipating the question and had wondered why it had been so long in coming.

"I think you are Beachan of Bargrenan," Harold answered.

His great-grandsire laughed. "Sharp-eyed hawk," he said affectionately, pinching Harold's cheek. "Wondered when it would come to him," he said as he continued on his way.

"That's no answer!" Harold bellowed after him.

Beachan of Bargrenan only held up his hand in a wave, then continued on his way without turning back.

Harold pressed on. He threw open the door to his parents' chamber. It was, he had to admit upon new observation, quite a luxurious chamber. Thick carpets were laid tidily upon the floor, and the walls were covered by equally opulent tapestries.

Things from his father's trades?

Harold suspected not. These were far and above anything he'd ever seen come in the back of a tradesman's cart.

"If I were the Sword of Angesand," he muttered, "where

would I hide myself?" He looked around him, then his eyes fell upon the headboard of the bed. He walked swiftly to it and ran his fingers over the intricate carvings. Aye, they were fashioned most suspiciously in the shape of a blade, especially that long bit there covered with trailing vines. And did not that crossed piece of wood look a good deal like a sword hilt?

He contemplated for a moment how he might liberate a blade from such a covering. Something sharp to dig with, aye, that would suit. He looked about him and scowled. If someone had just lit those candles on the candelabra near his dam's night table, he might have . . .

He might have been able to see.

Which he did now, in spite of those unlit candles, candles resting on a long, silver stand that was, oddly enough, sword height.

If you were a woman, that was.

Harold wondered why he hadn't seen it before. Indeed, it was as if a veil of un-noticing had been pulled off his eyes and now, for the first time in eight long years, he saw clearly.

There, in plain sight, driven into a round base of black granite, was a sword. A sword with a tracery of leaves and flowers—things Queen Mehar loved—flowers that looked a great bloody bit like his mother's favorite tapestry that hung in his favorite cozy chamber, truth be told. The hilt was a simple cross, adorned with more trailing, blossoming vines where they didn't interfere with the holding of the weapon. The hilt now wore a humble tray of polished stone on which sat a handful of candles.

The Sword of Angesand.

Harold turned and leaped upon the bed with all the enthusiasm of Murcach of Dalbyford's finest hunting hounds and pressed and prodded and poked at the headboard with the candle snuffer he'd found near the candles until—to his great astonishment—part of the wood fell down and hung

there by hinges. And what should be behind that wood—
that sword shaped wood—but a sword with a great, blind-
ing blue stone embedded in its hilt.

The Sword of Neroche.

Resting above his father's pillow, of all places.

He put his hand out to touch it.

"The blade is sharp."

He squeaked in fright and whipped around to see his
mother standing at the foot of the bed, hidden just a bit by
the bed curtains. Harold peered around the fabric. By Tappit
of Croxteth's crooked nose, had he never marked how queenly
his mother looked? He found himself suddenly quite unable
to form words—a rather alarming turn of events, to be sure.

His mother, Mehar of Angesand, Queen of Neroche.

She walked around the end of the bed, came to its head,
and leaned past Harold to lift the wooden façade back up. It
closed back over the sword with a firm *click*. Then his
mother looked at him and smiled.

"So, my son," she said gently, "your sight has cleared."

He babbled. He stammered. He ceased his attempts
at speech and merely stared at her in wonder. Then, he felt
his eyes narrowing. "Why didn't you tell us?" he demanded.
"Tell *me*, of all people."

She reached out and smoothed his hair out of his eyes.
"My young Harry, my trusted confidant, I didn't tell you
because I needed to protect you as long as I could."

"Protect me from what?" he demanded.

She gave him the look she was wont to give when he'd
asked a question for which she'd just recently provided the
answer. "Were you not listening this evening?" she asked
quietly. "Did you not hear whom it is we fight—"

She stopped at the sound of footsteps outside the door.
She put her finger to her lips and pointed to the shadows
near the fireplace. Harold bolted across the room and hid
himself behind a tapestry.

"Mehar? Ah, love, there you are."

Harold nodded in satisfaction at the sound of *that* name. So, he was right after all.

And then the full truth of it struck him with full force. He peered around the tapestry and stared at none other than Gilraehen the Fey, King of Neroche, son of Alexandir, grandson of Iamys, great-grandson of Symon, and great-great-grandson of Yngerame of Wychweald, who was the most powerful mage of all. Gilraehen.

His father.

"Alcuin says that he's seen nothing on the roads tonight—"

Then he paused and looked directly at Harold who was merely peeping out from behind the tapestry and was certain he'd been hidden well enough. He gulped.

His father didn't move. He merely stared at Harold in silence.

Harold leaped forward and threw himself to his knees before his father.

"My liege," he said, clasping his hands in front of him. "My king. Command me."

His sire regarded him with a quite noticeable lack of expression. "Your liege? Your king? What prompts you to offer me such obeisance, my son?"

"I saw both swords," Harold admitted.

His father looked at him for another moment or two in silence, then sighed deeply and cast his wife a look. "I suppose he had to see eventually. I'm only surprised Imogen hasn't been asking questions. Did you not see her the other day, snatching looks at the spell book of Wexham?"

"Aye," Mehar said with a laugh. "The next thing we know, she'll be turning Reynauld into a toad as payment for his chopping up her dolls for use as artillery bits."

Harold could hardly believe his ears. "Imogen? She possesses *magic?*"

His mother looked at him. "She is my daughter, Harry. I daresay that you might be a Camanaë exception yourself. Your sight has cleared quite early and it was no weak spell we cast over this palace of Tor Neroche."

Tor Neroche. *Neroche of the mountains.* Harold shook his head. Why had he never seen it before? Why had he never questioned his mother more fully about her past, or questioned his sire more fully about his? And to think he himself might possess magic. That he could believe, but the thought of anyone else in his family claiming the like, especially his sister, was too much for even him. He looked at his mother.

"But Imogen," he protested. "She's just so . . . so . . ."

His father cast him a mild look of warning and Harold turned away from his thoughts of disbelief that his sister could do anything more complicated than find ways to match purple with red and make it look appealing before he borrowed trouble. He smiled weakly at his father and found a wry smile greeting him in return.

"When did you intend to tell us?" Harold asked. If his father was looking that accommodating, he might get in a few questions whilst he could. "And won't Reynauld be surprised! An Angesand steed will surely be his!"

Gilraehen laughed as he knelt down on one knee and looked at his youngest son. "Aye, that is possible, though if he thought about it hard enough, he would realize that the ancient, hoary-haired steed he tends so carefully in that unassuming stall is none other than Fleet, Queen Mehar's winged steed."

Harold could hardly believe his ears. "Fleet?" he squeaked. *"That* is *Fleet?"*

"Who has sired many, many fine horses that you have watched your mother ride more than once. Perhaps you haven't marked her skill."

Harold gave that some thought. He'd been generally more concerned about the bug life crawling about in the mud than his mother's skill with beasts, though he had to admit upon further reflection, that she was a capital horse-woman. He nodded at his mother, then turned back to his sire for further answers.

"When did you intend to tell me all this?" he asked again.

Gilraehen the Fey laughed and ruffled Harold's hair af-fectionately with a hand that was scarred—Harold could see that now—but whole.

"You *did* intend to tell me, didn't you?" Harold pressed.

"Aye," Gilraehen said, "we would have. When it was necessary. When we were prepared to wage war. When we thought Lothar could be taken."

Harold rubbed his hands together expectantly. "Well, what do we do now? What is our plan?"

Gilraehen shot Mehar a look that Harold considered far fuller of amusement than the situation warranted, but he was getting answers to his questions and he was privy to the king's counsels, so he wasn't going to take his sire to task when there were still answers to be had. He waited patiently for further enlightenment.

"How do you feel, Harold my lad, about an adventure?"

Could life improve? Harold almost leaped with joy. "An adventure?" he asked rapturously.

"Aye, my son, an adventure. But," he added seriously, "it will not be an adventure for lads with no stomach for danger. It will require courage, sacrifice, loyalty to the highest degree. And a willingness to pay whatever price is necessary to ensure victory. And even then, we cannot be assured of victory during the course of our battle. The war will be long, for the enemy is cunning and has nothing to live for save his own misery. We may fight, only to leave the ending of the war to others."

"If it means I can fight with you, Father, then the ending does not matter."

"Then put your hands in mine, son, and pledge me your fealty. And then, I suppose, we must see to fashioning you a sword. Perhaps you might ask your mother. She's quite skilled at that sort of thing."

IT was quite a bit later that Harold went to bed. His brother was already asleep, snoring as he lay on his back, sleeping the sleep of the uninformed. Harold tried not to feel superior as he sought his own bed, but he failed completely.

He had pledged fealty to Gilraehen the Fey, King of Neroche.

He had discussed the making of a sword with Mehar the Queen, his very own mother and sword-maker extraordinaire.

His head was full of visions of glory, danger, mighty deeds that would be sung of for generations to come. And he, Harold of Neroche, son of the king, would be involved in all of them.

And if that wasn't an adventure of the first order, he didn't know what was.

Fallen Angel

SHARON SHINN

THE first time an angel kissed me, I was too young to remember. The Archangel Raphael had come to visit my parents, for he was a great friend of my grandfather Karsh, and he kissed me as I lay sleeping in my cradle.

The second time an angel kissed me, I was fourteen, and the Archangel Gabriel was complimenting me for a solo I had just sung at the Gloria. I was one of a handful of Manadavvi girls who had been chosen to sing that year, and Gabriel had given each of us a chaste kiss on the cheek after we performed.

The third time an angel kissed me, he was not an Archangel at all. He was a fatherless wanderer, the wildest of wild young men, and he kissed me as he suffered in exile for having killed a mortal man.

What made it worse was that the man he had killed was my father.

Actually, if I were telling the truth, I would have to admit that that was not the first time Jesse had kissed me, when I was eighteen and he was twenty-one, and I had come to find him shackled to a mountaintop. He had kissed me twice before, on a single autumn day, when it was clear he was only flirting and it was equally clear I had no business flirting back. I was a Manadavvi woman and he was a wayward, reckless, sullen boy completely without prospects. Manadavvi women were not permitted to love men like that—and we were certainly not allowed to marry them.

My grandfather Karsh was one of the richest men in Samaria. He owned so much property in the fertile northern plains of Gaza that, the story went, he could not walk from one end of it to the other in a single day. His house was so huge that it could accommodate a hundred overnight guests. He had more servants than family members, more money than love, and he hated the Archangel Gabriel. His entire life was spent scheming—how to make more money, how to acquire more property, how to outmaneuver his neighbor and best friend Ebenezer Harth. The Harths and the Karshes and the Leshes and the Garones and a smattering of other families made up the people collectively known as the Manadavvi, the wealthy elite in the country we called Samaria. For me, until I sang at my first Gloria at the age of fourteen, they made up the entire world.

"A Manadavvi woman owes a debt to the family and to the property," my mother told me more often than I cared to count. "You will marry a man your father or your grandfather chooses. He will be a Harth, perhaps, or a Lesh, or possibly a merchant's son. But only a merchant from Semorrah or Castelana. He must be respectable."

"Could I marry an angel?" I asked her one time when I was thirteen.

My mother frowned, as if considering. "Possibly," she

said. "Not just any angel, of course. If he was to be the next Archangel, then, yes, you could marry him. Or if he had been chosen to lead the host at one of the holds. He would have to be an angel of some distinction."

This particular conversation was taking place a few days before we were to hold a very large dinner party. We had just gone through every single item of clothing in my wardrobe to determine which pieces might be appropriate for me to wear at the afternoon tea and the morning breakfast that would bracket the main event. To wear at the dinner itself, of course, new gowns had been commissioned for both of us. Now we were looking through my jewelry case to see if I had the right necklaces, earrings, bracelets and rings to complement the outfits we had already chosen.

"But how will I know?" I asked, pulling off a short opal necklace and trying on a strand of pearls instead.

"How will you know what?"

"If the angel will be Archangel? No one has been chosen yet to succeed Gabriel."

"Gabriel has served a little over half his term, silly girl. The god will not need to choose another Archangel for seven or eight years."

"But then how will I know if the angel I fall in love with is good enough?" I asked.

She laughed a little, the merest sound of exhaled breath. "Silly," she said again, her voice soft and affectionate. "You won't be *in love with* this man you marry. He will be chosen for you because he is a proper husband."

"But I want to fall in love," I argued.

"Love comes after marriage for a Manadavvi woman," she said firmly. She began picking through my jewelry box to search for a suitable ring.

I looked in the mirror to try to read the expression on her face. She was looking downward and all I could see were her slanted cheekbones and the perfect fall of her loose, fine, honey-colored hair. "So you didn't love my father the day you married him?" I asked.

"Oh, I was quite pleased at the idea of marrying him," she said, her face still tilted downward. "Quite a handsome man was Joseph Karsh when he was only twenty-five! He still has that dark hair and those dark eyes, and his face was even more handsome when he was young." She glanced up, meeting my eyes in the mirror, and smiled. "You have the shape of his mouth and the color of his eyes, but you have my cheeks and my hair," she said. "Your grandfather said you took the best of us both when you were born."

I was frowning at her in the mirror. "But when did you fall in love with him?" I insisted.

She laughed. "I've had *life* with him," she said. "Three children and fourteen years of running his house. That's what a marriage is, Eden. It's not this sweet romance you seem to have concocted in your head."

"I want romance," I said. "I want to fall in love. I don't want to marry a Manadavvi or some other man just because he's rich."

She put her hands on either side of my head and turned me back to face the mirror. "Let me give you a little piece of advice," she said. "Never say that to your father."

IN fact, I rarely said anything to my father at all. He was as my mother had described—a handsome, dark-haired man, with intent brown eyes and a restless energy. As my grandfather was always scheming, my father was always striding— off to look over the fields of whatever crop was due to ripen, off to inspect some new shipment from Luminaux merchants, off to argue with the angels at the nearby hold of Monteverde. He was impatient, intelligent and frequently ill-tempered. The only time he seemed truly happy was when he had just completed some business deal that was extravagantly advantageous to the Karshes. He was impossible to like and—I finally realized after this conversation with my mother—impossible to love.

It had never occurred to me that others might hate my father as much as I did. Not that there was anyone else to ask. My brother Evan, five years younger than I was, looked like a smaller, angrier version of my father. *He* was only happy when my father allowed him to trail behind him through the fields or to the negotiating table, absorbing every word, every gesture that my father used. The rest of the time he was throwing tantrums and engaging in displays of temper. I avoided him whenever I could—easier now that I was almost a young lady. I spent less time in the schoolroom with my brothers, more time with my mother being groomed for my entrance into society.

My youngest brother, Paul, was only two, and so had no opinion on anything other than the food he wanted to eat and the times he did *not* want to go to sleep. He looked more like my mother than Evan did and had a much sunnier disposition. I admit I spent more time with him than I did with Evan, but I did not make much effort to interact with either of my brothers. We were not a close family. The five of us did not sit down to intimate meals; the children did not visit with the parents at the close of day to recount our adventures and lessons. The very patterns of our lives separated us—and once I turned thirteen, I had even less time to spend with my brothers.

From that time on, I was required to take part in the social events that regularly occurred at my grandfather's house. We often had other Manadavvi over to dine, for instance, and many river merchants were considered respectable enough to be included in the Karsh hospitality. Ariel—the leader of the host at Monteverde—was a frequent guest, and despite the fact that my father and grandfather would just as soon do away with all angels and their interference in Manadavvi schemes, she was always treated with the greatest respect. I met her for the first time at a small dinner held at our house shortly after I turned fourteen.

"So you're Joseph Karsh's little girl," Ariel said when my mother introduced me to her. Ariel was tall, energetic and full of laughter, and I liked her at once. "You're very pretty."

"Thank you, angela," I said politely.

She tilted her head as if to inspect me, taking in the shape of my face, perhaps, and whatever stamp of personality had laid itself over my youthful features. "Yes, I would think you would do quite well," she decided. "I'm surprised your father hasn't sent you off to one of the angel holds already to see what conquests you might make there."

"I believe my husband expects her to marry for property and not prestige," my mother interposed.

Ariel laughed. "Oh, so then he's looking to Semorrah, not Monteverde," she said, seeming not at all offended. "Well, I wish you good luck getting her to conform to your wishes. I tried very hard to steer my sister in a proper direction and she fell in love where it was most disastrous, so I am no longer quite so sure about the wisdom of arranging marriages. But perhaps you will have more success than I did."

"My husband almost always achieves his goals."

Ariel's eyes strayed across the room, where my father was locked in a combative conversation with someone I didn't know. The other man was well-dressed and haughty, so I assumed he was a Harth or a Garone who just hadn't come my way yet. "Yes, it is what one most admires about him," the angel said. Her voice was solemn but her face was still amused, and I thought, *Here is someone else who doesn't like my father*. But I was hardly in a position to ask her if I was right.

At dinner that night, I sat in the very middle of the company, away from all the most interesting conversation at the head of the table, where my father sat, and the foot, where Ariel was placed. I could catch a few phrases here and there; I could tell that the people sitting nearest Ariel were enjoying themselves immensely, while the people sitting by my father appeared to be engaged in heated argument. Those around me were the less important members of the group, the younger brother of a landowner or the third daughter of a merchant. We spoke to each other politely but mostly concentrated on our food.

Conversation only became general once, when a sudden lull across the table allowed my father's words to be carried across the room. "We'd sort it out quickly enough if the angels didn't stick their fingers into business that had nothing to do with them," he said.

All eyes immediately went to Ariel, who was smiling. "Ah, Joseph, without the constant supervision of the angels, the Manadavvi would impose repression upon the whole of Samaria," she said easily. "You would re-enslave the Edori, you would cheat the Jansai, you would require tithes and concessions from the river cities, and turn the entire world into a feudal state, with yourselves as lords over all. The angels exist merely to keep some balance in the three regions, and we do not care that you hate us for it."

My father seemed not at all discomposed to be caught out saying something so highly uncomplimentary to an invited—and powerful—guest. He leaned forward across the table, as if he could somehow annihilate the thirty feet of polished wood that separated them, and spit his words directly into her face. "The angels ceased to care about balance when Raphael was lost," he said intensely. "Gabriel cares nothing about the accepted order of the world. He cares nothing about traditions and natural hierarchies. He is a sloppy egalitarian who would rather watch the whole world fall to ruin than to see true leaders come to power."

"Gabriel is the wisest man I know," Ariel said simply.

"He saved us all from the destruction that Raphael would have loosed upon Samaria. I would follow Gabriel into a thicket of thunderbolts—and so would any other angel, and so would most of the other citizens of Samaria. You will not overthrow Gabriel, Joseph, no matter how much you hate him. If you ever hope to have any power in this alliance, you had better learn to work with the Archangel."

My father's eyes narrowed with real hatred. "If he expects an easy time of the last years of his tenure," my father said quietly, "he had better learn to work with me."

There was silence at the table a moment, and then someone near Ariel asked a question, and the conversation split into halves once again. This time, by concentrating more closely, I was able to catch whole, long segments of conversation between Ariel and her tablemates. Rather quickly they seemed to lose interest in my father's incendiary words and turned instead to gossip about matters in the angel hold.

"But tell me if the rumors are true," said one well-dressed woman who seemed to be a Harth matriarch. "That boy is in trouble again—the one who created such a stir last year at the Gloria."

Ariel grimaced. "I have no idea what to do with him next," she said. "I sent him to Gabriel after last year's disasters, but he wouldn't stay at the Eyrie. So he's back with me, and I'm completely at a loss. I don't know how to discipline an angel who doesn't seem to care about any of the punishments I might devise. I cannot come up with a dire enough consequence. I don't know how to control him."

"But who are you talking about?" another woman demanded. "I don't know these stories."

Now Ariel sighed. "His name is Jesse. His parentage is—murky. His mother was a young woman who showed up at Monteverde when the baby was an infant. None of my angels admitted to having any dealings with her, and she would never tell me who his father was."

"That's odd," said the Harth woman. "Most angel-seekers are only too proud to talk of all the angels they've ensnared."

"That's just it," Ariel said. "I'm not sure she was an angel-seeker. I had the impression—but I could be wrong—that she was a well-brought-up young woman, perhaps a farmer's daughter, who had caught the attention of an angel without intending to. She was quite lovely in a rather dark, exotic way. She may have been part Edori, in fact. At any rate, it occurred to me more than once that this angel may have forced himself upon her, and that she was too embarrassed or too enraged to go to him when she discovered she was pregnant. And once she had the child, and it was angelic, she came to me."

"But—" Now it was an older, patrician man who joined the interrogation. "But surely angels do not go about raping young women in the countryside? I mean, I know that not everyone holds angels in high esteem"—and here he glanced at my father—"but that is not the sort of behavior that I have ever heard attributed to them."

Ariel nodded emphatically. "No. You're right. I am the first to admit that angels have their flaws, but it is generally so easy for them to find a willing partner that they do not engage in such acts of violence. But if it is true—well—" She shrugged, and her wings shimmered and fell behind her. "I have a guess or two as to who might have shamed her in such a way."

The others sitting near her exchanged glances. "Not—not Raphael?" the Harth woman asked.

Ariel shrugged again, causing candlelight to dance down her feathers. "Possibly. Or an angel named Saul, who was his closest companion, and a despicable, loathsome creature. I was afraid of Saul myself—and generally, you know, I have no reason to fear anyone."

"So, this young man, what has he done that's so terrible?" asked the older man. I was glad he'd asked, for I wanted to know the answer myself.

Ariel laughed a little. "What hasn't he done? He is constantly fighting—with angels and mortals—bloody fist-fights that always end up with someone being severely injured. Once it was a *knife* fight! But it wasn't Jesse who pulled the weapon. And—oh, he gambles, he drinks. If I send him off on a weather intercession, he's gone for four days and I never have any idea what he's been up to until some merchant or farmer writes me to complain. There doesn't seem to be any great malice in him, just this—this—restlessness. This uncontainability. Life is too tame for him, I think. He wants worlds to conquer and enemies to overcome. And instead we live in a peaceful, prosperous country in which the only malcontents are wealthy landowners who have too much to lose to really descend to anarchy. I don't know what will become of him. He's only seventeen and he's already wreaked havoc in two holds. What will he do next? What isn't he capable of? That's what keeps me awake at night, once I stop worrying about the Manadavvi and how to accommodate them."

She was laughing again, and she had effectively turned the subject. I stopped listening to her conversation and started meditating on the words she had just spoken. I had limited experience of angels and no experience at all of restless young men, angel *or* mortal. But I thought this wild uncontainable Jesse sounded more interesting and exciting than anyone I'd ever encountered in my grandfather's house. I wished enviously that I might meet him someday, while he was still wild and untamed, and I wished still more that I was the kind of woman who would attract the notice of a man like that. I had no idea what kind of woman that would be, but I was pretty certain that a placid, docile, highly mannered Manadavvi girl was not the sort who would draw his attention.

*   *   *

IT was two years before I actually did meet Jesse, and in the interim, my life had expanded greatly. By the age of sixteen, I had become a fixture on the Manadavvi social scene. I had learned what colors to wear to flatter my dark eyes and pale hair; I had memorized all the names of the wealthy men in the three provinces, and their family histories and genealogical trees; I had attended dinners in Semorrah and theatre performances in Luminaux. I had spent one whole summer in Monteverde, one of many young men and women invited to the hold to cement allegiances and watch firsthand some of the political maneuvering that went on between the purveyors of power in Samaria. I had sung at two Glorias. I had been introduced to the Archangel Gabriel. I had danced with his oldest son. I had made friends with Ariel's daughter. I was highly polished, perfectly well-bred and totally bored.

I didn't realize it, of course. I thought I was happy. I thought I was living the life that poorer girls would envy as they married inferior men and lived in small houses and took no part in the great events of the day.

I never forgot Ariel's description of Jesse, though, and any time I was going to be at a gathering that included angels, I always looked for him. But he was not the sort of angel who would be invited to attend weddings in Semorrah or to sing a solo at the Gloria. He must have been there on the Plain of Sharon during both of those Glorias that I attended, but I did not meet him. He was not at Monteverde the summer that I lived there, for he had been sent to Cedar Hills as a punishment for some infraction. I heard his name often— young girls told stories about him and giggled behind their hands; older women whispered of his misdeeds and warned each other to keep him away from the girls in their charge. There were a number of tales about women who been led astray by his charms—he was nineteen now and had apparently added seduction to his other vices—but I never met anyone who claimed to have been his lover. I caught the echoes of his name in every hold and mansion that I visited, and the very syllables gave me a delicious set of shivers. *He was still wild. He was still untamed.* The more refined and artificial my own world became, the more I reveled at the news that someone else was still quite free.

And then I attended a summer fete in northern Gaza, and I met him, and my world changed.

We were all there to celebrate the wedding of Emmanuel Lesh's daughter to Luke Avalone, the son of a Castelana merchant. Emmanuel Lesh was not as wealthy as the Karshes or the Harths, but he had a better relationship with Monteverde and Ariel trusted him above all the Manadavvi. Any affair at his house was attended by all the elite of the three provinces, and it was no different for his daughter Abigail's wedding. Every Manadavvi in the country, or so it seemed, had been invited, as well as representatives from all the angel holds, and rich river merchants, and a few cultured Luminauzi, and even a Jansai or two. Someone said that five hundred people were attending the event, and I had no reason to dispute it.

My family arrived a few days early, as did many of the angels and the other honored guests. There were to be many events to entertain us—dinners, dances, theatrical performances, hunts and games. Present were Ariel with her daughter; Gabriel with his wife, Rachel, and his sons; angels from the hold of Cedar Hills; the Harths, the Garones, the Semorran merchants—everyone that anyone cared about.

With the contingent from the Eyrie came the angel Jesse. I did not know who he was at first. I had been there a day and I had just heard the commotion of new arrivals, so I had wandered down the wide white marble staircase to investigate. Gabriel and Rachel were standing near a heap of luggage, talking seriously with Emmanuel and his son. Just out through the great double doors I could spot a knot of younger angels, all teenaged boys, laughing and joking. One was Gabriel's oldest son, Gideon, with whom I had become friendly. I didn't know the other two, but I had long ago lost any shyness of angels. I pushed through the doors and stepped out into the bright light of a summer noon.

"Hello, Gideon," I greeted him. "Have you come for the wedding? It's so good to see you."

Gideon turned immediately at the sound of his name. He was a thin and awkward thirteen, too tall and still unsure of himself, but you just had to look at him to see the man he would become. He had his father's blue eyes and his mother's golden hair, and the bones of his body seemed to have been stretched too far, so that it was clear he would one day grow to an imposing height. His wings, though, were glorious— a vivid white that spilled so far in both directions that you thought he could fill a ballroom with them. "Eden," he said, breaking into a genuine smile. His voice trembled a little between the high register and the low. "I didn't know you would be here."

I made him an exaggerated curtsey. "You can always find me at the most elegant events of the season," I said in a haughty voice. "Naturally, I can be found anywhere the elite of Samaria congregate."

Two of the other boys turned away to discuss some topic that could only be dissected by men. The fourth angel remained standing to one side of Gideon and regarded me with a stranger's half-caught attention. He was clearly older than Gideon, with the solid build and effortless stance of a man used to his body, not a boy growing into his. His hair was black and thick, tangled by the wind of flight and a little too long for his narrow face. His eyes were a brooding green and his expression was sullen. I thought he was one of the most handsome men I'd ever seen, even before I learned his name.

"Do you know Jesse?" Gideon asked. "He lives at the Eyrie. Sometimes."

"Jesse?" I repeated, and I heard the squeak in my voice, which embarrassed me no end. "You live at the Eyrie?"

Jesse laughed, and Gideon laughed with him as if at some private joke. "Sometimes I do," Jesse said. "When I haven't been sent off somewhere less dangerous."

"I can't think of too many places that are less dangerous than the Eyrie," I said without thinking. My heart was still repeating his name—*Jesse? Jesse?*—and my mind was trying to come up with something interesting to say. I could tell already nothing was likely to occur to me.

Both the boys laughed again, even harder. "Yes, maybe I said it wrong," Jesse replied. "Sometimes I get sent off when I'm the one who's too dangerous for the Eyrie."

"But my father likes you," Gideon said. "He always lets you come back."

Jesse shook his head. "Your father wants me to fly away to the other side of the world and never return."

Gideon was grinning. "My father wants you where he can watch you every minute of the day. That's why you're here at the wedding and not back at the hold."

I spared a moment to think that the Archangel Gabriel probably would not be best-pleased to learn that his oldest son and the most incorrigible young angel of Samaria had apparently formed a fast friendship, despite differences in age, parentage and general expectations.

"I think it'll be a fun wedding, though," I said, still unable to come up with any but the most inane conversation. I could talk to a Manadavvi lordling for three straight hours and never once seem stupid, but I didn't know how to converse with a handsome young angel of questionable character.

Jesse laughed and looked away. Gideon rolled his eyes. "If you like balls and formal dinners and pointless conversation," the Archangel's son said.

"Well, I do," I said.

Jesse turned his eyes back our way. "We're not far, though," he said to Gideon. "We can go to the water's edge tonight or tomorrow. You'll see."

"See what?" I demanded.

Now Jesse looked at me. "The ocean. Gideon's only seen the water off the western coast. But it's so calm there. You can't appreciate the ocean until you've seen it off the northern edge of the continent. It's so beautiful, it's scary."

Gideon grunted, as if to convey his doubts, but the phrasing caught my attention. *It's so beautiful, it's scary.* I thought the same words might be applied to Jesse himself—though he had not done anything particularly scary yet. It just seemed possible that, at any moment, he might.

"I'd like to see the ocean," I said.

Jesse's dark eyebrows rose. He was still looking at me, but I couldn't tell what he was seeing. A spoiled, silly daughter of privilege? A pretty blond girl with a dimpled smile? Someone intriguing, someone annoying? A stranger who interested him not in the slightest?

"Would you?" he said. "Then you can come with us when we go."

AND that was how I ended up going on an expedition that would surely have enraged my father and disturbed my mother, had they known about it, as we headed out to view the sea. Gabriel's son and Ariel's daughter were respectable enough to please both of my parents, and my mother and father could have had no objection to the other two mortals who accompanied us, a girl and a boy about my age, siblings in one of the extended Harth clans. But they would not have been pleased to know that the troubled young angel Jesse was one of our number, or that he was the one who carried me from the Lesh house to a slaty gray cliff overlooking the northern ocean.

The flight took half an hour, for we were only about twenty miles from the sea. In deference to the summer clothes of the mortals, the three angels flew low to the ground,

seeking out warmer air, but it was still a cold flight. I had
been carried in an angel's arms before, many times, while I
stayed at Monteverde and visited the Eyrie, but I didn't remember any flight being quite like this. Jesse held me close
to his body, so that I was always aware of the heat of his skin
and the tireless, effortless, almost automatic working of his
wings. He didn't bother to speak to me, so most of the way
I fretted that he was sorry he had invited me on the trip,
sorry he had drawn me as a passenger—but as we landed
and he set me carefully on my feet, he gave me a dazzling
smile. It was full of mischief and pure uncomplicated pleasure, and I smiled back for all I was worth.

"Thank you," I said.

"I enjoyed it," he replied and turned away to greet the
others.

We had come to rest on a high, rocky promontory attached
to Gaza by a rough and nearly impassable strip of land. A few
scrubby trees and dispirited flowers poked their way up
through the hard soil, but for the most part, the cliff was hard,
flat and unadorned. Its only claim to beauty lay in the view.

For it overlooked the ocean, and the ocean, from this
place, was magnificent. It lashed and foamed against the
cliffs with no buffer of beach to impede its headlong motion. The water seemed to snarl against the rock, and then
claw upward in white fists of foam. Farther out, the vast surface of the ocean seemed to boil with a perpetual internal
rage; it sent up great jagged plates of water to war with oncoming waves and create a clashing of white-edged fury.

I was mesmerized. I could only stare out at the fierce continual combat and wonder at the forces that drove the water
to such senseless passion. Why did it not lie calm, like the
water in the ponds on my grandfather's estate? Why did it
not roll in on slow, leisurely waves, as it did off the western
coast? There, the ocean was an impressive but hardly fearful
sight. This was nature in a much more raw and frenzied

state. I would not be desirous of setting off in a boat to cross these treacherous waters.

"It's pretty," the Harth girl said, casting one cursory look over the sea. "But I'm hungry. Gideon, do you have the basket of food?"

Gideon had come to stand beside me, silent as I. He nodded and pointed to a level stretch of rock where the angels had laid down their various burdens—some blankets, a satchel of food, a few canteens of water. He didn't answer her in words, though, and after waiting a moment, she tossed her head and stomped off to where the provisions were piled.

Ariel's daughter Persis swept up to stand beside me. She was about my age, thin, brown-haired and bossy. It was clear she would be leader of the host at Monteverde once her mother stepped down. "Marvelous, isn't it?" she said to Gideon and me. "It doesn't really look this way anywhere else."

"It does if you fly out from the coast a ways," Jesse said. He had drifted back toward us, as if irresistibly drawn by the call of the ocean. "Miles and miles, I mean—so far you can't see the land behind you. Then the water almost always looks like this. So powerful and so vast it makes you feel helpless and small."

Persis glanced at him. "Then why fly out that far?" she demanded. "I'd be afraid. What if I lost my way? What if I got caught in a storm and couldn't fly back? What if I fell into the ocean?"

"Then you'd drown," Jesse said.

There was a short silence after that.

Gideon was the first to turn away. "I agree with Persis. I don't need to go courting reminders of death. If I flew out that far, the whole time I'd be worrying that I would drop in the ocean and die. I can think of a lot of other things I'd rather be doing."

He and Persis joined the mortals sorting through our

provisions. I stood beside Jesse for another five minutes and watched the raging restlessness of the sea. "Thank you," I said again, finally breaking the silence. He smiled again, watching me, and he nodded. He didn't say anything else. We turned back to join the others.

We had left the Lesh compound in early afternoon, promising our parents and other guardians that we would be back in time for the evening's festivities—a dinner and a ball. I had to concentrate to remember what activity we were missing during our outing—a hunt, I decided, organized to catch some of the wild boar that were plentiful in this part of the country. I couldn't begin to say how much happier I was to be here, with this group of people, rather than off on such a ride.

"I'm hungry," said the Harth girl. "Let's eat something."

"I'm cold," said her brother. "Can anyone build a fire?"

There was general laughter at this. "What do you think we are, Edori?" asked Gideon. "We don't spend our lives traveling across the country and camping out every night. I don't think there's an angel in the three provinces who knows how to build a fire."

"I do," Jesse said, and knelt on the hard ground. "But we'll need some fuel."

I agreed with the Harths; I was both cold and hungry. Angels, with their higher body temperatures and general indifference to weather, might feel perfectly comfortable on this windy cliff, but I was beginning to shiver. "What kind of fuel?" I asked. "I'll help look for it."

So Jesse sent us off to find dry dead branches and spindly twigs—rather a search in this inhospitable place—and finally we had gathered enough wood to satisfy him. He had told the truth: he knew how to start a fire, a skill I had never seen practiced by anyone in my social circle. Within minutes, we had a welcome blaze dancing away within a circle of rocks. The girls spread the blankets around the fire, and we all settled down before it.

"Now food," said Persis, opening the satchel and distributing its contents. No one had thought to pack plates and silver, so we handed around loaves of bread and chunks of cheese, tearing or biting off suitable portions, and passed them to our neighbors. The water containers were similarly shared. Usually I'm a fastidious eater and don't even like one of my little brothers to sip from my glass, but this afternoon I was so grateful for heat and food and water that I didn't mind the communal style of the meal. I bit off a large mouthful of cheese and handed it over to Gideon.

He grinned at me. "Never thought anything could taste so good, did you?" he asked, in his pleasant, uncertain voice.

"Wait till sometime when you're really hungry," Jesse said, breaking off a chunk of bread. "If you haven't eaten for a whole day, or two, and finally you come across a place with food. Then you'll eat anything—carrot scrapings, beef fat, stale bread, old wine—and think it tastes like a feast."

We all looked at him. "When did you ever go two days without food?" Persis demanded.

Jesse grinned, chewed his bread, and swallowed. "Lots of times," he said. "When I was off wandering."

"Away from the holds and the cities?" the Harth girl asked, as if she could not imagine that any land existed between these points of civilization. "Where did you get the food, then?"

Jesse shrugged. He was sitting cross-legged on the ground and his wings bunched out behind him, bulky and muscular. "At a farmhouse sometimes. At an Edori campsite sometimes. I've eaten with the Jansai now and then, but I like the Edori better. The Jansai are—" He shrugged again.

"My father hates the Jansai," Gideon remarked.

"Well, *my* father thinks they're the key to Samarian wealth and commerce," the Harth boy shot back. "And that *your* father has set out to ruin all the trading alliances of the three provinces with his attitude toward the Jansai."

My father had expressed much the same opinion, but I was not about to say so now. Anyway, Persis took immediate and competent control of the conversation. "Well, we're not going to sit here and ruin a lovely day by arguing our parents' politics," she said. "Let's talk about something else."

"I'm still cold," the Harth girl said and held her hands out to the fire.

She was sitting between Jesse and Persis, facing the ocean. My guess was that Jesse had chosen his spot for the view, and she had chosen hers for the company. It made me dislike her, suddenly and strongly, though up until this point I had had no opinion of her one way or another.

Persis shook her head. "You thin-blooded mortals," she said, teasing. "You're troublesome no matter where we take you."

"I'll give you my coat," her brother said, though he looked chilly, too.

But Jesse shook his head and lifted one glossy wing to lay it across her back. I was sitting across from them and saw the look of sleek gratification that crossed her face. "It's breezy," Jesse said. "They're probably all cold. We should put up a windbreak for as long as we're sitting here."

And the other angels nodded, and suddenly an amazing thing occurred. We had haphazardly settled ourselves around the fire but had happened to arrange ourselves with mortals interspersed between angels. Now all the angels lifted their wings and interlaced them; suddenly, the whole circle was contained in an overlapping basket of satin-smooth feathers. I felt Gideon's wings across my shoulders and against my cheek, and, over his, Persis's adding a layer of warmth and silk. Instantly, the force of the wind was cut; the fire's heat bounced off those quilled white surfaces and pooled before us with redoubled strength. I felt warm, I felt protected—but even more, I felt ever so slightly decadent. There was something sinful about the touch of those luxurious wings, something seductive and alluring. Gideon and Persis were my friends, and I had no romantic interest in either of them, and yet there was something about the play of feather across skin that made me shiver and grow giddy in silent delight. It had never been a secret that mortals were easily infatuated with angels, though I had never been particularly susceptible before. But that day, on that remote clifftop, beside the primitive passion of the ocean and the elemental beauty of the fire, for the first time I realized what power angels exerted over mortals and that I would happily succumb to it under the right circumstances. Maybe it was the hunger, maybe it was the cold, maybe it was being sixteen and among people both more beautiful and exotic than I, but at that moment I felt completely helpless and completely besotted with the angels in our circle. It was like being drunk; it was like losing volition in a dream. I closed my eyes and leaned my shoulders ever so slightly into that caress of velvet, and I shivered again when a wing feather kissed my cheek.

"It's getting late," Persis observed, her pragmatic voice breaking a long silence. "I don't know how much longer we can stay if we're going to get back on time."

"If we want to get back on time," Jesse said.

"Well, I do!" the Harth girl exclaimed. "If I miss the ball tonight, my mother will—well, I don't know what she'll do, but I think I'd be a lost girl roaming the fields of Gaza before night's end."

Jesse gave her a lazy smile. "You might like the life better than you think."

She smiled back up at him as if she couldn't help herself. "Only if someone were taking care of me."

"We can stay another half hour or so," Gideon said. "They won't be back from the hunt yet."

"I'm still cold," the Harth boy said.

Gideon nodded. "It's the wind. It never stops."

Persis shrugged; I could feel her feathers slide and tangle against Gideon's across my back. "Oh, well, we can stop the *wind,*" she said carelessly, and Gideon laughed.

"I'll start," he said, and without another word he launched into song. Within a few measures, Persis had come in on a descant line and Jesse on a bass harmony. The music was sublime, eerie, a complicated three-part paean to the god. I listened in open-mouthed silence. I knew, of course, that the angels used musical prayers to control the weather, singing to the god to beg for rain, or sun, or calm, or storm, but I had never heard the prayers performed. I had never sat so close to any angels, wrapped in a coverlet of living down, while they sang these unearthly and sacred passages of supplication. I felt as if I were standing on the god's doorstep, listening to the divine music of his door chime, asking for entrance into heaven. I shut my eyes, and I felt the wind die down, and I shivered with cold ecstasy even as the world grew warmer.

"That's done it," Jesse said, abruptly breaking off the song. "Even the waves have grown quiet."

"That was pretty," the Harth girl said. I remembered that she had used the same word to describe the wild ocean, and I wondered at her complete and unredeemed vacuity.

Gideon laughed. "We don't usually call the sacred songs *pretty,*" he said. "They're just necessary. They're just songs we know."

"I prefer the masses," said Persis. "They're so thunderous."

"I prefer the prayers that call down lightning bolts," said Jesse.

Gideon and Persis cried out against that.

"You can't sing those! Not straight through!" Ariel's daughter exclaimed. "They're too dangerous."

Jesse hunched his shoulders; I saw the movement cause his wingfeathers to tickle the back of the Harth girl's neck. "I suppose," he said.

"If you've been praying for lightning—" Gideon said.

Jesse gave him that brilliant smile. "Not lately."

"I never heard any of the prayers before," I said. "I thought this one was—so beautiful." Like the Harth girl, I found my vocabulary failing me. "I've been to the Gloria, and I've heard Rachel and Gabriel sing the masses, and that was splendid, but this was—I can't describe it."

"And are you warmer?" Gideon asked.

"Yes, I am, thank you."

"Then the prayer has achieved its goal."

"Not that it matters," Persis said. "We really do have to leave."

I don't want to go, I wanted to say, and unless I missed my guess, the same sentiment was written on Jesse's face. But he remained silent and so did I. The Harths jumped to their feet and began smacking dirt off their clothes. Gideon and Persis more slowly stood up and began packing up the items we had brought with us. Jesse and I were left facing each other across the fire. Neither of us had moved. He tilted his head a little, watching me again, and a small smile began to play around his mouth.

"I can take you back later," he said. "We don't have to go just yet."

I was tempted. So tempted. For a moment I was willing to trade every luxury of my life for one evening on a cold clifftop with this handsome and dangerous angel. But it was the certain knowledge that my life would be irretrievably thrown away if I did such a thing that made me sigh and shake my head.

"My father," I said, and nothing else. Jesse nodded and pushed himself to his knees. With a few quick motions, he put out the fire and scattered the stones. By the time I stood up and looked around to see if there was anything I could do to help, there was almost no trace left of our visit to this place.

"Jesse. I want you to carry me back," the Harth girl was saying in that imperious way most Manadavvi cultivated, as if they knew their wishes were always paramount. I waited for him to tell her we would all fly back paired as we had been on the outbound journey, but he merely gave her that devastating smile and nodded.

"Are we all ready, then?" Persis said. "Gid, I guess you've got Eden. Let's be on our way."

And a moment later, Gideon had taken me into his thin arms and leapt into the chilly air. He was so much frailer than Jesse that for a moment I thought my weight would pull us down from the sky, and I clutched his neck with a little squeal. But almost immediately he found his rhythm and his altitude, and we were soaring southward, back toward the Lesh house, toward fertile land and elegant civilization. I would have been happy enough to fly in silence, thinking over everything I had heard and felt that afternoon, but Gideon asked me a question about my grandfather, and I responded, and we ended up conversing idly for the whole flight back. We arrived just as late summer twilight was beginning to paint the Lesh mansion with a fiery gold, and those of us who cared about such things noted in some apprehension that we would barely have enough time to dress for dinner. Five of us scattered through the main corridors of the grand house. Jesse released his burden, watched us all scurry off, and then disappeared back through the double doors of the front hall. I was fairly certain that I would not see him that night at either the feast or the ball, and I was conscious of a bitter disappointment that almost entirely swallowed my fear of encountering my father before I had dressed for the evening's events.

THE dinner was lavish and impossibly dull. I would have been bored almost beyond endurance except for the fact that

I was so hungry—a consequence, I supposed, of brisk sea air and illicit excitement. So I ate a great deal of every dish offered to me, ignoring my mother's scandalized look, and made inconsequential conversation with the young men seated on either side of me. One was a Fairwen heir from Semorrah, supercilious and instantly unlikable; the other was from a minor Manadavvi family and not really worth my time, though he was far more pleasant. I didn't give either of them much attention.

Once the feasting ended, the dancing began. I stayed close to my mother at first so that she could direct or approve of my choice of partners, but I could see her relax her usual vigilance after the first hour in the ballroom. Here we were, among the most exclusive set of people imaginable, at a private ball in a Manadavvi mansion; what was there to guard against? So, as soon as I returned from a waltz with the Harth boy, she took me aside to whisper in my ear. "I think I'm going to join some of the other women in that little anteroom by the dessert table. Come find me if you need me. Otherwise, dance with whomever you please. I'm sure you'll have a wonderful evening."

I was less sure of that, though I wasn't sorry to be relieved of her attention for the rest of the night. My father had already disappeared, off to argue politics with his Manadavvi cronies. But, as she had surmised, there was little chance I would get in trouble with any of the remaining guests. I had already searched and searched the crowd with my eyes. Jesse was not among the dancers on the floor.

In fact, only a handful of angels were. I had been informed before that dancing—like swimming, horseback riding, and any number of other pursuits—was an almost impossible feat for an angel to perform. Wings were all very well for skimming across the sky and even for standing about looking gorgeous, but they got in the way during ordinary athletic pursuits. Still, I would have given up riding and dancing if I could have grown wings.

Gideon, one of those few angels in the ballroom, materialized at my side moments after my mother left. "I suppose it's too much to hope that you don't want to dance," he said.

I grinned at him. During the flight home, for some reason, he had seemed to shed the magic he'd acquired as we sat around the fire, and now he was just Gideon again—awkward, kind, thirteen years old. "Has your mother insisted that you invite *every* mortal girl onto the dance floor at least once?" I teased.

He nodded glumly. "My mother's not very interested in pomp and rank," he said, "but she very much believes in being fair. If I dance with one girl, I have to dance with all of them. She doesn't want anyone to feel left out."

"That's kind of her."

"So I have to *ask* all of them, but they don't have to say yes," he added in a hopeful voice.

I laughed. "But I do want to dance with you. I want to see how an angel manages such a thing."

He sighed and held out his arms to take me into a very chaste embrace. We stepped onto the dance floor and into a waltz. "The secret is to hold your wings very, very tightly to your body," he said.

I wrinkled my nose. "Does that hurt?"

"No, but it takes a lot of concentration. It's as if you're trying to hold your stomach in all night. Sometimes you forget. And you're pretty tired by night's end."

"You're a very good dancer, though. You must have been practicing since you were quite young."

He sighed a second time. "And you wouldn't think so," he said. "Since my father doesn't care about impressing the wealthy families, and my mother doesn't have any social graces at all. But both of them have insisted that we learn all sorts of boring accomplishments. My mother says that learning to dance is like learning to use a sword—it's a weapon when you're dealing with certain members of society, and you always need to know the weapons of your opponents." He shook his head. "Sometimes my mother talks like a lunatic."

I laughed again. "No, she's right. If you're going to deal with Harths and Karshes and Fairwens and Garones, you're going to have to participate in activities they consider important. But I never thought of my social skills as an arsenal."

We talked more as we twirled and paraded around the dance floor. I caught a number of jealous looks tossed my way by the young women of the company, and I couldn't keep myself from responding by laughing even more often and smiling at Gideon with an entirely feigned possessiveness. He was an angel; he was the Archangel's son; he was acceptable by any Manadavvi measure. Despite his youthfulness, no doubt many a scheming mother had dragged her daughter here simply to make sure she had a chance to meet Gideon. There was no mistaking Gideon's strength of character and seriousness of nature. He was much too young to be named Archangel when his father's term ended in three years, but he would doubtless become leader of the host at the Eyrie, a position of considerable prestige and power. A girl could do far worse than to ensnare Gideon while he was still young.

As the music came to an end, he gave me a courtly bow and I responded with an extravagant curtsey. "That wasn't so bad," he confessed. "Maybe you'll dance with me again later unless my mother lets me leave the ballroom."

"I will," I said. "I wish Jesse was here so I could dance with him, too."

He shot me a look that I couldn't read, though it seemed troubled. Because I was foolish enough to pine after Jesse, or because Jesse's behavior always filled his friends with worry? "I don't think Jesse dances," he said. "He's probably outside somewhere, prowling the grounds. He doesn't like to be cooped up inside big houses like this. He hates—" He waved his hand to indicate the whole of our surroundings.

"Ostentation," I suggested.

Gideon nodded. "Exactly."

"Well, I won't look for him, then. I hope you enjoy the rest of your evening."

He grimaced. "I'll try."

I didn't know if he would be able to obey my admonition, but I did know that I spoke a lie to him: I did plan to look for Jesse. I just didn't plan to do it inside the ballroom.

I edged toward the doorway that led to the main hall, glancing around casually to see if my mother or father had reentered the room. But no, I appeared to be quite unsupervised. Two more steps and I was at the doorway; a pause, another glance around, and I had ducked outside.

The hallways of the Lesh manor were long, shadowy, lit with elaborate but inadequate sconces, and made of the smoothest marble imaginable. I felt myself gliding along those shiny, polished surfaces like a sailboat along calm waters. Where might Jesse be? If the stories told about him were true, he could be down in the wine cellars, getting drunk with the butler, or over in the kitchens, gambling with the servants. Or out back in the orchards, seducing a Manadavvi heiress. I shivered a little in the corridor and asked myself what, by the love of Jovah, I really thought I was doing. But I kept moving forward, my thin slippers sliding soundlessly along the expensive floors. I paused in the conservatory, thick with the heavy green smell of plant life; no one there. I checked the library, where a solitary old man read before a snapping fire; Jesse was not in sight. I glanced inside salons and music rooms and billiard halls. Jesse was nowhere.

But he was not a tame indoor creature. More likely he would be strolling the grounds, circling a decorative pool, or fluttering like a trapped moth inside one of the gazebos set up across the lawn. It was too dark, and these attractions were too far, for me to attempt to find them alone. Instead I went to the roof, to see how much of the grounds might be visible from this vantage point.

Jesse was there.

He was perched like a gargoyle on the brass railing that ran around the upper level of the mansion. His wings were spread to aid his balance, but he seemed to have achieved the perfect equipoise, for not a muscle, not a feather, quivered in the silver light of a high full moon. His feet were flat on the railing, his knees drawn up in a crouch; his arms were folded on his knees, and his chin rested on his wrists. For a moment, as he sat there so thoughtful and so still, I thought I was mistaken. I thought he was indeed a statue, an angel of onyx and alabaster, commissioned by Emmanuel Lesh and set here to guard over his house and his fertile lands.

I stopped a full ten feet away. I didn't speak, just in case he was real and my words startled him into tumbling off the railing. He didn't move. Moonlight fell on us like sheets of ethereal rain.

Then he spoke without even glancing in my direction. "Tired of dancing so soon?"

A silly laugh trembled in my throat. "I—the dancing was—I decided to come out for some fresh air," I said, garbling my sentences.

He leaned his head back as if to consider the sky. "It's a beautiful night," he agreed. "Everyone should be out on a night like this."

I came a step closer. "It was a beautiful day, too," I said. "The flight to the ocean—I really enjoyed it. I wanted to thank you for letting me come along."

Now he turned his head to look at me, though nothing else in his pose changed. "Always happy to take a pretty girl on an outing," he said.

"I'd like to go back sometime," I said I was talking to put

words out into the air between us, to keep the conversation going. I didn't know exactly what I wanted to say to him, what I wanted to hear from him. I just knew that I wanted to be next to him, included in his circle, touched by his dark aura. "To see the ocean."

He raised his brows. "It's even more beautiful at night," he said, "when you're so far from land that the whole world looks black, above you and below you. Except for the stars, which seem as thick as rain. And the thunderbolts, which light up everything."

I swallowed. "The thunderbolts?"

One quick movement and he had jumped from the railing to the roof. His wings swept behind him like luminous shadows. "Want to go see? Now?"

"See? See the ocean? Now?" I repeated, my voice a little faint.

He nodded. "There and back in a couple of hours. Who will miss you?"

Potentially, anyone. My mother, my father, Gideon, my host or hostess, or any of the strangers these people might want me to meet. But in reality, probably no one. I was supposed to be safe in the ballroom of a Manadavvi stronghold, where I could come to no harm. Who would worry about me tonight?

"I—I suppose no one would notice if I was gone."

"Then let's do it," he said. "Let's go."

I felt a shiver pass over me and attributed it to the night air, warm as it was. "Dressed like this?" I said, indicating my sheer ballgown with its low neckline and lace sleeves.

He nodded to the far edge of the railing. I could just make out a dark, shapeless form lying across it, like a bolt of fabric carelessly laid aside. "Put that on," he said. "It'll keep you warm."

I stepped over to the shadow and picked it up. A woman's cloak, decorated with a jeweled clasp at the shoulder and smelling still of the owner's citrus perfume. "Who left it behind?" I asked.

Jesse grinned. "Could have been anyone, I suppose."

So one of my first guesses had been right: he had eschewed the pleasures of the ballroom for the much greater pleasures of dalliance. I wondered which of the women in residence at the mansion had enjoyed his attention this night, though by the cut and fabric of the cloak, I could see it was not a serving maid who had been meeting Jesse out in the moon-kissed dark. I was not so eager to be his second— or third or fourth—conquest of the evening, and I hesitated, the cloak trailing from my hands to the marble beneath my feet.

He misread my indecision. "We don't have to go. Not if you're afraid of what your father might say."

I tightened my hold on the cloak and slung it over my shoulders. The smell of lemon was very strong. "How will he find out?" I said, tossing my head and pretending I was very bold. "No one will see us go, and no one will miss me while I'm gone."

"Excellent," he said, and came to stand beside me while I was still basking in my own bravery. "Then let's be off."

And without another word he scooped me up in his arms and leapt over the railing.

I smothered a scream and clung to him, feeling the pull of the earth trying to drag us down in the moment before his wings found purchase in the air. The long edges of the cloak trailed behind in the wind; the lights of the mansion fell away. Below, the upraised arms of the trees chastised us for foolishness, and the scattered ornamental ponds, reflecting the moon, winked in complicity. Within a few minutes, we were so high above the dark ground that I could see nothing at all.

Nothing below and nothing but a radiant net of stars above. I had never before taken flight with an angel after dark, and I would not have expected the experience to be anything like this. I wrapped my arms more tightly around Jesse's neck and felt a combination of terror and exhilaration wipe my mind clean of any coherent thought. The world was wind and darkness and a whirl of constellations.

And Jesse.

We didn't speak during that short flight, but I was aware of every shift of his muscles, every beat and upsweep of his wings. His arms around my body seemed absolutely sure; I felt as safe as I ever had standing in the middle of one of my grandfather's limitless fields. He was the only point of motion in a stark and frozen world of black ether and spangled light. He was the only sentient creature, the source of all change and all life and all desire.

Even with the cloak on, I was cool, though I could feel the heat of Jesse's body through my thin dress. By the time we reached the sea, I was so attuned to the currents around us that I could sense the change in the consistency of the air—now thick, damp, and heavy with the scent of salt. I stirred in his arms. "We're here?" I whispered, as if someone could hear me if I spoke aloud.

He nodded. "At the water's edge. But we're going farther out."

He continued flying without pausing. I lifted my head and peered down. It was almost impossible to see the ocean below us, opaque and mysterious, but here and there moonlight glinted off the slanted surface of a restless wave. There was such a sense of grandeur surrounding us—of vastness—of so much space and air and water that I could not calculate it all. I felt tiny and frightened and delighted all at the same time.

And then Jesse began to sing.

I did not recognize the song, a haunting, minor prayer decorated with sharp and urgent staccato phrases. His voice seemed as dark as the night, as untamable as the sea; it seemed to fit in this wild landscape like the cry of the gulls

and the hiss of spray. I felt his chest rise and fall as he gathered more air and expelled it in even more beautiful song.
I felt the strain in his shoulders as he held me before him
like an offering to Jovah or some more foreign and barbaric
god. I saw his wings move behind him as if they were
sweeping darkness away from us, or brushing it more densely
over our heads.

The sky split with a sizzle of white. It shocked the world
into a phosphorescent beauty, then dove into the ocean like a
hand clutching for treasures. Utter darkness again, even
blacker in contrast to the light. Another dazzle of lightning—
then another. Jesse continued to sing. Darkness alternated
with mystical light in a terrifying show of might and destruction. Each streak of light plunged far under the surface
of the water, illuminating the blackness with a bloom of
pure opal, and in an instant disappearing. Thunder rolled
with a continual menace across the louring sky.

We hung suspended in that circle of dangerous light as
thunderbolts danced around us and fell like calamity into
the sea.

I don't know how long that display went on—it felt like
hours—but suddenly Jesse abruptly stopped his singing.
The last lightning bolt shivered into the water and evapo-
rated. The sky ceased its grumbling and the curtains of the
night seemed to draw closer around us, darker and more
impenetrable. The air smelled like chemicals I could not
identify, wild and full of fire. I heard the patter of rain moving
across the water.

"I'm freezing," I whispered, suddenly aware that every
inch of my skin was numb.

"It's late," he whispered back. "I better get you home."

That was it. We did not speak again. I felt his arms
tighten around me as if he would lend me more of his body
heat, and then he wheeled around and headed for land. Or
I hoped he headed for land—at this point I could not have

told if we were flying east or west, heavenward or seaward. My mind was so full of patterns of light and darkness that I could not distinguish shapes or directions. I assumed that Jesse, more innured to marvels, would be able to find his way home.

It was a couple hours past midnight by the time we landed back on the roof of the Lesh mansion. Jesse set me carefully on my feet, keeping one hand on my shoulder in case I should find myself too dizzy to stand. For a moment we stood there face-to-face, watching each other in the dark, each waiting for the other to speak. I felt as if we had witnessed a great tragedy or the most profound event in human experience; I felt that we had both been so changed by this occurrence that we would be forever linked by the power of its memory. I did not know how to express any of my thoughts.

"No one else has ever seen that," he said, his face and his words so solemn that I knew he was feeling at least some of the devastation and elation that were flooding me.

"Thank you," I said at last—the third or fourth time I had said those words to him. His face relaxed in a smile.

"That's the best I have," he said. "Nothing else I could ever show you would impress you so much."

"I think you're wrong," I said. "Everywhere you go, you seem to be trailing thunderbolts."

He laughed aloud at that. "Doesn't that frighten you?"

"Oh, yes," I breathed. "A little."

He shook his head, smiling now. "Girls like you are meant to make brilliant marriages with respectable and very wealthy men. What are you doing out on a rooftop with me?"

I shook my head. I wasn't sure I could answer that question even to my own satisfaction. "Men like you make girls like me forget all the lessons they've learned," I said at last.

He hunched his shoulders and turned away. For a moment he looked sullen and defensive. "For a night maybe, they forget," he said. "Not for a lifetime."

"And when's the last time you thought about spending a lifetime with a girl?" I asked.

He turned back, his eyes narrowed, parsing through the various charges in that simple question. I tilted my head up so the small moon could throw its glow on my cheekbones, catch the blond luster of my hair. I allowed my lips to part, just a little, just so they looked full and inviting in the starlight. I waited for him to want to kiss me.

A man's voice and a woman's laugh broke the night's quiet, and the door to the rooftop swung open. Before I had even had time to think, Jesse had tugged up the hood of my borrowed cloak, drawing it over my hair, and pushed my body behind the shelter of his wings. I heard booted heels and slippered feet hit the marble of the roof. I heard a man's exclamation and a woman's voice.

"What—who—oh, Jesse, what are you doing up here so late at night?" I didn't recognize the speaker by her voice, but she sounded sophisticated and mature. A Lesh relative perhaps, or some other well-bred matron. Why would an older woman of Manadavvi lineage be on friendly terms with the wayward young angel?

"I could ask the same question of you," Jesse said, the smile in his voice sounding entirely genuine.

That laugh again, merry and a bit naughty. Whoever she was, she knew how to flirt. "Is there someone standing behind you? A young lady, perhaps? I think I see the hem of a dress beneath the shadow of a cloak."

"Someone who needed a little cool air and now needs to return to the ballroom before the last waltz is played," Jesse said.

"Then you'd best hurry her on downstairs, for the orchestra is about to pack up its instruments."

It was hard to tell in the dark, but it seemed he gave her a swift, mocking bow. "The roof is yours," he said, and shepherded me through the doorway. Not till I had hurried down the first ten steps toward the top floor of the mansion did I pull off my hood and unclasp the cloak.

"Jesse! Who was that? Did she know who I was?" I whispered.

"She didn't recognize you and I see you didn't recognize her. Better that way," he replied, urging me down the stairwell to the next story. One more floor to go. "I can still hear the music playing. Probably best for you if someone sees you leaving the dance floor."

"You could dance the last number with me."

A grin in the dark. "I don't think so."

"But will you—"

"Hush," he said and appeared to be listening. "Voices in the hallway. Step outside as soon as they've passed. I'll just wait here in the stairwell."

"But if you—"

"Hush," he said again. We were silent long enough to hear the voices fade away. He pushed open the landing door and nearly shoved me into the hallway. His hands, hooked in the collar of my borrowed cloak, pulled it back with him into the stairwell. "Quickly. To the ballroom. Dance with someone."

"But you—I want to—I mean, will you be around tomorrow?"

I could see his grinning face framed by the closing door. "I imagine we'll all be around till after the wedding," he said.

"But—" I said again, but I spoke to the closed, gilt-and-cream-colored door. I knew well enough that if I opened it again, Jesse would have disappeared. "But will I *see* you tomorrow?" I whispered. "Will I get my kiss then?"

No time to be standing here having one-sided conversations with doors. More voices were coming down the hall from the direction of the ballroom as people began to trickle away from the dance floor. I glided back down the marble halls, back in the direction of light and music and color. I slipped inside the doorway and made my way around the perimeter till I was deep inside the room. No one seemed to notice my arrival, just as no one had seemed to notice my departure.

Well, one person. "Eden!" Gideon's voice exclaimed in my ear, and I turned to see the Archangel's son smiling down at me. "Where've you been? I looked for you a couple of times."

"Oh I was dancing, then I was eating, then I went outside for a little bit when it got too hot in here," I said nonchalantly. "Have you been dancing all night? Have you had fun?"

"Dancing, yes. Fun, no," he said. "But I've made my mother happy, and that counts for something."

I laughed. "It counts for a lot. Are you done dancing for the night? Or do you have enough energy to do this last one with me?"

For an answer, he held out his arms, and I stepped into his very correct embrace. By now, the dance floor was only about half full, and most of the performers were tired; this final waltz was pretty languorous in pace. Gideon and I chatted happily throughout it, whispering comments about the other people on the floor and those we did and didn't like. I glanced across the room once to see my mother's eyes on me. She stood by the door, as if she had just stepped through it to look for me, and she was smiling in approval. I lifted my hand from Gideon's shoulder to give her a friendly wave, and she waved right back.

THERE was no opportunity to see Jesse for the first half of the following day. The young women were all herded off together into Abigail Lesh's quarters to spend the day with specialists imported to work on our hair and skin and nails. It was an activity I normally would have enjoyed, for I loved fashion as much as the next Manadavvi girl, but today I wanted to be roaming the mansion grounds, looking for Jesse. There was no escape, though. A special lunch was brought to us, and harpers and flautists entertained us with wistful music while we ate, then it was back to beauty and self-indulgence. When we parted in mid-afternoon, many of us were commandeered by our mothers and forced to lie in our rooms for an hour or two to improve our skin tone and our dispositions. At dinner, another fancy affair, we were seated by clan and lineage, and I could not even spot Jesse's wings amid the welter of Harth finery and Fairwen ostentation. No chance that Jesse would attend the musical event in the evening; no chance my mother would allow me to skip it. I sat dutifully by her side for that whole interminable evening and spent all my energy hating every single singer, every single harpsichordist who climbed on the stage to perform.

The evening ended early, for the morning was to begin with the great event of the whole gathering—the wedding. As I lay in bed that night, unable to sleep for irritation, I reflected that it was a little odd that I had been at the Lesh mansion three days and not said a single word to Abigail. She was only a few years older than I was, a pleasant but rather unremarkable young woman, and we had been friendly enough in the past. And I was, after all, here in this house specifically to witness her marriage; I would have thought I would have found a moment to talk to her privately and wish her well. Perhaps my only chance would come at the luncheon that would follow the ceremony tomorrow, as all the guests queued up to give their congratulations to the newlyweds.

As it happened, no one was able to speak to the happy couple the following day. There was no wedding. Abigail's youngest sister had risen at dawn to help the bride dress and had found Abigail locked in the arms of the angel Jesse. Her shriek of alarm brought half the household to her sister's doorway, and the rage of Emmanuel Lesh could be felt reverberating through every slab of marble in the house. Guests hastily decamped, packing up their bags and calling for their carriages before noon had even tumbled across the meridian. I sat in my father's coach, stonily staring at the northern Gaza countryside rolling past, and wondered if Abigail Lesh wore lemon verbena perfume when she dressed for dancing and engaged in forbidden romance.

IT was a year before I saw Jesse again.

I heard echoes and whispers of his name from time to time, tales carried back from friends and strangers. He had gone to live in Luminaux for a few months, taking up wood carving in one of those famous ateliers. He had traveled with an Edori clan. He had disappeared for a while, no one knew where, perhaps to camp on the ruined mountain where the old angel hold of Windy Point once had stood. It was possible that none of these tales were true. It was possible they all were.

I thought about him often, knowing full well he never thought of me. I had told no one about that night of fire and water, rage and beauty, but I could not erase its spectacular images from my mind. I could not forget the wordless sense of intimacy that had existed as we hovered over the ocean, watching lightning knife through the waves. I scarcely knew this man, and yet he haunted me like a lover renounced in bitter pain. I knew I might never see him again, and I knew I would not forget him.

That year was a busy one, for I was well and truly part of Samaria's social circle now. I was invited to every important event held at Monteverde or any of the Manadavvi holdings. I even traveled to Semorrah and Luminaux and Cedar Hills for the grandest occasions, and naturally I went to the Gloria

again that year, though I did not sing. I spent the spring with
the Fairwens in Semorrah and flirted with the sons of merchant lords. I stayed at the Eyrie for a couple of weeks that
summer and dallied with the angels. I thought, at the age of
seventeen, that life offered a great many bright and careless
diversions, and none of them mattered to me very much.
Now I was bored, and *knew* it, but I didn't realize my life was
soulless and shallow. Or rather, I thought that was what
everyone's life was like—certainly the life of everyone I knew.

When I was home, and when I paid attention, I could see
a shadow falling between my mother and my father. Or perhaps that shadow had always been there and I was only just
beginning to discern its outlines. These days, while my
brothers were still relegated to the schoolroom, I was part of
every social function held on the Karsh estates, present at
every formal dinner and invited on every outing. I spent
more time with my parents that year than I ever had before,
and I began to see how strained their relationship was. They
might sit side by side at a long, elegant dinner table and not
speak to each other once. They might stand at the door,
greeting arrivals for a ball, and never exchange a glance or
reach over to put a hand on the other's arm. The few times
I saw them alone or in private, they were exchanging sharp
accusations and tense denials.

It was not clear to me what their arguments were about.
There could be no money worries among the Manadavvi,
and my father had never seemed interested in other women.
Perhaps he was not interested in my mother, either, and her
desire for affection, for any response at all, led her to nag at
him till he rounded on her in quick anger. Three or four
times I saw him knock her aside with a violent motion.
Once I saw him strike her roughly on the shoulder with a
closed fist. More times than I could count, that year, I came
upon her in her bedroom or her sitting room, sobbing into
her folded hands. The only time I tried to comfort her, she

turned away from me and begged me to leave the room. After that, when I came upon her weeping, I said nothing, merely crept back out of the room.

One day in mid-summer, I was outside on the front lawn with my grandfather and my father and my mother and half the upper servants of the house. We were looking up at the façade of the centuries-old mansion and debating whether we could, as my father wanted, add a wing on the eastern hall without destroying the symmetrical beauty of the place. My mother and the steward were arguing for a wing to be added to the back, where it would be invisible from the front walkway, though it would require tearing out all the kitchens and most of the servants' quarters and cost three times what an eastern wing would cost. My grandfather was saying testily that he did not think we needed another room in the house, no, not a cellar or a broom closet. I was wondering if I would be able to move into the new wing in my own suite of rooms, so far from my brothers that I would never have to see them again.

Suddenly the housekeeper whirled around and looked up and shaded her eyes; and then the steward turned; and then the butler, and the bailiff, and my mother, and then me. My father and grandfather were still conferring, so they did not see the sight that greeted our eyes—a contingent of angels, sun-white and iridescent in the afternoon light, massed over-head and slowly drifting down to land. The bountiful spread of their overlapping wings seemed to fill the lawn; it was as if winter had come early, laden with snow. I saw the black-haired Archangel Gabriel in the lead, Ariel of Monteverde at his right shoulder. I knew before any words had been spoken that whatever news they bore could not be good.

"Joseph Karsh," Gabriel said, in the voice that could soothe the god or bring the mountain down.

My father spun around to stare at him. My grandfather, turning more slowly, glanced from the angel to my father and back to the angel again. His face looked troubled but unsurprised. My mother's expression was one of deep apprehension.

"Angelo," my father replied, inclining his head very slightly in acknowledgement.

"Joseph Karsh, a committee of angels has convened to discuss with you infractions you have committed against the laws of Samaria," Gabriel said. He spoke with the rhythm and intonation of a herald announcing portentous tidings—disastrous tidings—and his face was unflinchingly solemn.

My father stood straighter, very tense, his hands balled at his sides. "I have committed no infractions," he said. "I have lived inside the law."

Ariel stepped around Gabriel, and her face and her voice were both more compassionate than the Archangel's. "Joseph, you have not," she said quietly. "Let us go inside and discuss these matters in private."

"I will hear any accusations leveled against my son," my grandfather said.

Gabriel's blue eyes settled on him. "Anyone may hear us and bear testimony if they wish. We have evidence I do not think you will be able to controvert."

"There is no evidence. I have done nothing wrong," my father said.

My mother turned for the house. "Go to the small dining room," she said. "I will have someone bring in refreshments."

"They won't be here very long," my father said.

"Oh, yes," Gabriel said, "I think we will."

IN fact, there were angels at the Karsh estate for the next ten months. Gabriel and Ariel did not stay so long, of course, but they were there three full days. I have never heard such shouts and recriminations as rumbled around the house during that period of time. Much of the shouting came muffled through the door of the small dining room, where the angels were holding their conference with the men of my family. Some of it came from other levels of the house— arguments between my father and his father, between my mother and my father, among all three of them at once. To escape the noise, I spent as much time as I could in the upper story of the house, actually seeking out the company of my brothers. Paul, of course, did not even realize that trouble was afoot. Evan, now twelve and a quick-witted though mean-spirited boy, understood what was going on better than I did.

"He's been making illegal deals with the Jansai," Evan explained to me. "Trading in certain goods without declaring them so he can avoid paying taxes to the angel holds."

"Then why aren't the Jansai in trouble?"

Evan shrugged. "They probably are. None of the Jansai can stand the Archangel, and they are constantly scheming to outwit him."

"Why would our father try to do such a thing?"

"Because angels levy unfair taxes against the Manadavvi."

"Unfair how?"

"Too high. We are not allowed to keep a reasonable percentage of our profits. It's Manadavvi money that pays for most of the upkeep of roads across Samaria, did you know that? Manadavvi and river merchant money. Our father is sick of paying for the privileges of the poor."

It was clear to me that Evan shared my father's views on the inequity of the taxation system. As for myself, I had never given it any thought—could not have told you, actually, who paid taxes on what goods and what the percentages were. It had not occurred to me to wonder.

When Gabriel and Ariel departed three days later, they left behind one of the angels from Monteverde, a solemn fair-haired woman about my father's age. Evan told me that Diana was to stay for five or six months, monitoring our father's financial transactions and sitting in on every business deal he conducted. He did not have to, though he did, detail for me my father's extreme rage at the installation of this supervisor. But the message had been clear: Accept an angelic overseer, or forfeit any right to conduct business in Samaria.

I don't know if I can adequately describe the tension in the household in those following months. When my father was present in a room at all, he glowered with such a barely contained, constantly refueled fury that no one wanted to catch his attention or attempt any conversation with him. My grandfather—the only one in the household not afraid of him—would occasionally rasp out derisive comments along the lines of "If you hadn't mismanaged things so badly, we wouldn't be in this predicament now," and the two of them would begin quarreling. My mother looked more haggard and weary every day, her pale skin stretched with worry, her blond hair piled in ever thinner braids on top of her head. Three of the house servants, who had been with us ever since I could remember, gave notice. None of the new cooks would stay. No one was hungry anyway, so all of us grew thin on a diet of kitchen scraps and grievance.

We could not possibly entertain in such a situation, and my father refused most of the invitations that came our way. I was still sent out to various balls and weddings and social functions, but I enjoyed them even less than before. Everyone knew of our disgrace, of course, and I was aware that matrons and their daughters whispered about me when they thought I did not notice. Not that their own husbands and fathers had not practiced similar deceitful tactics, which Evan assured me more than once. They had just been more discreet, or less greedy, or more conciliatory when the angels came calling.

The scandal did not ruin my social standing as much as I might have expected. I was still a Karsh, after all, the only marriageable daughter of my house, and our family was still wealthy beyond imagining. This affair might be a humiliation for a year or so—at most, a generation—but such disadvantages could be overlooked when a young man was seeking an alliance with money, land and a business network that stretched across the entire continent.

Even so, it was clear to me that I would probably not secure a bridegroom any time in the next few months, and I found the thought peculiarly liberating. My mother had been married at the age of eighteen and had borne her first child a year later. I had had every reason to expect that my own adolescence would end abruptly this year when my father informed me that he had chosen the man I was to marry. Wretched as it was in my father's house at the moment, I was not so eager to be bartered over to another imperious, foul-tempered man and assume all the responsibilities of adulthood. I was actually rather relieved to be given another year of freedom.

And it was not because I harbored any illusions of marrying for love or even continuing a doomed romance with a most ineligible suitor. During the summer and fall of that year, I hardly thought of Jesse at all.

Until he came to our house bearing messages from the Archangel.

IT was a windy autumn day, and the ivy climbing to the turrets of the mansion had turned a passionate red overnight. I was up in the schoolroom with Paul, playing some tedious board game with him but happy to avoid the usual tensions in the lower reaches of the house. A movement outside caught my eye, and I glanced out the window in time to see the unmistakable glamour of angel wings dropping down.

"Visitors," I said to Paul, standing up and shaking out the folds of my gown. I had dressed rather casually that morning—I usually did, these days, since we rarely had company—but I didn't suppose this new arrival had come to see me anyway. "I'd best go down and see if Mother needs my help."

"Come back and finish the game," he commanded. "When you're done."

"If I can," I said, carelessly ruffling his hair. "Don't move any of the pieces while I'm gone."

By the time I made it downstairs, I could hear my mother's voice in my father's study. I only caught a few words—"A packet of letters, I think, from Gabriel"—before I heard his explosive reply. I hurried a few steps on to the private parlor where angelic guests were usually installed. I doubted my mother had had time to offer food or refreshment to the messenger.

When I walked in, he was standing by the tall windows, looking out at the artful scattering of autumn colors across the back lawns. I could not see his face.

"Did my mother have a chance to offer you something to eat or drink?" I asked in my politest voice. "I'll be happy to have something sent to you."

He turned swiftly, his wings brushing the curtains behind him, and we stared at each other in silence for a moment. "I thought this might be your house," he said, when it was clear I was unable to speak. "But there are so many Karshes—I wasn't sure."

I put my hand to my throat, just like the heroine in a melodrama. "Jesse," I said, "What are you—" I shook my head, not completing the question.

"I've been at the Eyrie for a few weeks," he said, his voice negligent, deliberately so, I thought. As if he did not want to admit how much it meant to him to be admitted back into the angel ranks, as if he did not want to discuss whatever exile he had undergone in the preceding months. "Gabriel asked me to carry something here."

"You've been—I've heard such stories about you," I said.

He grinned and his whole face relaxed. I was staring at him, taking in details. He was no taller than he had been last summer, but he looked bigger, sturdier, as if his body was turning its attention to muscle and bone now that it had done with height. His narrow face looked sharper and more permanently formed, as if Jovah had said, "No more experimenting with the expressions and attitudes of youth. This is your countenance, and from here on out, everything you do will be permanently engraved upon your face." I supposed he must be twenty now. A man by any standard.

"There always seem to be stories about me," he agreed. "Most of them aren't true."

"Which ones are?"

His grin widened. "Which ones do you like best?"

"I know which one I didn't like," I said.

Instantly, his face grew serious again. He glanced at the door, as if to make sure my mother had not reappeared. "I didn't bother to explain that to anybody," he said. "But I could. If you're talking about Abigail Lesh."

I stepped closer to him, though most of the room still separated us. "I am," I said. "And I'd like to hear the explanation. Because it looked very bad, indeed."

"Abigail—" he began, but then we both heard footsteps in the hall. I turned quickly, in time to see my mother step into the room.

"My husband will need some time to look over the letters," she said in a low, strained voice. "Would you—is there someplace I could put you so you can rest from your long flight? I can have a room ready for you."

"Thank you," Jesse said gravely. "I might take a walk in your garden. Do you think he'll have an answer for me before nightfall, or should I plan to find an inn for the night?"

"Oh, surely we can put you up here," my mother said. "It's not as if—Diana is here, after all, and where there is one angel, there may as well be two. I do not mean to sound unwelcoming," she added.

Jesse's solemn face lightened into a smile that caused even my anxious mother to smile back. "I am well aware that Joseph Karsh is not enamored of angels," he said. "I don't want to cause any more distress in the house. Tell me what would be best and I'll do it."

"By all means, spend the night," she said. "Join us for dinner. Diana will be glad of the company—as will we all."

Jesse inclined his head. "Then that's what I'll plan for. Can I still walk in the garden?"

"Of course you can! Eden, go with him. I'll tell the cook to expect a guest for dinner."

A few minutes later, Jesse and I were strolling through the garden, though it was not much to look at this time of year. A few hardy roses still offered their soft, saturated colors for admiration, but most of the shrubs and flowerbeds were full of bare stalks and shriveled leaves. I knew exactly how far you had to walk down each path before you were out of eyesight of someone watching from the mansion, and I led us at a fairly brisk pace to the point of privacy. We sat on a stone bench and watched a stone cherub pour imaginary water into a fountain that had been emptied for the season.

"Now," I said. "What about Abigail?"

He gazed before him, careful not to look at me. "I'd met her a few times. We were friendly. Sometimes I get along with women and they tell me things."

"You almost always seem to get along with women," I said dryly.

"She was dreading this marriage. We'd been at a party— oh, six months before—and she told me she thought her father was going to try and wed her to Luke Avalone. And that she hated him, and that she'd begged her father to look for another groom. She seemed hopeful that he would. I didn't hear from her again until I learned she was marrying Luke Avalone after all. Gabriel brought me to the wedding but I didn't have a chance to see Abigail alone until that night—the night of the ball."

"She met you on the rooftop," I said, "and left her cloak behind."

He nodded. "She begged me to come to her room that night. Said maybe between us we could think of something to stop the marriage. I told her I'd fly her away, take her to Luminaux or Semorrah or anywhere she wanted to go. And I think she considered it. I think she tried to make herself believe she could leave everything—her family, her friends, the life she knew. But when I got to her room after I left you, I could see she wouldn't go. She was too afraid. She just sat there and cried in my arms. Till her sister came in and found us."

"Surely it must have occurred to you—or to *her*—that someone was going to discover you in her room."

He shrugged. I thought I saw a small smile come to his mouth, but he was still looking straight before him and I could not be sure. "It crossed my mind," he said. "She didn't seem too worried about it. I let her make the decision about how long I should stay."

"So she got what she wanted anyway," I said, taking a deep breath. "She didn't have to marry Luke Avalone, and she didn't have to leave her home."

Now he turned to look at me, his green eyes considering. "In my experience, most Manadavvi women do," he said.

I was confused. "Do what?"

"Get what they want. Even if they get it in a devious way."

I stared back at him. "They have to be devious," I said quietly. "No other ways are open to them."

"You should talk to a Jansai woman," he said. "If you want to meet someone who has no power in her life."

"No one talks to Jansai women," I said. "Their husbands and fathers keep them hidden from the world."

He shrugged and glanced away. I wondered just exactly how he had managed to meet a Jansai girl and what the outcome of that encounter had been. "So what is it you want, Eden Karsh?" he asked me, still looking in the other direction. "And how deceitful would you be to get it?"

I was silent.

He swung his head back and looked down at me. "Or don't you know yet?"

"What I want or what I'd do?"

"Both. Either."

I shook my head. "I've always been a dutiful daughter. I've always had everything I needed, everything I wanted. Someday my father will pick my husband and I'll marry, and I assume I'll be a good wife. What do I want? I want that husband to be someone who isn't cruel, someone whom I can like or at least admire. I don't expect that goal to be impossible to achieve. So far, I haven't met anyone that I would beg my father not to give me to in marriage."

He was still watching me. "That's pitiful," he said.

I bristled. "What is? What's pitiful? My life?"

"What you want from your life."

"I'm not the one causing chaos in three provinces," I said. "I'm not the one who is so restless and so unhappy that everywhere I go, trouble follows. I think by the end of it, my life will be filled with much more contentment than yours will. I don't think I need *you* to pity *me*."

"At least at the end of my life, I won't look back and say, 'Why didn't I do this? Why didn't I try that?'"

"Why didn't I go drinking with the Jansai? Why didn't

I go traveling with the Edori?" I mocked. "Why didn't I kiss this girl at midnight on her wedding day and cause her to be cast off by her family?"

He looked at me sharply. "That's not what happened to Abigail."

"No," I admitted. "They sent her away to her aunt in Semorrah, where she met a Fairwen boy. They were married three months later."

His face lit with that dangerous smile. "So you see, I am not just an agent of chaos and trouble," he said.

"It's still chaos," I say, "even if it resolves in calm."

He shrugged elaborately. I felt his wings rise behind me, brush against the back of my shirt and rustle to the ground again. "If calm is what you want," he said.

I burst out laughing. Before I could answer, Paul came racing down the garden path, calling out my name. "Eden! Eden! Mother wants you both to come in for dinner. Ebenezer Harth and his wife have come, and Mother wants you to change clothes and be beautiful."

I came to my feet. "The Harths? They haven't been here in a month."

Paul nodded. "Mother's excited. So come in, please, she says, and let's all get ready."

I nodded at Jesse. "Two angels at our table for dinner tonight. It gives us consequence."

"Even though your father hates angels?"

I smiled. "Even then."

UNFORTUNATELY, even the presence of two angels and two elite Manadavvi could not turn my father into a sociable creature for the night. He had never bothered to mind his tongue around Diana, of course, and Ebenezer Harth was a long-standing ally who shared many of the same views, and apparently my father felt no compulsion

to modify his behavior on Jesse's behalf. Thus, for most of
the meal, we were treated to various tirades on the ineffi-
ciencies of modern taxation systems, the greed and waste-
fulness practiced at the angel holds, the inferiority of
Luminaux workmanship, the duplicity of Semorran merchants, and the general superiority of all things Manadavvi. He spoke carelessly to Ebenezer Harth, insultingly
to Diana and sharply to my mother, while entirely ignoring me. Ebenezer Harth didn't seem to notice; he agreed
emphatically on all the financial points and seemed bored
when the topic turned in any other direction. My mother,
of course, was mortified. Jesse's expression was impossible
to read.

But as we all stood up after the meal, planning to move
to one of the salons for another round of scintillating conversation, Jesse made his way, without seeming to plan it,
across the room to where my father stood.

"And you, you're like all the angels," my father growled
at him, draining his wineglass and setting it down beside
his used plate. "Think you're so much better than everyone
else. Think everyone in the three provinces has to bow down
before you. I say you're dirt under my feet. You're supported
by Manadavvi dollars and dependent on Manadavvi good
will. I say those dollars and those days of good will have just
about dried up."

Jesse smiled at him. He was only slightly taller than my
father, but his body was more solid and his wings gave him
additional bulk and menace. It was only just now clear to
me that he was furious. "I hope the god's coffers are drained
to the bottom the day you die," he said in a soft, pleasant
voice.

"What? Why? What do you mean?"

"Because otherwise you won't be able to buy your way into
Jovah's arms," Jesse said. While everyone stood there in
stunned silence, he made a quarter turn and addressed Diana.

"I'll be at the inn just south of the Karsh property, on the main road," he told her. "Bring his letters to me in the morning, and I'll make sure they get to Gabriel."

And he nodded at the rest of us and stalked out. The room was so still that I thought I heard the slam of the front door behind him, the sweep and flutter of his wings as he took off. No one moved or spoke until my father snatched up his wineglass and flung it against the wall, where it shattered into more pieces than there were acres of land on my grandfather's estate.

TWO weeks later, Diana left us, unable to endure my father's company any longer. To replace her, Gabriel sent an angel named Adam—and instantly everything was better.

He was a slim, dark-haired man with deep-set brown eyes and an inviting smile. His wings were sharp and elegant, every quill edge seemingly honed to a knife-edge, the trailing points as long and fine as a gentlewoman's hands. His voice was mellifluous and soothing; he laughed often. To be in his company was to be instantly put at ease. Where Diana had skulked around the mansion looking gloomy and remote, Adam made friends everywhere. The servants were instantly his partisans, my brothers adored him, and my mother—who had seemed so defeated and lost in recent months—revived to sociability under his influence. Even my father, who hated all angels and particularly angels foisted on him by the Archangel, could not help responding to Adam's amiable presence.

"Angels are a parasite on the inherent structure of the social order," my father shot at Adam one night over dinner. "They don't farm, they don't mine, they don't trade, they don't labor. Yet we're forced to treat them like minor deities and support their existence with the profits of our own labor and our own trade."

"The angels are intermediaries between you and your god, but let's put that aside for a moment," Adam responded in his genial way. "Let's cite more concrete examples of their worth. Angels can control the weather on Samaria. They can pray for sun, they can pray for rain, they can extend your growing season artificially by as much as a month or two. Which improves your harvest, which improves your profit, which increases your wealth. How can you say angels are parasites when they're directly responsible for pouring coins in your hands?"

My father loved a good argument; he replied with zest. "Ha! Without the angels, I might have a shorter growing season, *but* I'd have no taxes to pay. Therefore my net profit would be higher anyway."

Adam sipped from his glass of wine and grinned. "Without the angels, there would have been no growing season at all two years ago," he said. "And without the angels, there would have been floods across lower Samaria fifteen years ago—which could have wiped out half the farms on the southern coast, *and* the mines, *and* washed away Luminaux. Angels prayed those storms to a standstill."

"That's true," my father said grudgingly.

"And who do you think keeps the Jansai in check? Who do you think regulates the roads and forces fair trade throughout the three provinces? Do you really think your own caravans would be unmolested if the angels didn't guarantee your safety?"

My grandfather bristled. "Jansai and Manadavvi have always been partners."

My father added, "We have no cause to fear Jansai traders."

"And you have no reason to despise Gabriel as you do," Adam said gently. "The Manadavvi have thrived under his rule. Even the Karsh clan is wealthier now than it was ten years ago."

Apparently this could not be disputed, for my father merely shrugged and didn't answer. My grandfather said with some energy, "And changes aren't so far off, anyway. Another two years, and Gabriel's time will be over. The next Archangel may look more favorably on our situation. We can afford to wait."

Talk turned to speculation about who the next Archangel might be, a topic that Adam seemed to find particularly intriguing. It occurred to me to wonder if he might consider himself eligible for that office. I was a little hazy on the details, but I thought an Archangel was generally between the ages of thirty and forty. He held the position for twenty years, during the prime of his life. I was not sure what qualifications the god looked for when assessing candidates—strength of character, one assumed, strength of will. Gabriel certainly had both of those. I was not so sure that Adam did.

For, oddly, I was the one person in the household who had not entirely succumbed to his spell. I couldn't have explained why. I was deeply grateful to him for the change he had wrought in the mood of the mansion, and I was pleased to see how he coaxed smiles from my mother. I had been amazed when Evan had come rushing in one day, shouting about the glorious flight he and Adam had taken over the whole of the Karsh estates. I had been amused to find my grandfather deep in discussion with him, calculating grain prices and shipping times, and of course my father's reaction to him astonished everyone. But I had never quite warmed up to him.

He had tried to win me over—might even believe he had. He had had dozens of conversations with me about the social elite of Samaria, and I had to admit he was the best gossip I'd ever met. He could tell hilarious or malicious or touching stories about every wealthy family in the three provinces, and from him I learned more about life in an angel hold than

I had discovered even during the weeks I'd lived in one. One afternoon he sat down with me and drew up a list of the twenty-five most eligible suitors to my hand, dividing them by category: merchant, landowner, river family, angel.

"How old are you again?" he asked me.

"I'll turn eighteen a few weeks before the Gloria."

He tapped his pencil against his paper. "If you were willing to wait another three or four years, you could hardly do better than Gideon."

"Gideon!" I exclaimed. "He's a boy!"

Adam cocked his head. "He's going to be a powerful and thoughtful man."

"He seems so young."

"What do you think of Joshua from Cedar Hills?"

I shrugged. "He's always friendly enough, but he's not very interested in me."

"Maybe not an angel, then. What about the merchant connections? Fairwen's oldest, or that handsome Avalone boy?"

I enjoyed the exercise and all of Adam's candid comments, though the whole conversation was just a touch disquieting. It was hard to say why. Perhaps because I found it strange that Adam would care about such things, or that he would want to talk about them with me. Or perhaps because, after we'd exhausted all the names of the eligible candidates, he tilted his head again and smiled. "Maybe you'll marry none of these fine young men," he said. "Maybe you're the type who will marry to break her parents' hearts."

I thought of Jesse and felt myself blushing. I shook my head. "I'm a good daughter, and I always obey my parents," I said.

"Too bad," he said, smiling. "The most interesting girls are the ones who don't."

Or maybe that wasn't such a strange thing to say.

At any rate, however I felt about him personally, I

appreciated Adam's presence in our house. As the weeks passed and fall turned to winter, he convinced my mother to begin attending social functions again. We were at Monteverde three times that season, and she even went to Luminaux for a wedding. He mediated a meeting between my father and Gabriel—the first time the two men had spoken in five months—and though it did not go as well as Adam had hoped, it did not go as badly as my father had feared. He brought gifts to Evan and Paul and continued to take both of them on short flights around the property.

He was the first one to offer my parents congratulations when my mother, blushing, made the announcement that she was pregnant again.

My brothers and I, sitting with the rest of the family around the dinner table, merely sat there open-mouthed when she told us the news. My father, to whom this clearly was not a surprise, sat beside her looking fatuously pleased with himself. My grandfather did not look like he cared one way or another, as he continued spooning up his soup. He already had my brothers as heirs; he did not have to worry about inheritances.

Paul spoke first. "But you're too old to have another baby!" he blurted out.

My father's smile disappeared. "She's barely thirty-seven," he snapped. "Plenty of women are much older when they have children."

"But what about us?" Evan demanded. "Eden marries, I inherit the property, and I make sure provision is made for Paul—but what about this one? If it's another son? How many more brothers am I going to have to support?"

My father's scowl grew blacker. "You should be grateful if it *is* a son, more assurance that the property will never fall into hands outside of the family," he said. "And if it's a girl—well, there are plenty of alliances left to be made once we've decided where to settle Eden."

"But—how are you feeling?" I asked my mother. I did not want to reiterate Paul's ungracious words, but she *was* a little old to be bearing a child, and her health had never been robust. And she had seemed so frail in the past year or so that more than once I had wondered if she might be developing a serious illness. "Have you been sick in the mornings? You've seemed tired, but I never thought—"

"Fine," she interrupted. "I was sick a little at first, but now I'm hungry all the time." She laughed. "I'm sure I'll be as big as the mansion itself by the time the baby comes."

"And that will be when?" Evan asked. He was still pouting but, mindful of my father's eyes on him, was trying to appear more positive about the announcement.

"Six months from now," my mother said. "In the summer."

Adam, who had sat silent all this time, now stood up and swept his pointed wings behind him. "This is grand news, indeed," he said in a solemn voice, and lifted his wineglass toward the ceiling. All of us hastily snatched up our own drinks and made a toast in my mother's direction. "To you—to your health—to the child you bear. My heartfelt congratulations."

He sipped from his glass, then stepped around the table to plant a kiss on my mother's cheek. She smiled and blushed again and looked as happy as I had ever seen her. My brothers and I, recognizing a successful gesture when we saw one, also went over to give her our kisses. When I leaned in to press my lips against her cheek, I noticed that my father's hand was holding hers under the table. I kissed him as well, for good measure, which surprised him so much that for a moment he didn't know what expression to put on his face. Then he smiled at me and nodded.

"This is good news for the Karsh clan," he said, speaking to everyone but seeming to address me.

"Joyful news," I said. "I can't wait till summer."

*   *   *

BY the time summer came, however, none of us were quite so joyful. Adam left us in the spring, called back to the Eyrie by an Archangel who clearly did not care what made a Karsh family happy and what did not. The good news was that Adam had recommended, and Gabriel had approved, the notion that my father no longer needed angelic supervision. Thus we no longer had an outsider sitting at our family dinners and overseeing my father's business transactions. This pleased my father no end, but the rest of us found we were a little sick of each other's company. I was delighted to get away to Monteverde for a couple of weeks. Evan made his own visit outside the family walls, spending some time with the Fairwen family in Semorrah to learn the ways of river trading. When he came back, he was more insufferable than ever, going on about ship cargos, hull requirements, portage problems, and other even less interesting topics. Paul and I ignored him when we could, but my father and my grandfather seemed to find him invaluable, and the three of them could constantly be found together, discussing business.

My mother was very near the end of her term by the time Evan and I returned from our travels. No matter how healthy she had been earlier in the pregnancy, she was not doing at all well now. She had gained more than fifty pounds and always looked deeply uncomfortable; her face was invariably drawn into a slight frown, as if she was never completely out of pain. She moved slowly and awkwardly around the house, and once she sat down she was reluctant to rise again for any reason. I developed the habit of bringing a food tray to whatever room she happened to be sitting in around meal time, but this late in the pregnancy, she had started to lose her appetite. "I can't," she said more than once when I tried to convince her to eat. "I'll just—I can't."

A month before my mother was due to deliver, my father

installed a midwife in the servants' quarters, and this woman didn't seem at all worried about my mother's lack of interest in food. "She'll be fine, baby'll be fine," said the midwife, who was as old as my grandfather and the most serene person I'd ever met. She seemed strong as a peasant, despite her age, and had the most capable-looking hands imaginable. I could picture her cooking, sewing, farming, woodworking—there seemed to be nothing she would not be able to accomplish with those hands. I was glad she would be there to help my mother, but I still could not help fretting, just a little, about the difficulties of the labor to come. I knew some of the damage a baby could inflict on its way into the world, and I worried every day about some new disaster that could occur in the birthing bed.

As it turned out, when the baby was born, I realized I had not worried enough—and certainly had not worried about the right things.

MY father and my grandfather were out inspecting the fields when my mother's labor pains started. The midwife had brought in her daughter to assist her the day before, "having a feeling," she said, "that the event is coming soon and might not go so smoothly." She commandeered the services of two of the upstairs maids, not letting them into the birthing chamber, but sending them scurrying around the house to fetch water and linen and other more mysterious items. I was not allowed inside, either, but I waited as close as I could, in the room adjoining my mother's, and listened to the sounds of grunting and moaning and weeping that issued from inside. This was dreadful, worse than I'd imagined; I never wanted to have a baby if it meant going through all this. But the midwife's voice remained calm, gentle. Not by a word or inflection did she indicate that anything about the labor was frightening or even unusual.

Until, about two hours after the process had started, she emerged to find me lurking just outside the door. "Ah, you're still here," she said in her unruffled voice. "Good. I want you to do me a favor."

"Is she all right? She sounds—so horrible—"

"All women sound so when they're trying to push a baby out," she said tranquilly. "But there is a complication I wasn't expecting. Nothing for you to worry about, but I'd like you to do something for me. Raise a plague flag over the house, will you? We need to call down an angel."

I stared at her. Her wrinkled face seemed entirely peaceful, her eyes were unflecked with horror. "A plague flag," I repeated. "A *plague* flag. But—if she's all right . . . if nothing's wrong . . . I don't understand."

"It's just that I think we're going to need an angel here," she said. "The sooner the better. Do you know how to raise a plague flag?"

"There's a special pole on top of the house," I said. My heart was beating painfully fast and my mind was blank with terror. "I can—the steward can help me. Or the butler. We'll—it'll be up in a few minutes."

She nodded. "Good." She reached out to touch me on the cheek, but reassurance was one thing that capable hand could not provide. "Don't worry," she said and disappeared back into the room.

Well, of course I was worried. I raced down the steps, calling in a panic for the servants to come help me, come *now,* there was trouble, my mother was dying. As soon as he heard what was needed, the butler dispatched two of the footmen to find and hoist the plague flag. It was a huge rectangle of bright red fabric, designed to catch the attention of an angel flying overhead. It signaled anything—sickness, death, emergency—any crisis beyond the ability of mortals to solve. I could not remember a time in my life we had ever needed to fly it, but my grandfather told tales of calling down angels when illness wracked the household or rain threatened to flood the fields.

And the midwife had determined we needed an angel now.

I tore back up the stairs to see how my mother's situation had changed and found my way barred at the hall by one of the servants. "She doesn't want any of us inside," the girl said. "She said to tell you everything will be fine."

"Everything will *not* be fine," I said sharply. "Why can't I see my mother?"

"She said you should watch for angels instead."

"But—it may be hours—it could be *days*—before an angel comes flying over the house—"

"I think she doesn't want you in the room."

I protested a while longer, but the maid did not relent. Moving more slowly now, I turned down the hallway and headed to one of the unused bedrooms on this level of the house. Stepping out onto the balcony outside the windows, I leaned against the railing and watched the sky overhead. It was a fine, warm day, thick with sunlight. From this vantage, I could see the yard and gardens, lushly green. I could see the long, looping avenue that led from the main road to our front door. And I could see miles of sky overhead, empty of clouds, empty of angels. I craned my head to watch in all directions.

It was late afternoon before I saw the first movement on the horizon, and then it appeared in a less welcome direction—a cloud of dust on the road, no doubt raised by my father and my grandfather on their way home. Would the midwife allow my father in the room with my laboring mother? How could she keep him out? Would she tell him the truth about whatever danger of death or infection threatened my mother? What would he do then?

When they got close enough, I could make out the figures of my father and grandfather, bent low over the horses' necks and riding hard. They must have seen the plague flag; they knew, whatever it portended, it was trouble.

When the riders were only a few minutes away, angels descended upon the house.

My attention had been so fixed on my father that I had forgotten to keep up my constant scanning of the sky. So I was startled when the winged shadows fell over my face and I suddenly looked up to find three angelic figures suspended in the air before me. One was Ariel; two I did not know.

"Eden," Ariel called. "What's the trouble here?"

I gestured wildly as if I could sweep them inside with my hands. "My mother—she's in labor—the midwife demanded that we call down an angel, but she won't say why."

Ariel's expression altered; she exchanged quick glances with her companions. She nodded at the male angel hanging in the air beside her. "Go on downstairs," she told him. "Greet Joseph Karsh at the door. Tell him we have been called down to aid his wife. Don't tell him why."

"But why have you?" I demanded as he canted his wings and dropped down toward the ground to meet my father.

"Step back inside the window, will you?" Ariel asked, not answering my question. I backed into the house. She beat her wings with a swift, hard motion, came close enough to touch her feet to the railing, balanced for a moment, then jumped onto the balcony. The female angel with her copied her motions; in a moment, they were both inside.

"Where is the birthing chamber?" Ariel asked, all business.

"What's wrong with my mother?" I whispered.

Ariel smiled at me and, like the midwife, laid a hand against my cheek. This kind gesture reassured me no more than the midwife's had. "Nothing's wrong," she said. "But things are about to get unpleasant."

"Please," I said, still whispering.

She studied my face a moment. "I am guessing that the

midwife has realized that the baby your mother is carrying is angelic. Not your father's at all."

I just stared at her. Downstairs, I could hear a commotion at the front door, the sound of my father's voice raised in argument with the third angel.

"And angel births can be very difficult for the mother. But even more—they can be, if they are unexpected, very difficult for the man who believed he was the child's father."

"Adam," I breathed.

Ariel nodded. "Most likely. He has fathered a number of children in high-ranking households across the three provinces. I am sorry for this, Eden. But the midwife did right to call us. We will protect your mother. And we will take the baby back with us to the hold. No mortal can raise an angel child. We will offer your mother the choice of coming with us or remaining here. I am afraid life at the Karsh household is about to become very strained, indeed. Now where is the birthing chamber? We must arrive there before your father."

Silently I turned and led them out of the spare room and down the hall. The servant girl guarding the door fell back in relief when she saw Ariel and her companion. "There's been screaming," the girl offered. "I've never heard anything like it."

"I have," Ariel said. And, pushing past the maid, she entered the chamber that had been forbidden to me. I heard one sharp, despairing wail from my mother, and then the door closed between us again. The noise from below was growing louder, or else my father was drawing nearer, shouting at everyone as he charged up the stairs. I leaned my head against the wall of the corridor and closed my eyes, waiting for the world to fall down around me.

*   *   *

THERE followed the most ghastly week of my life. I cannot describe the way my father's face turned from fear to fury when Ariel emerged from the labor room and coolly told him what she had told me. I do not want to think about how he launched himself in an attack on the angels, how he was physically restrained, how he became a prisoner in his own house while my mother gave birth and recovered. I don't want to dwell on my own apprehension and confusion and rage and sadness during those days. I don't want to re-live that time at all.

I was only allowed to see my mother once, for she was very weak. Even I knew how rare and difficult the birth of an angel could be; many women died during that violent passage. My mother had not died, but she had come close, and even five days after her son was born, she could scarcely speak or stand. But she had asked for me, and they had let me in. It was late afternoon, but the curtains were mostly drawn and the chamber was dark. I could barely make out her ghostly face against the white pillow. I could barely see the small, wrapped form lying beside her on the bed.

"Eden," she whispered when I tiptoed in. "Oh, I have missed you these past few days. Do you hate me? Do you forgive me? Please come kiss me and say it will be all right."

At that I stumbled the last few feet across the room and dropped onto the bed beside her. "I've been so worried," I sobbed. "I was so afraid. How could you do this? How could this happen? Did you love him? Will you leave us? Oh, Mother, I am still afraid—"

She shushed me and stroked my hair and let me cry into her shoulder. "I'm so sorry," she said, over and over. "So sorry. And yet I love my son so much already, I would do anything to keep him safe—"

When I grew calmer, I sat up and we talked for nearly an hour. She did not want to discuss Adam and the time she had spent with him. She merely said, "I do not regret it, not one hour, and I do not regret whatever turmoil comes after."

"You never loved my father," I said.

She looked at me. "I tried," she said. I nodded. He was not, in fact, a man that anyone could truly love.

"Are you going to Monteverde?" I asked.

She nodded. "I must. They will take him whether or not I go, and I have to be with him. You can come, if you like. Ariel has said so."

It was as if light blossomed inside my chest, rendering me luminous and giddy. "I can? To live with you among the angels?"

"The boys, too, except—except—I do not think that Joseph will let them go."

"He might not let me go either." I took a deep breath and forced my excitement to die away. "And I cannot come. Not just yet. Once you are gone, and your angel child with you—I must stay a while. There will be much to do in this household to set things right."

She sighed and laid her head back on the pillow. "Things will never be right in this household," she said. "They never were. Only when Adam was here."

And even then, I reflected, everything had been wrong. I did not say so; it was clear she was too weary to talk any longer. I sat beside her another few minutes, watching her eyes close and her face loosen, listening to the easy sound of her breath as she slept. Then I bent over her body to look into the small, closed face of her sleeping son. My half brother. An angel. I lifted a finger to trace the smooth, delicate skin over the tiny features of his face. Still sleeping, he frowned and twitched away. I pulled back my hand and stood up. Once I had kissed my mother on the cheek, I crept from the room. I did not see her again for two months.

Those were grim months at the Karsh house, and more

than once I was sorry I had decided to stay. My father's mood was so foul that my brothers and I frequently forsook family meals and got all our food at odd hours from the kitchen. My grandfather seemed shrunken somehow, suddenly old and tired beyond description. I was the only one who seemed capable of running the household, so I gave the cooks their menus, the house servants their instructions and the gardeners their directions. I ordered household goods, paid tradesmen and answered all correspondence. The steward became my confidant and the butler my ally. Together the three of us kept the house running and the inhabitants fed. But none of us enjoyed it.

My mother wrote often, constantly renewing her offer to have me come live with her. I knew I could not forsake my father's house, but I missed my mother—and I longed for some entertainment, no matter how brief and restricted. Since my mother's disgrace and my father's violent reaction, no one came to visit us anymore, and very few invitations were sent our way. Evan did go spend another week in Semorrah, and I went to a local dinner or two, but in general we were not up to making the effort of socializing. We were too exhausted and we were too mortified. Even the Karsh family would need some time to recover its standing after this blow.

It was a nasty fight with my father that made me decide to leave, at least for a little while. I can't remember what set him off that night—the flavor of the soup, perhaps, or the spices on the meat—but he raged through dinner and then stood in front of me and shouted in my face for a good five minutes. When I tried to leave the room, he grabbed me by both shoulders and shook me until my vision failed. My grandfather finally knocked him away from me, while Evan shoved me out of the room for safety. I was shaking as I made my way upstairs to my room. I went directly to my closet to pull out my luggage, and that night I packed for a trip to Monteverde.

But life at the angel hold was just as strange in its own way.

First, my mother had changed. She was totally absorbed in the new baby, scarcely willing to leave the room if he was awake and might need her attention, and so she was distracted and weary. She did not seem unhappy, though, or even particularly penitent, and it was soon clear that the pampered life at the angel hold suited her well. Not that life as a Manadavvi wife had not had its share of luxuries, but here she had no responsibilities except to care for her child. She did not have a husband to appease, a household to run, neighbors to visit, an image to maintain. She was merely a mother who had been offered unlimited resources and assistance. She was tired but content.

Second, my own status was a little unclear. All my old friends greeted me with their usual affection, but I felt awkward, as if I was the one who had committed a scandalous act. Now and then I thought I caught people gossiping about me in the halls or smirking when they introduced me to a stranger. Let me be clear, it was only mortals who behaved this way—the angels all seemed to think it was perfectly natural that my mother would have wanted to take an angel lover and bear an angel child, and their attitude toward me changed not at all. But I knew that I was not destined to live the rest of my life among angels, and that their values could not govern mine. I was a Manadavvi woman, destined to marry a Manadavvi heir, and I needed to find my place again among my peers.

Third, Adam came and went at the hold and did not seem to think I would hate him. He was stationed at the Eyrie but flew north to Monteverde every week or so on errands for the Archangel. He appeared quite friendly with my mother, though not at all devoted to her; he was more interested in his son. It did not seem as if they had resumed their relationship or that either one particularly wanted to, and neither did they seem to feel any animosity toward one another. I was the only one, it appeared, to harbor any hostility at all.

I was alone one day on one of the open plateaus of Monteverde when Adam happened to stroll by and see me. Monteverde had been built in a low, pretty series of mountains that were easily climbed and often clogged with visitors ascending to the hold. The buildings were spread out over several acres and interspersed with small parks and merchant establishments. The view down the mountainside was spectacular as the landscape shaded from green peak to variegated flatlands below. I loved to sit by myself on one of the benches overlooking the scenery, and I was not pleased to be joined by anyone—particularly Adam.

"Are you enjoying your visit to the angel hold?" he asked in his friendly way. "I know your mother is happy to have you here."

I shuttered my face and gave him a neutral look. "Yes, it is always good to spend some time at Monteverde," I said.

He leaned his elbows on the retaining wall and looked out over the countryside, rich with the reds and golds of autumn. "Will you be going to the Lesh wedding in a few weeks? Most of those young men we talked about will be there. It might be time for you to start looking for a husband."

"My father will find a husband for me," I said in a constricted voice.

He shrugged, and his wings rose and dipped around him. I felt one silky quill brush my toe. "Your father doesn't always appear to have your best interests at heart."

"My father—" I said and then stopped abruptly. "My father has a great deal on his mind at the moment," I said carefully. "And I don't know if I will be at the wedding or not. My life has not admitted of too many diversions in recent months."

He gave me that warm, easy smile. I was astonished at how much I despised him at that moment. "A girl as pretty as you is a diversion herself," he said. "Go to the wedding. Have fun. You're too young to be mired in disasters of other people's making."

"And you're too old to be making those disasters," I said quietly. Rising to my feet, I hurried away. He didn't respond and he didn't follow.

Three days later, two much more welcome angels put in an appearance. I was outside again, this time in a small grassy square that connected two of the Monteverde buildings, and I was thinking that it was cool enough for me to want to go back inside.

"There she is," I heard a voice say, and I looked up to see a pair of angels headed my way. One dark, one fair; one a grown man, the other a boy. I jumped up, delighted to see them both.

"Jesse! Gideon! Oh, I didn't know you were coming here! How have you been? How long are you staying? Gideon, you've gotten so *tall!*"

I gave Gideon a hug and a kiss on the cheek, because I always did—and then I hugged and kissed Jesse as well, because it would have seemed strange not to. His arms took me in a closer embrace than Gideon's had; he turned into my kiss and laid his mouth ever so briefly against mine before letting me go.

"We hear you've been having rather a rough time of it," Gideon said. "None of the angels seem to realize what a scandal this is, but my mother said you'd be feeling lonely. She sent me to come see you, and Jesse wanted to come along."

"That was kind of her, and kind of both of you," I said. "Oh, it's so good to see you. Come tell me everything that's been going on."

We headed to a small restaurant tucked up against one of the hold buildings and ducked inside out of the chill. Jesse ordered drinks for all of us, and we sat and talked for hours. Laughing references of Gideon's made me think there had been some trouble on Jesse's part in recent months, but Jesse didn't explain and I didn't ask. Gideon's own life appeared to have consisted of an escalating series of commitments and responsibilities; it was clear he was being groomed for some leadership role. But the responsibilities seemed to lie easy on his shoulders, which were already wide enough to assume a heavy load of other people's cares.

We stayed out late that night, picking up a few more companions as we made our way from the restaurant to a tavern that Jesse knew of. For the first time since I had arrived at Monteverde, I felt that I was among friends, and I enjoyed myself immensely. I had a few more glasses of wine. I laughed a great deal. I sat close enough to Jesse to lean my back into his shoulder and to feel the protective satin of his wing as it curled around me. We didn't return to the hold till well past midnight, and both Jesse and Gideon escorted me down the hallway to the door of my mother's suite. Gideon bowed and kissed my hand. Jesse glanced once, mischievously, at Gideon, then kissed me on the mouth again. I giggled and waved at them both and disappeared inside the room. I fell on my bed without undressing and slept till almost noon.

At which time I discovered that my father had arrived. And he was not happy.

I only learned later what had brought him to Monteverde in the first place, for he hated the angel hold and all its inhabitants. He had received a letter from my mother, begging him to allow her to see Evan and Paul, and he had responded furiously with two letters of his own. One to her, denying her any right to ever see her other sons, and one to me, demanding that I come home. Mine mysteriously went astray, though I came to suspect that my mother had destroyed it before I had a chance to see it. When I did not reply or return, he came to Monteverde to fetch me.

I didn't know he was there until I went to the nearest

dining hall, seeking breakfast or lunch or whatever they might be serving at that hour. The dining hall was one of the many large, open rooms designed to make it easy for residents to congregate, and at the moment it was about half full with a mix of mortals and angels. My mother was seated at one table, holding her baby and laughing with Adam, who stood beside her, smiling. Ariel was over by the buffet, three or four other angels in tow. Jesse was a few tables from my mother, in conversation with two mortal girls, but he gave me a grin as I walked in. I smiled in return and headed to my mother's side, deciding I would ignore Adam's presence.

"I just woke up," I said, yawning. "Is there something you need me to do?"

"Well, you could—" she said, and then shrieked in alarm. The world blurred to violence and motion as someone yanked me backward by the hair and began yelling invective in my ear. I felt blows fall on my face, on my shoulders, as I screamed and twisted and beat futilely at my attacker. My mother was crying at the top of her lungs. Adam, who had snatched the baby protectively to his chest, was shouting for help. I felt bruises blossom on my back and my neck twist so brutally that for a moment I could not breathe.

I had recognized my father's voice and I did not doubt that he would be willing to kill me.

Abruptly as the assault had started, it ended, with my father's hands being wrenched away. I fell to the floor, clutching my throat, aware of raised voices all around me and angel wings slicing between my body and my father's rage. Coughing and crying, I forced myself upright, trying to assess what was happening. At first, all I could see was the shape of white wings flung over my father's bent form as a dark-haired angel choked him to silence. *Adam,* I thought, but then I realized Adam was still beside my mother, still holding his son. Ariel, Gideon and three other angels rushed up, thrusting aside my rescuer and batting my father back to the floor when rage made him try to rise again.

Jesse, I realized then. Jesse had crossed the room and saved me before anyone else had made a move.

"Joseph! Joseph, listen! Calm yourself! This must stop! Joseph Karsh, I swear I will have you locked away if you cannot control your rage—"

That was Ariel, right in my father's face while the two other angels stood behind him, holding his arms. Jesse snaked past her to give my father a hard punch to the cheek. "If you touch her again," he said, his voice low and intense, "I swear I will kill you."

Ariel pushed him impatiently to one side. "Jesse!" she exclaimed. "You're not helping! We need to calm him down and sort this out."

"He practically strangled her!"

"And he will be punished for it. Get her out of here— and her mother, too. We'll talk to them later."

"You're a whore's daughter!" my father shouted at me, trying to kick his way free. I saw Gideon's strong young hands tighten mercilessly on my father's arm. "Don't try to return to my house! I disown you! I disinherit you! You *and* your faithless mother! Let me see that devil's child! I should have twisted his neck while he lay sleeping in my house—"

Jesse started forward again but Ariel blocked him. "Out! Out of here! All of you—give me some space," she commanded. "I need the senior angels here to help me. The rest of you, go."

The room cleared out pretty quickly, though no one went far. Mostly we stayed on the bright square of grass just outside the dining hall. Everyone was buzzing with excitement and retelling the story to the people in their own groups. I stood with my mother and Adam, rubbing my throat and shivering with shock.

"Eden, I'm so sorry," my mother said to me remorsefully. She held the baby in one arm and tried to cradle me with the other. "Had I known—he's angry, of course, but maybe he—"

"He's a lunatic, and he's dangerous, and I hope Ariel knows how to deal with him," Adam said darkly. "He's not only a disgrace to the Karsh name, it's clearly not safe to expose anyone to his temper. Especially the three of you."

Jesse came striding up, his wings taut behind him, still quivering with temper. "Let me see," he demanded and pried my hands away from my throat. "You'll be bruised for a week at least. You can see the finger marks."

"He's never hurt me before," I said, "not really."

"You can't go back," my mother said.

"I don't know what to do," I said unhappily.

"Ariel will take care of it," Adam said.

Jesse gave him a smoldering look. "*Somebody* will," he said.

NEITHER Ariel nor my father had emerged by the time the crowd on the square began to disperse. Still shaken by the ordeal, my mother and I returned to her suite, endlessly discussing what I should do next. Was I really disowned? Would I truly never see my father's estate again? But would I ever feel safe returning? If he refused to give me a dowry, would I be able to marry—at least as well as we had always intended? Though I was sure I *could* live at the angel hold as long as my mother did, was that where I really belonged?

There were no answers to any of these questions. I helped my mother put the baby to sleep and then suggested she lie down for a nap as well. Having slept till just a couple of hours ago, I was not tired, so I slipped out of the room and back out into the open spaces of Monteverde. The day was cool and fine, so I was not the only one strolling along the boulevards of the hold, taking in the sunshine, trying to order my thoughts.

These were still in chaos when I heard my father's voice call my name. I looked around, apprehensive, to locate him standing on an arched stone bridge that connected two of Monteverde's plateaus. "Eden!" he shouted again, waving a hand impatiently. I wondered if he had escaped from Ariel or merely convinced her of his ability to see reason.

A knot of people gathered behind me—witnesses, I suspected, to the events in the dining hall. "Eden!" my father shouted again, an edge of irritation tightening his voice. "I need to talk to you."

I hesitantly waved back. "All right," I called and took a few steps in his direction, glancing around to determine my best route to his side. In that instant, I heard an urgent shout behind me. My eyes went instantly to the bridge where my father stood—staring up at an angel swooping down on him. Someone screamed again—then everyone was screaming, running fruitlessly in the direction of the bridge. Too late, too late. The angel had snatched up my father, who writhed and twisted in his arms, and carried him over the low crags and peaks of the surrounding mountainside. Then, as everyone watched and dozens of voices took up the cries of horror, the angel released his grip and sent my father tumbling onto the rocky slopes below.

SHOUTING, screaming, running. Angels everywhere. Someone flew down to retrieve my father's body and lay it gently in the middle of one of the common squares. Ariel strode from building to building, calling a convocation of residents. Eventually we were all huddled outside in the bright but insufficient sunshine. Ariel stalked past the mortals as if we were not there, her eyes snapping from angel to angel as if she was doing physical count. I did not need to be told what she would discover when she was done surveying her host. Only Jesse was missing.

* * *

GIDEON came to my grandfather's estate to attend my father's funeral. My grandfather had made it very clear that my mother was not welcome, nor Adam, nor even Ariel, but he had not turned Gideon away when he arrived, bearing a long spray of white lilies in his hand.

"A bad business—a terrible business," my grandfather said to the Archangel's son, shaking his head and leaning his hand against a chair back for support. "Joseph was a hotheaded man—the god knows he was full of faults—but to die that way—at an angel's hands—"

"My father has punished the person responsible," Gideon said in a quiet voice.

"How?" my grandfather demanded, helpless and furious. "How does one discipline an angel? Do you lock him in a cell in one of those stone holds of yours? Starve him to death? Kill him outright? Your father would not do any of those things."

"He's been exiled."

"Exiled," my grandfather said in awful scorn. "How do you exile a man who can fly anywhere in the world he desires?"

Gideon glanced at me. Having a keen interest in this story myself, I had sidled close enough to hear. "He has been taken to one of the mountains that ring the Plain of Sharon," Gideon said reluctantly. "He has been left with food and water, and more food and water will be brought to him when his supplies run low. He cannot leave—he has been shackled on a long chain to the mountain itself."

My grandfather grunted, obviously pleased with this picture, though grief had made it almost impossible for him to be pleased with anything these past two weeks. "I hope he dies there."

"He very well might."

I thought Jesse might indeed want to die, chained to one place for days or years or the rest of his life. That wandering, restless, untamable young man, pinned to an isolated mountain on the edge of the world. I thought he might call down thunderbolts to strike him dead rather than spend more than a day or two in such a situation.

I sobbed through the ceremony, mourning I could not have told you what—not my father, whom I had not loved and did not miss, but the whole tragedy of his life, perhaps, and the disaster it had made of mine. My grandfather, at least, had not disowned me, but he told me bluntly that he was in no case to be arranging marriages for me or worrying about my place in Manadavvi society. "I've got the boys to take care of now and the property," he said. "You'll have to make your own way."

But I could think of nothing, no one, except Jesse, found guilty of my father's murder and exiled to a mountaintop by the Archangel himself.

I had no chance to talk to Gideon till after the service, and after the somber dinner that followed, and after all the guests—and there were hundreds of them—found a chance to stop by Gideon's chair to make idle conversation with the Archangel's son. I had no chance to talk to him until everyone was gone and the servants had begun to clear away the mess of the meal, and I had slipped out the back door to the gardens where I had whispered for Gideon to meet me.

He was waiting not far from the house, his wings spread behind him like a hovering ghost. I walked straight up to him and he put his arms around me, and we stayed entwined for ten minutes or more.

"I'm so sorry," Gideon said. "That your father—that Jesse—I'm just so sorry."

I pulled back and studied what I could see of his face by cold moonlight. "Take me to see him," I said.

He dropped his arms in astonishment. "Take you—to see *Jesse?* No! What are you—Why would you want—He killed your *father!*"

"If you don't," I said, "I will go to him anyway. I will walk from here to the Plain of Sharon, I will climb up every single one of those mountains until I find the one where he has been chained. I will climb until my hands are bloody, until the rocks of the mountain have cut through the soles of my shoes. I will find him, or I will die trying to find him, if you don't take me to see him."

"I can't do that," he said.

I turned away from him. "Then I will leave tomorrow to begin to look for him on my own."

He remonstrated; I walked away, my arms crossed stubbornly on my chest. He caught up with me, turned me with an impatient hand on my shoulder. "Eden," he said. "Why? Why do you want to see him? To forgive him? To chastise him? What do you have to say to him? I will take the message for you."

"I want to tell him I love him," I said.

Gideon stared at me in the chilly dark. He dropped his hand. "How can you?" he whispered. "Even now?"

"You're his friend," I said. "Don't you still care about him?"

"Yes, but it's not *my* father he killed! And however much you may have hated your father, you cannot condone—you cannot believe—there is *no* justification for what he did."

I turned away again. "I'll leave for the Plain of Sharon when you're gone," I said. "If you would at least tell me which of the many mountains has been turned into his prison—"

We argued for another half hour, circling around the garden. I was adamant and Gideon was desperate. "Very well," he said at last. "I have to go to Adar Lesh's wedding. I had planned to leave tomorrow anyway. Were you invited? Did you intend to go? I'll tell your grandfather that I'll take you with me. We'll detour to the Plain of Sharon, and you may have one hour to speak with Jesse. And then you must go on with me to the wedding. I'll bring you back, but we won't go by the mountaintop again."

"We won't have to," I said. I threw my arms around his neck and kissed him on the cheek. I could tell he was deeply unhappy about his decision, but I didn't care. "Thank you, Gideon. I swear you will not be sorry."

He sighed. "I'm sorry already."

I stayed up most of the night packing. No formal clothes, though, not the sorts of outfits you would expect to see a young woman wearing at an elite function. Sturdy shoes, travel clothes, an assortment of toiletries, medical supplies in case Jesse had gotten sick or injured, provisions of food and water.

And the heavy black ring that held all the keys to all the locks in the Karsh mansion. I had stolen it from the steward's quarters the instant I realized Gideon had arrived for the funeral.

WE took off for the mountaintop shortly after breakfast. My grandfather had greeted with little interest the news that I was, after all, attending the Lesh wedding. "I'll be back in a week or so," I said, kissing him on the cheek, hugging my little brother, nodding at the older one who was not interested in kisses or hugs from me. "Perhaps I'll have news."

"Travel safely," he said and turned away.

It took more than half a day to travel from my grandfather's land to the Plain of Sharon. We only stopped once, to eat, and talked very little. I was dressed in my heaviest clothes, but still I was cold, even when we landed to make a meal. I didn't complain. All I could think about was what I would say to Jesse.

It was mid-afternoon when Gideon angled downward, making for the circle of mountains that sheltered the Plain of Sharon. I could see their knobby brown heads bowing over the green valley of the plain. "Which one?" I cried into Gideon's ear, hoping he could hear me over the wind and the whuffle of his wings.

"Northern peak," he called back. "Right up against the sea."

That might have pleased Jesse, if anything about this confinement could have offered him a scrap of pleasure—the nearness of the ocean. My eyes picked out the mountain Gideon had indicated, and I strained to see any sign of life on top of it as we drew nearer. There—no, a shadow. There—no, a white patch of snow, not a dejected fall of clipped wings. There—yes, yes, *there,* an angel standing with his back to the water, his head tipped up, having spotted us long before I had been able to discover him. His arms were crossed; his face showed no emotion. I could see the thick, heavy chain that ran from a post in the ground to a black shackle around his left ankle.

"Leave me here," I instructed as Gideon touched down so lightly it was almost impossible to tell the difference between earth and air. "I want to talk to him."

"One hour," he said, letting me go and stepping back. He nodded at Jesse, but did not address him. "Then I'll be back."

"I'll be ready."

I waited until Gideon had flung himself back aloft before I stepped any nearer to Jesse. I watched his face as he watched me. His expression was shuttered, his green eyes hooded. If he felt remorse or shame or anger, he was not about to show it. He had been on this mountain for about two weeks. I thought he already looked thinner, his face more gaunt, his body starting to show its bones. I could not imagine that he would last a year here. Perhaps not even a month. I had not come a day too soon.

"Jesse," I said.

"What are you doing here?"

"I made Gideon bring me."

"I see that. Why?"

I dropped all my bundles on the ground and walked forward, just like that, till I was close enough to put my hands on his shoulders. He was dressed in casual clothes, a thin cotton shirt and leather trousers, and I could feel the heat of his skin through the fabric. "I wanted to tell you that I know you didn't kill my father."

He stared down at me and the guarded expression on his face did not change. "Everyone saw a dark-haired angel drop your father into a ravine. Everyone knows that I alone went missing. Why would you think the story was not true?"

"Because you wouldn't do it," I said.

He looked away. "Oh, yes, I would."

"But you didn't."

For a long time he didn't answer, but kept his eyes focused on that distant view. I wondered if he was looking at the ocean or the sky, or backward at that day in Monteverde. After a long silence, he sighed. "But I didn't," he said.

"It was Adam," I said.

He nodded, still looking away from me. "That was my guess as well. He released your father, then circled back, joined the others on the mountain peak. It took them all a while to gather, I would suppose—no one would notice who was there all along, who came running up afterward. *I* was the only one who didn't make an appearance at all."

"Where were you?"

He shrugged, his bones rising and falling beneath my hands. "I'd gone down to one of the little taverns near the foot of the mountain. Too angry to stay at Monteverde. Too angry to think. By the time Ariel found me—the story had been set. There was no way to change it."

Now I tried to shake him, but he was too tall and too strong for me to really influence. "No way to change it! You could have said—you could have told the truth! People must have seen you in the tavern—someone would have remembered you—"

"Yes, there was a woman in the tavern who saw me there. We talked all afternoon. But no one would believe her."

"Why? Why wouldn't they listen to her?"

His mouth twisted. "Because she's an angel-seeker with some reason to dislike Adam. She bore his daughter two years ago—a mortal child, not an angel—and Adam would have nothing to do with her. You can imagine how bitterly she speaks of your mother, who has been ensconced in Monteverde with all honor. And how much she hates Adam. Anyone would expect her to lie about me if it meant disaster might come to him."

"Someone else, then," I said impatiently. "The tavern owner, the men drinking at the next table—"

Humor flashed through his green eyes. "There was a man there who recognized me, but he'd as soon see me chained to this mountain for the rest of my life. I don't think he'd speak up on my behalf."

"But you could ask him! You could ask this—this angel-seeker! If you raise enough questions, if you create enough doubt, Gabriel will have to listen to you. He will have to consider that you were not the one who killed my father—"

"It doesn't matter," he said in a low voice. He shook himself free of me and paced away to the limit of the chain. "I would have done it. I should have done it. I hated your father and I was afraid for you. If he was going to die at someone's hands, it should have been mine. So if an angel had to be punished for the crime, why not me?"

"If an—but—but that doesn't make any sense! Why

should you suffer for what Adam did? Why would you lie for him? Answer me, Jesse!"

He turned to look at me, and now his face showed so many emotions that I could not sort them out. Fury, self-loathing, despair. "What else have I ever done that made any difference?" he demanded. "When have I not hurt someone—or shamed someone—or created disasters in my wake? Why not take the blame for this and let Adam go free? He's the better angel. He's the one who would be missed. What is my life worth next to his?"

"*He's* the better angel?" I breathed. "Adam? He fathered a child on a married woman. He abandoned his own daughter because she was not angelic. He *killed* a man—and he let another man take the blame! That's the sort of man you'd protect? That's the sort of angel you think is better than you? I never trusted Adam, but I'm terrified of him now. What else might he do, now that he has succeeded at such a crime? What might he do to my mother, if she ever guesses the truth? Once an angel has murdered one mortal, what's to stop him from murdering again?"

As I spoke, Jesse's face changed again, growing darker, angrier, full of its customary defiance. "Yes, I did think of it that way, but I—then I thought this was better—"

"You cannot throw away your own life for someone so dangerous," I said. "So many people are not safe if you are here and he is free."

"But what can I do now?" he burst out. "Trapped here like a hawk on a jess. Gabriel will not release me, Eden. He will not even hear me out. He wouldn't come here to listen to my words."

"You'll have to go to him," I said.

A slight laugh of disbelief. "And how will I manage that?"

"He's on his way to the Lesh wedding. Meet him there. Tell him everything. Give him the names of those who saw you in the tavern. He'll give you a hearing—he has to."

He lifted his left leg and shook it till the metal links rattled together. "It seems too obvious to have to say it out loud, but—"

I turned back to my bundles on the ground. "I brought the steward's key ring. There are a hundred keys on it, and one of them is bound to fit."

He stayed standing exactly where he was as I pawed through my bags, emerged triumphantly with the key ring, and hurried over to his side. I knelt beside him on the rocky ground and tried key after key on the hard black shackle. I was maybe a quarter of the way through the ring when a thin gold key slipped inside the eyehole of the lock and made a small, satisfying click. The fetter snapped in two. Jesse yanked his foot free and then stood for a moment staring down at it, or at me.

"Thank you," he said at last, reaching down a hand to pull me to my feet. "I don't know why you would do so much for me."

I gave him the answer I had given Gideon. "Because I love you."

His answer was to pull me against him and give me one hard, dizzying kiss. I reached up to put my arms around him but he drew back, stepped away. "First, let me fix this," he said. Two steps, a purposeful beating of his wings, and he had taken off, soaring away from the mountaintop like a falcon that had gnawed its way free from restraint.

When Gideon returned a few minutes later, he stared around him with astonishment at the mountain peak that held only me, my luggage and an unlocked manacle. "Where's Jesse?" he said blankly.

"On his way to Adar Lesh's wedding."

IT was impossible to make it all the way from the Plain of Sharon to the northern edge of Manadavvi country in what remained of the day, but Gideon tried. He was so furious that for a moment I thought he might abandon me there on the mountaintop and head north alone. He didn't—but he didn't speak to me at all as we flew, faster than I had really thought possible, into the oncoming night. Even when it was full dark, we continued on—Gideon navigating, I had to suppose, by moonlight and constellation. I could not remember a time in my life I had ever been so cold.

Around midnight, spotting lights below us, we dropped into the welcome haven of a small town and took a room for the night. By dawn, we were on our way again. Gideon still wasn't speaking to me, and I gave up after offering two attempts at conversation and one apology. I just lay in his arms, trying to make my body as light as possible, and watched the autumn country scroll by below us.

It was close to noon when I realized we were almost at the Lesh property. This was a place I had seen from the air once or twice before, after all; I should recognize it from this vantage point. I straightened in Gideon's arms and peered down, noting that the roads converging on the mansion were crowded with horses and carriages.

"It's *today?*" I demanded, appalled. "The wedding?"

Gideon nodded. "This afternoon. A few hours from now."

Another Lesh wedding to be ruined by Jesse. I could not bear to think about that. "Is he here yet?"

"How would I know?" Gideon replied irritably. "He may have flown all night. And he may have flown faster. But I hope we've beaten him."

When, a few minutes later, we arrived at the Lesh property, we saw no sign of the errant angel. Gideon came to rest in one of the wide, flat lawns that sloped gently away from the main house. Just now it was laid out with rows of chairs and festive white tents, and well-dressed people were milling about holding fruit-colored drinks. An outdoor wedding, it would appear, despite the coolness of the season. I glanced down at my bulky jacket and hideous brown trousers, borrowed from Evan. Obviously, I was not dressed for the event.

"There's my father," Gideon said, waving someone over.

"Oh—no—" I stammered. I was not nearly ready to face the Archangel.

"You have to tell him what you've done," Gideon said. I turned and saw, to my horror, that it was not only Gabriel headed our way, but also Ariel and two or three other angels, curious about our odd late arrival.

Adam was among them. He was smiling at me, his eyebrows raised in a question, wondering, no doubt, what could have sent me here in such a fashion and in such an ensemble.

"I can't talk to them," I said in a low voice. "Jesse has to explain."

"You can start the explanation," he said.

They had arrived at our side before I had time to formulate my thoughts, and suddenly I was surrounded by a white wall of feathers, regal and impenetrable. "Eden, we never thought to see you here," Ariel exclaimed in her warm voice. "Is something wrong? Has something happened to your grandfather?"

"No, everything is—I didn't plan to—"

"She has something to tell you," Gideon said darkly.

Gabriel looked at me, his eyes so blue they challenged the sky. "Not bad news, I hope," he said seriously.

"It's about Jesse," I said.

"Jesse!" Adam exclaimed. "Eden, I know you have a fondness for him, but you must realize—surely—"

The words tumbled out. "He didn't kill my father," I said.

Gabriel's black eyebrows rose. "That seems very unlikely," he said.

Gideon was staring at me. This was the first time I had said the words aloud to him. "If you don't think Jesse did," he said slowly, "who do you think it was?"

"Nonsense," Ariel said briskly. "Eden, I'm sorry for you.

I'm sure you are very distraught. There are many young girls who fell in love with Jesse only to find out he was not what they thought he was. But so many people saw him with your father—and he never once said he did not commit the act—"

"He didn't do it," I said fiercely.

Adam laid a hand on my arm. "Dear Eden," he said softly, "don't let him break your heart."

Gabriel still seemed serious and entirely calm. "Let's ask him," he said.

Which was the first any of the rest of us realized that Jesse had arrived.

He was hovering over the back lawn, spiraling slowly down, and he appeared to be looking for someone—Gabriel, Adam, perhaps even me. Even from this distance, I could see that his face looked haggard, tired from the long journey, but creased with stubbornness. He knew that I was the only person in the world who believed him. He had come here burdened with almost no hope.

I pulled free from Adam's touch and waved wildly. "Jesse!" I called. "Over here!"

He pulled in his wings and slanted in our direction. "How did he get loose?" Ariel demanded. "And why come here? Why not fly somewhere to freedom?"

"I released him," I said. "So he could tell the truth."

Gabriel, who should have been watching the supposed criminal land three feet away, instead still had his eyes on me. "And who do you think killed your father?" he asked.

Jesse answered. "It was Adam," he said.

There was a moment of absolute silence.

There was a moment when everyone spoke at once. Ariel said, "No, he didn't," just as I said, "Adam killed him," just as Jesse added, "I can prove I didn't do it." Gabriel held up his hands to enjoin silence, and everyone subsided.

"This is a grave accusation," Gabriel said, his eyes now on Jesse. "Why should I believe you have not manufactured a charge against another angel just to abate your own punishment?"

"There were people who saw me—that day—who know I could not have been up on the mountaintop when Eden's father was thrown to his death," Jesse said.

"Yes, but Adam would not have done such a thing!" Ariel exclaimed. "To even suggest it—"

"He hated my father," I said. "He was afraid my father would harm the baby."

"And he was probably right!" Ariel replied in a heated voice. "The way your father talked—"

Gabriel silenced her with a gesture. "Am I to understand Joseph Karsh actually threatened the child?"

"Yes," I said. "My father said he wished he'd strangled him when he was first born."

Now Gabriel turned his icy blue eyes in Adam's direction. "You heard him say this?"

For a moment it appeared that Adam could not decide whether to respond with easy laughter or outraged anger. "Yes, I heard him say it," he finally replied, choosing to shrug carelessly and speak lightly. "I was furious at the moment, but was I really afraid of Joseph Karsh? Not at all. And I certainly didn't snatch him from a Monteverde bridge and thrown him into a canyon."

There was something false in the timbre of his voice, something in his words that did not ring true. Whatever it was, Gabriel heard it, too. His blue eyes narrowed and the lines of his face grew more severe. "I do not think we have reached the bottom of this," he said coldly. "When this wedding is over, we must all return to Monteverde and conduct a proper investigation. I do not want the wrong man to be left chained to the mountaintop."

"That man should not be me," Jesse said.

Adam made a quick, violent movement, so unexpected that no one could avoid him. "It will not be me, either!" he cried, snatching me against his body and holding me hard. As the angels stared at him, stupefied, he snarled, "Stand back! Stand back, all of you!" I was too astonished to fight as he dragged me a few paces away, and the others appeared too surprised to move. "I will kill her too if you try to stop me," he hissed. "Don't follow me."

And he pulled me closer against his chest and leapt into the air.

For a moment I was sure we would plunge back to the earth, and I screamed as his grip tightened around my body. His wings beat the air furiously—the sky whirled around my head—the lawn spun dangerously close. And then we were aloft, racing away from the beribboned white tents and the gracious lawns and the crowds of people staring up at us, their drinks still in their hands. The ground fell away alarmingly fast; the cold sky enveloped us in a malicious, eternal wind.

I crushed down my impulse to continue screaming, to wrench my arms free and start beating him around the face and chest. We were so high now that if his grip loosened, I would fall to my death; the less I did to anger him, the better my chance of survival. Which seemed very, very slim in any case. I had no idea where we were flying at such a rapid pace that my lungs hurt and my cheeks were scratched red by the wind. I couldn't imagine that we were bound for any place that would be particularly comfortable for me.

We had been flying for maybe ten minutes when I became aware of a phalanx of angels all around us. I wriggled against Adam's hold to try to get a better look, hope burning painfully in my chest. Yes—to the right of us, Ariel; to the left of us, Gideon. I could barely see Gabriel behind us and Jesse below. Gabriel I knew could outdistance any angel from the three holds, and I thought Gideon, too, could fly faster than Adam. But they could not knock him from the sky, or try to crowd him off his course, for fear of the harm he might do to me. So they paced beside him, silent, implacable escorts, ready to follow him to the very edge of the world.

Which, I soon realized, was exactly where we were heading.

I smelled the salt breeze before I saw the ocean, wild and wind-whipped here at the northern tip of Samaria. I couldn't control a small shriek as Adam passed over the last promontory of land and kept on flying, heading out into the infinite, unmarked territory of the sea. Dearest god, sweetest Jovah, he was going to fling me into the ocean, from which no angel could rescue me; he was going to cast me into the raging and boundless sea. Now I did begin struggling, panic making me stupid, whimpering against his chest. He merely clutched me so tightly that I could not breathe and continued flying.

We were miles and miles over the ocean, so far that I could not believe there was still land behind us. There was only water, icy and black, and sky, remote and blue. He flew so far that there was nothing in the world but ocean, and then he opened his arms and let me fall.

I screamed and fell into an angel's arms. Still falling, down and down, the water rushing up so fast that it seemed to be lunging for us. We fell so far that his wingfeathers tore through the waves, lashing up a spray of foam. I screamed again, and saltwater spit across my tongue.

And then we were rising, slowly, agonizingly, breaking free of the sucking hunger of the sea. I sobbed and flung my arms around the angel's neck. I felt him press a kiss into my hair as he reached a safe altitude above the rocking sea.

"Look," he said, but I had not needed to hear his voice to know that the angel who held me was Jesse. "Watch now."

I lifted my head and followed his gaze. There were still four angels flying farther out to sea, but the one in the forefront had increased both his lead and his altitude. Indeed, now he seemed to be climbing higher and higher, as if he

had given up his race across the water and instead had decided to flee toward the sun. The three trailing angels had
slowed down, pulled back, refused to follow his ascension.
"Watch," Jesse whispered against my ear.

And as I watched, Adam folded his wings back, angled his
head down and made a sharp, graceful, perfect dive into the
sea. The water washed over him and left no trace. No one, not
even the scolding gulls, could wring out a cry of horror.

WE found, when we returned to the Lesh property, that the
wedding had been postponed. I think even Adar Lesh felt
the events unfolding around her were more exciting than
the vows she was about to take. Gabriel brushed past the
bride's father and the clamoring crowd of Manadavvi and escorted Jesse and Ariel and Gideon and me into a private
room inside the house.

"Now," he said, in a voice there was no gainsaying, "the
entire story, please."

It was quickly told and soberly received. "You're a fool,"
Gabriel commented when Jesse explained why he had not
defended himself to begin with.

Jesse shrugged. "I didn't expect to be believed. Least of
all by Eden."

Gabriel's eyes, blue and inescapable, once again were
turned on me. "Yes, her part in this is most extraordinary. I
suppose she has found a way to explain to you why she
trusted you when no one else did."

Jesse was grinning. "Yes, angelo."

Gabriel nodded. "You will come to the Eyrie, both of
you, for a time," he said. "Eden, it is clear you will be spending more of your days with angels in the future, so you must
get more used to us. Jesse—I know no other way to apologize than by making every effort to get to know you now, to
learn about strengths that I have heretofore failed to see."

"I have managed to conceal them from almost everyone," Jesse said wryly.

"That time is past," the Archangel said. "Gideon, tell our host that we will be ready to see this wedding go forward in a matter of moments. Ariel, do you own something more appropriate that Eden could wear? Allow me to be the one to tell the story of today's events. The rest of you"—and here he actually smiled as if amused—"drink a few glasses of wine and try to enjoy the day."

Jesse put his arms around me, and then, like a waft of enchantment, his wings. "That, angelo, will be easy to do."

Gabriel was still smiling. "A few moments," he warned. "And the wedding proceeds."

At that, he escorted Ariel and his grinning son from the room. I turned into Jesse's embrace and we explained, in gestures more detailed than words, what sort of terror we had endured that day. He had saved my life, and the only coin I had to pay him with was a kiss; I had rescued him from ignominy and disgrace, and a kiss was what he used to settle his debt. Paid in full—the account most satisfactorily settled.

That day, when an angel kissed me, I didn't know exactly what my future held, but I knew that my life had changed forever.

An Elegy for Melusine

CLAIRE DELACROIX

Chapter One

THEY are not the audience I would have chosen, but I have few choices left these days. If naught else, I have learned to make do with what I am granted—that lesson, apparently, will serve me to the end.

So be it.

I watch them from a narrow window, awaiting my moment. They are more like birds than women, these two, their elaborate garb reminiscent of the fine plumage of birds in courtship. They twitter like starlings, they cackle like hens, they rustle their skirts and huddle together. I suspect from their foolish chatter that they are no more clever than the doves in the rafters.

In my time, they would have never survived childhood.

In this time, they are the ornaments of wealthy men, truly no better than peacocks upon gilded chains. For their own sake, I hope their husbands get children upon them shortly. Such women do not fare well once they have been savored but failed to satisfy.

But then, my children caused all my woes.

The pair halt upon the threshold and peer into the shadows of the old stone castle. I try to see the place with their eyes, not gilded with memories of mine. There is moss on these floors of fitted stone, and undoubtedly there are mice in the dry brown vestiges of the fragrant herbs that had once been thickly strewn about here and there. The merry trickle of water echoes from somewhere within the walls, water that has almost certainly invited itself in through a nook somewhere. A rogue beam of sunlight shines through the broken roof and sets the dust motes to dancing within it. Real doves twitter in the half-rotted rafters, hidden by the shadows of what remains of the roof.

But still, there is grace in the keep's proportions and majesty in its very size. There is elegance in the arches embellished with a mason's carving. The beauty of this abode can still be found here by those with eyes to see.

This pair has no such eyes.

"Is this not terrifying, Marie?" whispers one, her eyes wide.

"Blanche, we have entered the castle of Melusine!" says the other. They cling to each other, shiver elaborately, then step into the keep's darkness together.

I barely restrain my sneer. What fools they are! I tread behind them, clinging to the shadows, loathing every word they utter. I debate my prospects but they are few. I have faded too far and weakened too much.

This pair will have to suffice.

"It is hundreds of years old," whispers Blanche, the timid one.

"And said to have been built in a week, for all of that." The one called Marie looks about herself with what might be awe.

"By Melusine," they intone together. The sound of that familiar name upon mortal lips makes me smile.

"How could your Bernard even think of destroying it?" asks Blanche, rapping her companion on her sleeve with a fan made of peacock feathers.

"He says he will build me a larger and finer keep," says Marie, lifting her young chin with a pride that will undoubtedly betray her one day. "He says it will be more luxurious even than Toussèvres."

Blanche's eyes narrow tellingly and I guess that she is the lady of this Toussèvres. Blanche walks farther ahead, the amity between the pair somewhat destroyed by these competitive comments. They make their way through what had once been the great hall, their trailing skirts stirring the dust.

"Melusine could see the future because she was a demon," says Blanche as they carefully lift their skirts and climb the mossy steps.

Marie clears her throat, unwilling to be outdone. "Indeed, she knew how to save Raymond's reputation after he accidentally killed his liege lord. She only did so to ensure the success of her dark scheme."

Now they compete over the details of the history of this castle, each vying to recall more than the other. The result sounds like argumentative starlings or willful jays.

"She built his name, and the repute of his home, and gave him ten sons to further spread his fame," says Blanche. "The great crusading family Lusignan issued from Mère Lusine, or Melusine."

"Her grandson was King of Jerusalem."

"Her son was King of Sicily."

They pause at the crest of the stairs and I will them to choose the arch to their right. They do so, granting me no small satisfaction that my powers yet linger, though in truth, there was half a chance they would have chosen it at any rate.

They barely spare a glance to the carving upon the lintel, so laden is it with grime and dust. I know it well enough to see the long current of a woman's hair, the sweet ripeness of her young breasts, the powerful coil of her serpent tail. I reach up and brush it with my aged fingertips as I pass beneath it.

Their steps falter on the threshold of the room into which I passionately wish them to go. Perhaps some old potency lingers here—it certainly does for me.

I cannot enter this chamber without hesitation, even now, and it is not one that I enter of my own volition. I know, though, that it is the proper place to share this tale for the last time.

Indeed, it is the only place that will suffice.

"Do you think it was here?" asks Blanche in a whisper.

Marie nods. She takes a deep breath and crosses the threshold. Curiosity about the mark reputed to be upon the sill draws them. They halt before the window, look down and shiver in truth.

There is no sunlight in this chamber, as the sole window faces north. I can see the deadened branches of the forest through its arch, the last vestiges of snow beneath the dark boughs, the roiling blue-gray clouds of a storm gathering in the distance. I had oft thought that one could see to eternity through this window, that detail forgotten until this moment.

My throat tightens with a hundred bittersweet memories, too painful to ponder, too precious to forget.

Blanche reaches out a tentative fingertip to the shape of a woman's foot, apparently carved in the gray stone of the sill. "But Melusine was a demon, a devil disguised as a beauteous woman."

"*La Belle Dame Sans Merci.*"

"She had a heart of stone. She beguiled Raymond, to better work her witchery upon the world." Blanche glances about herself, perhaps sensing that they are not alone.

"She made him vow to never look upon her on a Saturday, when she took her bath, because it was then that her true nature was revealed." Marie seems to take a grim delight in the details. "It was then that she reverted to a serpent from the waist down and a woman from the waist upward."

"It is said that every son she bore him had an unholy flaw."

Marie nods. "Geoffroi Great Tooth, born with an enormous tooth."

"Horrible, born with his third eye between the other two."

Marie lifts a finger. "Save Fromont, the sole normal son and his father's pride."

"Until Fromont took his monastic vows, and Geoffroi slaughtered him, burning the monastery to the ground and killing all the monks, not only his brother. And Melusine defended his wickedness."

"So Raymond, who had spied once upon his lady, denounced her before his entire court. He called her what she was and blamed her for bearing him such a monster of a son."

"'*Most false serpent!*'" the two women cry together, the condemnation sending a shiver to my very marrow.

"He denounced her as the demon that she was and cast her out, as she so rightly deserved," says Blanche with such satisfaction that I long to do her injury.

"She stepped on the sill and took flight as a winged serpent, woman no more because her evil scheme had been discovered."

The pair lean on the sill and look out over the deadened forest. "And she was doomed to remain in that form until Judgment Day." Blanche clutches her heart while Marie crosses herself.

"Mercifully, no such demons walk among us any longer,"

says Blanche. They eye each other, neither wanting to be the first to suggest that they leave.

I conjure the form of an old woman as my vehicle, not caring what it costs me, and step from the protective cloak of the shadows. I feel the very moment their gazes land upon me, as surely as a touch.

"That is not precisely how I recall the tale," I say, and truly, I enjoy how they jump backward in their alarm.

"Old woman! Who are you and how did you find yourself here?" Blanche demands. She snaps open that fan of peacock feathers and fans herself furiously, as if she was merely surprised to find a trespasser upon her husband's lands, not afraid.

"Have pity," I say. "I am but a good woman who seeks shelter from the forest within these old walls."

"But you would challenge our story?" asks Marie. I see now that her face is sharp and avarice gleams in her eyes. She is shrewd perhaps, rather than clever. She will be unattractive soon, for greed has a way of stretching a woman too taut to be pleasing.

"I said only that it was not the tale that I recall." I feign need, as it will soften them. I cringe as if fearing they might strike me and stretch out a gnarled hand to entreat. "I would but share my version of the tale of Melusine, share it for a crust of bread."

The women exchange the arch glance that the wealthy so oft share in the presence of poverty. Yet more intriguingly, they are convinced that they will never be less than affluent, that the gods will play no tricks upon them.

I decide it is not worth the trouble to peer into their futures to discern the truth. The sharpness of Marie's features and the flatness of both their bellies tells me enough.

"Of course," says Blanche, settling on to the bench beneath the window and arranging her skirts.

"I see no harm in such indulgence," says Marie. She

arches a brow. "Though I cannot imagine what difference you can make to the tale. It is so well-known, after all."

"Your version of it is well-known, that I will not dispute," I say. "But it was not always told thus. It was not always believed that Raymond unveiled and foiled Melusine's dark scheme." I hold up my hands, knowing that with this single detail I have their attention in thrall. "Once it was recounted that it was her love for him that proved her undoing."

"Oooo! Tell us!" cries Blanche, her eyes shining.

Marie arranges her skirts with care, preparing herself to be entertained by her inferior. Her smile is condescending. "Tell us the tale that you know, old woman."

I begin the tale with ease, for I know it and its beginning as well as I know my own name.

SO much had been foretold, but of Raymond's beauty, Melusine had had no warning.

She had known that his steed would be a dappled stallion. She had known that he would be garbed in fine mail, and that his tabard would be the blue of sapphires. She had known that his insignia would be a dolphin, that it would be embroidered in white upon that tabard, that it would similarly embellish his red shield beneath an annulet, that open circle signifying that Raymond was the fifth son of the Count of Forez.

Melusine had expected that her quarry would be riding from the hunt, that his blade would be stained with the blood of his patron, that he would arrive at the very hour that Venus cleared the horizon on the night that the moon waxed full. She had seen all of this in her dreams.

Every detail conformed to what she had been told to anticipate, yet still the sight of Raymond de Poitou nigh stopped her heart.

She had not known that a mortal man could be wrought so well.

Melusine was not accustomed to being startled by mortals. Mortals, particularly mortal men, were slow of wit and heavily wrought. They were earthbound, concerned only with what they could see and hold, distrustful of the glimmers of the world Melusine called her own. They smelled of blood and flesh and earth, which was as revolting a combination as might be imagined. As a rule, mortals were as alluring as a creature one might find in the damp shadows beneath a stone.

This knight was handsome, as if he were indeed fey, and he was distraught, as if all the merit of the world was lost. Even more curious, the revulsion she always felt when she came in contact with mortals was absent. Against her every instinct, Melusine was intrigued.

Raymond had discarded his helm, and the trails of his tears were evident. His hair was dark, as dark as obsidian, thick and wavy. He was tanned, his flesh a vigorous golden hue uncommon to the fey yet attractive. He was much taller than she and wrought as well as a mortal man could be wrought.

He rode directly past Melusine and her sisters, no more than an arm's length away. The fey trio drew back instinctively, though they had not yet chosen to step through the veil to the realm of mortals.

Raymond halted at the fountain just beyond them, but only because his exhausted horse refused to continue. The stallion halted, sides heaving, and planted his heavy feet stubbornly against the soil.

"Onward!" cried Raymond. In apparent oblivion of his master's command, the steed bent his head and drank. "Hoy! Jupiter, run!" He tugged the reins, dug his spurs into the stallion's sides, all to no avail.

The horse drank, unhurriedly and with great satisfaction.

"And why should my fortune change now?" Raymond shouted. He shook his fist at the sky, then buried his face in his hands and surrendered fully to his despair.

He wept as only a man unaccustomed to shedding tears can weep, as only a man who believed himself alone could surrender to his unhappiness.

Melusine had never seen a man—mortal or fey—weep, no less weep as if his heart was rent beyond repair. Warrior's tears were potent for their rarity.

His grief puzzled her. She had never anticipated that Raymond would regret the deed he had been fated to do. He was fated to kill his uncle and benefactor, and she had assumed that was because Count Aimery's death was his unspoken desire. Thus, she had felt no qualms at proposing a bargain with him, one that would serve to the advantage of both of them.

Her determination faltered that Raymond should be so vulnerable as this, that he should be so troubled by what he could not have changed. Was it just to make a wager with a man so distraught?

Her sisters drew closer, doubtless intrigued that she hesitated. They were as vipers, these two, and quick to mark a shortcoming.

"Why do you linger? This is your chance, bold sister," whispered Melior.

"He is comely enough for a mortal, after all," said Palestine, the malice in her tone revealing that she would have willed it otherwise.

"Show us how readily the curse can be broken, you who are responsible for its infliction."

"You both joined me in our deed," Melusine reminded them.

"It was *your* idea to avenge our mother thus," said Melior.

"Our father broke his pledge," Melusine said. "The Fates decreed that retribution must be made."

"And yet Melusine, bold enough to enforce the will of the Fates, is afraid of this mere mortal?" Palestine's words were mocking.

Melior gave Melusine a nudge in the direction of the mortal realm. "Has your valor failed you, Melusine?"

"Show us how the release from our mother's curse is won, Sister," said Palestine. "If you dare."

Melusine had never been able to suffer a challenge. She slipped through the barrier of the fey realm and approached her salvation.

They would make a wager, she and Raymond, just as had been foretold, and she knew already who would gain the most. No matter what he chose, Raymond's terms would last solely his lifetime, a mere blink of the eye for Melusine.

While she would possess her heart's desire for all eternity.

The price, to her thinking, was fair.

THERE was blood upon Raymond's tabard in greater quantity than Melusine had noted earlier. It was Count Aimery's blood that dripped from his scabbard, dripped as if Raymond had sheathed his blade without cleaning it. His sword was obviously fine, graced with an elaborate hilt and a gem as a pommel. His oversight more clearly showed his anguish, for Melusine knew the reverence in which mortal men held their weapons.

Compassion touched her own heart, though she could not indulge in such weakness. She had her own freedom to win and Raymond was no more than the means to her goal.

"And what manner of man does not grant a courteous greeting to ladies?" Melusine asked with a levity she did not feel.

Raymond started, then stared at her as if she were a figment suddenly manifest before his eyes.

And Melusine was startled in turn. His eyes were an uncommonly vivid blue, the hue of the sky where dusk touches the darkness, where the stars first become visible.

They could have been fey eyes, wrought of a patch of that starlit sky. His tan made his eyes seem an even more vibrant blue. His lashes were long and dark, his features striking.

Her heart skipped in a most unusual manner.

Melusine smiled and glanced back to her sisters, who had also slipped through the veil. They were adorned as fine ladies at a king's court now, jewels sparkling on their brows and at their throats.

Melusine raised a hand as if sharing a jest, letting laughter fill her words. "Truly, the manners of men have become sorry, indeed, if a fine knight cannot grace three noblewomen with a fair greeting."

Her sisters laughed. "What dire course the world does pursue," Melior said.

"How sad," Palestine pouted, "when men cannot hail ladies with good grace."

Raymond looked between the three of them, clearly astounded. "But I was alone," he murmured. He shook his head, like a man awakening from a dream, then fixed his gaze upon Melusine. "It is the midst of the night, in the midst of the forest. How do you come to be here—and why?"

"I could ask the same of you, sir."

Raymond frowned, wiped his eyes, then doffed his gloves. His manner was polite but cool. "My apologies, lady, for my oversight. I assumed myself to be alone in the wilderness." He made to turn away, making it clear that solitude was his choice.

Melusine caught his sleeve in her fingertips. "And yet you are not alone."

That sapphire gaze lingered upon her and Melusine guessed that he was shrewd. Indeed, his expression changed slightly, perhaps with the realization that the otherworld touched his own. He was not a common mortal, this one. "Where am I?"

Melusine spread her hands to indicate the glade around them. "At a spring in the forest, one which my sisters and I choose to frequent."

"Upon whose lands do we stand?"

"These lands are soon to be claimed by one Raymond, presently a knight sworn to the service of Poitou and fifth son of the Count of Forez." She watched as he started visibly. "He is destined to be Lord of Lusignan."

His eyes narrowed. "You know my name."

Melusine inclined her head in acknowledgement. "It was foretold that you would arrive here at this time, Raymond of Poitou." She met his gaze steadily, covertly grasping his steed's reins. "The Fates decreed that you would arrive here without your patron and liege lord, Count Aimery, Lord of Poitou, as well as why that would be." She dropped her gaze pointedly to his stained scabbard.

"You cannot know the truth!"

"Your own blade confirms it."

Raymond took note of the blood upon his scabbard and garb, perhaps for the first time, then recoiled. He inhaled sharply and might have ridden away, but Melusine gripped the reins fast.

"How can you know of this deed?" he demanded, even as he tried to work the leather from her grip. Melusine held fast. His voice caught, thick with that grief again. "How could any soul have foretold it? I meant him no harm! Aimery was my patron, my friend. I would have harmed myself afore him!"

Melusine saw the scene then in her mind's eye, saw it with startling clarity. "Anger betrayed you, as it has before," she said. "You meant to strike the boar, you meant to save your lord from certain death. But in your vigor, you struck Count Aimery instead of the wild beast."

His eyes widened, their color pronounced in his fear of her. His whisper was hoarse. "How can you know this?"

"I know much of you, Raymond of Poitou, including how you can see this matter resolved to your own advantage."

"It will be resolved by my death, which is hardly to my advantage," he said bitterly. "No one will believe my tale, though it is true. Am I not the Count's nephew? There are no witnesses of my innocence save the Count and the boar."

"Did Aimery not tell you what he saw in the stars this evening?"

"You cannot know what he said to me." There was less conviction in his tone than previously.

"He told you that he could not understand the evidence before his own eyes," Melusine continued. "He told you that a man who killed his benefactor this night would gain wealth beyond belief, though that made little sense to him."

The knight paled.

"Do you think your lord, Aimery, was the only one gifted to read the stars? Their message is clear indeed."

Raymond regained a measure of his composure, though still he was uncertain. "Who are you in truth?"

"I am the one come to grant you your heart's desire."

He looked at her, truly looked at her, and his gaze was hard. "You are fey," he said, snapping the reins from her grip and gathering them as if that was sufficient cause to end their discussion. Melusine neither confirmed nor denied his guess, though her silence clearly displeased him. "Your wager has a dark price, of this I have no doubt." He cast a suspicious glance over the glade, then crossed himself. "God only knows where I have found myself this night."

"You have found the aid that you desperately need this night, no more than that." At his arch glance, any lie regarding her nature died upon Melusine's lips. "I would make a bargain with you, for there is something I desire of you and something you can grant to me. The price will not be so foul as you dread."

He hesitated.

Melusine saw more than she would have wished to see in his magnificent eyes. She saw that grief was not new to Raymond, nor was misfortune, and that distrust was a mantle he had learned to assume. She felt a sudden kinship with him, a dawning sense that it had been no accident that he had been chosen for her.

"Are you so anxious to be convicted and killed as that?" she whispered. She peered within his heart and was disappointed to find a typical desire lurking there. "I can see you wealthy, as you yearn to be, with a fine estate and no taint upon your name."

"In exchange for what?"

"Marriage and fidelity."

"Who is your father?"

"The King of Albion," she said, for it was true. She saw a respect dawn in his eyes. The King of Albion was mortal, of course, and Melusine saw that Raymond's fears of her fey nature were diminished.

Still he was curt, tempted but suspicious. "This, then, is your wager? My aid to you in exchange for your aid to me?"

Melusine nodded, noting how he considered the prospect. "In return for my aid, you must wed me. We must live as man and wife."

A smile touched his lips then, his gaze turning appreciative as it slipped over her. "This then is the sum of it? Marriage?" He chuckled, much amused. "Truly I have lost my wits to have assumed I met a fey woman!"

The twinkle in his eyes was beguiling, indeed. Laughter suited him far better than wariness, and Melusine had an uncharacteristic urge to touch this mortal.

"Perhaps you are but a clever demoiselle," he teased, "one who listens where she should not and uses what she hears to her own advantage."

Melusine granted him a scathing glance. She was insulted that he could so readily think her mortal—no less that her objectives were common and unimportant. The truth of her nature, to her thinking, was abundantly clear to any soul of sense.

She had a measure of temper herself and in this moment, it was riled.

"And it was foretold that you were a man with your wits about you." Melusine pivoted and walked toward her sisters. "Go then, go and meet your death."

Silence told her that she had surprised Raymond. Doubtless he was unaccustomed to women rejecting his charms! She had thought that only the fey were possessed of such pride.

"What of your heart's desire?" Raymond called.

"My heart will craft another." Melusine lied. "I have all eternity to wait, after all." She granted him another cool smile. "You would appear to have much less time to concern yourself with such matters. How rapidly do you think the Count's heir will declare your guilt?"

Raymond swore with astonishing vigor and she glimpsed the fury of his temper. Melusine turned her back upon the sight, unafraid, and strode back to her watchful sisters.

She was not surprised when she heard Raymond dismount, not surprised to hear his steps fast behind her, not surprised when he seized her elbow and spun her to face him.

His touch sent such sparks through her that she gasped. He was indeed taller than she was, and his smile was more troubling than she had hoped.

The man meant to charm her, 'twas clear, and Melusine would have preferred if she could have recoiled from his touch. She was confused, for this should have been simple, yet his effect upon her made it complicated, indeed.

She glared at him, too angered by her own response and his surety of it to feign a demure nature she did not possess.

"Tell me more of your wager," he cajoled.

"I see no point in such discussion."

"Perhaps I do."

"Perhaps I do not care."

Raymond chuckled. Melusine caught her breath when he touched her chin, tilting her face so that he could look into her eyes. His charming smile and twinkling eyes undermined her annoyance with him. This mortal had more than a measure of allure, to be sure.

"Tell me," he murmured. "Please."

Melusine took a deep breath, knowing that she had to cede this to him, and looked deliberately across the glade. His touch upon her arm was not as unpleasant as it should have been. Indeed, a tingle emanated from his touch, spreading over her flesh like a wind through the grasses.

"The wager is as I have told you," she said. "The sole constraint I would ask of you, should we agree to make this wager, is that you never look upon me or ask after me on a Saturday."

A frown touched his brow. "Why? What will you do?"

Melusine granted him an exasperated glance. He chuckled at his own folly and shook his head.

So the man could laugh at himself. That was no small thing. Melusine found herself smiling in return.

As they eyed each other, heat was kindled between them. Melusine could smell his flesh and hear the pulse of his blood, but she did not wish to pull away. He traced the curve of her bottom lip with his thumb, an unexpectedly pleasurable caress.

She spoke quickly, breathlessly, to ensure that her terms

were clear to him. "If you make this pledge to me and break it, you will lose everything I have aided you to gain, including your wealth, your land, your fame."

"What of my sons?" Raymond mused, his expression turning mischievous. "There is no merit in wealth and lands without sons to inherit it."

"Sons?" Melusine echoed, horror welling within her.

"Do you not offer my heart's desire? Mine is all you have offered, and sons."

"But . . . but that means that we will have to lie together . . ."

He smiled with that roguish confidence. "Indeed. Is that not a part of marriage?"

Melusine could barely speak. The prospect of being despoiled by a man's seed, of lying beneath him, of blood and semen and sweat, made her feel faint. She could not imagine any fate more vile. But Raymond looked determined. "One son," she suggested.

"Ten. The world is unpredictable, lady."

Ten sons! Ten couplings at least. Melusine could not summon a word to her lips so great was her dismay. She fought the urge to deny him, knowing the price that denial would bear.

Yet she was tempted, dangerously tempted, to grant him his will.

Raymond bent and brushed his lips across her temple. Melusine shivered and glanced up, puzzled anew by his effect upon her.

"I shall endeavor to see you pleasured," he whispered, his breath hot against her cheek. "Upon that you can rely."

Lost in his gaze, Melusine found herself curious. Raymond traced a line along her jaw with his warm fingertip, that seductive mischief in his eyes. For the price of her own salvation, perhaps she could fulfill his yearning for sons.

She nodded, her mouth too dry for speech.

"Are we agreed, then?" he asked, his acceptance so ready that she was surprised. "A holding, ten sons, wealth and no stain upon my name, in exchange for marriage and your privacy each and every Saturday. I would accept your wager, lady, and hold you to your terms, if I might know your name in exchange."

"Melusine," she said, her voice soft and unsteady.

"Melusine," he repeated with satisfaction. Later, she would know that she had been lost in that moment, that his utterance of her name was more potent than the strongest spell. "Lady Melusine, consider your wager made."

Before Melusine could reply, Raymond kissed her to seal their agreement. It was the first kiss Melusine had ever tasted, the first time a mortal had laid his lips upon hers.

The unbearable sweetness of it reassured her that the burden she had accepted would not be too much to bear.

Chapter Two

MELUSINE washed Raymond's blade, his garments and his scabbard in the fountain. The waters eased away the dried stain of the Count's blood, as if it had never been there. Her sisters, meanwhile, cast a fine dust over the trail of blood that marked Raymond's course to the glade. They enjoyed the detail of those ten sons overmuch, to her thinking, and she ignored them.

Indeed, Melusine could think of little beyond her awareness that Raymond stood half-nude near her. The hair upon his chest looked rough and animal to her gaze. His flesh smelled of sweat and blood and carrion. She could taste earth upon her lips. Yet she was drawn to him, as surely as a fish upon a lure, and she could not explain her attraction.

Nor could she explain her agreement to his terms. Ten times his seed would spill within her. Ten times a mortal child would fill her womb. He could not have chosen a detail that would make her more firmly earthbound, more securely fixed in the realm she would spurn.

Could she keep this pledge and not forget all it was to be fey?

Raymond watched her, wary again, perhaps sensing the turmoil of her thoughts. Melusine returned the scabbard and tabard to him, ensuring that their hands did not brush in the transaction. She saw that this displeased him. He dressed with haste, his disgruntled gaze fixed upon her.

He held out his hand for his blade.

Melusine did not relinquish it. "You must trust me fully."

Anger flashed in Raymond's eyes. "Even though you mean to keep my blade, granted to me by my grandfather's own hand? You ask much of me."

"As you expect much from me. You shall have it returned to you in time." Melusine spoke firmly, knowing a warrior would respond to her commanding tone. "Ride now, ride east upon this very path until you reach a wide road. Take it to your right and ride with all speed. You will reach the gates of Poitou with the dawn."

"And then?" Raymond was vexed yet.

"Tell them that Count Aimery has been struck down by a boar."

He shook his head. "They will not believe the tale without his corpse."

"So you shall take them to it. Return upon that very road with a party to retrieve your liege lord, ride upon it until the sun is at its zenith, then look into the forest to your left. Not twenty paces within the forest, you will find your fallen lord."

"There was no road," Raymond said irritably. "We were lost in the thickness of the forest when the boar assaulted us, and lost precisely because there was no road. Your directions are folly!"

"And your pledge to follow my dictate is a thin one."

"You ask me to believe much that is uncommon."

"I am saving you from death," Melusine reminded him. "Much uncommon must occur to achieve such an end."

Raymond glared at her for a long moment, then heaved a sigh. He folded his arms across his chest and smiled ruefully. His anger fled, his mood changing as abruptly as the sun darts out from behind thunderclouds, and Melusine found herself charmed. "I am not accustomed to finding Fortune matching her steps to mine, Melusine."

"I am not Fortune."

His eyes twinkled. "I suspect you are more fair."

Melusine felt herself flush. "You will find Count Aimery's corpse, just as I have bidden."

Raymond nodded slowly, then shoved a hand through his hair. "But there is yet another detail," he said, his tone more reasonable than it had been before. "They will know that I tell a falsehood by the shape of the Count's wound. It was cleanly made by a blade and any fool will discern as much."

"Your trust is meager," Melusine accused quietly. "We shall gain nothing without it."

"No one can change the shape of a wound."

"Have faith. Faith can accomplish much indeed."

Raymond donned his gloves, dissatisfied again. "Be warned that I will see you hung beside me if this strategy fails."

"It will not fail." Melusine saw no reason to tell him the truth, that he would never again find her unless she desired as much. "Go, for the road already begins to fade."

Raymond swung into his saddle, pausing to look down at her. He was concerned now, his mood shifting yet again. Truly, these emotions held mortals in thrall! "When will I see you again?"

"When you have done as you have pledged, and I have

done as I have pledged." She inclined her head to him. "Until then, Godspeed to you."

"That salute will not suffice," he muttered, then bent to catch her nape in his gloved hand. He kissed her deeply then, his tongue slipping between her teeth, his rough caress feeding that newfound desire within Melusine. Indeed, she found herself participating in his embrace with a fervor that should have startled her.

She was breathless when he lifted his head, breathless and flushed. He grinned then, a reckless grin that made her heart skip in a most uncommon fashion.

"*Au revoir,* Lady Melusine." Raymond touched his spurs to his steed and rode into the deep shadows of the forest.

Melusine stood, deaf to her sisters' mockery, staring after Raymond until long after the thunder of the stallion's hoofbeats had faded. She tasted his mortality upon her own lips and marvelled at what she had done.

What had this knight awakened within her?

WHAT fool's wager had he made?

Raymond rode along the road as Melusine had bidden him, guiding a company of the Count's men to some point, he knew not where. Already he had heard the whispers of discontent with his tale of Aimery's demise, and he was well aware that not all believed his innocence.

That the road glimmered slightly just beyond the periphery of his vision did little to reassure him.

He had thought it all a jest. He had thought some pretty demoiselle played a trick upon him—the daughter of the King of Albion, no less—for no living soul could pledge what she had and keep the wager. He had agreed to her terms, not truly expecting that much would come of it.

But the road had been there, just as Melusine had foretold, and it was curious, so curious that Raymond was uneasy. He had followed her dictate for lack of a better tale, though now he wondered at the wisdom of it.

Even now, he could effortlessly summon the recollection of her. Her hair was long and fair and had glinted in the moonlight as if wrought by a silversmith. Her eyes were a green more verdant than the deepest forest pool. He liked her wit. He liked that she did not believe him to be a fool. He liked how she tasted, so sweet and fragrant that he had half believed she had not been truly before him.

Had he ever seen a demoiselle so fair? He should have credited his initial thought that she was fey. He should not have been so readily persuaded to grant his pledge. In her absence, he fretted as he had been incapable of doing in her presence. The rippling ribbon of fairy road beneath his steed's hooves taunted him.

What if she had lied to him? The fey were known to do as much, especially to win their way in some wager.

What if Aimery's corpse was not as Melusine had declared it would be? What would he tell his fellows then? They would think him deceitful or cunning. Aimery's son Guillaume rode in the company and Raymond knew that his own future rested in the hands of the Count's heir.

What would he do, where would he go, if Guillaume cast him out? There was no doubt that Guillaume would not suffer a traitor in his hall, or even the man who had forgotten the location of Aimery's corpse.

Raymond could not decide whether it would be worse to find all as Melusine had foretold. What dark powers did she hold within her grip, if she could so change the world at will?

What manner of bride would he find in his bed if he kept his vow? Sweat beaded upon his brow and a cold trickle of dread meandered down his spine, though the day was temperate.

He knew when it was midday, though not by the angle of

the sun. Nay, there was a prickling at his nape, a conviction that he was watched, and indeed, the fey road seemed to fade ahead of their party. Raymond looked to the left of the path and—to his relief and trepidation—did see something within the woods.

"Here," he said, his voice husky as it seldom was. His finger shook as he pointed. The men led their steeds into the undergrowth, some dismounting to stride through the thicket. Raymond did not lead the way, though he found Guillaume fast beside him.

"This must be difficult for you, old friend," the Count's son said quietly. "To return to the site of an ordeal is a challenge for the most stalwart warrior. I know the regard that you had for my father."

Raymond said nothing, letting Guillaume think what he would. It was worse, in many ways, that Guillaume was determined to think well of him. They had grown up together and for the first time, Raymond found the younger man's admiration of him an undeserved and unwelcome burden.

The men shouted. "It is our lord, the Count!"

Raymond hastened forward, anxious to see the truth. It was Aimery, just as he had fallen, in the same garb and the same pose, and an entirely different place. Aimery was just as dead as he had been when Raymond had left him, and the knight felt his grief wash over him again. There was no hint that Aimery had been moved, and indeed, when they rolled his corpse over, the ground was stained beneath his body with his blood.

As the ground had been where he truly fell. 'Twas impossible, yet before his own eyes all the same. Raymond crossed himself, gooseflesh dancing over him as he watched. He did not wish to see, yet he could not look away.

The men peered beneath Aimery's body, grimacing at the wound, and Raymond feared that he would be unveiled as the liar he was.

"What a monster that boar must have been," declared one man. "Look at the damage wrought by its tusks. The wounds are so wide and so far apart."

"So deep," whispered another and shuddered.

"You should not look upon it, my lord," the first counseled Guillaume, who had paled. "Your father had no chance of survival."

Stunned, Raymond stepped forward to see. There were indeed two wounds where once there had been one, and both were ragged as if wrought by tusks and not a sword. He crossed himself again, his gaze rising to the woods.

"Praise be to Aimery," murmured the first man, echoing Raymond's gesture. "May his soul rest in peace." The men all crossed themselves and spontaneously recited the *Paternoster*.

Raymond's flesh prickled all the while. Melusine was here. He knew it well. She lingered to see the result of what she had wrought and he could not hide his fear of her and what she had done.

What price for this feat would she demand of him in truth?

"The boar!" one of the squires shouted from a distance.

All of the men pivoted, fearing in that moment that they were under assault.

"The dead boar is here!" cried the boy again. A ripple of relief passed through the company. The men trudged toward the boy, Raymond among them, and one whistled at the size of the boar.

It was the same beast, he would have wagered his life upon it. It had been larger than most, uglier than most, and blessed with a rare abundance of fur. But instead of raging and snorting as it had when he had seen it last, the boar was dead. Its eyes were yet open, those distinctive eyes. Even in death, one remained angry red and one silver gray.

Raymond bent and touched its flesh, needing to be certain. "It is truly dead," he marvelled.

"Aye, and it is a veritable monster," said one man. "This one may haunt your dreams for a long while, Raymond. I have never seen the like of him."

"It must have been overwhelmed by its battle with Aimery." The other men nodded agreement, several commenting on the length and thickness of the beast's tusks.

"We had best make a meal of it," said Guillaume. "There will be hundreds come for Father's funeral and we will have need of all the meat we can muster. Perhaps this flesh will be sweet in exchange for the high price it commanded." He snapped his fingers, tending his duty despite his obvious dismay. Boys hastened to do his bidding.

As the boar was lifted, a gasp echoed through the company. Raymond took a step back and blanched.

Melusine had told no lie, though she returned his blade in a most uncommon manner. It was plunged completely into the boar, the jewelled hilt gleaming in the dappled sunlight.

Raymond swallowed, astonished. The other men clearly recognized the blade, for they hooted.

"Praise be that Raymond was with our lord!"

"You are modest, indeed, my old friend," Guillaume said, his voice hoarse. "You said nothing of this brave deed."

Another man gripped Raymond's shoulder. "It takes a rare spirit to face such a fiend, especially in the defense of another."

It was upon Raymond's lips to deny that he had ever done as much, but the entire company murmured assent. They clapped him upon the shoulder, gruffly congratulating him for his valor, and the moment for honesty was passed.

Indeed, with his blade as it was, a denial would have been beyond credibility.

"I did not know for certain that the beast had died," he said as he bowed his head.

"I thank you, for dispensing justice in my stead." Guillaume glanced between Aimery and the boar. "My father was well served to have a man like you pledged to his hand." He embraced Raymond, tears glistening in his eyes, and Raymond felt a fraud.

The others assumed, of course, that he was modest. He was surrounded and congratulated yet again. The others carried away the dead boar, still chattering about his valor.

Raymond lingered where the boar had fallen, his grip tightening and loosing on his stained but recovered blade. He had not merely been absolved of the killing of his uncle but hailed as a hero.

It was beyond expectation.

It was precisely as Melusine had foretold.

It was a lie. His own memory of events caught in his throat. He had tried to defend Aimery, but he had not succeeded. The praise of his fellows felt tainted for he knew himself to be unworthy.

His gaze fell upon Aimery's corpse, now being lifted to a bier to be carried back to court. Raymond looked at the blood stains upon the ground. He had lost a comrade and a patron, a friend whose loss would not easily be filled. He turned and retched into the undergrowth of the forest himself, spitting with vigor when he straightened. He wiped his blade upon the leaves and returned it to his scabbard, then wiped his face with both hands.

He would never have willingly injured his patron, not for all the gold in Christendom. Though Melusine might grant him his heart's desire, the price was too high.

He cast a glance over his shoulder, still aware of Melusine's presence. "This is a foul way to make any earthly gain," he whispered unsteadily. "I rescind my agreement. I will not benefit from my lord's loss. I break with our wager, let your vengeance be what it may."

He might have departed then, but Melusine appeared so

suddenly that he was taken aback. She might have stepped through a curtain, but there was no curtain in these woods.

Raymond knew then with whom he bargained.

"Demon!" he whispered, uncertain the others could see her though they might hear him. He crossed himself with vigor, then walked away, not sparing her another glance.

The men mounted and urged their steeds back to the road. Raymond noted that the road shimmered even more than previously and that it had faded completely beyond this point. He guessed that none would ever be able to find the site of Count Aimery's demise again. They would make legends of it, they would tell tales of Raymond's valor, and Raymond alone would know the truth of it among men. Fame would be his, but it would be based upon a lie.

When he died, he might well gain a kind of immortality, snared as he would be within the tales of his fellows.

The prospect sickened him.

Perhaps, if he prayed fervently enough, if he avoided the forest, Melusine herself might not be able to insist upon collecting what he had promised. In her absence, he knew he could be resolute.

Perhaps he had best leave Poitiers.

Soon.

MELUSINE nigh roared with frustration. She could not pursue Raymond, not now, though she knew he meant to spurn her and their wager. The taste of the earth was upon her tongue and she felt the familiar shiver beginning in her very bones.

The sun was already lowering to the horizon and the morrow was Saturday. Melusine had an obligation she could not evade, one that could not be forgotten, one that would not be denied.

She hastened to a forgotten corner of the forest where her

shame would not be witnessed. One day per week, the portal to the world she preferred was barred against her. Her curse trapped her in the wretched mortal world while it wrought its price. It was a painful reminder of her fate if she could not break the curse.

Melusine was so tired from her labors of this day that she barely made her refuge in time.

The change came with the shuddering vigor that always took her by surprise. She fought it, struggling against its wickedness as always she did. Her effort made no difference—it never did. The silvery touch of moonlight only made the change more horrific, though she had never had the fortune to metamorphose in the dark.

It was a detail of the curse, wrought by her own mother, that Melusine must witness the price of her deed.

And witness it, she did. No living soul could have torn her gaze away from the unnatural change, no less its relentless speed.

The scales first appeared upon her hips. They grew upon her flesh with startling vigor, like a gleaming pestilence spreading before her very eyes. Even as they claimed her flesh and replaced her skin, her legs were drawn together by a force she could not deny. Her thighs and shins were sealed each to the other, then changed shape, becoming one thick tail. That tail grew as quickly as lightning could strike, coiling in the water where her feet had been just heartbeats before, thick and serpentine.

It was agony to endure and Melusine grit her teeth. Her legs might have been sliced to ribbons from hip to toe, for the vigor of the pain. Her flesh might have been flailed to a pulp, for the fire that burned the length of it. She was singed, she was changed, she was wrought anew in an alien guise. The scales gleamed once her tail was formed, shone in the moonlight, arranged in stripes of argent and azure.

And through it all, she tasted earth. The dark secrets of

the soil were upon her tongue, the mysteries of the chthonic
mortal world itself. She knew the terminus of every tunnel,
the locale of every snake and newt and mole, the destination
of every root. She knew the secrets of death and regenera-
tion, she held the keys to Hades and to Hell, she could have
swum the river Styx. She could have summoned a mortal
soul back from the dead.

Melusine rejected all of it. The earth was not part of the
fey world she knew and loved. The fey lived in air and water
and left earth and flame to mortals. She was half-mortal,
'twas true, and this curse had been wrought to remind her of
her crime against her mortal father; but she would not accept that legacy willingly.

The mortal world was inflicted upon her and foreign, and
though she must endure it, she would never welcome it or
allow that there was any merit in its presence. She would
step into that world, for as long as she was compelled to do
so, but only to win eternity in the domain she loved.

And in the end, she would be rid of this tail. Raymond
would have his castle and his wealth and his ten sons, and
she would have a freedom that would endure long after he
had rejoined the earth.

She must persuade Raymond to her cause. She could not
be trapped within the mortal world for all of eternity, she
could not accept such an exile.

Melusine touched her lips, which still burned from his
kiss, and simmered with anxiety to see him again.

BEFORE Sunday's dawn touched the horizon, Melusine realized that she was no longer alone. She jumped in alarm, her
tail swishing in the pool, then her mother's chuckle sounded.

"Fear not, daughter mine. It is only me."

Melusine had learned well enough to fear her mother, or
at least her mother's wrath. She settled cautiously into the

water as her mother appeared on the bank before her, studying the older woman for some hint of her mood.

Presine seemed merry enough, which was perhaps a warning in itself.

"Have you come to gloat?" Melusine asked. "Or to ensure that your curse is effective?"

"I know my curses to be effective." Presine waved a hand, conjuring a stone bench behind herself. She sat down and met her daughter's gaze. "It is my lessons that oft prove evasive. Have you learned anything?"

"Solely that my mother is as a viper when defied, and beyond reason with regard to my father."

"You three should not have imprisoned him in a mountain."

"He should not have broken his pledge to you! Did he not vow to never look upon you in childbirth?" Melusine folded her arms across her chest and glared at her mother. "Though you were too weak to demand compense for his crime, I am not."

Her mother tilted her head to regard her and spoke softly. "What of forgiveness?"

"What of the honor of keeping one's word?"

Presine shook her head. "You have learned little as yet, I see, but perhaps that will change in time."

"What is that to mean?"

"That forgiveness has its place, as does love. We fey have little use for such emotions, and, indeed, we believe that mortals can teach us little that we do not know. Their very mortality, though, makes them value life as we do not."

The day had been long and chilly, and her thoughts had been plagued by the recollection of Raymond's burning touch. Melusine feared that she was softening to mortals, just as her mother had, but she feared the import of that even more. Thus, she spoke with greater impatience than she should have done. "I value my life, and value it more when I am not plagued by this tail."

"You are not fully fey, daughter mine, and that tail should remind you as much once a week."

"Half-fey is sufficient by the old laws to live as fully fey."

Presine nodded acknowledgement. "But the half you have from your father cannot be so readily forgotten as that. Had you not retaliated against him, you would have become fully mortal. Mortal blood is stronger than fey blood and takes dominance over time."

"No! You never told us as much!"

Presine's smile was wry. "I doubted that you would appreciate the revelation."

"Then I am glad indeed that I took the vengeance you refused to take, for I would be fully fey, for all time."

"Would you?" Presine shook her head, then looked up at the last of the stars. "Our time passes, Melusine, and soon there will be no place for us. The realms of fey and mortal draw apart, and the thread that holds them in tether together frays a little farther with every passing day. It will snap, not long from now, though the exact day cannot be named. Once it does break, I suspect that the fey realm will be all the paler for its isolation."

"I have heard naught of this."

Presine shrugged. "Nonetheless, it is true. You can see the evidence of it in the scorn of men for us and our realm, in their disregard for our powers. Ensure that you choose your realm before that fateful day, for there will be no passing between the worlds from that day hence."

With that, her mother disappeared. Melusine wished she could follow her through the veil and demand more details, but her tail kept her prisoner in this world.

Her mother's warning made Melusine anxious. She knew full well where she would choose to spend eternity, though now she could not be certain that she would have sufficient time to break her curse. She watched the sun rise with impatience, for she had much to accomplish. She had a wedding to arrange, and ten sons to bear, as quickly in succession as possible.

But first, she had a man's heart to win.

RAYMOND knelt in the chapel, clutching the vial of holy water he had requested from the priest. It was no credit to him that he had crafted a lie to win the priest's agreement to this, but a man had to do what was necessary to protect himself.

The bells had ceased their ringing, the faithful had been summoned and the priest had begun the procession when Raymond had the sense that something was awry.

He felt a ripple in the air, a parting of the clouds of incense, a slight chill touch the back of his neck. He glanced back covertly, narrowing his eyes against the shine of thousands of candles in the shadows.

A woman stood in the portal, wrapped in a dark cloak of heavy wool. He could nearly feel her gaze slipping over the congregation and he had the sense that he was being hunted.

Melusine. His heart began to pound. Before his marvelling eyes, she dipped her fingertips into the font by the portal and wrought a cross upon her forehead with the holy water.

This would show the truth of it!

Nothing happened. Raymond blinked. He had been so certain that she was the spawn of a demon, so certain that her wicked soul meant him ill. How could this be? She hastened down the side aisle and knelt beside Raymond just before the priest began to sing.

"How . . . ?" he began in indignation.

Melusine shushed him, raising a single fingertip in

admonition. "Heed the Mass," she chided, as if chastising a noisy gossip. She folded her hands before herself, bowed her head and joined the prayer with conviction.

Raymond was confused. Demons were always denounced by the sacraments and it was well-known that holy water repelled them. But he could see the glisten of holy water upon Melusine's brow. He watched her lips move as she participated in the prayers.

Had he been wrong? Desire unfurled within him at this most unwelcome time, tempting him. He recalled the brief glimpse of her face and found himself too aware of her heat beside him. He gripped his vial of holy water.

Melusine took the bread of Christ's body upon her tongue with nary a flinch. She crossed herself and murmured the prayers as one long accustomed to the ceremony. She recited the *Ave* and the *Paternoster* perfectly, her manner as sweet and chaste as a madonna.

His resistance to her abandoned him along with his certainty of her diabolical nature. Her flesh was soft, her lips ripe, her complexion touched with the flush of a new rose. Her cloak did not hide the fullness of her curves and he burned with recollection of her kiss. He watched the delicacy of her fingers as she gestured. He was beguiled by the soft murmur of her voice.

"May God be with you, neighbor," she said to him when the service ended and she rose to her feet. Raymond knew he did not imagine the enchanting smile that touched her lips.

And then she was gone, leaving the chapel in a swirl of wool, her scent lingering behind to torment him.

He had too many questions to let her depart so readily as this. That was why he was compelled to pursue her.

At least he told himself as much.

As if she guessed his intent, Melusine moved quickly through the church. Raymond had to run to catch her. His progress was impeded by many who wished to congratulate him on his kill and his loyalty. Melusine easily outpaced him and he feared he might lose her.

He lunged out of the sanctuary and into the thin sunlight in time to catch a last glimpse of her as she rounded a corner in the market.

Raymond ran. He leapt across the square and seized her elbow. She met his gaze, laughter in her own, not surprise.

"I thought the Host would declaim an unbeliever," he said in a hoarse whisper. "I thought the fey could not take communion."

"And I thought mortal men put value in their pledges," she said, then arched a fair brow. "It seems we both have erred." She might have stepped away, but he tightened his grip upon her.

"Pledge to me that you will not flee. Not yet."

She met his gaze, as uncompromising as Aimery had been with a transgression. "Because my pledge is worth more than yours?"

Raymond shoved his hand through his hair. "It is no sin to break a pledge made with a demon, especially when one has been deceived."

"I am not Satan's spawn." Her scorn was unmistakable.

"Indeed, you can be no demon, for you have attended the Mass."

She smiled and leaned closer to him, placing her hand upon his chest. "You need not fear me, Raymond. I believe all the creed that you believe, and more besides, more that you have never heard."

"Will you drink this?" He offered the vial of holy water.

She smiled, removed the stopper and drank it dry, with no ill effects. Her eyes sparkled at his astonishment. "You place little value in faith, Raymond. Your God gives you succor because you believe in him."

"And this holy water does not injure you because . . ."

"Because it is water, no more and no less." She raised a fingertip. "All water is blessed. All of this world is blessed. I acknowledge that blessed state and thus it cannot injure me." She pressed the empty vial back into his hand and made to turn away.

"What do you believe, Melusine?"

She paused and he saw a frown touch her brow. "A more honest creed, perhaps. That each will act according to his own advantage, that each will pursue his own ends."

"Regardless of the cost to others?"

"All ways intersect and all actions provoke reactions. No one can predict all of the repercussions of any given deed."

Her words were not reassuring, not to a man who feared what he had done and what his pledge would bring.

Her expression changed suddenly then, as if she guessed that she only fed his doubts. She regarded him coyly, the glorious green of her eyes veiled by her fair lashes. It was an utterly feminine expression, one that awakened his desire once again.

She eased closer and placed her fingertips upon his jaw, her lips curving into a knowing smile. "Tell me the truth of it, Raymond of Poitou. You said that you were unfamiliar with Fortune. But is it true that Fortune always neglected you, or is it you who have always spurned her kiss?"

Before he could reply, Melusine reached up and brushed her lips across his own, coaxing the heat within him to an inferno.

And she spoke a truth, to be sure. Here was the opportunity he had always longed to have, the chance he had known he would never receive. Truly, he had seen time and again that men make their own luck. A beauteous wife, a holding, wealth and ten sons seemed a fat gain for granting a woman her privacy each Saturday.

Perhaps his folly was in refusing the gift Melusine could grant to him.

"I cannot wed without a holding to my name," Raymond said, his voice sounding thick to his own ears. He raised a hand and dared to touch the silk of her hair, dared to utter her name. "I have no estate, no title and thus no right to wed, Melusine. That must come afore the nuptials."

She regarded him steadily. "Have you the will to wed me, then?"

He nodded slowly, his resolve growing with every passing moment. "I render my debts and I keep my vows, upon that you can rely."

"How fortunate that I know how you can obtain a holding." When he began to smile that she would not reject him, Melusine raised a cautionary finger. "*If* you trust me."

Raymond nodded. "You will not surprise me so readily again."

"Then what you must do is this. The Count's son and heir will offer you a reward for killing the boar that killed his father."

"Guillaume has already done so."

"I shall hope that you did not modestly decline."

"I said that I would have to think upon the matter."

"Good. You must tell him this very day that you desire a holding. You must ask him for all of the land that can be encompassed by a hart's hide, no more and no less."

"But that is not enough to keep a mouse!"

Melusine granted him a stern look.

Understanding dawned upon Raymond. "Doubtless this is your strategy, to test my trust of you."

"The man has found his wits, after all," Melusine said, smiling when he chuckled.

Raymond let his thumb move against her upper arm, tracing a circle. He felt her shiver, but she did not pull away, and he dared to be encouraged that this match could serve them both well. The prospect emboldened him mightily. "And after I have done as you have bidden?"

"Ride back into the forest, by that very road you took yesterday. You will come upon an old man, who will offer to sell you a hart's hide bigger than any in Christendom."

"And I shall buy it."

"No. You will declare it to be inferior and ask if he has another. You must insist upon buying the second hart hide shown to you and no other, regardless of how poorly it looks."

Raymond nodded. "For there is more to it than meets the eye."

"Indeed. And when you have it, take the sharpest knife you possess. Slice the hide into the thinnest ribbon that you can, beginning from the outside edge and cutting in a spiral."

"And that fine ribbon will encompass a larger parcel of land. How clever you are!"

Melusine smiled but did not pause her instruction. "Take the ribbon to the woods and unfurl it as you will. Begin with the fountain where we met, and ensure that it is encompassed within the circle you make. Take witnesses with you, then ask the Count's son to grant you all the land that you encircle."

"It still would seem that precious little land would be so surrounded, no matter how thin I cut the hide," Raymond said. "There will be something uncommon about this hart hide, I wager."

Melusine only smiled.

And Raymond believed. He bent and caressed her cheek with the tips of his fingers. "I will not fail in this, my lady. I shall tell the Count's son that I must have a holding now for I am most anxious to wed." He smiled at her, anticipating a merry nuptial night between her thighs. "It is, after all, no less than the truth."

And this time, when he kissed her with possessive ease, the lady hesitated only a heartbeat before she rose to her toes to return his embrace. Her tongue dueled with his own, her fingers twined in his hair, drawing him ever closer. Raymond knew then an utter conviction that he had chosen aright.

Accepting Fortune's due promised to be an easy burden to bear.

Chapter Three

THE midday meal was in progress when Raymond reached the Count's hall. He spied his brother, Fromont, seated at Guillaume's left, and grimaced. Doubtless Fromont had come to see what could be gleaned from the Count's holdings, under the guise of paying his respects. Raymond had no desire to speak with his brother and tried to slip unnoticed into the company. He sat upon a bench at the back of the hall and had time only to nod to his fellows before Guillaume's voice rang out.

"Raymond! Come! You must sit with me at the board!"

"I am content here, my lord," Raymond replied with a smile.

"And I am not," Guillaume said, with more than a measure of his father's charm. "Come, do not spurn the honor I would show you."

Raymond excused himself and made his way to the high

table, trying to smile as those present offered their congratulations on his valor. He felt a fraud, more so when he reached the high table and spied the boar itself, roasted and holding an apple within its mouth, being carved.

"The finest cut for the Count's defender," said Guillaume. The company applauded while Raymond took his seat, awkward with praise he knew he did not deserve.

"My brother is unaccustomed to such favor," Fromont said. "It is only reasonable, as he has never done any deed with success in his all his days."

"You know little of your brother since he came to my father's hall," Guillaume said coolly. He smiled at Raymond. "I am not surprised by his valor, for I have seen it often, nor am I surprised that he is as modest as a good knight should be."

Fromont snorted, but contented himself without making further comment. Raymond managed to eat enough to ensure that others did not note his distaste for the meat. He could not look at the carcass without recalling Aimery's insistence upon killing it, and the misfortune that had ensued.

"You are quiet this day," Guillaume said.

Raymond grit his teeth. "As much as I welcome your stewardship, the hall feels empty to me in your father's lack."

Guillaume smiled sadly and looked down at his trencher. "You speak the truth, as always, my most trusted friend." He turned a bright glance upon Raymond. "In my father's memory, as it would surely please him, I would offer you anything as reward for your defense of him."

The meat stuck in Raymond's throat. He knew what he should ask, knew what Melusine expected of him, but he felt he had no right to do so. "The meat will suffice," he said hoarsely.

Fromont made an exasperated laugh. "As witless as ever he was," he muttered, but Guillaume ignored him.

"I must insist, Raymond," Guillaume said, his voice low with intent. "My father will surely haunt me if I do not see this due rendered. Choose, or I shall choose for you."

Raymond's head snapped up in alarm at this prospect. "As much land as can be encompassed by a hart's hide," he said, his words tumbling over themselves in their haste to be heard.

"What nonsense is this?" Fromont demanded.

Guillaume watched Raymond. "Are you certain, my friend? Your price seems small."

"It is all I desire, my lord."

"Why?" Guillaume lowered his voice. "You may remain at Poitiers for so long as you desire. I will always have need of a loyal man in my household. Think upon the favor you would ask, my friend, and do not waste it on a frippery."

"But I would wed, my lord. I would have a small holding that I might honorably ask for the lady's hand."

Guillaume laughed with delight. "There is the finest news I have heard this day! No wonder you are not yourself. Has she seized your heart truly?"

Raymond could only nod and stare at his uneaten portion of meat.

"Well, who is she?" Guillaume nudged him. "I must know her!"

"I fear you do not, my lord, though with your aid and God's grace that omission shall be repaired shortly."

"Splendid!" Guillaume called for more wine. "A toast to Raymond and his lady fair!"

"YOU are even more witless than I recalled," Fromont began as soon as he and Raymond had ridden out of the stables. "All of Poitiers yours to take, and you ask for this folly!"

Raymond tried to ignore his brother's bitterness. Indeed,

he wished he could have evaded his brother's determination to accompany him. "It is all I desire."

"Then you are more addlepated than even Father believed. You could have been Count of Poitiers!" Fromont flung out his hands. "You could have ruled all of this! There are those saying that you deserve no less, and Guillaume could not have denied it to you."

"It is Guillaume's inheritance." Raymond looked carefully for the road that seemed to appear and vanish, the road that Melusine apparently could summon. He spied it just where it had been the day before, but only when they were almost past it. Raymond turned his horse quickly and took the path, earning a curse from Fromont but no relief from his tirade.

"Poitiers could have been yours. If you did not want it, you could at least have thought of your own kin." Fromont spat onto the road. "Three brothers yet there are at Forez, each and every one of them chafing for a scrap of land. I have to look over my shoulder all the time, so fearful am I that I will be struck down in darkness by the most ambitious of them."

"Who is the most ambitious of them?"

"Whosoever is in a foul mood. Whosoever has been denied some small thing by me. They are all ambitious and they all loathe me." Fromont arched his brows. "You might have spared a consideration for your own brother, for me and my welfare."

"I have ensured that you do not have to provide for me."

Fromont snorted. "Hardly that! How much land do you intend to surround with this hart's hide? Enough for a privy, perhaps?" He laughed, much entertained by his own jest.

Raymond ignored his brother, for there was an old peasant man beside the road ahead. He was removing the hide from a large dead hart. He had killed the deer, in direct violation of the forest laws, though he did not appear to be frightened by their approach.

"You should be flayed alive for your impertinence!" Fromont said to the old man, who eyed him with disdain. "You have no right to hunt such a beast on the Count's own land and you know it well."

"The Count has no reckoning of this territory," the old man said. A shiver slipped down Raymond's spine. He noted a glimmer around the old man, a shimmer that might have been wrought of frost and starlight.

The old man returned to his labor. The meat glistened as he worked, the hide appearing uncommonly supple in his hands.

"I would buy a hart's hide from you," Raymond said.

"At least you have the sense to buy a large one," Fromont said.

"This one will be large, indeed," the old man said with satisfaction, more than half finished with his task.

"Have you another?" Raymond asked.

The old man granted him a sharp look. "You do not want that one. This one is much larger."

"Let me see the other one."

"I am too busy to fetch it this moment."

"I will wait." Raymond dismounted, cast the reins over his steed's head and let the horse wander. The old man regarded him, not troubling to hide his irritation, and Raymond smiled. "There is no need to hasten."

The old man fussed. His knife moved without its former precision and he nicked his thumb. He swore vehemently, then cast his knife aside. He dug in his pack with haste, then flung a darkened hide at Raymond so quickly that the knight barely managed to catch it. "There! Is that worth your waiting?"

Raymond spread the hide before himself and knew a moment's doubt. It was moth-eaten, this one, and old, with a faintly unpleasant smell. It was no more than half the size of the other.

He recalled Melusine's conviction, though, and the deed she had accomplished with his own blade. He must show his faith in her.

"How much do you wish for it?" he asked.

Fromont snatched his shoulder and shook him. "Are you mad?"

Raymond stepped away from his brother's grip. "I desire this one."

"Why? You will not even have a privy to call your own! What manner of woman will wed a man who cannot offer her a privy?"

The old man watched this exchange with interest, but named a price promptly when Raymond met his eye.

"Thievery!" Fromont said.

"Aye, it is twice as much as I would take for the larger one." The old man clearly hoped Raymond would take the other hide.

"This will serve me well." Raymond paid the disgruntled peasant, over Fromont's strident objections, then mounted his horse and rode back to the hall.

"Madness!" Fromont shouted behind him. "You deserve every misfortune heaped upon you, upon that there is no doubt. I shall disavow you as my brother, for you are too stupid that we could share any blood between us."

Raymond said nothing, for the prospect suited him well enough.

FROMONT had very little to say the next morning, however, when Raymond unfurled the ribbon he had cut from the hide. The narrow band of hart's hide seemed to be endless, and when it was all laid out, Raymond had encompassed not only the fey fountain but a territory miles and miles across.

The company who had come with Guillaume as witnesses gaped in astonishment.

"It is a marvel," said one.

"It is sorcery," whispered another, who crossed himself.

"I do not care. Let it be so!" cried Guillaume. "Well done, old friend! I feared deeply for your lady and yourself when first you revealed this scheme. And this fair land, I confess, is one I have never noted before. You have chosen wisely and have won no less than you deserve."

"But what of this bride?" Fromont asked. "Her countenance must be as bewitched as her counsel."

Raymond, jubilant that Melusine had fulfilled her pledge so well, had no care for his brother's insinuations. "You shall meet her in a fortnight, in this very place. We shall be wedded here, and shall abide here." He remembered her prophecy. "These lands shall be known as Lusignan. You are all invited to join my bride and me and make merry at our nuptial feast."

The company applauded, but Fromont shook his head. "Who is your bride? From whence does she come?"

Raymond had no intent of answering those questions. "What need have you of such details?"

"Can you not celebrate your brother's success?" Guillaume asked.

Fromont scowled. "A man cannot believe all he is told, especially by a woman who provides trickery like this hide."

"I bought the hide. You witnessed as much."

"From her man, upon her counsel, I would wager. You did not happen upon that old man by chance! You led me there, knowing full well what you would find." Fromont leaned closer to whisper. "What manner of woman will you wed, brother mine?"

"A beauteous one, as all shall see in a fortnight."

Fromont snorted. "Not I! Cast aside your life and your salvation, if you must, but do not ask others to share in it.

We part this day for all time if you insist upon such folly."

Raymond met Fromont's gaze. "So be it. My pledge to my lady stands true."

Fromont spat on the ground. He left the company and took to the road alone. Guillaume put a hand upon Raymond's shoulder in sympathy. Raymond was embarrassed that he had seen Fromont's poor manners.

"Raymond, about this lady of yours," Guillaume said, his words brimming with laughter. "Has she a sister?"

The company chuckled at this and made to return to Poitiers.

"Fromont is only jealous that your new holding is so fine," Guillaume said. "Any man with blood in his veins would covet such a prize."

"I thank you for the granting of it."

"My father would seem to be smiling upon you, old friend, for the Fates have turned in your favor with his demise."

It was a reminder of Aimery's own prediction that Raymond did not need, but he forced a smile nonetheless.

THE first day of the wedding feast dawned sunny and fair, for Melusine had arranged as much. She had labored long and hard to conjure all that was needed for these days of merriment, all that was needed to persuade Raymond that the wager would be as he had hoped and to convince his fellows that success was Raymond's indeed.

For three days and three nights, she would host his guests and family. It would be a wedding that all would recall, a wedding with finery fit for recounting over and over again. Peacocks and swans had been prepared for the meal, both cooked and redressed in their feathers for presentation at the board. There were roast chickens aplenty, and stags and pigs, and eggs prepared every which way. The board would groan with the meat.

Pastry had been shaped into dozens of follies, like partridge pies with pastry "partridges" sitting atop the filling.
Sweet almond marzipan had been colored and shaped like
fruit, the confections sure to delight the guests. There was
wine from every province and ale for those who preferred it
and hippocras to end every meal.

Melusine had ensured that every detail was so rich as to
befit a king, all the better to show that her new husband had
finally been granted his due. She hoped that all would meet
with Raymond's favor.

She would like to see the wariness leave his eyes.

She would like to see him smile.

Melusine smoothed her silken skirts at the sound of hoofbeats and gathered her maidens about herself just as the first
of Raymond's party left the woods. Raymond rode alongside
the newly invested Count Guillaume, the trap on their
steeds gleaming in the sunlight as brightly as their mail.
Pennants flew above the party, all the guests dressed in their
finest garb and jewels.

It was as naught compared to the finery of the fey.

Melusine smiled at the mortals' collective gasp of astonishment. This had been but a field when last they visited the
fountain. Now a hundred silken tents were pitched in a
meadow jostling with flowers. Ostlers strode forth to take
the horses, and fair maidens brought cups of sweet wine to
welcome the guests. A thousand birds sang in the trees, and
the fountain sparkled with music of its own. There were servants aplenty in the meadow, each garbed in lustrous silk,
each beautifully wrought. Many sang, their voices sweeter
than lutes, and the women had flowers braided into their
hair.

The largest tent in the center was tall, wrought of azure
silk that shimmered in the breeze. The walls were rolled up
and tied with silver ribbons, the tables set within gleaming
with silver cups and plates for the wedding feast. To the left

was a smaller tent, striped azure and silver, within which Melusine had anticipated Raymond's every desire upon his nuptial night. To the right was a red silken tent, hung with gold, the Count's banner flying from its peak.

The mortals were astonished, and so they should be, to find themselves in an earthly paradise.

Melusine took an embroidered tabard over her arm and strode to meet her guests. She had left her hair hanging loose down her back, though a measure of it had been entwined with golden ribbons. She wore a kirtle wrought of silk as blue as a summer sky, which shimmered in the sunlight like fine metal. It was embroidered with silver lions upon the hems, and the tabard which she carried was wrought of the same silk and embroidered to match. A silver circlet rested upon her brow and the sleeves of her chemise were visible—that garment was wrought of so fine a linen that it might have been the gossamer of cobwebs.

The stars glimmered in her betrothed's eyes and she caught her breath at his delight.

Raymond dismounted and bent low over her hand, his lips brushing her knuckles even as he held fast to her fingertips. "Lady Melusine! You are more beauteous each time I see you."

Melusine inclined her head, well aware that the others surveyed her openly. She was uncommonly glad to see him again as well.

"Welcome, my lord," she said to him. "I hope that all I have prepared pleases you this day."

"My lady most certainly does," he whispered, for her ears alone, his eyes twinkling. He did not release her hand when he straightened. Melusine felt the warm pulse of his blood when his palm pressed against her flesh, the beat of it making her flush in anticipation of their first night together.

Ten sons.

Raymond introduced her to Count Guillaume. Melusine

did not recall the names of the others she met that day, the insistent pulse of Raymond's touch driving all from her thoughts.

"And what do you carry?" he asked.

Melusine felt her cheeks heat that she had forgotten her own intent. She offered the tabard to Raymond. "I made this for you, Raymond, for our nuptials." Her words faltered as they customarily did not. "That you might wear the colors of Lusignan on this day of days."

"Lusignan!" Guillaume repeated. "It is a fair name for a fair holding."

Raymond smiled then, smiled with pleasure, and Melusine's heart fairly stopped. "For me? Truly, you wrought this marvel for me?"

She wondered how often anyone had granted him a gift and guessed the answer afore she completed the thought.

"May it be the first of many marvels the two of you create together," Guillaume said heartily.

If only he knew the truth of it. She and Raymond exchanged a secretive smile, a lover's smile, filled with an awareness that warmed her heart.

"Come!" she said. "We have prepared a tent for you, Count Guillaume. Raymond and I will take our vows this day, and a feast has been prepared for afterward. If you would like to retire first, all is prepared for you."

Guillaume bowed. "I thank you for your thoughtfulness, Lady Melusine."

As the Count strode away with his servants, Raymond caught Melusine fast against his side. He whispered in her ear, his voice filled with an excitement he could not hide. "Who are all of these people? From whence did they come?"

Melusine smiled. "They are your vassals, of course."

"I have no vassals!"

"You have claimed Lusignan. These are the vassals of

Lusignan, and they will pledge to both you and I during these nuptials."

Raymond glanced about himself, marvelling. "This place is from the realm of the fey, is it not? You have conjured it, as surely as you conjured the road, as surely as you have conjured these vassals."

Melusine shook her head, glad that she could be honest with him. "Little of merit can be conjured of naught. I would have to be far stronger than I am to conjure all of this and maintain the vision of it for three days and nights."

"Then what? How?" He was intrigued, fascinated but not repelled.

"The realm of fey and the realm of mortals lie entangled, Raymond, some places within one domain and some within the other. A few, like the forest Broceliande, exist in both. Others, like the isle of Avalon, have been in both at times, but in just one in others. Lusignan is not conjured, but summoned. I have summoned these territories from the realm of the fey, to keep my pledge to you. Lusignan has crossed the divide and will remain in the mortal realm for so long as our wager is kept."

He nodded, his gaze trailing over his new holding even as his fingertips traced the embroidery upon the tabard he held. "And if I break my word to you, it all shall slip across the divide once again, disappearing as if it never had been?"

Melusine nodded. There was no need to tell him of her mother's news, for there was naught any soul could do to halt the course. And who knew? Raymond might be as dust afore it occurred.

The prospect made her breath catch in her throat.

THE nuptial vows had been exchanged, the marital feast had been savored, the toasts to their health had been drained and the new couple were finally alone in the tent that held their nuptial bed.

Melusine saw Raymond's trepidation. He watched her, his uncertainty mingled with his desire, and she knew that he feared to find some horror beneath her skirts.

How ironic that he sensed her Saturday nature, though he had never glimpsed it, heard tell of it, or seen it.

And he never would, unless he broke their pledge. The prospect chilled Melusine, and made her doubly determined to win his love.

Sadly, she did not know much of this mortal mating. She had long preferred to match wits with men, not suffer their touch, and she refused to think of what she had known would have to happen this night. She unlaced her kirtle and cast it aside, unaware that the candlelight shone through her chemise.

She was aware that he watched her avidly.

"There is naught to fear, Raymond. I am wrought as you would desire," she said quietly. She unbound her hair and laid upon the bed on her back, prepared for however this deed proceeded.

Raymond did not move.

Melusine cast him a smile, then closed her eyes again. "I am prepared. Do what you must to create sons."

Raymond, to her astonishment, laughed. He sat on the edge of the mattress, his weight making it dip. Melusine looked up then and caught her breath, for he had discarded his chemise. He was close, very close, his flesh bare and tanned, the hair thick upon his chest.

His eyes danced and a smile pulled at the corner of his mouth. It seemed that he fought the urge to laugh at her. He braced his hands on either side of her and smiled down at her.

"You have not done this afore," he said, with no accusation in his tone. "But surely you have heard whispers."

She shook her head, uncertain what he meant.

"How do the fey mate?"

"With laughter, with words." How could she explain how the fey wrought children, spinning them like tales out of the ether? It was a process few understood fully.

"Not with flesh upon flesh?"

Melusine could not fully suppress her shudder of distaste. She looked away from him, not wanting to insult him. "You may proceed," she said, closing her eyes and hoping the deed would be finished soon.

Raymond chuckled. "Your participation would be welcome."

"But it cannot be necessary."

"Is it not?"

Melusine could not resist the sound of his voice, not when he sounded so merry. She opened her eyes and was snared anew by the sparkle of his eyes.

Her own pulse quickened.

Melusine swallowed and dropped her gaze, noting then what he found so amusing. His enthusiasm for the deed seemed to have waned. "I thought you found me alluring."

"Not when you lie like a corpse." Raymond stretched out beside her and caught a tendril of her hair between his finger and thumb. He twined it about his fingers as he spoke, his voice not unlike the low murmur of a brook. "I would meet abed merrily, Melusine. I would see you pleased, as your touch sees me pleased. I would have us grant pleasure, each to the other, and be able to tell our sons that they were wrought in joy."

"I do not know how to do this."

Raymond smiled, an expression as potent as any spell. "You have only to tell me what you like."

"I do not know."

"Aye, you do. You like laughter and camaraderie. What else?" He bent and touched his lips gently to her shoulder, then met her gaze.

"A lighter touch would be more pleasing," she admitted, her heart in her throat.

He kissed her shoulder again, his touch as gentle as a butterfly landing upon a flower, and Melusine gasped.

"Did you see the folly set before the duke?" he murmured, his breath teasing her skin.

Melusine shivered and smiled despite herself. "He thought it was a bird in truth."

"It was so wondrously crafted."

"You must not forget that he had drunk heartily of the hippocras."

Raymond chuckled. "He insisted that it chirped."

Melusine laughed in recollection of the plump duke's foolishness. "And forced his fellows to listen to the confection."

"Did you note how Guillaume pretended to hear it? He had the others half persuaded."

"But each time he swore it chirped, the duke insisted it did not." Melusine found herself laughing. She leaned her head against Raymond's shoulder, savoring the recollection as much as the sound of their laughter entwined together.

"It was a fine feast, finer than any I have ever had." Raymond propped himself up on his elbow, his eyes gleaming, and closed his hand around her breast. "I thank you for your labors."

Melusine could not breathe, particularly not when his thumb slid beguilingly across her nipple. Raymond kissed the hollow of her collarbone and she sighed. A tide of desire grew within her, silencing her objections. She knew that it would shortly carry her away, that it would overwhelm her fey reservations.

And she did not care. She wanted to share all Raymond had to offer. She locked her fingers into the thickness of his hair and drew him closer.

"There," she urged when his kiss found a spot that made her tremble.

"Aye, there," he agreed, closing her fingers around his strength.

Melusine's eyes flew open at his apparent enthusiasm. He chuckled, his fingers sliding into the soft heat of her. She moaned, quivering at both the surety of his caress and his happiness.

"We can make magic together, my Melusine," he whispered.

He was mortal. Her response should not have been thus, but Melusine knew it could not be denied. When Raymond kissed her again, she surrendered fully to the sorcery of his embrace, without a single regret.

AFTER three days of feasting and three nights in Raymond's embrace, Saturday dawns upon Lusignan. The bride is absent. Melusine hears Raymond's words, as at a distance, and is relieved, even as the old evil claims her body.

No sooner does she wish that she understood him fully than there, in the refuge of her forest glade, Melusine dreams a mortal dream. It is someone else's dream, someone else's memory.

It is Raymond's memory.

She sees a small boy, dark of hair and blue of eye, a boy too small to be so wary. It is clear that he is fey, for he is wrought small and fine and there is starlight in his eyes.

She peers into the boy's past and recoils from a mere glimpse of his mother, a beauteous fey, but one captured and abused by Raymond's father. The mother escaped her abuser and abandoned her sole child, wanting naught of mortals or half-mortals again.

The father does not welcome the burden.

Melusine winces and looks back to the child Raymond. She sees his four older brothers, his indifferent father, their flesh hanging heavily upon their bones. She sees the hovel in the woods in which they lived, she sees the gruel Raymond was offered to eat, she sees the lice within the pallet where he slept and in the rags in which he was garbed. She sees that he is loathed, because he is different.

Her heart twists.

She sees the Earl of Forez—so the father calls himself— summoned to the court of the Count of Poitou. Count Aimery, the man killed by the boar, is younger in this memory, virile and hand- some. It defies belief that he and Raymond's father are brothers, but indeed they are.

She sees the Earl of Forez's jealousy when he enters the Count's fine hall and knows his poison will find a target.

"How unfortunate that all your wealth is destined to waste, Aimery," he says to the Count. "As you have not a single son to carry your name."

She sees the Countess blanche at this rude reference to her barren womb; she sees Aimery close his hand protectively over his wife's trembling fingers. "I shall make you a wager, Brother," Aimery says with uncommon grace. "I could take one of your sons beneath my hand and lighten the burden upon you."

The Countess catches her breath and color touches her cheeks.

The Earl of Forez laughs harshly. "I will grant you one of them willingly. Be warned, Aimery, they eat a cursed amount, each and every one of them, and there is not a one among the wretched lot who will come to any account."

Melusine sees the Countess grip her husband's hand, hope mak- ing her radiant again.

"Choose," Aimery bids her softly.

She leaves him, descending to the floor of the hall like a jewel come to life. She is a beautiful woman, if burdened by disappoint- ment in her own failure, her skin creamy and her lips red. She is dressed richly, so richly that she glistens as she walks, like a fey queen, though Melusine knows that wealth is as nothing to her.

All the Countess desires is a son, for a son will please her beloved spouse. She would give any trinket, do any deed, if only she could grant Aimery his heart's desire.

She may have such a chance.

The older boys kick Raymond behind them, for he is the smallest, and they have drunk heavily of their father's hatred.

But the Countess is not deceived. She has an eye for merit, this mortal. She bends and beckons to Raymond. He hesitates, clearly fearing a trick. Melusine sees evidence that he has told her the truth, that Fortune has not oft been his companion.

The eldest, Fromont, kicks him soundly, ignoring the Countess's sound of dismay. "Forgotten your manners, runt?"

"Not I!" *Raymond spares a telling glance to his brother's boot, then steps forward. His face burns crimson, probably with the awareness that every eye in that hall is upon him, but he does not falter. He bows low before the Countess.*

Melusine can fairly hear the thunder of his heart.

"At your service, my lady," *he says with a solemnity beyond his years. His brothers chuckle and mimic him, his father guffaws.*

But the Countess is charmed. She offers her hand to him, as filthy as he is. "Come to me."

Raymond swallows and does as he is bidden. His hand shakes as he reaches to her. He does not touch her but leaves his fingers just before hers, aware of the grime upon his flesh.

The Countess smiles and closes her hand around his with resolve. "And what is your name, child?"

"Raymond."

"Raymond," *she repeats with satisfaction, then turns to smile at her husband.* "Raymond will be tall and handsome, I wager."

"Do you offer a child in truth, Brother?" *Aimery asks.* "Will you spare Raymond, to gladden my lady's heart? I will see him fed and clothed and trained as a knight."

Raymond's father spits into the rushes. "I would be well rid of one less mouth to feed. Take him! He is the most worthless of the lot."

"You will never make a knight of him," *whispers Fromont viciously.* "I am the only one who will be a knight!"

"The world has need of more than one knight," *Count Aimery says, then he smiles at the frightened boy his wife has brought before him. "Welcome, Raymond. Welcome to Poitiers. Join us at the board, for from this day forth, I pledge that I shall treat you as my own son."*

The boy is led to the head table by the Countess, his astonishment as clear to the company as the resentment of his kin.

Melusine hears the faint echo of hope in the boy's heart, the hope that his luck had finally changed for the good. She wonders how a child so chosen, plucked from the mire against all odds, could still consider himself to be a stranger to Fortune's kiss.

The glimpse of another memory grants her the answer.

Within the year, the Countess ripens. She is gay, sparkling with joy. She tells Raymond that he has brought her greatest desire to pass. Melusine cannot tell whether the young boy understands what is happening, why the Countess's belly is so round, why the Count insists that he will keep his word to Raymond.

Raymond is awed yet by his surroundings, but he grows taller in this household.

A third memory, a vivid one, visits Melusine as the moon rides high over her secluded pool. It is clearly an event that scarred Raymond, for Melusine feels the recollection as polished as a stone that the fingers cannot leave be. She heeds it with care, hoping to learn something of his secret thoughts.

It is dark, night in the hall of Poitiers, but no soul sleeps. A fire burns on the hearth, though none gather near it. Fat candles burn low, the flames sputtering in the melted beeswax. It is warm in the hall, the air filled with the smell of blood and beeswax and the pulse of mortal hearts.

And a sound that cannot be evaded, the screams of a woman in labor. This is beyond Melusine's experience, this task of bringing a child to light, though she has heard tell of it. Her mouth goes dry, for she too will endure this ordeal.

Aimery is pacing, his anxiety echoed in a watchful young Raymond's eyes. "All women scream thus when bearing a babe." Aimery tousles Raymond's hair, but his words lack conviction.

Aimery is afraid. Melusine smells his fear and marvels at it. The fey have no fear. They are shackled with few of the emotions that so entangle mortals. She is both fascinated and puzzled.

But not for long.

The screams stop so abruptly that every soul in the hall—and there are many in the shadows—catches his or her breath. Aimery and Raymond turn as one to look to the stairs, just as every servant in the hall glances up.

The midwife appears, cradling a bundle. She is as brown and wrinkled as a midwinter apple and her smile is toothless. "A son!" she cries in triumph. "A hale and healthy son."

The company cheers, more than one commenting that the lady will be pleased. Melusine smiles in her turn that the Countess will have her yearning fulfilled. The servants prepare to congratulate the lord, but he pushes them aside in his anxiety.

"And my lady wife?" Aimery demands.

The midwife closes her eyes and turns away. The hall falls silent on a gasp of disbelief.

What is this?

The midwife's voice is thick. "Her last wish was that the boy be named Guillaume."

"Nay!" The Count runs up the stairs, shoving the midwife aside to enter his wife's chamber.

"She bade me remind you of your pledge to Raymond," the midwife says softly. A trio of women in the hall, elderly servants all, begin to weep.

"Margot!" Aimery's shout echoes throughout the hall. "Not Margot! Say she yet lives."

But she does not, and every person in the hall knows what he refuses to believe. More than one weeps quietly. The midwife rocks the child who has begun to cry in his turn. Small Raymond turns back to the fire, a frightened boy uncertain of his future yet again, his eyes filled with tears.

Fickle Fortune! Only now does Melusine begin to understand the price of the mortality borne by those in this realm. Though she has known affection, it has never been so potent as this. These people mourn the loss of a beloved, mourn in a manner unknown to the immortal fey.

They mourn because Death has stolen one of their number away, stolen the Countess for all time. Is love more potent for mortals? Is their love more poignant for the fact that it can be lost at any time? Is this the compensating gift granted to them, in exchange for their inevitable demise?

In the silence of the forest, Melusine wonders. What is it like, to be as beloved as Aimery's Margot? What is it like for mortals to twine their hearts together, to make one from two, to pledge fealty each to the other for so long as they both shall live? A desire lights within Melusine then, a yearning to know the truth of it.

The sun gilds the horizon and Melusine changes form, with the usual relentless pain. This time, though, her tears are not shed solely for her own agony. She weeps for the Countess Margot, cheated of seeing her greatest dream come to fruition. She weeps for Aimery, who surely desired a son but not in exchange for his lady wife.

And she weeps for Raymond, a boy taught too often that Fortune could not be trusted to favor him for long.

Chapter Four

WITHIN eight days of their nuptials, the forest around the greatest hill in Raymond's new domain of Lusignan had been cleared away. The laborers had emerged from the forest, arriving silently one morning without warning. No one knew them or from whence they had come. They spoke little, but they worked with unholy vigor.

Raymond chose not to ask for details.

The laborers dug enormous ditches, beneath Melusine's command. They laid foundations and crafted a dungeon deep and wide. They began to build a stone wall, a wall that grew higher and higher with such remarkable speed that people came merely to marvel at it. Two commanding square towers rose above those walls.

The walls were rife with arrow slits, and the top of the wall was a crenellated battlement. Three men could walk side by side along the crest of the walls, arms outstretched and fingertips barely touching. There were three gates, each protected by a heavy portcullis and numerous cunning vantage points for archers.

Raymond had not guessed that his wife had known so much of military matters and defense.

There was a chamber within the keep, close to where the lord's chamber would be, and curiously, it was completed first. It had only very high windows, so narrow that a bird could barely peek within them, and it was to this chamber that Melusine retreated each Saturday. Raymond did not know what she did there, and he told himself not to care. It was sufficient for him to know that she was close at hand, not disappearing into the forest alone.

Having grown accustomed to Fortune's lack, Raymond knew to embrace her gifts when they appeared. He found himself laughing at small things, and his lips seemed to be curved permanently in a smile. Raymond found himself, standing in the fields, merely watching the laborers at their craft, marvelling that this should be his. He greeted each morning, not with wariness, but welcoming its possibilities. One day he found himself whistling and realized that this new effervescence within him was happiness.

Melusine could not help but know that he credited her with the change in his life and circumstance. Raymond was besotted with her, fascinated with the rounding of her womb. He seduced her each night, learning what she favored and what she did not, taking delight in her pleasure.

It was more than the mating itself; they became fast friends. They nestled together in their tent at night and spoke of nonsense, of names for the child, of what he would look like, of whether the babe would indeed be born a boy.

Raymond was determined to show himself worthy of his lady's gifts. He strove to be a fair lord to his vassals. He oversaw the courts himself and was visible amongst his people. He listened to them, considered their desires, ensured their defense. He planned a mill and a pond for breeding fish; he vowed to clear acreage for farms and pastures.

Raymond believed his marriage was a good one. He courted his wife both day and night that she might be persuaded of the same.

IT had been some nine months since their nuptials, when Melusine came to Raymond in the fields. She carried a gift for him in her hands and hoped desperately that he would favor it.

"What is this?" he asked, kissing her cheek in affectionate greeting as was his custom. "This child has made you as soft as a rose petal," he whispered and she felt herself flush.

"I have wrought you a gift," she said, then she fought a smile. "With my own hands, even." He feigned such amazement that she laughed, and she proudly showed him the needle pricks upon her fingers. He kissed each one dutifully, prompting her laughter at his playfulness.

"It must be precious, indeed." Raymond shook out the burden of cloth and gasped in wonder. It was a pennant, long and slender and wrought of silk.

"It is a pennant for Lusignan. I designed the insignia," Melusine said hastily when he said naught. "I hope you find it fitting."

"Fitting!" Raymond laughed aloud and shook it out into the wind. "Melusine, it is magnificent! Look how long it is, how bold the colors!" The vassals near him commented with enthusiasm, but Melusine had eyes only for Raymond's smile.

She had chosen a background of ten horizontal stripes, alternating azure and silver, though she hoped he did not ask the reason for their color. Atop the stripes, she had embroidered a red lion, thinking it appropriate.

"It is glorious, Melusine. I will be delighted to bear this

mark upon my shield." He examined it in wonder, exclaiming over the quality of the embroidery, then stared at her in understanding. "A pennant? Does this mean that the castle is complete?"

Melusine nodded and smiled. She offered her hand to him and he seized it, pressed a kiss upon the back of her hand, then placed it upon his elbow.

"Let us unfurl this banner where it belongs." He led her to the keep, ensuring that her way was unobstructed and letting her lean upon him when she grew tired. The babe was heavy these days, and she appreciated his gallantry when she felt so graceless and large. They strode beneath the portcullis to the cheers of their vassals.

"Truly, this is all to be our own?" he asked.

"Truly, Raymond, it is no less than you deserve." Melusine rose to her toes to kiss his cheek. He turned so that her embrace met him full upon the lips, much to the pleasure of the company.

Melusine gasped and it was not from his kiss. She had had small contractions these past days, enough to make her catch her breath. But this one had nearly taken her to her knees.

"What is it?" Raymond was immediately concerned.

"The babe." She was flustered. "Your son intends to arrive shortly." Melusine closed her eyes and caught at his arm as another contraction clutched her womb.

Her waters broke then, the dark puddle spreading across the stone floor. Melusine leaned against Raymond, needing his strength. She could hear the reassuring thunder of his pulse and found comfort in his warmth. She wished she could bear the child there, in the circle of his arms, but she knew it was not to be.

"This was not the way I would have first entered our chambers," Raymond teased. "You need not fear. I shall see the banner hung this very morn. You and the babe can look upon it when you are able." He caught her in his arms and climbed the stairs, trying to tempt her smile all the while.

She saw that he was frightened as well, but could say nothing to reassure him. They were no sooner in the lord's chamber than the ladies were pushing him out the door.

Then the pain began in earnest. It was worse than that of her weekly transformation because it endured so long. Melusine found herself screaming as the Countess had screamed in Raymond's memory. It was barbaric, to bear children as beasts of the forest bear their young, but she would fulfill Raymond's terms.

Or die trying.

The prospect terrified Melusine as little else could. It was purely mortal to procreate this way and she supposed she could only have done it because she was half-mortal.

But could she die in the deed, as the Countess had?

If she did die partaking of this mortal folly, would any mourn her loss?

MELUSINE'S first son bawled mightily upon his emergence into the world. It was past midnight and Melusine was exhausted from her efforts. She lay back upon the pillows, hearing herself pant like an animal even as the blood ran from her.

"What a large babe!" the midwife said. "It is no wonder you labored so long and hard, my lady." The women gathered closer as Melusine felt only relief that the ordeal was finally over.

And she was yet alive.

She had only nine more times to do this deed. She closed her eyes, feeling the extent of the ache within her. She listened as the women commented upon the babe's size and vigor.

Then there was silence, and Melusine knew that something was amiss. She sat up as best as she was able, fully aware of the sweat upon her brow and the blood upon her flesh.

"Let me see my son," she commanded. She had to demand him again before the boy was laid in her arms.

She immediately saw why they had hesitated. This child she had created within her womb was not wrought poorly, but his eyes, his eyes were troubling. They were not the eyes of a mortal babe, nor those of a fey child, and the very sight of them sent a shiver down her spine.

One eye was angry red, the other silver gray.

They were just as the boar's had been, Melusine realized with a start, like those of the boar that had killed Aimery. She knew a foreboding then that the truth that she and Raymond had buried would force its way to light, one way or the other.

Why else would her child remind her of that boar? Why else would she suddenly feel guilt that the truth had been disguised, that proper compense had not been made?

Melusine shook her head, willing such nonsense to disperse. She was tired, no more than that.

"His name is Urien," she said, the words as dust in her mouth.

Raymond came into the chamber then, impatient with the women who would have kept him from his wife's side. Melusine saw the anticipation upon his face, saw the happiness within him, but there was no point in hiding the truth.

They had wrought this together, after all.

Melusine offered him the bundle that was his son. She watched, heartsick, as revulsion filled his eyes. He took the child, but with reluctance. Melusine knew with immediate certainty that he blamed her for the child's flaw. She turned away, stung, and kept her darkest fear from him.

Let him believe the taint was hers.

She would do better with the next son.

MELUSINE'S wish was not to be.

Oblivious while her second son filled her womb, Melusine

built the city of Lusignan outside the castle walls, her workers casting it up with a speed that left all speechless. She added a tall, ornate tower to the keep itself, desperate to show her husband how she cared for his favor, how she would prove herself worthy of their wager.

When it was completed, Raymond's smile did not reach his eyes.

Her gifts were worthless. Melusine felt a despair such as she had never known. She felt an affinity with the Countess and could only hope that this child was wrought more fair.

Raymond carried her again to the bedchamber when the pains began anew, kissed her brow and wished her well. A thousand things remained unsaid between them as the pain claimed Melusine.

To no avail.

Hugues's flesh was so fiery a red that it might have been cut from the heart of the sun, and, indeed, touching him left burns upon his nursemaids. Though he did not resemble the boar, there was something of a beast about him.

Melusine conceived promptly again, though that did not slow the frenzy of her pace. She established the towns of Mel and Partenay while her belly rounded, determined to show her spouse that wedding her was not without merit.

But Raymond became grim and distant, despite his polite acceptance of her earthly gifts. They did not whisper abed any longer, and indeed, he did not always share her bed. Once he knew she had conceived, he slumbered elsewhere. Melusine ached with loneliness for his company, for the sparkle of his smile.

There was but one way she could win either again.

Guy had one eye that was lower than the other, but otherwise was finely wrought. A ghost of a smile curved Raymond's lips when he examined his son and Melusine dared to be encouraged.

Raymond returned to her bed, professing his certainty

that the "ill-fortune" affecting their children was diminishing. Melusine resolved that she had not accepted the fullness of her wager with sufficient joy. She greeted him abed with enthusiasm and surrendered utterly to the pleasures of mortal loving.

Of course, Raymond's seed took root again, and did so with astonishing speed. Haunted by the prospect that she might die in labor, for it grew more difficult each time, Melusine worked tirelessly. She established the town of Rochelle, upon the coast. As always, Raymond knew how to make the best of her offerings: he licensed a shipping trade in wine from that port, which added many tithes to the Lusignan coffers.

Anthony was born with a bleeding gash in his cheek. The midwife said it was like a wound wrought by the claw of a lion and set to tending it. Melusine thought it more like the gash of a boar's tusk. She knew, deep in her heart, that the wound would never heal in all his days and nights.

It never did.

Nor were the shadows dispersed in Raymond's eyes. He did not laugh as much as he had in the early days of their marriage. His brief certainty that all misfortune was behind him had died, leaving him somber as he had been when first they met.

Melusine bent her attention upon her sons, scarred as they were, ensuring that they were a credit to their father. She raised them to be courteous, to be valiant and true, to keep their word and speak their thoughts. If one could overlook their physical flaws, their natures were worthy, indeed. Melusine persuaded Raymond to take Urien as a squire, to begin the boy's knightly training. The boy fairly blossomed beneath his father's attention and was so quick a study that Raymond was impressed.

Then Raynold was born with only one eye. Time proved that he saw more clearly with that single eye than most people do with two. That was not sufficient to sate his worried parents.

Their couplings became silent now, quick, dutiful and devoid of joy. The matings that had once created such joy became a misery and an obligation. Melusine felt the full weight of her earthliness without the compense of Raymond's love. Indeed, her weekly metamorphoses became more painful than they had ever been, more redolent of the earth.

Geoffroi was born with a great square tooth already protruding from his mouth. Melusine took one look at him and buried her face in her pillow, unable to evade its similarity to the tusks of boars. Were boars not said to be born with their tusks intact?

Raymond returned to the marital bed grimly. The pair did not look into each other's eyes, they did not tease each other, they did not waste time with the pursuit of pleasure. Melusine suspected that she was not the only one counting that they had four more children to bring to light. She half feared she would give birth to a boar itself, should this continue.

Raymond no longer defended Melusine against the whispers of her nature that they oft heard. She dared not voice her suspicion that it was his deed turned against them. It would have been too much for the man to bear. Already he saw his wish for ten sons tainted. Despair sat between them at the board like an uninvited and unwelcome guest that could not be ousted.

Melusine was despondent when she rounded again, and Raymond barely acknowledged the news when she told him.

Their seventh son, however, was the son who changed all.

THE babe was beautiful.

Melusine could not believe it. His hair was dark, like

Raymond's, his eyes a merry blue, his lashes dark and thick.
Though she had examined the babe a dozen times, she could
not find a flaw upon his flesh. He had not so much as a mole.

But there was something about this babe, something
that cast a shadow over Melusine's joy. She smelled a poison
in him, though she could not name it or its source.

Perhaps she would have preferred that any flaw he bore
was visible, not hidden in his heart. Perhaps she was too suspicious to accept Fortune's kiss, as Raymond once had been.

She was still struggling with her response, still holding
the babe, when Raymond came to her side.

"What is amiss with this one?" he asked, indifferent as
he had not been when first they wed.

"Naught," Melusine said. She offered him the child,
withholding her doubts, until she saw his response.

"He is perfect!" Joy suffused Raymond's features. He
held the boy high and laughed, turning in place while the
midwife chided him. He bent and captured Melusine's chin,
then kissed her deeply. "Praise be, Melusine! The curse is
behind us, finally."

Her heart thumped to see him so pleased. "So it would
appear."

"We shall invite every soul to his christening!" Raymond
was exuberant. "We shall have a feast to rival that of our wedding. We shall have everyone gaze upon his beauty, share
our joy."

"As you wish."

Raymond hesitated at her bedside, bouncing the child in
his arms. "Might I ask a boon of you, Melusine?"

She shrugged, unable to shake her foreboding.

"I would name him Fromont, for it is a traditional name
in my family." Raymond took a deep breath. "And I would
invite my brother to the christening. Perhaps he should be
godfather. It is time that we put old wounds behind us."

"As you wish," Melusine agreed, closing her eyes when he

bent to kiss her cheek. She was tired, tired to her very bones.

And she feared she knew now what taint the babe Fromont bore. It was the toxin of Raymond's half brothers and father that she smelled upon the child.

It was jealousy, and though she could not guess whether this child would carry it or cause it, she feared its import.

THE third day of feasting happened to be a Saturday.

It had been a folly of planning on Raymond's part. He had not forgotten about Melusine's weekly departure, but had been so delighted with his new son that he had overlooked it. Truly, if she had been of more aid in the arrangement of events, as was her wont, it would not have happened.

But Melusine seemed very weary after this birthing and was slow to rise from her bed. In his determination to resolve all and leave her the time to recover, Raymond neglected that one detail. He supposed, in hindsight, that they had gone their own ways for so many years, that he had become less aware of her daily doings.

Raymond awakened on that day, not surprised to find her gone and the door to her private chamber locked against him. He took the babe Fromont from the nursemaid and carried him down to the hall, smiling upon his other sons as he went. His brother and the babe's namesake was already at the board, his manner such that Raymond knew he would make trouble this day.

"Is your wife too lazy to be the good hostess this day?" Fromont demanded by way of greeting.

"It is no sin for a new mother to rest."

"Slovenly is what our father would have called it. A woman should be about her tasks within days of bearing a child."

Raymond felt a flicker of temper, but he damped it deliberately. He bounced his son, and savored the ale and bread brought to him. Fortune had smiled upon him again, and he would not fail to appreciate her charms.

Fromont grew ever more agitated as time passed. "Does your lazy wife insult her guests?"

"Of course not." Raymond smiled. "You shall see her at chapel on the morrow, no doubt."

"On the morrow!" Fromont snorted. "Does she mean to neglect us all of this day? What manner of hostess is she?"

Several of the other guests eyed each other, their doubts awakened by Fromont's nonsense.

"Melusine is tired from the delivery of our child," Raymond said firmly. "You will sate yourself with my company on this day."

"All the day, she will rest," Fromont said. He rolled his eyes. "Truly I should like to be the Lady of Lusignan, the better to lead a sluggard's life."

His squire snickered. The hall became silent.

Fromont leaned close to Raymond. "Is she oft absent like this?"

"What matter to you?"

Fromont tapped a fingertip upon the board. "I shall tell you what matter to me, brother mine. I have heard that the Lady of Lusignan is never seen on a Saturday. I have heard that the Lord of Lusignan is bewitched by his wife, too enchanted to demand of her an explanation."

"You have heard nonsense."

Fromont sat back, his expression sly. "I have heard that the Lady of Lusignan has a lover, that she spends a day abed with another man once a week and her husband has not the wits to ask after her absence."

Anger flickered within Raymond. "You cast aspersions upon the character of your hostess. That is foul manners in any court."

"I repeat only what others are saying." Fromont smiled. "And I do so because I care for your welfare, Brother."

"You have never liked Melusine," Raymond said, his voice rising hot. "I will not listen to whatsoever you say against her."

"I have always been skeptical of your lady, I must admit." Fromont sat back. "I have always suspected that she is fey. There is something ethereal about her."

Raymond feared to hear his own suspicion uttered aloud, before the company. He could not name Melusine's nature with certainty and in truth he chose to avoid the matter, even in his own thoughts.

"Certainly, your holding seems to have been conjured from naught, and all has been built with unholy speed . . ." Fromont snapped his fingers. "As if by magic."

"Melusine has found diligent laborers."

"Yet the lady does not seem to have aged in all the years you have been wed. How long is it now? Twelve years? And not a silver hair is there upon her brow." Fromont chuckled. "While you, brother mine, have more than a few."

"Who knows what women do in their vanity?" Raymond said, summoning a smile with an effort. "Perhaps she spends her Saturdays removing those errant silver hairs."

Too late he realized that he had confirmed Melusine's weekly absence. Fromont's eyes gleamed with malice.

"Perhaps." Fromont surveyed the hall. "If she were fey, she might well be on her knees in the chapel all this day, doing penitence for her nature to earn the Lord's forgiveness."

"You repeat the nonsense of old women."

"Perhaps." Fromont's gaze dropped to the babe in Raymond's arms. "But what if these sons of whom you are so proud are not of your own seed?"

The very thought sent a shiver through Raymond and sharpened his anger.

"They cannot be of your own seed, Raymond, not with such monstrous scars."

The possibility grew more plausible to Raymond.

"What if the flaws upon them are a mark of God's disfavor? What if they are an indictment of adultery?"

The very prospect infuriated Raymond, firing his temper as it had not been roused in years. The notion made dangerous sense. He knew that Melusine had not been anxious to meet him abed. Did she prefer to mate with another man?

Whose sons did he raise as his own?

Fury that his wife cuckolded him blinded Raymond to the trouble his brother stirred.

Fromont lowered his voice and tapped Raymond's arm. "What if Melusine couples with demons each and every Saturday? Should you not know what occurs within your own hall? What manner of a man would not put a stop to such doings?"

How dare Melusine so deceive him?

How dare she steal from him the sons she had pledged to bear?

Raymond pushed the babe into a nursemaid's arms and rose abruptly from the board. He strode from the hall, anger hot within him, and made his way to the chamber of her treachery.

Fromont was right. It was time Raymond knew what occurred within his own hall. No door should be locked against the Lord of Lusignan.

NO sound came from behind the door. No light glimmered beneath it. Raymond dropped to the floor but found he could not peer beneath the door. It was crafted by some fey means to ensure that none could glimpse whatsoever occurred within the chamber behind it.

That made it perfect for an assignation. Why would Melusine have bothered to craft it so, if her secret had not been foul?

Raymond would not be swayed, not now that he was

determined to know the truth. He took his dagger from his belt and embedded the point in the wood of the door. He silently spun the sharp weapon, gradually cutting away the wood. A dent appeared, then the dent grew deeper. Finally, his blade broke through the thickness of the wood, and he worked at the hole until it was the full diameter of the blade.

He hesitated for a heartbeat.

Melusine would never know that he had looked. Raymond told himself as much, shook off his foreboding, then put his eye to the hole.

At first, Raymond saw nothing amiss. Melusine was bathing. Indeed, she was alone in the chamber and that relieved him mightily. She sang softly to herself.

Raymond's anger faded to naught and he found himself admiring the beauty of his wife. He had not looked upon her leisurely in years, and now he indulged himself. He liked the ripe curve of her breasts, the rosiness of pregnancy that yet clung to her flesh. Her skin would be softer than silk, her hair smooth beneath his hand. He was tempted to join her there, to make merry in the bath together, and he raised his fist to knock.

Then Melusine reached for a cloth that was just beyond her grasp. She raised herself out of the water and Raymond's knees fairly gave out beneath him.

His wife had a tail.

He blinked but the sight remained. From the navel down, Melusine was wrought as a serpent. Scales of azure and silver covered a long twining tail that replaced her long lean legs, its stripes the same colors Melusine had chosen for the banner of Lusignan. Raymond shuddered in revulsion and leaned his brow against the door, unable to look upon the horror of her any longer.

This was what Melusine did not want him to see. He was momentarily tempted to spurn her, to cast her out for the monstrosity that she was.

Then he found himself thinking of the kindness Melusine showed to their scarred sons, how she had taught him to look beyond the physical marks they bore to their noble natures. Raymond had to admit that she was right. Their sons were gracious and well-mannered, their prowess at arms exceeded only by their skill at poetry. Though the shock of his first glimpse of each of them had been profound, he loved them all now.

Though none as much as he loved little Fromont.

Raymond's heart wrenched. Melusine was his wife, his lady and his love. She had saved him from death. She had kept her pledge to him. She was loyal and just, kind and honorable. With her aid, he had made far more of himself than ever he might have otherwise. Her counsel was good, her patience was uncommon. Melusine had brought him joy and hope, such as he had never known before.

Raymond loved her. The realization astonished him, all the more because he was utterly convinced of its truth. Still the balance between them was a poor one: Melusine had granted Raymond his heart's desire.

And he had rewarded her with treachery.

Raymond stepped away from the portal, ashamed of his weakness. He sealed the hole with wax and returned to the hall, newly determined to prove himself worthy of his lady's affections.

Once there, he turned to his older brother. "You worry for naught, brother of mine!" he said. "My lady wife slumbers alone, as I told you, as a women tired from bearing a child will do. You make a tale where there is none."

"She should join us in the hall, then, if nothing is amiss."

Raymond's temper flickered again, though it was directed more truly this time. "Hasten yourself, Fromont. Any man who speaks ill of my lady wife is not welcome in my hall." He lifted a cup of wine to his lips. "Begone afore I drain this wine."

Raymond saw then the jealousy that had prompted Fromont's denouncement. It was Lusignan's wealth that attracted his brother's venom, no more than that.

Guillaume had warned him once, but Raymond had let his temper lead him to an error.

Never again.

BUT Melusine knew what he had done.

Raymond realized as much when his lady came to their chamber just after first light. She was hesitant, uncertain as never she was, and he immediately guessed the reason for it. She came to the side of the bed and looked down upon him, her expression sad, her fingertips trailing across the linens. 'Twas as if she took leave of him.

His heart in his mouth, Raymond smiled at her, feigning ignorance. "Good morning, lady mine."

Melusine jumped. "I did not know you were awake."

"I have waited for you, for your heat beside me in our bed."

She studied him carefully, reluctant as he had never seen her. "I dreamed that you were angry with me."

"Dreams are folly," he said, pulling back the linens for her. "You should know better than to heed their nonsense. How could I be angry with you, with seven fine sons to my name?"

Wariness lit her eyes. "They are not all fine."

"They *are* all fine," he insisted. "They are an honor to us both in their chivalry, their bravery and their skill. I do not doubt that they will win great fame and beauteous wives in their time."

Still Melusine did not touch the bed. "Forgive me. My dream was most unsettling." She crossed the chamber, her fingers knotting together. "What of your brother?"

"Fromont has left and has been bidden not to return."

She glanced over her shoulder, surprised.

"His wicked words are not welcome at Lusignan."

Melusine turned back to the window, clearly uncertain.

"We should grant a stirrup cup to our departing guests."

"They have feasted beyond expectation for three days and nights. I would let the castellan bid them farewell. Come to bed, Melusine."

"It is too soon, Raymond, too soon after the babe."

"I would hold you close, no more than that."

Still she did not come to him.

Raymond rose and, when she did not turn, caught her shoulders in his hands. He kissed her nape, loving how she still shivered slightly at his touch.

"Your dream is backways 'round, my beloved Melusine," he whispered, pulling her back against his chest. "I have a gift for you, one I have been saving too long."

He retrieved the silk bundle from its hiding place in his trunk. He did not tell her that he had purchased the gift in anticipation of the birth of their first son, but had been too devastated by the sight of Urien's eyes to give it to her then. He half-suspected Melusine would guess as much.

She unfurled the silk, so carefully that she might have expected to find an asp within it. She caught her breath when the jewel lay in her palm, then looked up at him. There was a shimmer of tears in her wondrous eyes. "You bought this for me?"

"I met a jeweller in Paris, on one of my journeys there. He had the most uncommon skill. Do you like it?"

She shook her head and said naught.

Raymond reached out and touched the gilded gem, unable to resist it even now. The gem was a great freshwater pearl, as large as his thumb, yet wrought in a curious curved shape. The jeweller had used the lustrous pearl as the tail of a figure of Neptune, creating a fine filigree of scales that held the pearl captive, making the rest of the figure out of gold. Neptune had tiny emeralds for his eyes and the tines of his trident were topped with garnets.

Raymond wondered suddenly if he had found the piece so alluring because he had guessed something of his wife's nature. Melusine watched him, clearly wondering much the same.

"I could not resist it," he said, shaking his head at his own impulsiveness. "It cost a small fortune, I must admit." He met her gaze guiltily and pushed his hand through his hair. "We did not, in fact, lose so much coin in the trade of wine as I had told you. I lied, Melusine, that you might not guess that I had bought you such a gift. I had to bring it to you." He smiled, hoping she would forgive him, and forgive him for more than that lie.

Melusine touched the stone with her fingertip. "It is most unusual," she said, her voice soft.

"It is beautiful. It is magical. I could not leave Paris without possessing it for my own." Raymond met her gaze deliberately, hoping she would glimpse what was within his heart. "Is it any wonder that it reminded me of you?"

Melusine smiled then, a smile that lit her eyes. It was the greatest gift he had ever been granted, for that smile told him that she would not leave.

"You speak wisely, Raymond, for the castellan can see to our guests. I would savor a few hours abed in your embrace," she said, reaching to caress his jaw. "I thank you for the gem."

Raymond was buoyant. He had been forgiven, beyond all expectation, and it was more, far more, than he deserved.

Chapter Five

❧

THERE was winter upon Raymond's brow when Melusine saw her mother again.

To be sure, her mother was the farthest matter from her thoughts. She had heard that foul rumor again, the one that troubled her so much, and she knew not what to do. Melusine climbed the stairs to the lord's chamber as snow swirled outside the narrow windows.

She had to do something, though she hesitated to ask Raymond's counsel. This matter would strike to his heart. Fromont, who had always been studious and serious, had joined the monastery at Maillezais—and this over Raymond's objections. Still the gleam in his father's eye, Fromont had taken a plump endowment to that monastery. He learned quickly, he always had, and Melusine had not doubted that his vocation was genuine.

Which was why the rumor about Maillezais troubled her so.

Three more boys had been born to her after Fromont, bringing the tally to Raymond's desired ten sons. The eighth had been another monstrosity, as if all the goodness of her womb had been devoured by Fromont. Born with three eyes and of so violent a temperament that he tore her womb even on his departure, Melusine had named him Horrible. The ninth, Raymond, and the tenth, Thierry, had been blessedly normal mortal children, though neither could dislodge Fromont from their father's affections.

Presine startled Melusine, no less by her presence than her welcoming smile.

"What is this?" Melusine asked. "You have not been glad to see me for years."

Presine laughed. "How long have you been wed, daughter mine?"

"Thirty mortal years." Melusine shook her head, marveling at how quickly the time had passed. "I have learned something of forgiveness in that time."

"Have you? You were always a clever child." Presine hugged her unexpectedly. "You were not just the eldest, but my greatest joy. That is why I came to warn you."

"Of what?"

"I told you of the worlds drawing apart. In these days, the thread frays with ever increasing speed. The moment of parting is upon us and I would not have you trapped in the mortal realm."

"Would you not remain with Father?"

Presine laughed at the very thought. "In a mountain? Nay! He has been dead these twenty years."

"I did not know."

"It is of import no longer. I cannot mourn him for all of my days as mortals mourn for all of theirs. I am young yet," for a fey, and there is much yet to savor." Presine smiled and offered her hand. "Come with me to the domain of the fey, Melusine. You have always preferred that realm. I would not have you lost beyond the divide."

Melusine hesitated, thinking of this matter of Maillezais yet unresolved. It was easier to consider that than the notion of leaving Raymond.

"Is your wager not rendered in full?" her mother asked. "Have you not delivered ten sons and all the wealth your spouse might imagine?"

"Of course." Melusine eyed her mother. "What of my own curse?"

"You had only to compel a man to love you for all of his life, without breaking his pledge to you. Has Raymond broken his pledge?"

Melusine looked away, unable to lie. Her mother chose to interpret that rather differently than it was meant.

"Ah, and he has stolen your heart in keeping his word so well! This is how you have learned of forgiveness." Presine laughed merrily. "You were always one much concerned with the merit of a promise. I am certain that the curse can be lifted, especially if you are in the realm of the fey and the divide has occurred."

Melusine was not so certain.

Worse, she did not want to leave.

Not yet.

"Come now, before it is too late!" Presine urged impatiently.

Raymond's tread sounded on the stairs, slower than it once had been but still beloved for its familiarity. Melusine turned, anxious as always to see him again. They had been apart all this day and she yearned for his embrace, as she did most every night. Tenderness assailed her and she half smiled, imagining the light that would claim his eyes when he saw her.

She had done well to forgive him.

Presine whispered in her ear. "There is no time for farewells, and they will serve naught at any rate. Disappear, you know that you can."

"It would break his heart if I abandoned him without explanation," Melusine argued, knowing that it was her own heart's breaking that she dreaded.

She loved Raymond. The truth stunned her with its simplicity, and she knew then what she had to do.

"He is mortal," her mother said. "Like your father, he will not have long to endure any pain."

Melusine turned at that and confronted her mother. "Nor will he have long left to savor this world. You defended my father once, against me, and bade me forgive him."

"I was angry that you defied me." Presine shrugged. "There is nothing eternal between men and fey—so we are taught and so it is true. Come with me, and be among your own kind."

Melusine did not move. "I will be among those I love, for so long as I can endeavor to do so."

Presine was aghast. "But you could be trapped in their realm!"

A tranquility filled Melusine, a satisfaction that her beloved drew nearer, a certainty that there was nowhere she would rather be than here, awaiting him. "So be it. Farewell, Mother."

They stared at each other, shocked that they might never have the power to see each other again. A sound filled the walls, erupting from everywhere and nowhere, a great tearing. The divide was upon them.

Presine offered her hand one last time, but Melusine stepped away. Her mother shook her head and then she was gone. The rending grew to a deafening roar, then fell silent. It was as silent as the grave, silent save the measured tread of Raymond's steps. Nothing looked different, but Melusine could feel an absence that had not been there before.

The realm of fey was gone.

Forever. The door opened behind Melusine even as she struggled with the truth of it.

"You look troubled," Raymond said.

"I am only concerned about a rumor I heard this day." He drew his chemise over his head, older and thicker than once he had been, though still hale and strong. "Tell me of it."

The words caught in Melusine's throat, for she was certain they would cut Raymond deeply. He could not be objective about their son Fromont, so much did he love the boy.

And she did not want to trouble him this night. She did not want to argue, or even debate.

She wanted to sleep, secure in his embrace, for the world she savored was lost to her for all time. She shrugged and spoke lightly. "I should not heed rumor, much less repeat it. Come to bed, Raymond, and force such frippery from my thoughts."

He smiled, as roguishly as ever he had. "My lady's wish is as my command." He caught her up in his arms and tickled her until she laughed helplessly, then they tumbled into bed together.

And Melusine had no regrets for the choice she had made.

MORNING brought the return of their crusading sons—for Christmas was nigh upon them—and a hall bursting with noise and merriment. The wine flowed as abundantly as the tales.

Urien told of how he and Guy had aided the King of Cyprus, and how their deeds had inspired awe in the men there. Despite their valor, the King had been wounded in the assault. Upon his deathbed, the King had granted not only his realm but his most beauteous daughter to Urien's hand.

Ermynee already had borne a son, Greffon, and Melusine delighted in meeting her first grandson.

Not to be outdone, the brother of the King of Cyprus had endowed Guy with the kingdom of Armenia, and his lovely daughter Flourie too was ripening with child, though she flushed mightily when Melusine commented upon it.

It was clear to all that both sons were as smitten with their brides as their brides were with them, and Melusine and Raymond exchanged a smile of pride.

"You raised them well," Raymond said, pressing a kiss to Melusine's knuckles.

Anthony and Raynold had travelled together to relieve a besieged holding in Luxembourg, discovering only later that the daughter of the duke of that place was its reigning authority. So grateful was this damsel named Christian that she wedded Anthony. Raynold had then accepted an invitation to defend Bohemia against the Saracens, winning both the hand of that king's daughter, Eglantine, and the crown of Bohemia for his triumph.

Geoffroi recounted how he had defeated the giant Guedon in Rochelle. Ever aware that his father found fault with him, Geoffroi took great pleasure in reminding Raymond that he had tried to dissuade him from this task.

"It is true," Raymond agreed easily. "I thought the fiend too doughty an opponent for you and I feared for your survival. You are too young to be lost to us."

"But I was not lost," Geoffroi said with satisfaction. "You underestimate me, Father, as always you did."

"And I am not displeased to have been mistaken." Raymond chuckled and called for another cask of wine to be opened. A great fire burned merrily upon the hearth and there was much laughter in the hall. A roast stag was carried to the board at midday, followed by dozens of other delicacies. Melusine seized a quiet moment after the meal to speak with Geoffroi, with whom she had always had a kinship. "I would ask a favor of you."

"Any deed you can ask of me, I will do, Mother."

"I have heard a rumor, one that upsets me greatly. I would know if there is truth within it before I cause your father concern."

"You know that I shall do your service first and foremost."

"It is whispered that the monks of Maillezais have lost their way." Melusine licked her lips and spoke with care, aware of Geoffroi's bright gaze upon her. "It is told that they are lecherous, one and all, that they have encounters with the local women and that they are sinners beyond compare."

"But Fromont is there!"

"Perhaps he is beguiled. Perhaps he does not participate in such folly. Perhaps he errs and does not know it." Melusine gripped her son's hand. "Perhaps the rumor is a lie. Unearth the truth for me, before your father hears tell of it."

"I shall see justice served," Geoffroi said, a flicker of his father's anger in his eyes.

"No! I ask you only to learn the truth!"

But Geoffroi strode through the hall, deaf to her calls for his return. She could not catch him, this son of hers so much taller than she. Too late, Melusine recalled how Geoffroi and Fromont had long competed for their father's favor, though Raymond's eye had never left Fromont.

Too late, she feared what Geoffroi might do.

SHE had not long to fear.

Geoffroi returned within a week, the smell of wood smoke upon his clothes. There was fury simmering yet in his eyes though he stood triumphant in his father's hall.

"I have dispatched wickedness from your realm again,

"Father," he declared, his resonant voice drawing the attention of all.

"What is this?" Raymond asked, bemused by this son as so oft he was.

Melusine prayed that the portent pricking her flesh was wrong.

"The abbey Maillezais is burned to the ground," Geoffroi said, not troubling to hide his scorn.

"Maillezais? Surely Fromont is not yet there?"

"He was and he is."

Raymond clutched the board, his face ashen.

Geoffroi met the gaze of every soul in the hall, his conviction that he was right unshaken. "I went to Maillezais, to seek the root of rumor at Mother's request, and I found that rumor had not done the truth credit. I found those monks fornicating in the chapel. I found them gorging themselves, I found them sleeping, fat and sated in every corner."

Geoffroi sneered. "I found the gold stacked within the cellars, and indeed, evidence of every mortal sin practiced at that monastery. They defiled the very place on which the abbey was located and were an abomination to God."

Raymond crossed himself, his hand shaking. Every eye in the hall was fixed upon the jubilant Geoffroi. Melusine made her way to her spouse and touched his arm.

"Do not be angered, Raymond. It will serve naught."

He shook off her touch and stepped away from her, his gaze fixed upon Geoffroi. "What wickedness have you done?"

Geoffroi smiled. "I have done God's work this day. I have purged Maillezais of sinners. It is writ that heretics should be burned, and so they were, all of them. I barred the doors and stacked the wood high so that none could escape. I burned Maillezais to the ground and took the taint of its sin from this world. God will judge them now, and He will not be merciful."

Silence filled the hall.

"What of Fromont?" Raymond's voice was hoarse.

"Dead, like all his sinning fellows."

"Nay!" Raymond roared, the single word fit to raise the roof. He bounded toward his son, seized his tabard and shook it as if Geoffroi was no more than a boy. "You do this out of malice. You have always been jealous of the favor I showed to Fromont. Tell me you lie!"

Geoffroi lifted his sleeve toward his father's nose. "Smell the smoke. Ride to Maillezais and see for yourself. Ask my men."

Those men nodded as one, many of them clearly uncomfortable with what they had done. "It is true, my lord. Maillezais is no longer."

Melusine braced herself for Raymond's response, but she was unprepared for all the same.

He spun and shook a finger at her, bitterness contorting his features. "Most vile serpent! This is your fault, and your fault alone. I should never have taken your wager, never have suffered your kind in my bed. I should never have believed you, never have let you beguile me. You are fey and you are monstrous. Naught of any merit ever came from your womb! Look, look what your wickedness has wrought!"

Every gaze fixed upon Melusine. She stood alone in the center of the hall, her back straight, her chin high. She felt the assembly slide away from her, saw the recrimination and rejection in her beloved's eyes. She felt more alone than ever she had in all her days.

"Naught of merit? Not even Fromont?" she asked quietly.

Raymond looked down, unable to hold her gaze.

It was done between them, for he had denounced her before all. Melusine could not pretend that he had not broken his word to her, not before so many witnesses.

"My lady?" asked a servant.

Melusine pulled her sleeve away. "I am your lady no longer, not now that your lord has cast me out."

The woman's face worked silently for a moment, then she broke into tears.

Raymond pursued her, his steps increasing in speed. Melusine turned away from him, devastated by his rejection. She crossed the hall and climbed the stairs to the chamber that only she had ever entered. She threw open the door, well aware that they trailed behind her.

It did not matter now. Nothing mattered now.

"Melusine!"

Raymond was behind her but she did not want to look upon him again. He caught her elbow and compelled her to face him. Melusine met his gaze, afraid to see his revulsion at such proximity.

Instead she found despair. His eyes gleamed with fey lights, just as they had when first she met him, but the shadows were a thousand times darker than they had once been.

This was the gift she had rendered to her beloved.

At the painful truth of it, Melusine wept.

Raymond eased a tear from her cheek with his thumb. He framed her face in his hands and she felt his hands shake. "God in heaven, my Melusine," he whispered. "What have I done?"

He knew what he had done. Melusine stepped away from him, though it was the last thing she wished to do. In truth, she had no choice and they both knew it well. Her vision glazed with tears, she left his side, trembling beneath the weight of her disappointment.

"You will see me no longer," she told them all, her voice hoarse. "So it has been decreed and so it shall be. But one thing I will ask of you and that is that you do destroy one fruit of my womb." She pointed to Horrible, who had killed two nursemaids in his infancy, who she could not supervise if she was not here. "Do not suffer this son to live. I ask this of you and this alone."

With that, there was no reason to linger. Melusine lifted her skirts and strode to the window. The assembly fell back, their eyes wide. They could not disguise their newfound fear of her, though, and that was bitter. Just this morn, they had regarded her with respect and affection.

"Melusine!" Raymond cried, his voice anguished. "Stay!"

"I cannot."

"But you weep!" he insisted, then appealed to the gathered household. "All know that the fey cannot shed tears."

Many of the company nodded, as if their assent alone could change her circumstance.

"And all know that the sworn word of a man of merit is worth more than gold. Even I was fool enough to believe that."

Raymond had the grace to pale.

The pain was growing within Melusine's legs, spreading through her more vigorously than ever it had before. The change was upon her. She was devastated to realize that she would change before so many horrified gazes.

But there was yet a moment to flee. Melusine leapt to the broad stone sill beneath the window, felt it give and shimmer beneath her foot, then strode into the open air. The wind lifted her, rising beneath the leathery wings that had sprouted from her back, caressing the scaled serpentine tail that trailed behind her.

When she parted her lips to cry farewell to all of those she had loved, the harsh scream of a dragon was the sole sound she could emit.

She did not truly expect the realm of the fey to embrace her, but all the same, it was a shock to find that curtain sealed against her. She was indeed an exile.

All because she had dared to love a mortal man, because she had dared to believe that love could make all come aright.

* * *

BLANCHE and Marie twitter but I have no patience for their foolery now. Just the sharing of the tale has emptied me, emptied me for the last time. I have no anger any longer, no remorse, no sorrow. I have no regrets. I am as an empty shell.

Or the discarded skin of a snake.

In my mind's eye, I see the repercussions yet again. I see Raymond wither, his heart broken by his own deed and his last days filled with solitude and regret. I was there, but he could not see me, could not feel me, could not sense my presence any longer. Indeed, I flew around the ramparts, bemoaning his pending demise, though he alone did not heed me. It was unbearably sweet to hear my beloved call my name with his last breath, unspeakably bitter that he did not know that I was there.

I see my sons losing their every advantage, I see their children born with frightening deformities, their marriages sown with dissent. I see marauding armies claim precious Lusignan, the lands and vassals unable to retreat to the realm of the fey. So much I watch, powerless in memory as I was in fact to avert the course of events.

I see this old castle as it crumbles and fades over the centuries, claimed by mice and vines, filled with rain and wind. I know that I cannot bear to watch it fall on the morrow.

"So, now you know the true tale of Melusine," I tell these foolish girls. "How her mortal blood grew dominant, how her yearning for mortal emotions cheated her of all she held so dear."

Marie laughs, a little too loudly for her merriment to be genuine. "You cannot know the truth of it, old woman. It was said to have happened hundreds of years ago."

"If it even happened at all," adds Blanche. She casts me a coin, but that token will no longer suffice.

I will have my price of them.

I draw myself up tall and cast aside my cloak. For the first time in all my many days, I take joy in changing before mortal eyes. Horrified, fascinated, they cannot look away, yet they cannot stand to watch.

The scales begin to form over my flesh, no longer so young and supple as once it was. These scales march over my skin with the same voracious speed, but they are gnarled and dull, like the toenails of the aged. The silver and azure stripes are faded, no longer gleaming. My bare breasts no longer are pert and firm, my hair is no longer long and flaxen. It is all part of what I am. I show them my wrinkled breasts and my grayed hair. I show them the toll that heartbreak has had on an immortal.

I show them all that I am and all that I was and I laugh as they scream in terror.

I laugh louder as they try to flee. Such women as these do not deserve to live. With the last vestige of power within me, I change their shapes, just because I can. One becomes a partridge, the other a peahen, both female, both plain, both clucking and pecking futilely at the stone floor.

I lift my arms high, savoring this last heady taste of the power that once flooded my veins.

Power that once I took for granted.

Then I step on the sill, the footprint perfectly fitting my own even after all these centuries. My leathery wings unfold behind me, creaking as they beat against the air. I cry out as I fly around the high ramparts one last time, then I leave Lusignan forever. I cannot hold any form for long, but I take great joy in shocking as many mortals as I can.

As to where my heart will go after my form fades to naught, who can say? The memory of my beloved burns bright within it, and of regrets, I have not one.